"On my side of town, complexion and class are two issues that are as old as Africans in America. Long before the movie *Pinky*, beyond the concept of the Talented Tenth, and long after the flick *Imitation of Life*, these issues have stood out in the black community and have, in part, defined how we look at ourselves as well as others in our "family." In a story that sings, Jones has tackled both difficult and seemingly "silent" issues with honesty and class. A must read for people of any class or color."
—Eric Jerome Dickey, *New York Times* bestselling author

From the moment Sandra first shook that hand of flimsy
skin and thin bones she knew there was something
odd about Eulelie, and now she had it figured out. Eulelie
was too aware of herself, conscious of every step, every
word, every smile. Why?
—from *Passing* by Patricia Jones

passing

a novel

patricia jones

AVON BOOKS ◆ NEW YORK

AVON BOOKS, INC.
1350 Avenue of the Americas
New York, New York 10019

Copyright © 1999 by Patricia Jones
Cover illustration by Cathleen Toelke
Author photo by Derek Bacchus
Published by arrangement with the author
ISBN: 0-7394-0447-4
www.avonbooks. com

～ Acknowledgments

I want to thank my sister, Velma Adams, for everything you've done to help me to this point. Thank you for believing in me and my writing when I didn't even believe in myself. Mostly, thank you for being my sister. You always said it just took the right mind to find this book, and you were right. Eileen Cope, I thank you for your sense, and your sensibility. Thank you, Lyssa Keusch, for being such a clear-sighted editor. Having an editor with your vision makes me a very fortunate writer. I am so blessed that you and Eileen were a part of this process. To my husband, Derek Bacchus, thank you for your patience through it all. And thank you for being a source of strength in your quiet way. I love and appreciate you for all you do. Most of all, I thank you, Alexandra Bacchus, my daughter, my angel girl, for the smiles and tantrums that always kept me focused on what's important—you. Thank you, Daryl Long, for being my biggest fan since Boston U. You have been my steadfast friend. Lynelle Phillips, remember the days? Thanks for the girl-talk all the way from Baltimore. Colette Curtis-Edell, my first friend, thank you for your unwavering love that has stood the test of years and tears. Thank you, Barbara Brandon-Croft, my girl in Brooklyn, for the laughs that got me through the process. I went to Africa and came back with you, my friend for life. And I can't forget you, Linda Brandon. Thank you for everything you did to help me find

Eileen. Claire Wood, my sister of the soul, thank you for the way you have calmed me with just one word, and the way you love without condition. I thank my sisters and brother in Baltimore—Bettye Pettiford, Annette Dodson, Tom Jones. I hope you all know that your laughter and love inspire me. Thank you Donna "Nonnie" Hughes for your encouragement, and of course, your long-distance smile. Then there is my mother, Anna Jones. Thank you for teaching me how to love from my soul. Your love and your widsom are one, and it is God-sent. You have helped me find the faith in myself I needed to be a writer, so this book is as much yours as it is mine.

$\mathcal{P}$ROLOGUE

꧁A Race Divided Against Itself . . . Is Just Fine by Her

With a lazy stride that was Sunday afternoon, Lila, the eldest Giles daughter, made her way into the living room with the cacophony of clinks and clanks, tinkles and clangs, riding in behind her on a pillowy wave of the smells of Sunday dinner, and lowered herself into her mother's chair. It was the Sunday afternoon of a new spring day, not much different than any other Sunday in this city that moves, breathes, speaks, even smells with the essence of a small town. Baltimore. The midday sun illuminated the room in a way that made the mellifluous radio voice, which had already filled the room full, its lover. Lila was not very interested in the woman on National Public Radio who spoke in rich, dulcet tones yet in an anxious while vainglorious way about her urban garden. The voice floated about the room with talk of pansies and daisies and petunias—*and lamb's ears can make a wonderful little border plant*—wrapping Lila in its sensuous warmth. Lila leaned over to turn the volume a little lower, but never off—it was her mother's presence even when her mother wasn't there. National Public Radio and the *Afro Gazette*, Lila thought as she chuckled to herself, her mother's only connections to the real world.

Lila was settling herself into the chair to make it her own, at least for the moment, when she noticed how the silvery light of casted shadows and reflections sent into the room by the sun had put a mysterious spell upon the picture of her father, standing regally in his judicial robe, which sat amidst other Giles family pictures on the fireplace mantel. He had been sleeping the sleep of sleeps for nearly ten years now, and the only thing that comforted her while he slept into eternity was walking into that room to have his smile conjure sweet memories, to have his smile tell her that all would always be well. But the sun's spell had stolen his smile, her repose. She held her head this way, then that, then the other way, but still saw the same thing—her father smirking, not smiling, as if he had a secret. As if he disapproved.

It was too nightmarish to ponder a second longer, how her father could have been smiling just yesterday and all those days and years before and suddenly he was not. So she blamed it on the sun and let her eyes and mind slide into the photos beside her father's on the mantel of all those generations of Giles faces, most of whom had been dead many more years than she'd been alive. Those faces told stories of not just a family, but a line, a line of remarkable men and women who were the legends of which the Baltimores of America were made. They were all-seeing from up there on their perch, looking down on her, their future generation, with faces far too fair to be colored, yet they were. But when she thought of her mother, the mother who raised but did not bear her, the mother whose face would one day be on a mantel in someone's home filled with these same Giles ghosts, a thought most wretched crawled into her mind, though she wanted none of its devilment. It had to do with the possessive, actually obsessive, way her mother believed in the separation of the race, though she would never, ever say it so plain-spokenly; but it was in everything else she said, everything else she did. When Lila thought about her mother's world of acceptable and unacceptable blacks, her face, which had been filled with contentment, faded into an expressionless oblivion, like a bubble that doesn't so much burst as much as simply dissolve. As Lila let her mind wander down the steep, slippery slope of the path she hoped would one day lead her to making heads or tails of her mother, it always seemed to dead-end quietly with the unsettling notion that her mother was a black woman passing as a white woman, passing as a black woman. And to understand this conundrum was to try to understand her mother, Eulelie Giles.

ONE

~❧ Worlds / Apart

Eulelie looked guilty. Like a thief trying to steal in the night. Over both shoulders she checked, and scoped out everything oncoming—traffic, strollers, even two young men on bicycles. She was walking home from that conceptual aberration known outside of her world as simply the corner store, after getting the milk for the creamy gravy her son so loved. With the din of approaching motors, Eulelie could only pray that no one in her insular universe had witnessed her walk to, or presently from, the other side of Hilton Street, that other place beyond the reservoir, that other place where *other* black people who were not like her lived, all so that her son would not be without gravy at Sunday dinner. And her daughters had tenaciously refused to go.

The only thing that kept her mind off her inelegant situation was that reservoir. Once she reached that reservoir, shiny and still, placid as her heart felt when surrounded by her children, Eulelie could momentarily forget about what she'd just had to do, from where she'd just come. Behind her, and beyond the reservoir, lay nothing terribly special. Still, all she could think about was who could see, who would talk. Is there one thing a mother would not do for the love of her son?

A jittery concoction of fear and anger and even a tiny touch of sadness with roots running too deep to probe had spread a damp warmth across her forehead, in her armpits, under the waistband of her skirt, as she thought of the possibility of Dottie Pettigrew-Van Dyke, heiress to the *Afro Gazette*, seeing her. Would Dottie go so far as to put something like this in the *Gazette?* The *Gazette* was Baltimore's newspaper on all matters black, and Eulelie could just imagine the headline: LOOK WHO EULELIE GILES IS RUBBING ELBOWS WITH THESE DAYS. How would she ever live this down? Somehow, though, as she walked and thought, Eulelie managed to slow her leaping imagination long enough to allow common sense to prevail. People walk to the store every day, she reasoned. Even Dottie Pettigrew-Van Dyke runs out of milk. The *Afro Gazette* had published some outlandish stories in its day, but a walk to the low-brow part of Hilton Street was hardly newsworthy, not even for the *Gazette;* not even in a slow news week. But it wasn't just Dottie Pettigrew-Van Dyke who worried her. It was the Breckenridges, or the Ballards, or any of the women from the Black Barristers' Wives Social Club; that's who she didn't want catching her slumming on the other side.

Eulelie opened the screen door, the only thing that separated the sanctity of the Giles home from the rest of the world on this Sunday afternoon. "I'm back, girls," she said from the front hall with a wearied voice, looking particularly frumpy in her church suit, which seemed a size, maybe a size and a half, too big for her, as if she might be wearing some other woman's fine linen suit. Its roominess put an uncomely emphasis on her frail body, of which she seemed most unaware, making her look plainer than a plucked chicken.

Lila scrambled out of her mother's chair and went to the front hall. "Momma, my God! You look like you're in distress. Are you okay?"

"Of course I'm not okay, Lila. What do you think? I am *never* doing *that* again. I'm telling you, that other side of Hilton Street is another world. I should have driven. My heart beats a little faster when I even have to sit at that corner at a red light, and here I am crazy enough to walk down there. I'm telling you I should have driven." She pointed one long, thin, pale finger at Lila, then said: "Your father, the Judge, is probably turning over in his grave right now knowing I went down there."

Lila took the bag with the milk from her mother and passed it on to her sister Lucretia, who had come into the hall for it. Lila looked blandly at her mother, then said: "Well why didn't you drive?"

"Oh, Lila, you know how those people down there will plop their bottoms on your car before you're even good and out of it. I didn't even want to put myself in the position to have an altercation with any of them." Eulelie walked past Lila and into the living room, peeling her jacket off. She threw her hand in the air in a queenly, dismissive way and said to Lila, "I don't care. The next time we're just going to have to be without gravy. I will not do that again. I just hope nobody saw me."

Her ears strained to hear the radio. "Turn that up, will you, dear?" she asked Lila.

As the volume rose, a male voice, not too deep, but not pansy light either, filled the room with the adventures of spawning salmon in the Pacific Northwest. *"The salmon thrash their bodies against the water . . ."* he was saying. Nothing she wanted to hear.

But before Eulelie could settle into another of her tirades about those awful corner-hanging, car-sitting, fringe dwellers on the dark side of Hilton Street, the voice of her youngest, Linda, floated in to her from the kitchen.

"Momma, dinner's ready, where's Gil?"

So, This Is Momma Eulelie

Gil washed the last swallow of scotch and soda over his tongue before surrendering it to his throat, his belly waiting for the burn. Scotch and soda, as many as it took, was the weekly ritual in preparation for Sunday dinner with Mother. As he set the glass on the bar, a pleasure/pain grimace took hold of his face in poetic reply to the liquor scorching a trail straight to the deepest pit of his gut, where more pain, beyond the physical, lived. The wave of mellow calm that rippled to his brain made the pain worth taking. His eyes brushed over his watch with enough precision to see that time was not with him. Yet, instead of going for his wallet to settle up, he stared straight ahead at the bottles of spirits lining the wall. Gil was caught in the bony clutches of four women who made his life, all at once, bearable and unbearable, and he did not want a clear head to face them.

A voice, rasping with too many years of drink and smoke, bellowed from the other end of the bar, jarring Gil from his deep musings. "Hey Gil, can I get you a third?" Curtis, the bartender, had known Gil for a half dozen or so years. And a half dozen or so years were as long as Gil had been coming in the bar. They had a quintessential bartender-drinker relationship. It started out that way from the first night Gil walked through the door asking for a double.

"Yeah, man, give me another one," he said now. This made three. Usually Gil never had more than two of his Sunday scotch and soda. It would be a rough ride through dinner with Eulelie. Then, like a wisp of a breeze out of nowhere, he thought of his mother. Not Eulelie, the mother who raised him, the one he was on his way to see for dinner. Rather, he thought of the mother in whom he'd once lived. How is it that she took such a chunk of him with her when she died? He was only six. But his spirit was more lightsome when she was alive. She allowed it. She loved it, even lived for it. And he lived life from one silly prank to the next, that's what made him so special—when she was alive. But then came Eulelie's will. Eulelie's rules. That's what he'd known the longest. Bending four small children to her will. Rules of decorum—everyone should be as appropriate as the code, her code dictated. A code that was not written to include the basic nature of a young boy. And he might not

have held himself so tightly through life had she appreciated
the person he'd already become by the time she'd stepped
in to be his mother. That spirit had to be quashed.

Gil gazed into the glass of naked ice cubes where his life
lived, for the moment, and echoes of memories danced. He
was only six. And his mother was dead. And then there was
this woman he had to forthwith call "Momma." Well, one
Saturday afternoon, while his *momma* and father were out
for a new tradition—their Saturday lunch—Gil wanted to
initiate his new mother into his life by surprising her with
one of his pranks. So, he took his GI Joes, all ten of them,
and lined them up along the sofa. Running back and forth
to the door, anticipating the moment the car would pull up,
young Gil couldn't wait. She would think this was just the
funniest thing she'd ever seen. He knew she would.

Finally, on his fifth run to the door, he saw them. His
mother and father were coming up the walk. He had to
move fast. Gil ran onto the porch. "Momma, Momma!" Gil
said with excitement. "Some people stopped by to see you.
They're in the living room. They said they wanted to meet
you. They're from some club, I can't remember." Eulelie
stood a little taller—chest out, shoulders back, back
straight—then gave a quick pat to her hair. She knew not
who was sitting in her living room, but appearance meant
everything. She was the lady of the manor, the Judge's wife
and a woman of society, for goodness sake. When she
rounded the corner into the living room only to find ten GI
Joes lined up on her sofa, she simply stared without expression. Gil laughed so hard, not realizing that she was not
laughing with him, or even at all. "Momma, I tricked you,
and you fell for it." He just couldn't get over his clever trick,
laughing until he heard a voice far more stern than he'd ever
imagined. Far more icy than his *real* mother would have ever
spoken to him, or anyone.

"Gil, no one likes a silly boy. Take these men up to your
room and you stay up there with them until you figure out
why you don't play jokes on your parents."

Gil climbed the stairs with his arms filled with his soldiers. He checked over his shoulder, once, twice, three times. What was taking his father so long to defend him? After all, he didn't have a hint as to what he'd done wrong. Surely his father didn't know either. If Gil had moved any slower he would have been standing still. One step, then the other, then the other, as if his legs were logs. But it wasn't until he finally reached the top of the stairs that he heard his father say: "Eulelie, don't you think you were being a little too hard on him? Gil likes to kid around. That's just his way."

And without missing a beat, Eulelie quipped: "Gilbert, do you have any idea how difficult it is to raise another woman's children? Now this kind of silliness might have been fine for Gloria, but I won't stand for it. Children ought to know their place."

"Yeah, but Eulelie, he's just a boy, just a child," Gil heard his father say.

And as little Gil stood in the upstairs hall listening, he felt hope. He *was* just a child, she couldn't deny that. But she did when she said: "Gilbert, little white boys can be silly like that. They have that luxury because their skin is white. Little black boys don't have that luxury because life for them as men is hard. You know that. Now if my responsibility in this family is to raise a black boy into a black man who will be a part of the pride of this family, then you have to accept *my* way, and *my* rules."

Gil heard his mother walk off somewhere, it didn't much matter where. He went into his room, listening to his sisters playing without care in the backyard. He closed the door with a slow, depressed push, and it was at that moment that Gil's natural-born mirth was conquered by serious obedience to everyone, and practically everything.

Watching Gil's tortured face, Curtis felt he had to do his job, and poured Gil's third scotch and soda. "You know, man," the bartender said, "I think you're worrying too much about this thing. I don't know your muvah, but the talk around town is that she's a really classy lady."

"Classy. Yeah, that's her, classy. She's respected all around Baltimore in all the right circles, all right. Only thing is, most of the black folks in this town confuse class with snobbery. Or maybe they think you can't have one without the other. I don't know."

"Naw, I'm tellin' you, man. I've met a lotta snobby broads with no class."

"Well, that's something else. You don't know my sisters. They're snobby *broads* with class and they're still too much. All I know is that Momma is very . . ." He paused, in search of what best described her. ". . . genteel. I suppose that's the best word for her, but with all that, is this snobby attitude that says she's . . . that we're somehow better than everybody else. We're talking about a woman who goes religiously to the meetings of a social organization that actually calls itself Black Barristers' Wives and she loves it; lives for it, even though the name itself is the epitome of snobbery and exclusivity, or at the least an attempt at it. She's bred my sisters the same way. Tomorrow night, when I take Sandra over to meet Momma, my sisters will have their sacrificial lamb for their rite of passage."

Curtis leaned across the bar, bearing the sly grin of untold secrets. Intending to whisper, but not succeeding, he rasped, "Down in Cherry Hill where I come from, we call the kinda people you talkin' 'bout 'hinkties' and we call the language they speak 'ackalacky.' " He laughed, more to himself than Gil, with a chuckle that lived deep in his round belly. Then, sticking his pinky in the air and cocking his head sideways, he said in a high-pitched mock, " 'Okay, my good man, would you happen to have any ten-year-old scotch?' You know what I'm talkin' 'bout. Hinkties and ackalacky. Some combination, huh?" He paused as if remembering something he had long forgotten, then grinned in a way that made Gil want to know. "Back a while, there was this broad used to come in here all the time with her sister. The sister had some kinda funny name, like a car company or somethin'. Both of 'em ran their mouths a mile a minute talkin' 'bout nothin'. Both of 'em was the biggest freaks in Baltimore, actually downright trampy. They was real good for a real good time, you know what I mean. Anyway, that chick married some lawyer and now she's a member of that Black Barristers' Wives you talkin' 'bout. Sometimes I see her in the *Afro Gazette* sittin' up there actin' like Miss All-That and I think to myself how amazin' it is that this broad went from givin' dudes blow jobs right over there in that booth to bein' Miss Baltimore Socialite. I tell you, man, I bet most of those women ain't even half of what they tryin' to be."

Gil threw Curtis a sideways smile and drank his scotch in two large gulps. He set the glass on the bar gently, suddenly realizing this was it, that it was time to go. Leafing through the bills in his wallet, he picked out enough to cover his tab plus a generous tip for his friend, his wise shaman. He stood, snaking his arms into his jacket sleeves. Only when he stood up could his tall, lean build be appreciated for its well-apportioned beauty. But when he walked away, the illusion was gone like a vapor. His stick-backed straightness almost worked against his good looks. He possessed an august manner that kept his head always high and facing forward, making it seem that he just might turn his entire body to look left or right. His arms were almost unnaturally still by his sides when he walked, unless he was carrying something. And his face, when inactive, gave the impression that he'd just taken in a strong whiff of something unidentifiable, and vastly unpleasant. It was the kind of bearing that would make any woman he approached unsure whether he was one of those rare, decently mannered albeit slightly boring men raised right by a strict mother, or a sociopath of some sort.

"Thanks. I'll see you, man," Curtis said. "And good luck."

"Sure. You may see me later," Gil said over his shoulder as he left.

He maneuvered through the streets that were fixed so

firmly in his memory. The car seemed to know its own way. While he drove, Gil rehearsed in his mind how he would tell his mother and sisters about Sandra. The words he'd use wouldn't matter. They'd be excited at first, of course—he hoped. Finally, he's found someone who's made him happy. Thank God he's not gay, his mother was bound to think. At last he's ready to settle down and commit to marriage. But then they'd start to ask all the unsubtle questions. And if he answered, they would have exactly what they needed to know about her pedigree. Who are her parents? Where did she grow up? What church does her family attend? What social organizations does her mother belong to? Did she belong to Jack and Jill growing up? The questions would be coming from all directions, fast and furious. They would be the arbiters of her acceptability as a person to know, much less marry.

When he turned onto Hilton Street, a visceral burning overtook him. Maybe it was the scotch, maybe it was anticipation, maybe it was both. Either way, he was too close for comfort. There was no turning back, sick or not. And even if he wanted to, that house drew him like a magnet. The house, large and gray and stone. The only thing flawed about it was its company among others that were splendid in their own way, but not equally so. Two flower pots placed the perfect distance apart made the porch look sparse, untouched, but still welcoming. Just the right touch. The screen door, simple metal and mesh, not loud with flourishes that aspire to another level but fall short. His childhood home belonged in another time, under another sky. It was a home that, in that other place, under that other sky, could only have been the possession of a man of means, and of another hue.

Gil remembered hide and seek with his sisters. Backyard Easter egg hunts with them, and the children with whom they were obligated by his mother's law of gentry to play, suddenly pirouetted through his mind. Halloween, even in his adult years, saw the porch alighted at nightfall by two jack-o'-lanterns and the door hung with a welcome-to-fall wreath of dried corn and small gourds, and all those amber leaves carpeting the front yard made it officially fall. Then there was his father, who would make it home from work extra early just to be able to jocularly answer the door to the neighborhood children with "It's your lucky day, I've got both tricks and treats," then proceed with his coin-behind-the-ear trick, or some such other cornball prank. But Gil loved it; he waited for it each year. And then at Christmas, one white candle was lit in each window, tiny white lights salting the oak tree in the front yard—the tree that, even with a mature perspective, seemed just as large as it was when its shadowy windblown boughs scared him sleepless. In all of those months when there was more darkness than light, the soft cozy yellow glow through the windows gave the house the look of a refuge and fortress for a disquieted soul. Eulelie had some sort of special touch that made simple, meaningless objects conjure the kinds of feelings only a contented heart and soul can feel. And all of these memories met in Gil's mind to mean home—the only home that, so far, had ever been home. Everything looked so right through a tunnel, he thought. Just don't ever look under, behind, or around.

His sisters were sitting on the porch. Lila poked her head over the ledge to see if it was really him, her thin neck as long as a swan's. She jumped up, Lucretia and Linda following, and all three beamed bright smiles. He'd come at last, the most important—the only—man in their lives since their father died. Pathetic.

"Momma, he's here!" Lucretia yelled.

"Hi Gil. We've been waiting for you," Linda said, pouting. "We thought you'd be here earlier so we'd have more time together to talk before dinner. As it is, Momma's just going to want us to sit down right away and eat. You know how she is about eating right at five."

"I got tied up." Gil swaggered up the walk, taking his time, all of a sudden not caring about anything. The scotch had kicked in and put a mellow buzz right on the edge of his nerves where it was needed. When he got to them, he pecked at their cheeks, his lips just barely alighting. They talked all at once to him, hungry for his attention, just like a pack of yipping, yapping Chihuahuas.

"Look Gil, don't you like this dress? It's new. I just got it to wear to the sorority's spring tea dance." Lucretia twirled and posed.

"It's very nice, but why didn't you save it for the dance?"

"I wanted you to see it."

"Gil," Linda said, pulling him by the arm and away from her sisters. "You've just got to buy a table to the Black Barristers' Wives Cotillion. Lila's chairing the committee and I'm on her board. I told them that we could count on my brother to buy a table. You will, won't you?"

"When is it?"

"Gil, I've told you a thousand times," she said, cocking her head sideways, with wisps of her hair taking feathery flights with each movement of her head. It was cut in that boyish, Peter Pan style that was all too trendy, and much maligned by her mother for looking too much like every black-girl hairdo in Baltimore, but it worked well, nonetheless, with her size, which was petite to the point of being almost childlike. "I swear, Gil, it's as if you just never listen to me. It's the third Friday in May. Is that so hard to remember?" Linda whined, tugging at his sleeve for him to follow her into the house.

Ack, ack, ack, ack, ackalacky. That's all he heard as the three pairs of blush-pink-frosted, thin-lipped mouths swirled around his scotch-soaked head like fireflies at an evening barbecue. He had only the slightest clue as to what they were all chattering on about, but about one thing he was clear—it was important.

Lila took his hand with both of hers, trying to pull him the rest of the way into the house. Her hair was a flounce of roller-set auburn—natural auburn—curls, hanging just past her shoulders in a styleless do that framed her face, the color of underdone white-bread toast. Still, there was a doe-eyed virginal innocence about the thinness of her body that gave the impression of classic beauty. And when she stood perfectly still, she could make an artist's eye wish for a camera, or paintbrush and canvas. She pulled and tugged him into the house, her chicken legs looking as if they might snap under the strain. She didn't have a dress to model or tickets to a fund-raiser to sell him. All she wanted was that the two eldest be seated together at dinner.

Gil stepped into the house where nothing ever changed, as if the house was being preserved for some later time when gilded ropes would be draped across the doorways of every room for future generations to marvel at the way in which the Giles family of Baltimore once lived. The halls and the walls in all the rooms were still with an eerie presence, and it stood to reason that this house's connection to this family, and families being what they were, made its walls the holder of too many secrets and not a few lies. The whole house stood with the bearing of a museum—a place Gil loved visiting for history's sake, but would only live in again due to a bizarre and unpropitious twist of fate. There are homes that are lightsome with the effulgence of life. They are welcoming and open, with nothing to hide and everything laid bare to share. This was not so for Gil's childhood home. It was heavy with eyes in faded photographs. A home heavy with the solemnity of family tradition. It was all this ghostly Giles greatness that, animistically, was still ruling and running this home.

His mother met them in the front hall as they all walked in, each of her girls trying to be next to Gil. She held out her frail, pale arms, and he did what naturally came next. He hugged her like the good son of her expectations. But she pulled back quickly, her face twisted into a displeased frown.

"I can't believe you would come to dinner at your mother's house smelling like liquor," she said.

"Sorry, Momma. I just stopped off for a drink with a friend." *Hinkty, ackalacky. Hinkty, ackalacky. Hinkty, acka-*

lacky. Suddenly he could not get those words to leave him alone now that he was in the presence of the Queen Hinkty.

"Well, how many drinks did you have?"

"Just one, Momma, just one. Honest. I swear," he said, diverting his gaze so he wasn't looking her in the eye and lying.

"You just watch yourself, Gil. You know you have alcoholism in your bloodline. You know that brother of Gloria's drank himself to death."

"Momma, I'm nothing like him. It was just an innocent drink."

"You just make sure that's all it was. The Judge had a devil of a time trying to help Gloria out with that brother of hers." She loved that title *Judge* and everything it meant; so much so that she never referred to her dead husband as anything else—not Gilbert, not Gil, number two, not your father or your late father, not even dear or honey when he was alive. He was only Judge or the Judge. The affectation was contagious, as her three daughters had taken to calling him the Judge on occasion as well.

"Come on, Gil, you sit here," Linda said, her slender, angular face making her smile seem painful. And her skin was so pale that as her eyes shared the smile, bluish circles became conspicuous beneath them.

"Lila, turn off the radio for me, will you?" Eulelie asked. Lila hadn't come into the dining room yet, leaving her closest to Eulelie's radio.

"That was Mozart's Flute—" She stopped the voice in mid-sentence.

Lila came back into the dining room and took her seat next to her mother, which was where she always sat—at the head of the table that took up most of the room. With all eyes on Gil, they waited for him to bless the food. He was the man of the family now. When he finished, there was an *amen* in unison.

"Momma, this meal is incredible," Gil said. "I am still amazed at how well you can cook now."

"What's that supposed to mean, dear?" Eulelie said, puzzled.

"Well, it's just that you never cooked when Dad was alive. You always had somebody to cook for us. All I'm saying is that I never even knew you could cook until after Dad died."

"Whether you do it for yourself or not, every woman should know how to cook. It's all a part of good breeding, and of course, being southern."

"Gil, did Momma tell you?" Lucretia looked at him, then at her mother, then back at him with *good news* written all over her face. There was a chubbiness to Lucretia that fluctuated in degrees with various whim diets. The latest was a boiled orange-rind concoction she'd found on the Internet. She swore she was fitting into skirts and pants she hadn't worn for years. Nevertheless, her ample form contrasted with the rag-and-bone bodies of her more petite sisters. In a coquettish way that didn't seem natural, and most unbefitting a lady, she fingered the locket that hung around her neck, nestling itself against a generously padded collarbone.

"Tell me what, Lucretia?"

"Did she tell you that Lila's this year's chairwoman of the Black Barristers' Wives Cotillion Committee? Linda and I are on the board. Did Momma tell you?"

It's as if they don't even listen to each other, Gil thought. "Linda just told me, Lucretia," he said, looking curiously at her. Waving his hand over his shoulder in the general direction of the front door, he added, "Right out there on the porch."

"Oh yeah, that's right," Lucretia said, nodding like a loose-necked Kewpie doll, as if to jar her memory. "Well, anyway, this year they decided to turn the chair over to all the former debutantes who came out from Black Barristers' Wives, and they chose Lila to put together and chair the board."

"Yes, we just feel that our former debutantes should be

the ones to judge the qualities of a young woman wanting to be a Black Barristers' Wives debutante," Eulelie explained.

"That's right," Lucretia said. "After all, they're going to be representing those of us who have already come out through Black Barristers' Wives just as much as they'll be representing Black Barristers' Wives themselves."

"Well, Lucretia, that's really exciting. You must be very proud," Gil said in a patronizing tone. "And for Lila to have been made the chairwoman, I mean, that's just something else."

Suddenly, Lucretia took in a long stench of a whiff that was his arrogance. Most likely it was in the affected way a pause filled with so much of nothing danced between *just* and *something*. She glared at him with eyes that bled with hurt and disappointment, maybe even abandonment. But her words were somehow less stinging than her eyes. "I guess this all seems awfully provincial to you, Gil, but this cotillion is tradition. It's as much of a tradition as this Sunday dinner, which *you* show up for every week."

"I didn't say anything," Gil said with a defensive rise in his otherwise bass voice.

"You didn't have to say anything. You act as if we're boring you."

"Boring me?" Gil said with a condescending chuckle. "No, I'm just . . . I'm just here listening."

"I'm doing something different this time, Gil," Lila said. "Something special, something that will mean more to them than just being introduced to society. I have brought the concept of the debutante into the nineties with career work-shops, and talks by corporate women and women doctors and lawyers, you know, professional women. I think it's time our debutantes learn more than just the waltz and how to give the perfect soiree. I'm going to let these girls see that they don't have to *marry* doctors and lawyers, they can *be* doctors and lawyers." She could see Eulelie's doubtful face in the corner of her eye, but Eulelie could not dampen Lila's fire for change. "Momma doesn't agree with what I'm doing." Lila was the little girl who desperately, and not so secretly, wanted her mother's smile.

"Oh, honey, I think you're doing a terrific job," Eulelie said. "It's just that career workshops and career this and that is not what this is about. If these girls are given the right social graces, all that other stuff will fall into place naturally once they get a good education."

Lila hung her head in a way that almost spoke of defeat. Then she lifted her eyes to look at Gil and only Gil. "I think it's worthwhile, anyway. But I guess you don't think one way or the other makes much sense, huh?"

"Well, it doesn't matter what anybody thinks," Lucretia said. "Putting this thing together is no cakewalk. If you ask me, we have our work cut out for us. Some of these girls are just awful. Downright boorish. They're loud. Some of them chew with their mouths open. It is really hard to find a true lady in this crop. The amazing thing is that they all come from good families."

"And some of them are just plain ugly and don't try to do anything to fix themselves up," Linda said.

"It's not supposed to be a beauty contest, is it?" Gil said, his tone somewhere between silly and serious.

"No, of course not," Eulelie said. "But what she means is that some of these girls today just don't seem to have any kind of values for themselves."

"Yeah, exactly," Lucretia said, placing a mouse's portion of food in her mouth. "It's not a beauty contest, but we consider how much pride they take in their appearance. I mean, after all, that's a good indication of how a person lives their life."

"That's right," Linda said. "Like this one girl. She's really, really dark, and—"

"And that makes her ugly?" Gil snapped with disbelief. "What are you saying?"

"No, I'm not saying that being dark makes her ugly, but she has this really bad skin with these big bumps and dark marks all over her face. I mean, come on. Her parents can afford good dermatology for her. Instead, she just walks around in these big baggy gender bender clothes that make her look even worse. All of that, the bad skin, the tacky clothes, just screams out that she's not ready to be part of this whole thing."

Gil's ironic smile was more to himself than to anyone at the table, and he said, more to himself than to anyone else, "This whole thing."

A brief silence fell over the room, the kind where the sounds of knives against forks, and knives and forks against porcelain, seemed deafening. "Oh, I just think Lucretia and Linda are way too hard on these poor girls," Lila finally said. "I mean, these girls are from families that don't know anything about this kind of society life. And who's to say that they should? We were born into this so it's in our blood. These girls and their families are just doing the best they can. Most of them have parents who were the first generation in their family to be college educated. That makes a big difference. I think it's great that they want to be a part of it, and Lucretia and Linda just need to learn how to make exceptions and be more understanding in some of these cases."

"Do you three have dates?"

"Of course they do," Eulelie said, surprised he would even think her beauties could be dateless at any affair. "Lila's going with Celeste Breckenridge's nephew who's moved here from Atlanta. He's a doctor." She paused for Gil to be impressed, but it didn't seem to work. "Linda and Lucretia are going with the Crenshaw brothers, you know, Dr. Crenshaw's sons."

"I thought they were married," Gil said.

"*Were* married is right," Lila said. "They're both divorced now."

"Geez, they didn't stay married long."

"Well, things just didn't work out. It happens," Eulelie said, brushing it off. "Anyway, don't you read the *Gazette*, Gil? It was all in there."

"Their divorces were written up in the *Gazette?*" Gil said, tongue-in-cheek.

"No, not their divorces, Gil. Don't be so simple," Lila said. "Their divorces were simply mentioned when they were referred to as bachelors. The story was actually about how they'll be taking over their father's practice when he retires at the end of the year."

Gil took another bite of food without a word. "So, are they dangling on your lines, waiting to be reeled in? After all, it's obvious that Momma approves of them, and they do have, after all, the right stuff."

"Gil, don't be crass," Eulelie snapped.

Gil chuckled, mostly to himself, and mostly about the absurdity of it all. Then he turned to Lila, whose stares he could no longer ignore. What did she want now?

"You know, Gil," she said, "Lucretia was right. You act as if this is some sort of embarrassment to you. What's so embarrassing about dating divorced men? I know you, Gil, and I know that little squint you do with your eyes when something is irritating you, and you've been doing that thing with your eyes ever since we started telling you about the cotillion, and especially when Momma mentioned the Crenshaw brothers. I can remember a time not so long ago when you would sell two or three tables for this event without judging it frivolous. So if it embarrasses you to hear us talk about something so meaningless as debutantes and cotillions and divorced dates, then fine, we won't mention it again."

"Fine." Gil moved food back and forth on his plate, put a few bites in his mouth, took a sip of water, and looked around slowly, his nerve building so he could have his say. He was trying very hard to find a face at which he could speak. If he couldn't look at one of them without really looking at them, he would never get it out. Finally, he couldn't hold it in any longer. He had to just say it, get it over with, and let the chips fall all over the room. It was either that or listen to another war story about Lucretia's

and Linda's valiant efforts to keep the undeserving from invading the sanctity of high society.

"Look, you all, I've got some news of my own to tell."

They stopped eating, forks in midair. *What could this declaration be?* is what their faces said. Gil never had news at
Sunday dinner.

"I'm getting married."

"What's this, Gil? What did he say?" Eulelie was certain
she'd missed something. Certain his words didn't travel far
enough to reach her ears.

"I've been seeing someone wonderful, and it feels right,
so I'm going to marry her."

Their faces were blank. There was nothing that could be
said, at least not immediately. They looked shocked, puzzled,
somehow saddened; perhaps to know that they'd been
cheated. Cheated out of being in on the courtship, getting
to know his intended. They looked at one another, trying to
figure out who would say what.

"Well, who is she, Gil?" Lila was the brave soul who
finally asked.

"Her name is Sandra, Sandra Hightower, and she's who
I've been looking for all these years."

"Gil, dear, this is awfully sudden, isn't it?" Oh, there
would be no automatic blessing slapped on this.

"No, Momma, it isn't. I've been seeing Sandra for almost
two years."

"Two years!" Lucretia yelled. "Two years and we've
never met her? Why?"

Gil tried to find a way to answer her without telling the
truth. Fortunately, Eulelie let him off the hook, in a way.

"Gil, who are her people?"

"You wouldn't know them, Momma. By the way,
Momma, I'd like to bring her by for dinner. Can we use my
mother's good china?" It was a deliberate attempt to change
the subject, knowing what the mention of his mother did to
Eulelie. She never liked to be reminded that another woman,
the dead sainted woman who gave them life, was their

mother before her. Gil had learned how to touch that raw
spot early in life. This time, though, it didn't work.

Eulelie looked at Gil with squinted eyes and said, "We'll
talk about that later. What do her parents do?"

"Let's see," he said, as if having to think about it. "I
believe her father works at Sparrows Point, you know, Bethlehem Steel, and her mother works down at Lexington
Market."

"Sparrows Point, Lexington Market," Linda mouthed to
her sisters with a scowl.

His mother made no judgment, at least not one he could
hear, but she caught her daughters' antics and snapped:
"That's enough, Linda. Just cut it out." Then, without missing a beat, the inquisition continued. "Have you met her
parents?"

"Once or twice. They're good people."

"I see," Eulelie said. "Well, what church do they go
to, Gil?"

"I'm not sure, Momma. I think they go to some A.M.E.
church over in East Baltimore."

Eulelie ate the forkful of food that was getting cold as it
sat suspended over her plate. Her mind drifted to corner
storefronts and abandoned movie houses converted into
neighborhood African Methodist Episcopal churches, and it
seemed to her that there was one on every corner over in
East Baltimore.

Then Lucretia asked, "What college did she go to?"

"Towson."

"Oh," she said flatly. "Well, if you're not going to go to
a black college and you just *have* to go to a white one, why
go to Towson? And high school? Where did she go to high
school?"

"Merganthaler Vo-Tech," he said, looking to the ceiling
as if he were not sure. Gil continued to eat. Sharks smell
blood, he thought. Wild animals smell fear.

"MerVo!" Lucretia said with a lilt that conveyed her disdain. "She went to MerVo. Well, what assembly line does

she work on?" She and Linda laughed heartily. It was the lightest the air had been since Gil made his announcement, except Gil wasn't laughing, and neither was Eulelie.

"I said that's enough," Eulelie protested. "Both of you."

Looking at his momma, but speaking mostly to his sisters, Gil said: "Look, you all, they're just decent, hardworking people trying to make it. Now, I want to bring Sandra by here after work tomorrow to meet you, Momma. Is that okay? Is that okay with you three? Can we come for dinner?"

"Of course, dear. Bring her by," Eulelie said, with a forced smile that showed too much of her gums. It was so old it made him tired.

Lila and Lucretia said, in a low monotone, "Fine," one after the other. Linda, however, just continued eating.

Then Lila asked, "Does her family live nearby? And what kind of work does Sandra do?"

Gil was chewing and could not answer right away. If there really were a God, he thought, he would get a tough piece of gristle, or even choke on a piece of meat. That way they'd be too distracted to remember the question. But He had no such plans for Gil on this evening. Gil swallowed, took a swig of water, and said, "East Baltimore. They're not from this part of town. She grew up in East Baltimore right near Greenmount and North, and that's where her parents still live. But she lives out in the Loch Raven area now."

"And what does she do?" Eulelie asked again for Lila. "Is she a professional woman?"

"She's a paralegal over at Putney, Gaines, Woods and Coombs."

"Hardly your firm's competition," Eulelie said with a prideful snigger. "A paralegal. Why a paralegal?"

"Well, Momma, she's working now as a paralegal, but her plan is to go on to law school. Georgetown, possibly."

"That's not bad if it works out, I suppose. A two-lawyer family. Not bad at all, that is if she really is intending to further her education and her legal career."

"Yes, most definitely, Momma," Gil said without looking

at her. There was something particularly sinful about looking a mother in the eye and lying.

Well, the next thing everyone knew, out of the cloudless blue sky, the table rocked with a thunderous boom. Water glasses shook, but did not spill. Silverplate rattled on the plates on which they sat. The epicenter was quickly found. It was Linda, who was running from the table in tears screaming, "This is just awful! This is just the worst thing ever and I'll never accept it *Never!*" She ran up the stairs and slammed her bedroom door.

And with all that commotion, Eulelie, Lila, and Lucretia acted as if the pig were not smack in the middle of the parlor. Not one of them even tried offering an excuse. Eulelie didn't try to apologize. There was something in their silence, though, that left not an ounce of doubt that they too wanted to run screaming from the room; that they too wanted to slam their bedroom doors in utter defiance. The table became longer and wider in his imagination with each moment of silence that ticked by.

Then, as if those last five minutes of silence following the explosion had never happened, Eulelie said, "So Lila, I think I'll have Cornish hens tomorrow night for Gil and his friend. What do you think?"

"That would be just fine, Momma, and maybe you could make those honey and ginger carrots that are just so good."

"And will you make one of your pies, Momma?" Lucretia asked. "You know no one can walk out of here without a second slice of your pie."

All Gil could do was stare in bemusement. Did they not see the same thing he just saw? Their ability to deny the existence of unpleasantness was just downright odd in his mind. It's a southern woman's best quality, his momma once told him. He didn't want to be a part of their madness, but just by sitting there through dessert, through coffee, and Eulelie's plate of after-dinner mints, Gil became an unwilling participant in their game of the Emperor Has No Clothes.

"Well, I guess I need to be shoving off," Gil finally said.

"So soon? We haven't even had a chance to visit with you," Lila said.

"Yeah, well, I need to stop by Sandra's and let her know that dinner is on for tomorrow."

"Can't you call her? Doesn't she have a phone?" Lucretia said smugly as she sipped her water.

Eulelie pressed her lips together in utter annoyance, squinted her eyes, then said: "Lucretia, you may excuse yourself from my table if you insist on continuing with this rudeness. I mean it, now. We don't behave like that in this house."

"Sorry, Momma," Lucretia said sheepishly. But the piercing she felt from her mother's eyes told her that it was not her mother who deserved the apology. So, looking in her brother's general direction, but not at him, she said: "I'm sorry, Gil."

Gil didn't respond. Her disdain was what it was, and the only thing it succeeded in doing was hastening his departure. He barely got the last bite of roast beef in his mouth when he got up from the table with a swift force that caused another tidal wave in all the water glasses. He couldn't be around these *hinkties* a second longer, listening to all their *ackalacky*. "Momma, I've really got to run," he said, giving her a quick peck of a kiss, his lips scarcely lighting on her cheek.

"Okay, son. So tomorrow at seven. Is that a good time?"

"Yes, Momma. Seven is fine." Gil was already at the front door. Eulelie and her daughters had to move quickly to keep up.

"Gil . . ." Eulelie said in her singsong momma's voice that was always pitched several octaves higher than normal.

"Yes, Momma?" He was already off the porch.

"Don't you two be late, now."

"No, Momma. Seven it is," he said, smiling as he backed down the walk.

Maybe, he thought, she was at least open to meeting Sandra. Or maybe she just wanted them to be on time. It

was hard to tell, and too close to call to warrant pondering.
But in that deep quiet place in his heart where he could
always go for the truth, he knew they would swoop down
on her like four Serengeti buzzards, picking and pulling and
gnawing until there'd be nothing left but a few piddling
shreds of her former pride.

As he got into the car, he looked up at the second floor
and saw Linda in her bedroom window. It was dark and
there was no light in the room, but the curtain was pulled
aside and he knew it was her hiding in the shadows. He
waved, but she didn't wave back. She let the curtain fall
back across the window and walked away from it, leaving
her brother alone in the street waving at a phantom.

≫ Gil and Sandra, and Memories of Mother

Gil arrived home in no time. He seemed to travel at the
speed of light out Liberty Road with nothing on his mind
but the evening he'd just spent with four women from another era, from another world. Fresh out of a glacier. They
were still with him as he walked into his house. What was
this hold these women always seemed to have on him? Especially Eulelie, who could, in some way he'd never been able
to understand, get him to do just about anything.

He sat on the sofa and lay back, his mind filled with the
question of why his mother vexed him so. And then the
little boy was there again. The little boy who was nothing
but a fuzzy memory now. This little boy was so far away,
and the way back was down a long, interminable road. It
was the little boy who liked to play, and tell jokes, and
play pranks.

Imagination was a sin, and to show it, even a peek of it,
even more so. Like the last memory of actually playing a
game with his sisters. The four were in the front hall while
his parents visited with friends in the living room. "Let's
play talking barnyard," Lila said. "Let's all go and get our

stuffed animals and make up stories about them." And so they did, and when they met up again in the front hall, the only stuffed animal Gil could find in his room was a stuffed frog that had lingered around from somewhere in his past. The girls had far more: Lila had a rooster, a dog, a cow, a duck. Lucretia brought a cow, a chicken, a bear, and a pig. Linda brought four bears of varying colors and sizes. So they gathered them all in the circle in which they sat, each one waiting for the other to start the game.

"I know," Gil said, grabbing Lila's rooster. "My frog will be the duck and rooster's mother, and the chicken can be the frog's husband. And then—"

But before he could finish, Linda, the baby, who was always acting like one, screamed: "*No! No! No! No!* That's not right! A frog can't be a duck's mother and the chicken can't be the frog's husband. A frog wouldn't marry a chicken."

They all looked astoundedly at her, because she was truly disturbed by this notion.

"Why can't a frog be a duck's mother and a rooster's mother and the chicken be the frog's husband?" Gil wanted to know. "And just look at the duck and the rooster. They could be their baby because the duck could get his feet from the frog, and his feathers and stuff from the chicken, and the rooster could get his waddle from the frog, sort of, and his feathers and stuff from the chicken. Just think about it."

But Linda was having none of it. Now she was bawling her baby head off. "*No!* I quit! Gil's not playing fair."

But Gil, in defense of his creative family, said: "Well, look at those bears. If we're really going to play fair, then you can't play because bears don't live in a barnyard."

That's when Eulelie came into the hall to find out why her baby was crying. Just her presence made the explanations commence without her having to say a word.

"Momma, Gil's not playing fair," Linda said through a veil of tears and gasps for air. By now she had worked herself up into a bratty hysteria.

Then Gil, with an attempt he knew to be futile—after all, Linda was their Momma's baby—said: "Momma, I'm not doing anything. Linda's all mad because this frog is the duck and rooster's mother and the chicken is the frog's husband. It's all just a game, but she says that a frog can't be a duck and rooster's mother and a chicken can't be the frog's husband, but she has all these bears, and bears don't belong in a barnyard, but nobody's saying anything about that because it's all just a game."

But his explanation was ridiculous to her, because his reasoning, even within the setting of pretend, was bizarre and abnormal by any mother's standard. "Gil, what is wrong with you?" she said. "A frog *can't* be the mother of a duck and rooster and a chicken can't be a frog's husband. Now you just stop this silliness or I'll send you to your room."

"But Momma, it's just a game."

"I don't care, Gil. It just doesn't make sense. What makes sense is for the chicken and the rooster to be married, but a duck still can't be a chicken and rooster's baby because it's a different animal, and you know that. Now if you can't play in a normal way, then you just go to your room. In fact, go to your room anyway and think about why a frog can't be a duck and rooster's mother. I'm sick and tired of you and your silly ways."

Gil stomped up the stairs, crying tears of anger and confusion. Lila and Lucretia sat helpless and bewildered, wanting to defend their brother but fearing their mother. They just let it happen.

"See Gil, I told you," Linda said with a brat tone she'd worked to perfection.

That was the last thing he heard before closing the door to his room. He sat there, then, contemplating Eulelie's hold on him, much the way he sat now, so many years later, still as confused as that eight-year-old boy from long ago and far away. His mother and his sisters had taken up too much of his day, both in presence and thought, he thought now. It was time to get away from them, and there was only one way that always worked. He got up as if sprung, made a dash toward the steps, then took them two at a time until he reached the top. In his bedroom, he was met by the unmade bed in which he and Sandra made unimpressive love just the night before. Kicking fallen clothes out of his path, and a pair of sneakers that stood in front of the closet, he opened the closet door. He moved a box of folders to the side, took out a stack of files and set them on the floor, then found what he wanted.

It was an old red box that had faded to an odd shade of pink by years of exposure to something, sunlight, heat, it was hard to say. It had been kept in so many different places since he was a boy. Around it was tied an equally faded purple bow; faded just enough to be an unattractive shade of purple, but not so bleached that its purpleness could be mistaken. He took the box to his bed and sat, sitting the box down next to him. He opened it, and the scent enfolded him like the past. Lavender, that aroma that smelled like its color. It wasn't as strong as it had once been, but it was strong enough to bring back his memories. He picked up each lavender-scented memento—a bar of soap, a bottle of perfume, a jar of hand cream, a vial of body oil, even a package of incense—and lifted each to his nose, one by one. And that's how he pushed the perplexing thoughts of Eulelie out of his mind and away from him, at least for the meantime. Gil, with his box of lavender-scented memories, wrapped himself in thoughts of the woman who gave him life, until the doorbell ringing sent him back to the closet in self-consciousness to hide his mother-box. It was only Sandra, he knew, but not even she would understand.

When he got to the door, Sandra was leaning against the door frame as if she'd been there all evening. One perfectly formed leg slanted out from her otherwise straightened body, as if it were part of some sort of stand keeping her from toppling over. It was the natural way her leg fell when she relaxed against the door frame. She was dressed all in red, even her purse—even her shoes—a red so rich and pure of any other hue that she could have strung her neck with garland and twinkly lights and looked no more festive. Sandra was not a slave to trends, nor a label wench, but she was stylish, almost glamorous, and the style was all her own. Her hair was long, or rather, what she and most other black women considered long—hanging only to her shoulders. And she had so forced it to that length, that what touched her shoulders were mostly only thin, scraggly ends. Usually she kept it tied back, but tonight she wore it hanging, the way Gil most liked seeing it, with a red plastic headband framing her flawless face.

"Come on in," he said.

Sandra walked with the slouching indifference of a cat-walk strutter, her hips moving with a swing that made her A-line dress move with the drama of a clanging bell. And she had her own constant smell. Oh, the smell of her, a hint of roses lingering in echoes after she passed by, giving him a rush of warmth and reminding him of his mother and the scent of her purple beauty she'd left behind.

Sandra knew what the smell of her did to him, though she didn't know why. It was wacky, she thought, from their first date when she wore English Rose and he requested that she always smell of roses, and there was something endearing about this strange need of his. And that was part of his charm for her. He was her mysterious man in a film noir whose fetishes hinted at layers of secrets and not a few demons. She was intrigued because one day, she believed, when she'd least expect it, she would know; just as one day she hoped to know why he preferred her hair looking none too elegant, struggling to touch her shoulders rather than cut off short and pretty to grace her face. Regardless of how odd his craving for her smell, her hair, she believed it made him need her, and in that she found contentment.

"Long day, huh?" Gil said as his heart quickened with every step she took. Gil had never actually known anyone who walked like Sandra. The closest he'd ever come was a

video in a high-end New York boutique. He found it most
mesmerizing, downright arousing.

She plopped down, bag and all, on the sofa. "Yeah, the
longest. I'm sure glad it's over. I was running all around this
city today."

"Well, just relax. Can I get you something? You want a
glass of wine?"

"Yeah, that sounds good. The wine from last night?"

"Of course. I don't drink the stuff. You're the only wino
around here." He gave a half chuckle at his own quip, then
went off to the kitchen.

As he left the room, Sandra looked at him and smiled at
how everything about Gil was revealed in his walk. He was
a man who carried in his gait all the markings of his clois-
tered life as a boy.

When he returned with the glass of wine and sat down
next to her, Sandra's eyes were closed, but she wasn't sleeping. Her father used to play possum like that when he
wanted his children to sympathize with his fatigue and, es-
sentially, leave him be. She prayed Gil would be so gullible.

"So I had dinner at my mother's today. I told her that
we were getting married and that I wanted to bring you by
tomorrow for dinner," Gil said as flatly as if he were giving
her the time of day.

Like one of those dolls whose eyes pop open when you
suddenly snatch them upright, Sandra bolted forward, eyes
bulging. "You told her? What did you say? How did they
take it?"

"They were shocked, of course, but I think in time it'll
wear off."

"I don't know, Gil. I don't think you should have told
them we were getting married just yet. I think you should have
told them about me, then let me meet them, *then* told them
we're getting married." Sandra took a large gulp of the wine
and slouched back again.

"Well, it's too late now. It's done. Besides, what's the
difference whether I ease the news to them or just tell them

outright? They're going to find out anyway, so it's best just to get everything out there right away."

Sandra finished her glass of wine with several more long sips, then set it on the coffee table. She lay back, only to find Gil's hand waiting for her. Feeling him caress her ear, she clenched her teeth together, wanting to pull away, but knowing that would be too obvious. For some reason, he must have thought ear caressing was something she found arousing, because that's where he'd always begin. It was as if he'd read it in a book, or heard it on the street: *If you really want to get a woman in the mood, just trace her ear with your finger.* It was more than a little annoying, it was downright flesh-chewing. Something that got right under her skin right at the base of her neck and traveled clear to every nerve. What made it worse was that she knew what he wanted.

"You know what, Gil, I'm so tired, I just want to go to bed."

"So do I," he said, with shifting eyebrows and a smile that said a Marvin Gaye tune was playing somewhere in his mind.

"No, Gil, I'm serious now. I'm really beat."

Gil, though, pressed on, undeterred. This was part of the game, right? This was how love between them flowed, right from the beginning. She'd had a rough day, she was too tired, her side ached, her legs ached, her back ached. Then his passion, too strong, too intense, impossible to shun, would make her forget her ailments as she'd succumb with weakened body and softened loins to his passion. Right? Everyone, after all, used something to turn them on.

He kissed her, harder than she would have liked, then ran an awkward hand up her dress searching for the top of her panty hose. His fingers danced around the waistband, waiting for her to do what came next. She was taking longer than usual, so his hand found its way to her bottom, where it clasped around one buttock, its lusciousness clearly making his passion rise, as he kissed her that much harder. His lips made their way to her neck, and, lest they be there rubbing and kissing and grinding all night, she relented and opened the gates. Sandra freed herself from her underthings and let him in. She moaned at subconsciously timed intervals, groaned when he moved on to his pelvic shimmy that she knew he believed was particularly sensual. And as she lay there, each one loving the other the best they could, her mind drifted farther and farther into the next day when she would finally meet the woman who created this man.

$\mathcal{T}$WO

 A Lesson in Their Ways

Eulelie was on the cleaning woman's trail with an exacting haughtiness. She followed her into the living room, but then sat in her chair as if *Oh my, we just happen to be in the same room.* In the hall, she sat at the phone table, pretending to search for a number, but keeping the woman in one eye's corner. Then she busied herself in the most obviously fake way by sorting through mail—two-day-old mail that had already been sorted.

Eulelie actually believed her ruses were unobtrusive. Sadly, though, this day was no aberration for the cleaning woman. She had been keeping the Giles home clean for over thirty years, and not one day with Eulelie was any different than the one before. She didn't so much accept Eulelie's insulting ways as much as she coped, much the way she coped with Eulelie never calling her by name. When Eulelie addressed her, she simply started talking with the expectation of a response. Her mother had given her the name Belva some sixty years ago, more years than Eulelie had been alive. What would happen if one day she simply did not respond, if she acted as if she had no idea to whom Eulelie was speaking? It was obvious. Eulelie would just keep talking, keep asking the same question or giving the same order until she was heard.

"Look at this! It doesn't even look like you cleaned it,"

Eulelie said now, pointing her pale, arrow-straight finger in the direction of the vase atop the piano in the living room.

"I cleaned it, Mrs. Giles. You saw me clean it. I don't know what you mean."

"Did you pick it up and clean it with the Windex?"

"No. I dusted it with the duster."

Eulelie looked at her for several long, impatient seconds, expecting her to get it. "Well?" she finally said.

"Mrs. Giles, I just cleaned it on Saturday with the Windex. There's only so much dust that can collect in a few days." And she didn't move. The request was ridiculous, even for Eulelie. A standoff. "So, you want me to clean it with the Windex?" Belva finally said, realizing there was no way to win.

"Yes, I do."

Belva, in a huff she kept under her breath, went off to get the Windex. When she returned to clean the vase, Eulelie stood right there, making certain that her vase would not simply be passively dusted, but rubbed clean with the Windex. The cleaning woman gave her exactly what she wanted to see. She spritzed the vase and rubbed it, rubbed it again, and then rubbed it again. She held it up to the light to look for anything, smudges, her own fingerprints, anything Eulelie might find. Spit-shined clean. But then, just for the affect of it, she still squirted the vase again, and rubbed it again, and again, until the look of satisfaction was on Eulelie's face.

"There, now," Belva said, placing the vase carefully back on the hall table. She gathered up all the cleaning supplies. "Okay, Mrs. Giles, that's it for down here. Everything's perfect for your company tonight. I'll just go and do Lucretia's room, then I'll be gettin' on home," and Belva went upstairs too quick for Eulelie to bark another order. In fact, by the time Eulelie turned around, Belva had already disappeared into the late afternoon shadows of the upstairs hall.

Belva made her way down the hallway to Lucretia's room with a wearied waddle—as if her feet hurt, or her back ached, or her entire body suffered the dull lassitude of a woman working hard for a pittance. Though the door sat open, she knocked. The room was so vast, Lucretia could have been in there, somewhere out of sight of anyone merely standing in the doorway. No one answered. From where Belva stood, she could see what needed special attention. What on earth does this girl do to that mirror? she wondered. Smudges everywhere. If she didn't know any better, she'd swear that Lucretia had gone back to her old ways of speaking fake Spanish and then kissing herself in the mirror. She'd done this as a child and as a young teen, mostly in the bathroom mirror, and she never knew anyone else knew. But Belva heard her—more than once. Whatever Lucretia was doing to make those smudges, it had to be equally as strange as the days of fake Spanish and mirror kissing.

Belva went to the bureau and set her cleaning basket on its corner, pushing aside nail polishes and bottles of perfume. Coating the mirror with the blue liquid, she wiped before it even had a chance to make a clean dripping getaway. In just a few strokes she'd cleaned away Lucretia's mystery smudges. Then, out of her basket she plucked a dusting wand that she waved majestically over the bureau, picking up what little dust was there. A mirrored tray sat empty in the middle of the dresser where those stray bottles of nail polish and perfume mostly lived. Belva arranged them back on the tray, then waved her wand again, only this time she wasn't looking when it bumped from the bureau a black-and-white photograph of Lucretia as an infant, cradled in a pair of arms that belonged, clearly enough, to a woman—but the woman had no face. Glass broke.

Belva turned with surprise when she heard a gasp come from behind her. "Oh, my, Lucretia, I'm so sorry, honey," Belva said, already on her hands and knees collecting the shards of glass.

"Oh, God, Belva! How could you be so careless? Give it to me," and she took the frame and broken glass from Belva's hands. She inspected the picture by running the tips of her fingers over it like a caressing lover. "Well, it's okay. Just the frame was ruined. The picture's still perfect." She looked up at Belva's face, which hung with absolute despair. "Really, Belva, it's okay. But you know what, don't worry about my room. It's really not as bad as Momma thinks it is."

Belva took her basket of cleaning rags and bottles and left the room, passing Linda in the doorway.

"What was that? I heard a crash all the way down the hall," Linda said to her sister, dragging herself and her hard day's work over to sit next to Lucretia on the bed.

"It was this picture of me as a baby. See?" and she held the picture upright as if at show-and-tell. "These are Mommy's arms, you know. I don't know, but this picture is so special to me. I guess it affirms that I'm not just *here*, if you know what I mean. It tells me that I have a history. But more than all that, this is living proof that Mommy actually, really did, once touch me; hold me in her arms and love me the way mothers should."

Linda looked wistfully at the picture, then touched it. "Yeah, I know what you mean. I swear, I wish I had something like that." And the two fell into a silence that was filled with the thoughts of a woman they never knew. Filling the quiet were Belva's clomping feet descending the staircase.

When Belva reached the downstairs front hall, she found Eulelie in the living room sitting at her writing desk, checkbook in hand.

"Dear, did you clean under the beds today?" Eulelie asked.

"No, Miss Eulelie. You told me that you just wanted me to do some dusting and tidyin' up and scrub up the bathrooms for company. You didn't say nothin' 'bout cleanin' under the beds. Besides, I just cleaned under the beds last week. Don't you remember?"

"Yes, I remember, but I wanted you to clean under them again today. Well, it's too late now. I'll tell you what. I'll just take off ten dollars today. Is that okay with you?" Eulelie said, writing out the check before the woman could even respond.

It wasn't okay. How could it be okay? Belva wasn't the type for confrontational hissy fits. Boy, did she miss the Judge. Since he died, Eulelie would cheap her way out of what was owed by accusing her of skimping on the cleaning. Belva took the check, saying what she always said: "This is fine, Mrs. Giles. Thank you." She glanced at the check that was just a dollar more than an insult, tucked it away, and left.

After seeing Belva out, Eulelie went to the kitchen to see how her girls were coming with dinner. Lucretia and Linda were nowhere to be found, but Lucretia had prepared the hens and had already put them in the oven. Lila had cut up the carrots and set them aside to await Eulelie's magic touch. Eulelie sat at the kitchen table and sipped the tea Lila had made for her, which was now just a bit warmer than tepid. Eulelie stared into the air that grew more funereal as the minutes ticked closer to seven o'clock. Despair, worry, and fear were spelled out in each and every crease in her furrowed brow.

"Momma, what do you want me to do with these greens?" Lila asked.

Eulelie didn't respond.

"Momma? Momma?"

"Yes, honey?"

"These greens. What do you want me to do with them?"

"Are they cooked?"

"Yes, Momma."

"Then just put some salt and pepper on them and put them in a serving dish. Cover them with foil. They'll keep."

But Lila didn't move to follow the orders right away. She looked at Eulelie's droopy face and said, "Momma, you're worried about Gil, aren't you?"

"Yes, I am. I just don't know what he's doing. What he's thinking."

Just then the front door opened, and all hearts jumped.

This was the dreaded moment. Lila was the only one who could see into the front hall. Eulelie bracingly held her breath.

"It's only Linda and Lucretia looking out the door, Momma. Relax."

"What's going on? You two look like you've just seen a ghost," Linda said, walking into the kitchen.

"We thought you were Gil and that girl," Eulelie said.

"Don't you remember, Linda? Gil's bringing his fiancée to meet Momma," Lila said in that tone that sounded like she was talking to a child, or the insane.

"Yes, of course I remember, and I'm having no part of it. You all can go ahead and be hypocrites if you want, but I don't accept this, I never will, and I'm not going to pretend like I do." Linda took a banana from the fruit bowl centerpiece and sat down across the table from Eulelie. Sliding her pumps off of her feet, she breathed a sigh and said, "I'm tired."

"I didn't even hear you come in, Linda. How was your day at the bank, honey?" Eulelie asked.

"The same as always, Momma—white trash coming in there asking for money they know they don't qualify for and can't pay back. I'm going to my room. Call me when this mess is over," and Linda went off.

With squint-eyed doubt, Lila watched Linda leave, wondering if her sister really was planning to be so rude, so obstinate. She picked up a wooden spoon and tapped the counter absentmindedly, summoning the words to her voice. "Momma, you know, I was just thinking about a book I read a few years ago. In this story, this woman was married to a man whose mother just despised her, just hated her, you know, felt she wasn't good enough. Well, this man, he cheated on his wife over and over again, but this woman was unbelievably strong and forgiving, and she kept that family together at all costs. When the man's mother finds out about his affairs, her feelings about his wife change. And don't you know that on her deathbed, this man's mother begged his wife not to leave her son. She came to see that this woman wasn't so bad for her son after all."

The quiet was eerie. It seemed as if something big would happen, should happen. Her mother and sister were stark still, as if waiting for the real end to this story, as if waiting for Lila to fall all over herself laughing at the absurdity of such a tale.

When Eulelie finally spoke, her voice was low. "Lila, are you saying that one day, even on my deathbed, I will accept my son's marriage to the likes of Sandra, a woman from a family in East Baltimore we know nothing about? Are you saying to me that your mind would entertain the ridiculous thought that your brother may end up not being good enough for *her*?"

"No Momma, I would never say that! I'm just saying that maybe we're not giving her a fighting chance to gain our favor because opinions have already been set about who she is because of where she comes from and because her family's not like ours. I mean, I have to admit that I've pretty much decided that she's probably not right for Gil simply because their worlds are so different. I'm not proud that I feel this way. I think it stinks that I feel this way, but I do."

Well, what was there for her to say? Eulelie wondered. Her daughter had obviously given much more thought to the notion of accepting Sandra as a Giles than she had, so Eulelie simply continued drinking her tea in tiny sips, and when she got to the end, she looked up at the clock for the time. "Oh my Lord, Lila," she said. "Would you look at the time? It's already seven-thirty."

"I know, Momma, but it's okay. Everything is done and the table is set."

"Yes, I know, but where's Gil? I told him seven o'clock, and here it is seven-thirty already and he hasn't called to say they're going to be late. Well, I'm not holding dinner a minute longer. We're going to eat. This girl is going to get her first lesson in manners. When someone says dinner at seven, they mean dinner at seven. Lila, dish out the food. Lucretia, pour the iced tea."

Not a word was spoken through dinner, and just before last bites were eaten, the phone rang, its scream cutting through the silence with the violence of a machete. Lila jumped to answer it.

"Hello? Oh, hi Gil," she said, raising her eyebrows at her mother. "Momma, it's Gil. Gil, where are you? Uh-huh. Uh-huh. Well, we've already started eating. You know that Momma said seven o'clock. We waited until seven-thirty, and when you weren't here . . . Okay, well just get here when you can. All right, we'll see you then. 'Bye."

"What happened?" Eulelie snapped before Lila even had a chance to put the phone back on the wall.

"It seems as though Sandra got held up with her family. Something personal. Gil didn't go into it."

"I see," Eulelie said without emotion. "Well, get the pie and coffee. We'll have it in the parlor." She pushed away from the table and went through the French doors to the parlor to wait for the cloud of East Baltimore to fall on her home.

"Poor Momma," Lucretia whispered. "This thing is just enough to kill her."

Lila walked into the parlor carrying the tray with the coffee and Eulelie's sweet potato pie. Lucretia followed with the silverware and dishes.

Before putting everything on the table, before even sitting down, Lucretia said in her uppity Baltimore drawl, "I'll bet she's crude."

"Come on, Lucretia," Lila said. "We don't know anything of the sort, yet. I think we should just give her a chance and wait and see what she's like. We may even like her, right, Momma?"

Eulelie didn't respond.

"Well, anyway, I just can't imagine anybody from East Baltimore having enough class to be with our Gil." Lucretia said the words *East Baltimore* with such disdain, it was as if they had defiled her mouth, leaving a sour, rotting taste on her tongue.

"Oh, for God's sake, Lucretia, just leave it alone. Besides, I don't even want to think about the whole East Baltimore thing. It's just not that . . . I don't know, important, I guess." Lila lowered her head in confusion.

Then Lucretia turned to Eulelie, almost as if trying to give a final plea. "Momma, I don't even know why we bothered having the cleaning lady come in. All we had to do was throw some chicken bones and beer bottles around the house and she'd be right at home." Then she sat back on the sofa, crossed her arms and pouted like a willful brat.

"Lucretia, now I want you to cut that out. This isn't easy on any of us and you are not helping things at all. Just cut it out." But her fear was perceptible only in silhouette. It lived around the edges of a reality that told Eulelie her family was under attack by an enemy that she and her kind fought to keep at bay. Now the interloper was about to walk through her door to claim her conquest, and in the end make them one of her.

"Momma, do you remember when Gil graduated from Hampton? Boy, Daddy was so proud that Gil had chosen his alma mater." Lila smiled up at the ceiling.

"Oh, honey, how could I ever forget that day. The Judge grinned from ear to ear the whole day."

"Well, of course he was proud. His only son was not just graduating from his alma mater, but he was graduating summa cum laude. How many men can say that?" Lila paused, smiled to herself, then said: "But that's just how our Gil was, perfect in every way. Momma, do you remember how at the mayor's inaugural ball the year after Gil graduated from high school the mayor pointed Gil out in his speech as one of the future mayors of Baltimore? 'Maybe even governor of Maryland,' he said. And he wasn't just saying that because he was a friend of Daddy's. He knew Gil was brilliant. That moment sent chills down my spine. I mean, to have the mayor say something like that. I'll tell you, as all those eyes looked over at our table as Gil stood to receive his praise, I don't think I've ever been prouder, not even of myself, than I was of Gil at that very moment."

No one spoke for several long seconds. Then Lucretia said, "Well, I guess that's all over now. I mean, you don't become the first black governor of Maryland . . ." She didn't finish the thought.

Their eulogy was interrupted when they heard a car door close out front. All three heads snapped toward the clock on the mantel, which said 8:25.

Upstairs, they could hear Linda bolting to the window. No doubt she was peering through the lace curtains, sizing up this outsider from afar.

When Gil walked through the door with Sandra trailing behind, he knew exactly where his momma would be; and there she was, as stiff-backed as ever in her favorite wing chair beside the fireplace. He went directly to her and bent down to kiss her soft, gaunt cheek. Eulelie did not budge until Sandra stepped forward to greet her.

"Hello. It's a pleasure to finally meet you and your family," Sandra said with her smile, not too big but not at all halfhearted, that showed only her four front teeth, curling just enough at the corners to let the world know that she understood its irony.

Eulelie stood, extended her hand to this woman who was without a flaw and quite pleasing to the eye, any eye, even that of Eulelie, who really only appreciated the lighter hues of Negro skin. Nothing about her said East Baltimore to Eulelie. "Hello, Sandra. It's a pleasure to have you in our home." Eulelie studied her hair in a way that wasn't so obvious. Sandra's hair was pulled tautly back into a curled-under ponytail, so it was difficult for Eulelie to determine what kind of hair Sandra had.

"Thank you," Sandra said.

But when Sandra cocked her head to one side to accompany a smile, the light hit her in such a way that Eulelie saw her hair was straight as a bone, no thanks to anything genetic.

Sandra turned to Lila and Lucretia. "Hello, how are you?" she said, extending her hand.

"Fine, thank you," they answered. Lucretia, the stanchest protector of her brother, stared at Sandra with a face that said nothing. She settled back down on the sofa, already prepared to have nothing in common with this woman her brother proudly dragged in on his arm to meet their momma.

Eulelie sat back down in her chair, trying to find a way to turn the awkwardness that hung in the air into a pleasant conversation.

"Lucretia, go see what's keeping your sister."

"Yes, Momma," and off she went without a clue as to how she could even begin to convince Linda to at least give Sandra a chance. It didn't take long at all for Lucretia to return, without Linda, saying to Eulelie, "Linda says she's busy."

"Busy doing what?"

"I don't know. Just busy."

"Lila, go up and get your sister," she said, while shooting a polite but nervous smile in Sandra's direction. "Linda gets so distracted, you know. She's the baby of the family," she said to Sandra, without actually looking in her eyes.

Sandra smiled and looked up at Gil, who was sitting on the arm of her chair.

Everyone heard the bellow of Linda's voice waft down the staircase. "I said I'm busy!" She was agitated, defiant.

When Lila returned, as expected, without Linda, Eulelie, determined not to let Sandra think she had raised aberrant children, called to Linda in the sweetest voice she could muster. "Linda, honey, come on down and meet Gil's fiancée."

But Linda called back, "I'm busy, Momma," in that snappy, stubborn, bratty way that made everyone, even Sandra, know that she was not going to budge, no matter who came up after her.

"Can I get you a cool drink? Some lemonade, maybe?" Eulelie asked.

"Yes, please. I am a little thirsty, and I'm starving too. I know we're late for dinner, but if there's something I can nibble on, I would appreciate it," Sandra said. "I'm so sorry we're late, but my mother needed me to give my baby sister a big-sister talk. I'm sure you know how important family is, Mrs. Giles. When family needs you, nothing else matters."

"Oh, well absolutely. Your lateness was not a problem at all," Eulelie said through one of those smiles she might flash upon witnessing a well-dressed lady drinking champagne from the bottle. "Lila, go make Sandra a sandwich from some of that turkey breast." She looked over at Gil and said, "When you two weren't here by seven like you said, we just assumed you'd already eaten. Gil, do you want something?" Eulelie's smile dripped sugar too sweet to be tasty.

"No, thank you, Momma," he said so subtly, so apologetically, only Eulelie could see what he meant. This was not right, Gil was saying. His mother would judge Sandra badly for her request of food. He knew his mother would not understand that in Sandra's world, this kind of thing was not bad manners. In her world when in the home of a mother, you made yourself at home. Asking for food was a compliment, acceptance, comfort.

Lila heard her mother's command but was stunned into immobility. "A sandwich, Momma?" She looked at Eulelie with bug-eyed surprise.

"Yes, a sandwich. Slice off the turkey breast we had for dinner on Saturday, and there's some lettuce in the crisper and some tomatoes I just bought this morning in the basket on the table. Go on now. We wouldn't want our dear Sandra to starve to death." Southern charm. The room was thick with it. That's what it was all about. Indeed, Eulelie was incredulous over this woman's nerve. Who wouldn't be? A woman with good manners who was late to dinner would simply endure her stomach's rumblings and pass the noise off as a truck in the distance until she was offered food, and even then she would demurely turn it down and simply try to talk over her internal growls. That's how it was done in

her world, but of course it would be bad manners to tell
Sandra so.

Lila did what her mother asked, mumbling "Yes, Momma"
as she left the room.

After Lila went to fix the sandwich, Gil stood abruptly
from the arm of Sandra's chair and said, "I'll be right back."
He took the stairs two at a time as he went to see what was
taking Linda so long.

Sandra, left alone with Eulelie and Lucretia, fell under
Lucretia's protective stare. Lucretia couldn't take her mind
nor her eyes off the garish streetwalker red nail polish on
Sandra's fingers and toes that peaked out through sandal
straps. And the same color was smeared across her mouth.
A wrinkled forehead and pressed lips showed disapproval.

As Sandra sat crossing and uncrossing her ankles, she felt
watched. Those pictures on the mantel with their spooky
eyes that seemed to know things, but that wasn't it. The
eyes stuck on her were very much real, very much human.
Then just barely in the corner of her eye she saw Lucretia
staring almost with pure contempt at her nail polish. What
was it about the color red? Maybe it offended her in some
way. Maybe, Sandra supposed, Lucretia thought everybody
should wear the white-girl shade of pink she and her sisters
wore. Sandra couldn't tell, but the staring was unnerving,
given the situation. She tucked her fingers into a fist to con-
ceal the color, but there was nothing she could do about
her toes, which sat in clear view of those searching eyes, or
her lips.

Desperate for a diversion, Sandra said without thinking:
"Lucretia, I really like your shoes. They're very classic." And
immediately she could have slapped herself. Why, out of
all the things about Lucretia she could have invented to be
impressed by, did she choose her shoes? If Lucretia hadn't
noticed her red toenails before, she'd certainly see them now.

Lucretia didn't bother to compare shoes. She simply
crossed her short chunky legs, which were unflattered by

unadorned simple pumps the color of cream that showed the bulges of her toes, then said: "Thanks."

"It was nice of Gil to bring you by here today, even though this news is . . ." Eulelie wanted to be delicate. ". . . a bit unexpected, to say the least."

"You know, I told Gil that just this morning," Sandra replied. "I told him that you all didn't know a thing about me. That's why I'm really so embarrassed about being late, because I know it looks bad. I don't think there's anything worse than making a bad first impression on your fiancé's family. But like I said, there was nothing I could do since my parents needed help with my baby sister, who's acting like a typical teenager."

Lila returned with Sandra's sandwich. "Here you are," she said, offering Sandra the sandwich and a glass of iced tea.

"Oh, thank you so much," Sandra said, then took a heaping bite out of it before Lila even set the plate on the coffee table. She ate as if the sandwich was the first thing in her belly for days. Her bites were not so much bites as they were gluttonous chomps; not dainty in the least bit.

"Sandra, are you a Delta, or AKA, or anything Greek?" Eulelie asked.

"No, ma'am. I'm just black." A stab at humor that went flat, as she chortled at her own witticism. "Well, anyway, no, I didn't pledge any sororities. I didn't see much of a point to them. I don't really see what they do. Besides, I'm not much of a joiner, you know. I don't join clubs."

"Sororities perform quite a service in the black community. They work with youth, they feed the poor, they do quite a lot, Sandra," Eulelie said as if she, herself, were under attack.

"I guess once you're out of college they do. But when you're in college, they just seem to me to be cat-fighting social clubs. 'The Deltas are better than the AKAs. No, the AKAs are better than the Deltas.' That kind of mess. I just didn't need it." Then, all at once, her face seemed to lose all its form. And what that blank slate seemed to finally grasp, in the twinkling of a star, was that Eulelie, maybe even her daughters, were members of a sorority. That's why all the sorority talk. Was it possible to speak with a size eight foot in your mouth? "So, Mrs. Giles, are you a member of a sorority?" she asked, now that her foot was nearly choking her.

"Yes, I'm an AKA, and so are the girls. And I guess you know that Gil's a member of Alpha Phi Alpha."

"Actually, I didn't. I guess it never came up. By the way, Mrs. Giles, I don't have anything against fraternities and sororities, you know. I just don't think they're right for me, and especially not while I was in college. Then, I was concentrating on keeping my grades good to get out of school, and trying to hold down a job at the same time."

"Yes, I understand," Eulelie said.

But Sandra didn't have to be a part of their world to know she had just gotten a point taken away. Who is this woman, Sandra had to wonder, who acts as if she's playing a role? Putting on airs. From the moment she first shook that hand of flimsy skin and thin bones, she knew there was something odd about her, and now she had it figured out. Sandra put Eulelie in her mind as a woman too aware of herself; very conscious of every step, every word, every smile. Why? she wondered, and decided the question was not important enough to ponder.

"So, Sandra, Gil tells us you grew up in East Baltimore," Eulelie said. "What was that like?"

"The pits," she said while chewing the last mouthful of sandwich. When she swallowed, she explained, "There's nothing over there as nice as this. This is a really nice neighborhood."

"Yes, this is a nice community," Eulelie said. "This is the community of Hanlon Park."

Sandra didn't let it ruffle her. Fine, they lived in a *community*. What was the difference? She was just trying to keep the conversation going. "Gil tells me that your father was a judge," she said to Lila and Lucretia.

"Yes," Eulelie spoke up. "And, let's see, there was the children's great-great-grandfather and grandmother, George and Hattie Giles, who owned a shop where Hattie made tailored suits and custom-made dresses for colored men and women. They were born free during slavery, honey, so this was some accomplishment for two colored people back then. Then there's their grandfather, Gilbert Horatio Harding Giles the First, who was a doctor. He treated practically every black family in Baltimore during his time. You know, thanks to him, colored people in Baltimore didn't have to resort to crude home remedies, or go without treatment altogether when white doctors wouldn't treat them." Eulelie paused only long enough to breathe before resuming her history lesson of the Gileses. "And *his* father, their great-grandfather, Horatio Harding Giles, owned the only Negro funeral parlor in Baltimore at the turn of the century. All of them were trained professionally at Howard University, except for Horatio. He got his bachelor's from Howard, but never received a professional degree. All the Gilberts, including my Gil, got their bachelor's from Hampton. Gil is part of that legacy of Hampton and Howard. I, myself, come from a medical family. My father was a doctor down in South Carolina and a pillar of the community. Both my grandfathers were ministers. My mother was a teacher, one of her brothers owned a drugstore, and the other one was one of the first colored men to own real estate in our town."

"Is that right?" Sandra said, genuinely impressed, it seemed, but secretly wondering why Eulelie felt the need to turn the Giles family history into a lecture series.

"Yes, indeed," Eulelie said in the manner and language of sixty-something women. "I became a teacher, just like my mother, because I think that's some of the most important work a colored person can do in this world, you know, educating our own. Those who want to be educated. Of course, I haven't taught school since I got married. My family needed me."

Eulelie thought it was important that Sandra understand,

really understand, the importance of this family, so she went
on: "You know, about a year ago I read a story in the *Afro
Gazette*—do you read the *Afro Gazette?*" she asked, in a way
that said a yes would somehow be a point in her favor.

"Not really. Once in a while."

"Well, anyway," Eulelie said, as if put off, "it was a story
about a black woman who had set out to prove that she was
a granddaughter of George Washington, removed by several
'greats,' because she wanted to join the Daughters of the
American Revolution. And I thought, how odd, how all at
once funny and pathetic, that this woman would be prideful
of such a relation. She could have it, right along with the
Daughters of the American Revolution. I'm related to George
Giles. What do I need with George Washington, whose
blood would most likely have been passed on through that
ghastly pock upon our people—slave rape."

Sandra sat smiling, a smile that knew of worldly ironies.
It was all she could do to keep that smile from exploding
into a full-throated laugh. How all at once funny and pathetic, she thought, that Eulelie would hold slave rape with
such disdain, yet it was the sole reason for the bright skin
she held so high.

For Eulelie, all of this was meant to point out that of all
the extreme ways the Giles family could have gone—to the
abjection of poverty or to the wealth of millionaires—not
one dead Giles would have ever imagined the turn this
branch of the family was taking right now. The Giles family,
through all these generations, had come to have a reputation
of respectable gentility, almost nobility. Not rich, but not
poor by any standard, black or white. They were comfortable, very comfortable. An eminent line, they believed in
such things as passing names from generation to generation
to maintain the family's sense of honor and history. "We
have been a very renowned family for over a hundred years
now." *Oh, the sullying one woman can do to a family's good
name*, she seemed to be saying.

"Wow. Royalty," Sandra said with a ghost of a smile,

out of deference to this family's tree. "Hey, aren't you two teachers too?" There was nothing else for her to say.

"Yes," Lila said. "I teach accelerated fifth graders, and Lucretia teaches the fourth grade at the same school. It's funny, because some of the kids who have Lucretia in the fourth grade work extra hard in hopes that she'll recommend them to come to my class in the fifth grade. It's very inspiring, actually, to see children craving to learn and excel."

"So, Sandra," Eulelie said, "Gil tells us that you're a paralegal and that you're intending to go on to law school. Oh, and it's just the mother in me that wants you to finish chewing before you answer."

Though it was nearly imperceptible, if one looked deep into Sandra's eyes, it would be clear that she got it. Like Moses on the mountaintop, she got it. She wasn't good enough. She gave Eulelie and her daughters a baffled look. And then there was the fear, plain as could be in her flattened face. She showed it to the lionesses. In that place, that burning place in the back of her eyes where tears become sad, Sandra's will fought against their birth. She answered plainly after swallowing all traces of the sandwich. "I'm a paralegal, that's all. I have no plans to go to law school. I like what I do, and at the end of the day, my day is over."

"And that's good enough for you? You don't want any more from your career?"

"Mrs. Giles, I have a job and I like it. I could spend the rest of my life making my living like this because it's honest work, it's hard work, but for me it's work, not a career."

"I see," was all Eulelie could say.

"Well, how in the world did you and Gil meet?" Lucretia's mind couldn't begin to fathom how their paths would have crossed.

"It was lunchtime and I was sitting down in Hopkins Plaza. He came up looking so handsome in his suit. I could just tell he was a decent guy, not like a lot of weirdos that wander down there. You raised a handsome gentleman, Mrs. Giles."

"Yes, thank you, I know that," Eulelie said with a patronizing half smile, as if she had something to do with his good looks.

"So, anyway, I went over to him with my sandwich, asked if I could join him, and the rest is history, but just in case you don't know, he called me again, and again, and again." She laughed, still amused at this story of love found in the strangest of places.

"How nice. What a sweet story," Eulelie said. Then she shifted quickly to where she really wanted to be. "Now, Gil tells us that your father works at Bethlehem Steel. What does he do down there? Is he a metallurgist?" Eulelie asked, knowing full well he wasn't, but why she had to ask escaped even her own reasoning.

"A what? No, I don't think he's that. He's a machinist, that's all. He doesn't have some fancy title like metallurgist." Sandra paused and looked across the room for her words. Then, with her family under attack, she said: "My parents managed to put two of us through college, and they're making sure my little sister will go too. What more could anyone ask of two people who simply wanted to work hard to provide for their family?" And Sandra looked at the woman in a way that said she expected an answer to her question that wasn't really a question. She was as mad as a hornet with a shook-up nest, and didn't know quite where to place her anger. Yes, this woman infuriated her to no end, but at that moment Gil angered her most, because he'd brought her before his mother without the merest mention that these people thought she was nothing from nothing; and then was inconsiderate enough to leave her alone with them.

"So you're Gil's stepmother, right?" Sandra was hoping to change the subject and keep it changed.

"Yes, I am, but we don't talk in terms of stepmother and stepchildren in this family. As far as I'm concerned, I'm their momma," Eulelie said, with a guarded edge.

"Sandra, generally people don't talk about that to us. It's just not good manners," Lucretia said.

"Well, why? I mean, was your own mother some sort of wicked person?"

"No, of course not!" Lucretia snapped. "It's just that we don't remember our mother. Momma's the only mother any of us ever knew."

"But you don't talk about your mother?"

"Well, no. Why talk about somebody you don't know?"

"So that you can know her," Sandra said. It made perfectly good sense to her, but they just looked blank-faced at her, as if she were muttering in tongues. Sandra smiled at their strangeness, and at their world, which was even more peculiar.

"You see, Sandra, Gloria was the woman who gave birth to us," Lila said diplomatically. "She died when I was three. Linda was one, Lucretia was two, and Gil was six."

"The girls were just mere stair steps," Eulelie said, hoping Sandra would now understand.

"Daddy married Momma soon after Gloria died."

"So you call her Gloria?"

"Yes. What else should we call her?" Lila asked, halfway expecting, almost wanting, an answer.

"Well, anyway, Mrs. Giles, you said you're from South Carolina?"

"Yes, I am."

"Where in South Carolina? I have some relatives down there."

"Oh, I'm sure I wouldn't know them."

"Well, where are you from?"

"Columbia."

"We have some family there on my mother's side. Do you know the DeLoaches?"

"No, I'm afraid I don't," Eulelie answered in haste, without even giving herself a chance to actually hear the name.

"Well, what's your family's name? I'll ask my auntie. Maybe she knows them. She knows everybody. Especially society folks."

"For goodness sakes! What in the world is Gil doing upstairs? He should know by now that Linda is as stubborn as a mule. . . . I mean, what I mean to say is that when she gets involved in one of her projects, nothing in this world can pull her away," Eulelie said, skittering away like a cockroach in the night from the topic of her family in South Carolina. "Would you like something else to drink, Sandra?"

"Yes, thank you."

"We have Coca-Cola, we have more iced tea, we have lemonade, and we have apple juice," Lucretia said.

"Lemonade sounds just fine, thank you," Sandra said, handing her glass to Lila.

Taken aback, Lila took it and looked over at Lucretia, thinking her sister would go get the drink, but it was clear Lucretia had no intention of moving. "Oh, sure, I'll be glad to. I'll be right back."

Eulelie felt she had to set things right. She couldn't be seen as some sort of shrew, not even by the likes of Sandra, for not helping her children keep their mother in their hearts. She said: "Sandra, dear, I don't want you to be embarrassed about bringing up the fact that I'm not their natural mother. The reason no one ever brings it up is because these children look so much like they could be mine. Feature for feature, of course, they don't look anything like me, but most people think they're mine because we share the same pecan-colored skin."

"Well, I guess if you're only looking at color, but to tell you the truth, the color doesn't make them look like they could be your children. To me, they don't look anything like you."

"Is that a fact," Eulelie said politely, her thin skin about such matters almost punctured. "Well, I guess with the Judge's light skin and people's inability to see past color, most people who didn't know Gloria naturally assume that the Judge and I made these exotically colored babies. How lucky you are that color isn't a barrier to how you see the world." Every single word dripped with sarcasm.

"All of you have an exotic coloring," she said, and then left it at that.

"I suppose it is different," Eulelie said. "My mother was a Creole woman from New Orleans, so she was very, very fair. My father was half Indian, but the colored side of his family were all very, very fair as well. So I couldn't help but look the way I look. Everybody in my family has this blue-veined skin."

"Oh, that's something," Sandra said, for lack of anything else to say, as Lila returned, holding a glass of lemonade.

"And I'll tell you something else. People always seem to find their kind. When I first moved to Baltimore, I took one ride down this street, and when I got to that reservoir, I knew exactly where I wanted to live—right here on Hilton Street in one of these big pretty houses overlooking that reservoir. I knew that this was where I belonged. I mean, someone from my background wouldn't come to Baltimore and live . . . well, I could just tell that this was where people like myself and my family lived. Almost every day I would catch the Liberty Heights bus up here to Hilton Street and walk up and down the street just staring at that water. And don't you know, it was as if I had some sort of premonition. A year after I moved to this town, somebody asked me to go out on a blind date with a handsome lawyer. Well, that was all she wrote. One look at that man, and this house looking at the reservoir, and these beautiful children, and I knew that it was all meant to be my life."

"Wow, and I thought only white women had that kind of luck," Sandra said.

"Oh, honey, it's not luck. It's what I told you before. People just seem to find their own kind, no matter where they are."

"Maybe, maybe not. Look at me and Gil."

And everyone in that room knew that Sandra had caught up to their game. There was nothing any of the Giles women could say because they didn't even see it coming.

Upstairs, Gil had been distracted on his way to talk some

sense into Linda by a tug from the past—his old room. He didn't stay long on the path of his memories, but as he closed the door to the room, he carried some baseball caps he hadn't worn in over fifteen years but was certain he could use now. Walking to the door down the hall, he knocked once, twice, three times, and still he heard no voice from the other side beckoning him to enter. He opened the door anyway, and found Linda sitting in the corner, nothing in her hands, nothing in the room to indicate that she was in the middle of something. There was nothing in the room but the squeak of her rocking chair as she went back and forth.

"What are you doing?" Gil asked. "Why don't you just come on downstairs and join us?"

"I'm busy."

"Busy doing what?" Gil said, looking around the room once again for signs of her activity.

Linda didn't want to start an argument, but there was no way around it. She wasn't about to go downstairs to meet Sandra, and Gil wasn't going to stop pressing her to go, so there was only one solution.

"I'm busy thinking," she finally said after a few seconds of silence.

"Thinking? About what?"

"About what you're doing and why you're throwing away your life on a woman who doesn't deserve to carry this family's name. Who is this woman, Gil? I mean, she's not like us, the women you've grown up with."

There was no gradual buildup. Gil's temperature went straight from cool porcelain to hot steel. "What do you mean, 'not like us'?" he said. "Could you possibly mean that she seems too angelic and good of heart to be of this earth? No, I don't suppose you mean that?"

The anger in his voice startled Linda pop-eyed. "You know what I mean, Gil," she replied in a tone just as defiant and determined. "Her family isn't like ours. There's no lineage, no breeding."

"Breeding? What are we now, show dogs? You need to

get over yourself, Linda. All of you need to get over your-selves. I see the way Lila and Lucretia are looking at her. I guess Momma would look at her that way too if she weren't so damned *proper*."

"What do you expect us to do, Gil? First you tell us, out of the clear blue, that you're bringing this woman, who you're planning to marry, over to meet us. Then you bring her here and we see that she's all wrong for you and you expect us to just accept her anyway?"

"All wrong based on what? It's all based on some ridicu-lous snobometer that all of you have in your heads that you wouldn't know a well-bred woman if she came up and bit you on your well-bred ass. And I'll tell you something else. It's not like I brought her here and then you all decided that you didn't like her personality. Every one of you decided she wasn't acceptable the moment I mentioned East Baltimore and Sparrows Point and Lexington Market." Gil's voice was rising with each word. "You're a real piece of work, Linda. All of you are. You're all pushing thirty and still living here with Momma because that's what *well-bred* women do until the prince comes along. Well, let me tell you something. You need to prepare to spend the other side of thirty here too because I don't know if there are men alive perfect enough to live up to the standards set by the women of this family."

Linda's mouth formed that familiar pout that always took him back twenty years. Without saying a word, she jumped up from the rocker with so much force it almost flipped over. She threw herself on her bed and cried uncontrollably, managing to say, through her tears: "I'm nowhere near thirty. I'm only twenty-six."

Gil wanted to go to her, as he always did, and apologize; tell her it would be all right; tell her it was his fault. What sense would that make, though? He just turned his back on her, walked to the door, and was about to open it when he turned to make one last attempt to jolt his sister out of this netherworld of acceptable and unacceptable blacks in which they all lived. "Linda, you know, if you would give her a chance, you would find that Sandra is really a good and decent woman. Breeding is more than being accepted into haughty social circles and knowing not to ask for food until it's offered."

"It's also more than never having been arrested for stealing a car and never drinking a bottle of beer out of a paper bag. Gil, this family, the Gileses, we are the kind of black people who show white people without a doubt that we don't need them. We don't need their law firms, we have our own. We don't need their hospitals. We have our own. We don't need their high society. We have our own. Sandra and her kind, they're what this race needs less of because they keep us from moving forward."

She paused only long enough to bound from her bed and take Gil's hand for a final plea. "Gil, don't you see? If you marry this girl, you will be taking a giant step backward for the entire race. They way *I* see it, this is about more than just our family."

"Oh, so now I'm screwing up the whole race. I thought I was just putting a black mark on the family, but now I see. I'm being politically incorrect. Well, thank you for clearing that up for me. You know something, you're so damned . . ." And as he searched for the right word, the only word he could call her, the only one he could find, was *"Hinkty!"* Gil slammed the door behind him, and when he got downstairs, he went directly to Sandra. "We're leaving!"

She was shocked by his anger, but expected his command, having heard the yelling that came from upstairs. Judging by the look on his face and the edge to his voice, she knew he meant to waste no time. Besides, she was more than ready to go after the chat with Eulelie and her girls.

"Gil, honey, you haven't even had a chance to visit," his mother said. "Why all of a sudden do you have to go?"

They followed him out to the porch and watched as he rushed Sandra down the walk and into the car. Lila whispered to her sister, "What happened?" and Lucretia whispered back, "I don't know."

"Gil is overreacting, that's all," Eulelie said.

After closing the car door for Sandra, Gil turned and just stared quizzically at his mother. Sometimes, her knack at pretending not to notice unpleasantness made him want to slap her, like they did in the movies, jolting her from her stupor of denial. He knew she'd heard the commotion upstairs. "I'm leaving, Momma, because it's not enough, in youall's hinkty world, that a person has never been arrested for stealing a car or that they never drank a bottle of beer out of a paper bag. That's why!"

Eulelie didn't quite understand what he meant, but figured it had something to do with what happened upstairs with Linda. It didn't matter now, though. He pulled away from the house in such a hurry, he left his mother and two sisters standing in a cloud of fumes and dust. As they watched his small sports car get smaller, smaller, and eventually disappear into the mix of Hilton Street traffic, they knew without a doubt that he had never been this angry with any of them—ever!

"It's *not* enough," was all Lucretia said as she turned and went back into the house, leaving her mother and sister staring into nothingness as if they expected Gil to come back.

Lila took her mother's hand to draw her back in the house. "Come on, Momma. It's no use. Gil's got it in his head to marry this woman and that's that."

"I guess you're right." Eulelie slipped her arm around Lila's waist and said, "It's going to be all right, honey."

Just as she was about to open the door, Lila turned to her mother and said, "Momma, what on earth is a hinkty world?"

Eulelie just looked at her, smiling sadly.

$\mathcal{T}$HREE

 What's Apparent Is Not Always Obvious

Every night's sleep of her life in Baltimore was spent somewhere between shallow slumber and wide-eyed consciousness. When the Judge was still living, she'd just lie there, still as murky pond water, staring at the ceiling or the wall, careful not to stir him as he slept so soundly, his sleep undisturbed by demons. Since his death, Eulelie had taken either to sitting up in her rocker until the hellhounds tired of their torment, or creeping down to the kitchen for a midnight snack. In the summertime she blamed her sleeplessness on the oppressive humidity of the wet-blanket days that lingered into nights. In the winter the problem was cold nights that chilled to the very pith of her, and no amount of flannel nighties could lend warmth. In spring it was allergies, in the fall it was howling winds. She had the year covered with extenuation.

What always seemed to wake her was a recurring sleep-scene that was not really a dream and not exactly a nightmare. There were no rat-tailed demons or two-headed carnivorous monsters, or even a homicidal maniac, but it woke her with a booming timpani in her chest.

It began with Eulelie running through the streets of Baltimore being chased by herself. Eulelie, in her church suit and church hat and church pumps is being chased by a barefoot Eulelie in a ragged, scrubwoman frock and unstraightened hair—a most dreadful image of herself. They run and run, at first as if jocularly racing one another—who's the fastest. Then something changes, the pace quickens. A friendly relay or a frantic run-for-her-life dash? There was no telling now. Eulelie, panting and dripping with a lady's perspiration, can see over her shoulder that Eulelie, arms pumping and soaked with a scrapper's sweat, is gaining on her. She makes a jack-knife turn, almost running in the opposite direction, certain this will surely shake her wild self from her tail.

In Druid Hill Park she's moving like thunder up the park drive. Her feet are going *slap clack whack* against the ground. It's as if they're not even attached to the rest of her; as if they're not a part of the same body in which a frightened heart beats to the rhythmic click of a metronome ticking off sixteenth notes—and still it's not fast enough for her feet. Then for no reason, or perhaps a rock, stone, or pebble in her path, Eulelie falls flat. When she looks up she sees herself, and behind her the Reptile House, standing alone and looking as devoid as ever of anything living.

The door of the Reptile House opens and out step two women whose faces she can't make out through the shadow that seems to fall on them from nowhere. They call to her mockingly, with one saying, and then the other: *Tsk, tsk, tsk. Still running from yourself after all these years. Don't you know you're gonna get caught?* And when Eulelie blinks they're on a road she somehow knew, some strange, yet oddly familiar place that could be a small town or a small part of a small town, and the women are walking off down the road. That's the point, always, when she woke up.

She dreamed this every night, or at least it haunted her so frequently it seemed to be every night. Sleeping pills were out of the question—not an option. Pills dulled the senses and could cause the mind and soul to tell their truths. For the same reason she hardly touched liquor—Eulelie did not want to lose control. She resigned herself to the unfortunate fact that the part of her character that believed in truth was holding her hostage. At least there was some small part of her conscious mind, though, that had a conscience.

Eulelie felt she had to get out. Leave it there. Perhaps when she returned, the dream-spirit, or whatever it was that brought this bizarre image to her mind so frequently, would be gone. Closing her door softly behind her, she walked down the hall toward the front steps, but when she got to Linda's room, something stopped her in mid-stride. Voices. Two voices coming from the room where there should have been none. One was Linda's, but the other did not belong in her house, not at that hour. It was deeper, probably a man's, definitely a man's. She knocked once, quietly, and the voices hushed with a suddenness that made Eulelie all the more curious. Nothing. No response, no invitation into the room. Eulelie knocked again, slightly louder, but this time said in a whisper, "Linda? Linda, are you talking to someone?" She slowly opened the door to a darkened room bathed in the soft blue light of the television. Poking only her head in the room, Eulelie found Linda snugly ensconced beneath covers pulled up to her neck; like Eulelie's sweet little girl who was most comforted by warmth, even in dead-of-summer heat. "Linda, sweetheart, are you okay? I thought I heard you talking to someone."

"Momma, it was just the TV. I'm watching a movie. Did it wake you?" Her voice was serene and sweet.

"No, honey, not at all. Okay, good night," and Eulelie closed the door, never seeing, or maybe not wanting to see, the lumpy form of a man in the bed with Linda. What would the mind do without denial?

Eulelie descended the staircase gingerly, not wanting to disturb her other daughters, whom she believed must have been sleeping this early into the new day. At the bottom of the stairs she froze, her ears perking like a hunter's hound. Something, someone, was stirring on the porch. The screen door opened. A key slid into and turned in the lock. Fear would not let Eulelie move. Could this be happening? Could someone actually be invading her sanctum? But whoever it was had their own key. She thought she must just die right there on the spot in the same way a trapped and hopeless, helpless deer would. When the door opened, a figure stepped in, a figure her horror would not allow her eyes or mind to know. The hall lights clicked on. Eulelie saw Lila standing there with disheveled hair and a guilty, flushed face. She was surprised, too.

"Lila!" Eulelie exclaimed, clutching at her heart. "You nearly scared me to death. I thought you had come in already and were upstairs sleeping. It's two in the morning. Where have you been?" She really hadn't intended to ask, but it just spewed out on automatic, maybe due to the stress of fright.

"Oh, I was just out with some, uh, teachers from the school. We went to a movie and then for some, uh, pizza. And then, you know, we just talked and talked and lost track of the time." She giggled nervously through her explanation. Hopefully, she thought, her mother bought it. It was Lila's luck that her mother was in just enough denial to believe anything, especially with the creaking of Linda's rocking bed being heard throughout the house. Lila went to move past Eulelie to go up to her room, trying to stay out of smelling range. Eulelie could smell a patch of stink weed growing on the other side of town, and Lila was certain that had she gotten close enough, that smell of the sex she'd just had— that was in her hair and in her clothes—would smack her mother in the face like a cold morning chill.

"Well, good night, honey," Eulelie said as Lila climbed the stairs at a pace so slow she could have been in pain. "Are you okay, baby? You look as if your leg is hurting you."

"Oh, I'm okay, Momma. I must have pulled a muscle getting out of the car. I'll be okay after a shower and some sleep. Good night," and she disappeared into the darkness of the upstairs hall.

Eulelie turned off the hall lights and went on into the kitchen. Everyone was right where they belonged. She didn't need to turn on the light. Everything in its place, she could find her way to what she wanted in pitch-black. The oatmeal cookies Lucretia baked were done just the way Eulelie liked them—soft, chewy, and with lots of raisins, a raisin with every bite. Eulelie poured the milk in a heavy-bottomed glass—no plastic cups for her. Glass kept it colder. Nothing was better to Eulelie than cookies and milk late at night. It was one of those things that made life worth living. Just the simple idea of a late-night snack, just the ability to be able to have one, was a luxury she'd idealized since she was a young girl.

Eulelie started up the stairs with her nighttime goodies, careful not to spill her milk, which was filled almost to the rim. When she got to the top, she was stopped by the sound of the shower coming from the girls' bathroom. Lila. Eulelie smiled to herself, thinking about Lila's fondness for showers. It didn't matter how late she'd come in, she had to shower. She smiled, then went on toward her room, but her stride was halted yet again. It was the most peculiar sound— *squeak-creak, squeak-creak, squeak-creak*. At first she thought it was the wind in the attic, except that there was a rocking rhythm to the squeaks and creaks. Then quiet took her over as she remembered the way Linda rocked in her bed for sleep to come on the nights when her visitor cramped her up. She could have sworn, though, that Linda had just had her period two weeks ago when those *squeak-creaks* filled the dark midnight quiet of the house. Then again, there was no way to accurately keep track of the cycles of three girls. Eulelie thought no more about it, continuing down the hall. Linda had found a way to comfort herself during that awful time of the month, and that's all that mattered, regardless of how loud those *squeak-creaks* would get—and in the past, they'd gotten pretty loud.

The next day was one of those glorious spring days with not a cloud in the sky—the kind of sky that only a creator can make perfectly blue. A day where all of Baltimore should have been at Druid Hill Park, or Harbor Place, or Fells Point, or some other strolling place. Gil and Sandra made their way

down Charles Street at lunchtime, indulging in ice cream—
she busy catching the drips from her cone before they
splayed over her fingers, he methodically scooping from his
sensible cup. The day went well with ice cream. They each
metamorphosed into their long-ago selves, as the child's am-
brosia slid past their tongues to a soul-stroking place deep
within where it danced. But even this diversion would not
make their very grown-up problem go away.

Nothing could wipe from Sandra's mind the night before—Gil running down the stairs, ordering that they leave;
Eulelie's over-mannered smile as she responded to questions
about where she grew up and what her parents did for a
living, and what she did for a living. It all reminded her of
those people who end up lost in East Baltimore, driving
around with tight, terrified faces that said they'd drive till
they ran out of gas rather than ask one of *those people* for
directions.

Gil and Sandra walked to Hopkins Plaza, the place where
they had met. Frequently, they returned to reminisce. They
would have even sat in the same spot where they ate their
first lunch together, but there were three giggling teenage
girls sitting there. Some days were just not meant to be
relived.

"You know, Sandra," Gil said, "it's hard to imagine, I
know, but my mother and sisters have their good points.
They really do."

"I'm sure they do. They were subtle. They were nice to
me. It's not like they were nasty and told me point-blank to
get out of their home and your life."

"No, they wouldn't do that," Gil said, without saying
the rest.

"I'm not naive. I know I don't come from a society family
with a father who's a judge and a socialite mother who be-
longs to every high-brow club in creation, but I think I was
raised with morals and raised to be a good person. But to
tell you the truth, I don't think it's about all that. I think

they just don't like the idea that some other woman is taking their Gil away." She took his hand and held it, softly.

It would take something within biblical confines to make the women in his life accept Sandra, he thought. To let her believe for a second longer that they would do this to any woman who tried to take him away would be wrong. No one could be better for them than some doctor's, or lawyer's, or Indian chief's daughter from that incestuous little breeding pool in which his mother and sisters swam.

"Look Sandra, this is the real thing. We're not talking about a mild case of noses in the air. My mother and sisters are hard-core snobs, and it's all-encompassing—money, social status, family lineage, even skin color. The bottom line is, they are not thrilled that I'm marrying a woman who grew up off of Greenmount Avenue with lower-class, blue-collar parents. *And* you're dark-skinned to boot."

Sandra gave him a look from her classic bag of looks. Raised eyebrows, cocked head. He'd either said or done the wrong thing. "Are you calling me and my family low-class?"

"Come on, Sandra. You know there's a world of difference between low-class and lower class. You know I'm not calling you all low-class. I'm speaking strictly from a socio-economic point of view *and* from my mother's and sisters' perspective."

"My parents may not have gone to college, Gilbert Giles the Third, son of the Judge Gilbert Giles the Second, but they raised four good kids. None of us ever did drugs or went to jail. We just worked hard and did what we had to do. If that makes us low-class, then the standards for high-class are just too high for me." She threw his hand aside, got up and walked away, spitting fire.

"Sandra, come on," Gil said, running after her. "You knew what the deal was the minute they started asking you questions, and if you believe you didn't, you're only lying to yourself. You're too smart about people not to have known."

Sandra turned and faced him as he claimed her hand once more. She looked at him with round, tear-brimmed eyes he had seen only once before and vowed he never wanted to see again. "I love you, Gil, but I'm not going to have your family treat me like I'm trash everytime I'm around them. And you know what else, you could have told me how they were going to act before you took me over there."

"And what would I have said? 'My mother and sisters won't like you, Sandra. They'll think you're not good enough.' "

"Yeah, maybe something like that. Why not? It's just that I wouldn't have asked for that sandwich if I didn't think it would be okay. I thought I was going to a mother's house. A mother who would be as warm and sweet as her son." Sandra softened just a bit, then just as quickly tightened her jaw again. "Plus, Gil, why did you tell your mother that I'm planning to go to law school to become a lawyer?"

"Well, we talked about that, didn't we?"

"No, Gil, you talked about it and I listened. I told you then and I'll tell you now, and I hope I won't have to tell you again. I'm not interested in law school, I like what I do and I'm not planning to change it, not for you and especially not for your mother. I just don't understand why you had to lie."

Gil thought, then looked away, feeling childish, humiliated. "I guess so that my mother would be impressed with you in some way."

"Well she's not, so that's that."

They walked on together with nothing between them but a chasm where their hands once held to connect their hearts; and there were no words. Gil came across a small stone in his path he felt compelled to kick. It went a few feet then rested, still in his path. He kicked it again, and again, and it became a game, a game he could play with himself at the exclusion of her and the heaviness of talk. And that's how she knew that what they'd discussed not even a minute before had been willingly pushed from his consciousness.

"Gil, I need to know that who I am is enough for you,"

Sandra finally said, stopping short with the hope that that confounded stone would roll to some dark corner of the street and wait for the next escape artist to happen by. "Your mother, your sisters, are obviously impressed with careers. Well, I don't have a career, I have a job. That's all I will ever have, and I'm good with that, you understand. So, if it's your plan to turn a sow's ear into a silk purse with matching business pumps and suit, you've got the wrong woman."

"No, no, Sandra, you know that's not what I want. I mean, it would be nice if those things weren't so important to my mother, but they are, but I'm okay with you. I've known all along who you are, right?"

"I certainly hope so."

"Okay, so what's the problem?"

She thought for a few seconds, looking into his eyes, then at a group of passing women wearing the same wide, hoopy black skirt and white puffy-sleeved blouse. Waitresses, possibly, or perhaps members of some traveling dance troupe that stepped to the rhythms of early American folk music. Who knew, and who else but she cared? Sandra's eyes trailed them down the street until they were too distant to be interesting anymore. Then she said to Gil: "I don't know what the problem is, but I know there is one, and I know I'm not so low-class as to ask you to choose between me and your family. They should appreciate that." She laughed, mostly to herself.

"You don't have to ask me to choose," Gil said softly. "Somehow, everything will work out the way it's supposed to." He took her hand and they walked back up Charles Street, having said everything that needed to be said. For now.

Four

Detention was only fifteen minutes long, and Lila was watching the clock as each minute took its time ticking by. She dreaded the days, like this one, when her name made its way to the top of the list to take her turn in the detention room. It would make so much more sense if she prepared herself for the change in routine of home by four, start dinner, and watch Oprah, but she never seemed to do it. They always managed to take her by surprise.

Today there were only sixth graders in after-school jail, all boys, and they were there for fighting—each other. So, as soon as they reported to her, she separated them in the room—front, middle, back. Then she sat to eat her detention duty snack—an apple, half of a cheese sandwich, and orange juice.

Now, with only twelve minutes left in their collective sentence, she felt the urge to try to be the boys' referee. "So you three," she said as she stood and walked toward the blackboard, leaving her apple with only two bites, "what's the problem? Why were you fighting?"

All at once, three prepubescent voices piped up after their presence had filled the room with angry silence.

"Well, DeShawn, he . . ."

"Naw, Miss Giles, it was Tarik who . . ."

"DeShawn's a punk and he . . ."

Lila chuckled quietly, flashing back to her own childhood quarrels, which seemed like the end of the world until the next day on the playground, where everything was more than forgiven, it was forgotten. "Okay, one at a time. Tarik, why don't you tell me what happened first."

"Awright, well, me and Michael was playin' boogie-tag with everybody else and DeShawn said he wanted to play, so we said 'Awright.' So, we was playin' and I was *it*, so then I tagged DeShawn and then he had the boogie touch, 'cept he didn't want the boogie touch—"

"Nobody wants the boogie touch, Miss Giles, that's why you run away from it," Michael said.

"Okay, that's fine," Lila said. "Go on, Tarik."

"Awright, so anyway, he's all mad 'cause he got the boogie touch and then he's all mad with me. So he pushed me and said I had it back, 'cept I had my fingers crossed and he couldn't give it back to me."

"Yeah," Michael said, ready to pick up the story, "and then DeShawn started pushin' Tarik and then he pushed him on the ground and started yellin' at him, so I went over and told DeShawn that he couldn't play with us anymore and that's when he punched me in the shoulder. So me and Tarik kicked his butt."

"He started it, Miss Giles," DeShawn said about Tarik. "He called my mother a welfare bitch. That's why I pushed him down. Then Michael said the same thing."

"I see." Lila got firmly to her feet from where she leaned against the blackboard. She moved in closer to the boys, sitting atop the desk next to Michael, who sat in the center of the room. "Now let's just think about something for a minute. Let's just say that some awful creatures with fangs and claws and hair all over came out of nowhere, like in that movie, you know, and they decided they wanted to take over the playground."

The boys each gave an embarrassed chuckle that said they were too old for these little-boy stories. They shifted uncomfortably in their seats, never realizing that they were allied against Lila's story.

Sensing this, Lila said: "Stay with me, now. Now let's say these creatures have decided that they will abduct some children to teach them how to play on the jungle gym. So they take Michael and DeShawn. Tarik, would you try to save only Michael, or would you also try to save DeShawn?"

"I don't know. I guess I'd save 'em both."

"Why?" she asked.

" 'Cause they might kill them, or somethin'."

"That's right, they might kill them. But DeShawn's not your friend, right? So why would you care?"

"I don't know. I guess I'd save him 'cause, you know, I don't know, I wouldn't want him to be killed."

"Okay, and Michael, would you only save Tarik, or would you also save DeShawn too?"

"Naw, I'd save 'em both."

"And what about you, DeShawn? Would you save these two if the creatures took them?"

He said nothing for several seconds, and just when she thought he wouldn't answer her, he quickly nodded his head yes.

"That's right, and do you know why you'd all save each other? You would do it because they're different and you're all the same. You're members of the human race, they're not. That's what connects the three of you, and you all need to always remember that. If you can start right now, remembering this and treating people right, then you'll remember it always. Because, you see, if these creatures were to come here with ideas of taking over, it really wouldn't matter who's on welfare and who's not. All that would matter would be saving human beings."

The boys sat quietly with her point, each one giving clear signs that she had caused them to think. Then Tarik said: "That sounds good and all, Miss Giles, but grown people don't care about that human beings stuff any more than we do. Y'all cuss and fuss each other out, talkin' trash and actin' just like we do. I don't know, I would save 'em both from the aliens, but I can't say that I still wouldn't fight with DeShawn again, 'cause he's a jerk.''

The boys gathered their backpacks, as if noticing, all at once, that they had stayed two minutes past detention. And Lila, knowing nothing else to say to the wisdom that had just come out of this babe's mouth, simply dismissed them quietly. She went to the desk to gather her own things. And even as she walked to her car and started it to make her way home, this young boy's haunting words brought Sandra floating into her mind on a wave of Tarik's wisdom; and Sandra would not leave her. All of it had her wondering about the nature of grown-up children.

There's No Mistaking Home

The car crept through narrow streets that led home. This was the place she called home since she had memory, yet it was as if she were seeing it anew—through the eyes of four Giles women. She drove along, looking left, looking right, left, right, unable to believe her eyes.

"Hey, drive or park, you stupid bitch!" some woman yelled as she sped around Sandra. Everything, even the irate woman, stood out in a most acrimonious way.

Her face flushed with the heat of humiliation at the thought of having driven Gil through all this so many times, proudly taking him home with her. To her right was the playground that was like a ghost town, a has-been funland. Just as today, though, it was always occupied, with children dusty from romping on the grassless earth and teenagers losing their innocence in every way. And around them were the skeletal remains of what used to be swings and seesaws and tire swings. Everything that could be destroyed on that playground had been, years before—the swing set with lonely chains dangling as if they'd never known a tire, the seesaw, broken in half, which could no longer see, much less saw, the sliding board with missing rungs. Only the monkey bars, iron-clad and indestructible, stood in defiance. And as she looked to her left, she almost brought her car to a complete stop, as the prickly heat of embarrassment tingled in her armpits.

There it was, right there for anyone to see: poverty, the desperate kind. The kind where people live in homes they share with vermin. The kind where people sit on the stoops of houses where no one should live, where no one with more than a dollar would live. The kind where little ones in soiled and tattered clothes dart in and out of spewing fire hydrants because there's no other way to survive an oppressive Baltimore summer. Sandra knew every generation of these families on these streets. This was the neighborhood that suckled her. All of these people sitting on their stoops, young and old, men and women, were aunts and uncles and cousins with no common blood, but they helped raise her up just as lovingly as if her blood ran through their veins. She hated that inch of her soul that gave her eyes the vision of this place as something other than sweet home. The waves, the shouts, the *hey girl* as she drove by. She didn't deserve it. She was a traitor, betraying them in the worst way—by denying them, forsaking them in her heart.

Sandra parked, then flicked away a trickle of sweat that tingled on her temple. Mr. Milton, the landlord, was leaving as she got out of the car. He had been a regular in her life for as long as she could remember, coming around once a month to collect the rent. Over the years, she had watched his wrinkles multiply, his belly grow, and his hair turn to snow. But one thing never changed—he was still the kindest, most sincere white man she had ever come across.

"Hey, Sandra, how you doin'?" he said in his Bawlamore twang that was not as bad as some can be.

"I'm fine, Mr. Milton," Sandra said, with a distraction that could be construed as rude.

"How're things at the law firm?"

"Oh, just fine. Thank you for asking."

"Camilla and Eustace sure are proud of you. They talk about you every time I'm around here. They let me know what you're doing."

"Yeah, Ma and Daddy bore people all the time with stories, I know. Well, it was good seeing you, Mr. Milton," she said, opening her mother's door.

"Okay, I'll see you."

She stepped into the living room where the television beamed and blared for no one. Just as every person owns a particular smell, so too does every house. It's a stale bouquet layered with a history that triggers the olfactory memory. That familiar emanation that made this place home hit Sandra immediately. It was the smell of decades-old fried grease whose essence was permanently ensconced in the sofa, in the rug, in the drapes, and in every chair. And the picture of Jesus, yellowed by years of blessings, still hung over the sofa. But that smell, it was unmistakable. It was the smell she wore to school each day in her dresses. It was the smell that was distinctly home.

The television had become irritating shrieks. Baby sister Nicki had been there and gone. The solitary television was probably one of many unfinished projects in her trail, which led to her room, or next door, or down the block. She'd be back soon, maybe later. Who knew? The television marked her territory.

"Ma, it's Sandra. Where are you?"

"Up here," a voice called down from upstairs.

"What're you doin'?"

"I'm puttin' some things away. Here I come," and a pair of long, slim legs appeared. Then a pair of hips too narrow to have brought four children into the world, a generous bosom, and eventually a slender, smiling face with hanging skin, as if residual from some extreme weight loss. "What are you doin' here?"

"I'm just stoppin' by. What, I can't just stop by?" Sandra said with a teasing smile of a fake pout.

"Don't be crazy. Of course you can. Come on in and

have some dinner. Your father's on a new shift so he won't be in till late." She gave Sandra a smoochy wet kiss on her cheek. "Nicki just don't know how to turn off the TV," she complained while turning off the set. "She went down the street with her little friends and just left the darn thing runnin'."

"That's a fifteen-year-old for you," Sandra said. She sat down in one of those same red faded vinyl chairs that had been in that kitchen so long she couldn't remember when they weren't there. And the speckled-top table of some sort of material that could not be identified made the set complete. And no room in her mother's house was ever in perfect balance without that picture of Jesus—that same picture of him with hands outstretched, imploring peace—that hung in every room.

Sandra took a piece of corn bread from the platter on the table and buttered it. Days went by and years ticked off by the tens, and still everything came back to this kitchen table, waiting for dinner. Her mother put a plate in front of her filled with pork chops and gravy, lima beans and mashed potatoes, just like the old days. She had never really given it much thought until now. Memories inspired by senses of this exact same meal. It was her mother's law of meals—only lima beans and mashed potatoes with pork chops and gravy.

"These pork chops look good," Sandra said.

"They oughta, and they oughta taste good too. I got 'em fresh from work today."

Sandra took a look around the kitchen, chewing her first bite. "Ma, have you and Daddy ever thought about moving away from here?"

"What? No indeed. Why would we? This is our home."

"I know, Ma, but now y'all don't have three extra mouths to feed, and I would think you might want to live someplace that didn't look like . . ." She couldn't finish.

"That didn't look like what?"

"I don't know, Ma. It's just that you and Daddy could get a nice apartment somewhere. Somewhere nice."

"And go from a house to an apartment. Shoot, that just don't make no sense. It's good to have space in this house. It probably didn't seem like much when you kids were comin' up, and you girls were sharin' that small room, but it's plenty now."

"Maybe, but haven't you ever wanted to get out of this neighborhood? Haven't you ever wanted to live someplace pretty?"

Camilla put down her fork and stared at her plate. Then, slowly, she lifted her head, as if to look into the face of a stranger spewing words of another tongue.

"Sandra, where is all this comin' from?"

"Ma, haven't you ever just wanted to get away from the ghetto?"

"You look at this place around here and see a ghetto. I look around and see a community filled with kin. This is the first place we moved when we came up from South Carolina. It was all we could afford then. But now we wouldn't move from here for all the pretty places in Baltimore. Our life is pretty where it counts. These people around here make it the prettiest because they became the family I left down South."

"Ma, this place is depressing. Everything is dirty. *All* the houses look like they're falling down. We're just lucky that Mr. Milton has done right by us all these years in keeping this house up. Everybody looks so desperate, Ma."

"Nobody around here is desperate because we've all got each other. Don't you know when both of Ida Bell's children had to move back home with all their children, three each, Ida didn't have enough room for all the children to sleep, so guess what? Three of those little ones stayed next door to Ida's at Marie's. Those children were living with Marie for goin' on a year and she never once thought they were a bother."

"I know the whole neighborhood is like one big family, and I love that. But you don't have to lose that by moving to a better place."

"You know somethin'? I never thought I would hear somethin' like this comin' from any of my children. Your home is more than this house, and now none of it is good enough for you."

Sandra began to cry. At first it was hard for her mother to tell, but when her head went down and the light sniffles filled the room's silence, Camilla followed the instinct that rose up the day Sandra was born. It traveled from her heart to her arms and legs. She took Sandra's hand, which was just about to wipe away a tear. She said softly, "What on earth is wrong, Sandra? This just isn't like you." Camilla took a paper napkin from the plastic holder on the table and wiped the tears herself.

"Ma, I'm sorry. I love this place," Sandra said through ebbing tears.

"Well, what's goin' on? I know you like I know myself, and I know somethin' brought this on."

"Well, kind of. I met Gil's family. You know, we went over to where he grew up. It was unbelievable, Ma. They live in one of those pretty houses over there on Hilton Street right across from that reservoir. Their father was a judge and Gil's mother and sisters treated me like the devil at a church revival." She touched her fingertips to her forehead and sighed. Then she looked up, as if suddenly remembering something important. "Ma, if Gil had come here for the first time and was hungry and asked for something to eat, like a sandwich or something, what would you do? Would you think he was ill-mannered?"

"Ill-mannered? No, for goodness sake. I would think he was hungry."

"But would you give him something to eat?"

"Sandra, what kind of question is that? You know I would give him something to eat. What does that have to do with anything?"

"Well, when we got to his mother's, we were too late for dinner, so I asked for something to eat. Most mothers would fix something to eat without a second thought."

"Sure, most mothers would. She didn't give you anything to eat?"

"Yeah, she did, but you would have thought that I had just gone to the toilet in the middle of their living room."

"Well, don't pay that no mind. They're the ones who're ill-mannered. What exactly did they say?"

"It wasn't so much what they said, it was how they acted. They had these siddity attitudes, you know, like they were better. They live in a better neighborhood . . . oh, that's right, I forgot, *community*. They made sure I understood that where they live is a *community*, not just a mere neighborhood. They went to private schools and fancy colleges. And they looked real funny when I told them that Daddy's a machinist down at Sparrow's Point."

"Sandra, big deal. Let them think what they want. There are snobs all over the world, not to mention this city. You just keep on goin' 'cause you know who you are."

"Ma, I know there are snobs everywhere, and I've certainly run into them before, especially in this city, but I was never going to marry their son and brother."

"Well, what does Gil say? He doesn't think like they do, does he? Because if he does, you—"

"No, of course not, Ma. He's embarrassed."

"By you?"

"No, by them. He knows they're snobs. He just didn't know how to warn me about them before he took me over there."

A knock fell on the front door and then a key turned in the lock. Both heads snapped toward the door.

"Hey Sandra! Jimmy told me he saw you drive up." It was Margie, Camilla's next-door neighbor and closet friend.

"Hi, Aunt Margie," Sandra said.

"Margie, where you been, girl? I called you when I got home to tell you to come eat some of these pork chops with me," Camilla said, getting another plate from the cupboard.

"Well, that's why I'm here now. You think I'm gonna pass up your pork chops?" and she laughed a hearty, deep-throated smoker's laugh. She loved to laugh, regardless of whether others got the joke. "I had to run Miss Evelyn over to the hospital to visit her sister. She had a stroke."

"Miss Evelyn down the street?" Sandra asked, as if surprised, but knowing there was no other Miss Evelyn around. "Her sister's all she's got left, poor thing."

Camilla said, "That's not completely true. She's got all of us," and she flashed her daughter a knowing smile and wink.

"So what you two gossipin' about?"

"Nothin', really. Sandra just met her new soon-to-be in-laws and they snubbed her."

"Not our girl!" Margie's incredulity came through as she took her voice to an unnatural high. "They snubbed you in what way?"

"Oh, the usual way black society folks snub other black folks from around here. I don't come from the right part of town and didn't go to the right schools. Ma and Daddy ain't never went to college and ain't a schoolteacher or judge."

"Well, who the heck do they think they are? They not even worthy of havin' a sweet chile like you in that family." Margie sucked her teeth and rolled her eyes at the mere thought.

"His mother's name is Eulelie Giles and his father was Judge Gilbert Giles."

"Judge Giles! That was Gil's father?"

"Yeah, you knew his father, Aunt Margie?"

"Well, I didn't know him, but I certainly knew who he was; and I knew his wife."

"Eulelie? You know Eulelie? That's who we're talkin' about!" Sandra said excitedly.

"No, I don't know her. She's his *second* wife. I'm talkin' 'bout his first wife, Gloria. She grew up with me down in Cherry Hill. It was a real big deal in the old neighborhood when she married Judge Giles. Of course, he was just a lawyer when they got married, but that was still somethin' big for a poor girl from Cherry Hill to be marryin' not just a lawyer, but a Giles. He was a big man in this city. His

whole family was. I don't know much about this new wife
except that she's his second wife. Gloria died when those
children were just babies. I see this second wife in the *Afro
Gazette* almost every week. Camilla, you know who she is.
You've seen her."

"Girl, you know I don't even look at the society page of
that paper. What do I care about those folks?"

Margie saw last week's *Afro Gazette* lying on the chair in
the corner. She rushed to it and page-turned so fast you
would have thought her picture was in there. "Here she is,"
she said, shoving the entire paper in Camilla's face. "This is
Gil's stepmother."

Camilla's eyes squinted smaller and smaller, until they
were just barely open. It was impossible to make out anyone
in the *Afro Gazette*, but she knew this face. It had aged—
aged well—but there was no mistaking this woman. Grabbing the paper from Margie's hands, Camilla took it over to
better light. This was not someone she'd waited on at Lexington Market. This was not someone she'd met once or
twice whose face was now crawling out of the recesses of
her memory. Could this face in the paper be the spitting-
image twin of the woman she knew, or could this be the
most amazing coincidence ever in the entire scheme of fate?
Eulelie Giles was someone she'd once known, and fairly well,
only nothing seemed to make sense.

"What is it, Camilla?" Margie asked.

"Nothing, nothing. I just wanted to get a better look at
her." And for some reason, maybe confusion, maybe an in-
nate understanding, Camilla decided to say nothing more.

"So, Gil's mother was from Cherry Hill?"

"Gloria. Yes, indeed. And when she married into that
Giles family, she worked hard for poor folks, donatin' lots
of food and toys and things, and even comin' into the neighborhoods with doctors to vaccinate children. And she was
always givin' some kinda benefit. Yeah, Gil's mother was
really a good woman."

"Those girls don't talk about their mother. Gil doesn't

even know that much about her. It's as if she's some sort of stranger. I mean, I know that they were real young when she died, but it seems like somebody should have been keeping her memory alive to them.''

Then Margie's face curled up into a scowl. "I don't know about none of that. I do know, though, that that second wife came to town high and mighty. She saw that man and that big pretty house, honey, and that was all she wrote. She chased that man all over Baltimore till she got him, kids and all. In fact, I know that he was seein' one lady in particular when he first started to see Eulelie, and when Eulelie found out, she followed that woman home one day and threw a brick through her window with a note sayin' to leave her man alone. It worked too, I guess, 'cause she got him. She must have scared that woman half to death with her craziness.''

Sandra was dumbfounded. She had just gotten the low-down from Aunt Margie. Gil probably didn't even know anything about this. That's how it had always been with Aunt Margie, who seemed mystical, the way she knew about people. If you'd been in Baltimore longer than a day, Aunt Margie knew your business. It didn't pay to be anyone but yourself around her, because she could always tell the truth.

"Aunt Margie, how do you know all this? I mean, you said you didn't know her.''

"Oh, honey, people talk. When I was workin' over there on Dorchester Road cookin' for Dr. Ballard and his wife, I would hear the talk. Mrs. Ballard was always hostin' these afternoon bridge games with all these wives of black doctors and lawyers where about four or five different games would be goin' on at the same time. Well, before Judge Giles's wife got there, the other wives would just talk and talk about how his wife, you know, Gloria, wasn't even cold in her grave before this woman went after him.'' Margie nodded her head and twisted her mouth in that way that let them know that her word on Eulelie Giles was final.

Sandra, eyes bugged with surprise, said: "So, Aunt Margie, you're tellin' me that she swooped down on him like a buzzard?''

"Chile, the grass hadn't even grown over Gloria's grave."

"But isn't that kinda low-class, doin' something like that? I mean, she acts like she never took a wrong step in her entire high-society life." Sandra crossed her arms and rolled her eyes. Disgusted.

"The rules in those circles are completely different. Sure, lookin' at it the way we do, it's in bad, low-life taste 'cause we got morals and manners. But for them, that kinda thing's only low-life if she hadn't gotten the man."

Sandra was left positively nonplussed after hearing this. She tried to speak. "But . . ." She desperately wanted to speak, to say something that would make it all make sense in her own mind. Her eyelids fluttered at the same speed as her thoughts. She chuckled, sighed, then broke into uncontrollable laughter. Margie and Camilla looked at each other for the answer.

"Sandra, what's so funny?" her mother asked.

But Sandra couldn't answer right away, she was so tickled.

"It's funny, that's all," she said, wiping the tears—tears of laughter this time—from her eyes. "Think about it. None of her children know about this. The story she tells them and everybody else is so clean and proper. She would just die if she knew *I* knew the real story."

"But now, don't you go tellin' Gil," her mother said adamantly. "Don't go stoopin' to her level. People got all kinds of reasons for lyin' to themselves that don't have nothin' to do with nothin' but an ache in their soul, so I know you won't be careless with what your Aunt Margie just told you. I know you won't use this against her unless you're backed into a corner, and let's just pray it doesn't come to that. A lot of people could stand to get hurt," and Camilla just left it at that.

"Oh no, I'd never dare. This is something best kept under my hat. That is, till I *have* to use it." And though Camilla and Margie said nothing and asked no questions, they knew what Sandra meant. One thing they knew for certain about their girl was that she was hardly one to cower in a corner when backed into one. She was deceptive in that way. Right now, she was a huntress hunting with one bullet, and she knew she had to have a clear shot.

Just then a buzz, low-pitched and ominous, pierced the air. It was what passed as a doorbell. "I'll get it," Camilla said. "You two just eat."

When Sandra heard the voice at the door, her heart fluttered with love that still felt giddy and fresh. As hard as she tried, she couldn't stay put. She couldn't wait for him to find her in the kitchen. She had to go to him.

"Hi! I didn't think I'd see you tonight. What brought you all the way over here?"

"I was looking for you, and I figured this is where you'd be, so here I am," Gil said.

"This is a good man, girl. Any man who would run all over the city lookin' for you is a man you got to hold on to," Margie said, her rasping laugh punctuating her words of wisdom. "You know, Gil, we was just takin' 'bout you."

"All good, I hope," he said.

"Gil, you know, I just found out that Aunt Margie knew your mother."

"You know my mother?" he said, shocked, and somehow not believing it.

"Yeah. We grew up together in Cherry Hill."

Gil looked confused for several long seconds, then he said: "Oh, you knew my mother *Gloria*. Yes, she did grow up down there. Okay. Wow, what a small world."

"I was just tellin' them that your mother was quite a lady. She married into such an affluent family and she was still as down-to-earth as ever. She never forgot the old neighborhood or anybody anywhere who was down and out and needed help."

"Really? Well, you know, Aunt, umm . . . Margie, I don't

know too much about my mother. I was very, very young when she died and I don't remember that much about her."

"Yeah, I know that, but nobody ever told you what kinda woman your mother was?"

"No, I guess my father and stepmother never felt there was a need to tell us. After all, we had no memories of her."

"But still . . . well, anyway, sit down here and I'll tell you about her."

Gil awkwardly pulled a chair up to the table and sat. Part of his soul wanted, actually needed, to hear every single detail about her. Another part of him, the part where Eulelie hovered, felt overwhelming guilt, as if he were about to commit an ultimate sin. Betrayal. Still, he had to hear what Margie had to say.

"Well, she was a beauty. All you have to do is look in the mirror and you know that."

"I look like my mother? I was always told I look like my father."

"Sure you look like her, especially around the eyes."

"You've never even seen pictures of your mother?" Sandra asked.

"Yes, sure I have, but they aren't very clear. It was hard to see how she really looked. It was hard to study her face."

"Well, aside from being a beauty, she was funny and smart, and like I said, she had a heart of gold. She could drink beer with slobs like us and champagne with the folks your stepmother hangs out with, and she did. Even though she grew up in Cherry Hill and they ain't have no money, she had class. And even when she married your father and got outta the old neighborhood and was really livin' the classy life, she didn't make the rest of us feel like we didn't have class. I'll tell you somethin' else you prob'ly didn't know. Your grandmother, your father's mother, worshiped the ground that girl walked on. Even though Gloria didn't come from generations of black socialites, they loved that girl and her parents to death. Did you get to know Gloria's parents before they died?"

"Yes, I did. They were good people, but again, I was eight when they died. There was no other family of my mother's to speak of, so my mother's memory died with them."

"What about your father?"

"When my father married my stepmother, he was her husband." Gil didn't feel the need to explain, so he said nothing more.

When the front door opened again, Sandra knew, just by the way it creaked, who was entering. "Daddy?" she said.

"That can't be your father. He's not due home for another hour or so."

"Daddy?" she said again, this time getting up to see for herself.

"Yeah, little girl, it's me," her father said.

She ran to him, just like when she was really his little girl, and threw her arms around him. "Daddy, Ma said you wouldn't be here for a while. I thought I would miss you."

"Yeah, little girl, well I was supposed to be on a new shift, but then my foreman comes around, tells me I could knock off early and go back to my usual seven to three shift tomorrow. I tell you, they treat you like a yo-yo down there."

"Well, we're glad you're home," Camilla said, hugging and kissing him as he came into the kitchen. "Come on and eat dinner. The pork chops are still warm."

"This is what you call a good woman." He was hugging and pawing her like a young lover. "You see this, Gil? I want you to love my daughter as much as I love this woman."

Gil, still standing, drummed nervous fingers against his leg, where they hung, waiting for the moment to pass. As if looking away would make it go away, Gil let his eyes wander out the window to find a sparrow perched on the limb of a skimpy-leafed tree, but not even that little bird, with the infinite possibilities of what its day was like, could distract Gil. Eyes, heavy with expectation, were bearing down. This was his moment, inevitable in every relationship, where a man's love is placed side by side with an ideal.

" 'Course you love her this much," Eustace said, sparing Gil the awkwardness of choking out an answer. "I seen it. It's there."

Gil smiled with half of his mouth, then said: "Yep, sure do." And that should have been the end of all the talk of good women and perfect love and such; so he thought.

"Well, his mother sure don't love her," Aunt Margie said, rolling her eyes yet again at the thought.

Camilla, with a tightened nervous jaw, shot her jittery eyes at Gil, then at Margie, hoping to shut her up. It was too late.

"What you talkin' 'bout, Margie?" Eustace asked.

Sandra tensed, a tiny vein pulsing on the side of her neck. She pressed her lips together as they, of their own will, formed a smile that told of a heart that had begun to leap. A part of her, a tiny part, didn't want to talk about Eulelie right there in front of Gil. With one glance, though, just one moment's look at Gil, and that other part of her heart, the part that was only human, took over, wanting Gil to feel all the humiliation and shame that should come along with being the child of someone like Eulelie. After all, Sandra thought, if Eulelie's living room were a crime scene, she would certainly be the chalk-outlined victim. Surely Gil knew this.

"Well, Daddy," Sandra said plain-spokenly, "Gil's mother doesn't think I'm good enough for him or her family. She thinks we're low-class 'cause y'all live around here and I grew up around here."

"Is that right?" Eustace said, without even a rise in his voice. "Oh well, there's people like that all over the world. She ain't the first to call my family low-class, and she sure as heck ain't gonna be the last." And that was that. Eulelie Giles wasn't worth the breath and wasted words it would take to badmouth her.

But Sandra could not accept his placidity. She watched

him eat without a care, free of bruised pride. He was positively untouched. It was in the way he chewed, the way he
cut his meat, the way he drank his Coke. Her father seemed
at peace with every corner of his simple life. "Daddy, that
don't bother you?" Sandra finally asked.

"What don't bother me?"

"How Gil's mother is actin'?"

"Little girl, what do I care? That woman don't make one
bit a difference to my day-to-day life." He took another bite
of meat and chewed it, and just before swallowing said:
"Now I tell you, your grandfather and grandmother, your
aunts and uncles, all said I wasn't good enough to marry
your mother, and that hurt, I ain't gonna lie. But if for one
minute that little girl over there had said that she was too
good to marry me, I don't know what I woulda done wit'
myself. All that counts is *who* counts, little girl. Remember
that," and Eustace glanced, for just the barest second, over
at Camilla, but that second was filled with more love than
one heart could contain.

Gil saw it. The blindest of the blind couldn't miss it. The
Hightowers love, raw, bare-souled, put Gill ill at ease, as if
he were a voyeur into an intimate moment not meant for
every eye. And then he felt the emptiness. It was the vapid
feeling he always felt, in some place too deep for him to
determine where, when he thought of the vacant glances and
meaningless silences his father and Eulelie shared. Eustace,
with that one stolen look at his wife, painfully reminded Gil
of how his father was merely married. Gil shifted his weight
to the other leg and looked around with the pained, strained
grin of embarrassment. "Look Sandra, I need to run," he
said.

Sandra was too caught up in the same bliss that had sent
a harrowing pang to every part of Gil's heart that could feel.
Gil called her name again, and she, with a snap of her head,
heard him this time.

"I've got to run," he said, this time into her face.

"Oh no, Gil!" Sandra said, getting over to him in one

hop. She tugged at his arm, saying: "Don't leave just yet. Come on, sit down. You haven't even bothered to sit down."

"Yeah, I know, but I wasn't planning to stay long anyway. I just thought I'd run by and see you while I can. I've got a lot of work to do on that case tonight. Well, good night everybody," and Gil left the kitchen with Sandra on his heels.

"Sure you won't stay?" Aunt Margie called after him as she thumbed, then shuffled, a deck of cards. "We're gonna play cards soon as Eustace finishes dinner."

"No thanks Aunt . . . uhhh . . . Margie," Gil said, his voice trailing to an awkward halt. He never quite felt comfortable calling her *Aunt* Margie. He didn't grow up with her in the way that would necessitate being worthy of such a privilege. And to call her simply Margie seemed disrespectful and presumptuous, at least that's what he'd learned from his mother.

In the living room, Sandra tried to say all that she didn't want her family to hear when she pleadingly took his hand, but Gil didn't seem to understand. With a face creased with worry, Sandra said in a whisper: "Gil, please. Please don't leave. Look, I'm sorry about telling Daddy about your mother, but Aunt Margie brought it up. Besides, Momma would have told him, anyway."

"No, that's not it at all," Gil said with an earnest-looking smile that he simply could not manage to make honest. "I've really got to go, Sandra. I'll call you tomorrow." He left a tight kiss on her lips and vanished to the other side of the front door with that stiff-backed, proud way of his that, as he left, was a little bit stiffer, a little bit prouder, and suppressing a whole lot of angst.

FIVE

The Giles sisters sat in a room that was not an official waiting room, but had been turned into one by virtue of their presence as they waited on the man who would cater the cotillion. This was only the second interview of the day, and already their patience had been nearly tapped—with the whole experience and with each other.

Lila was the angriest, and Linda was the object of her ire. The youngest Giles was only keeping with her typical self. Still, Lila kept a cold shoulder turned to Linda, and Linda turned one on her in the everlasting minutes it took for the second caterer to come and save them from having to ring one more bell of yet another chef. The last one was bad enough to make them want to forget catering and cook the food themselves.

His name was Larry Boxer, and Lila had found him through the principal of her school, who raved so much about the man's cooking that Lila didn't want to miss out on what could have been the best. The three sisters got to his kitchen all at once, but in separate cars. A shingle hung over the door frame said: LARRY BOXER'S CATERERS—IT AIN'T NO BOX LUNCH. They looked at the sign, then at each other, trading crooked smiles that said they each recognized the simple-minded corniness. They were worried, but Linda went ahead, grabbing the doorknob, which would not turn.

"It's locked," she said to her sisters.

"This isn't a walk-in-off-the-street kind of business, Linda," Lucretia said. "You have to ring the bell."

Only a few short seconds after ringing the bell, the door swung open to reveal a thin-haired white man, somewhere in his thirties, who was smiling pleasantly.

"Hi, I'm Larry Boxer. Which one of you is Lila Giles?" he said.

"I'm Lila," she said with a quiet stammer of shock. Her assumption had been that he was black. There was nothing that would have brought her to that presumption—maybe because her principal was black—but when she pictured it, she saw a black chef working for them.

"We spoke on the phone," the man said, extending his hand as part of his greeting.

"Yes, well, it's good to finally meet you," she said. What else was there to say?

The sisters went through the door single file. Larry Boxer had walked on ahead of them, guiding them to the room where they'd talk.

Linda hung back for Lila, and taking her by the arm, said, "You didn't tell us he was white."

"Yeah," Lucretia said.

"I didn't know," Lila said. Then she snatched her arm away and snapped, "What difference does it make? Food is food."

"Not all food," Linda whispered to herself.

They followed him into a room filled with boxes and shelves of pots, pans, and cooking utensils they'd never seen before. He asked them to have a seat around a square table.

"This is my combination storage room, office," he said with a laugh. "I would show you the kitchen, but we're in there preparing for a big party tonight."

"Oh, that's fine," Lila said.

Larry Boxer flipped through the pages of a legal pad he had on a clipboard. "Okay, let's see," he said in an accent that was clearly not Baltimore. "Now Lila, when we spoke, you mentioned that you wanted salmon served with whipped potatoes and a spinach dish, right?''

"Yes, that's right. That's just to give you an idea of the kind of menu we're looking for. And it would be nice to have a sorbet between the appetizer and the main course. And of course a cheese plate before dessert.''

"We want it to be a very elegant meal," Lucretia said.

He wrote furiously on his yellow pad. "I see. Well, I have to tell you ladies, what you want would truly be an elegant meal, but it's also going to be expensive. *Very* expensive. So, if I may, I'd like to suggest you think about maybe a roasted chicken menu. I can make you an incredible mango chicken breast with a rice pilaf and seasoned vegetables, or something like mixed vegetables.''

Lila said nothing right away, letting him think she was actually mulling it over. It was the polite thing to do. Then she said, "No, I think the salmon is what we want. Definitely salmon.''

He let out a nervous laugh that slid right to the edge of Lila's nerves with such force it made her heart jump.

"Lila," he said, "I have to tell you, salmon is going to cost you a lot of money. Look, I've fixed this same dish for the Kappa Alpha Psi fraternity, you know, the black fraternity, and they loved it. I fixed it for a fund-raiser I catered for the Urban League last month and they all raved about it. The Delta Sigma Theta group, the black sorority, I've fixed it for them too.''

Lila shifted in her seat in a way that showed how agitated she was growing. She looked to her sisters for help, but they were looking equally nonplussed as they stared him down. "You know, we've never even discussed the cost of things, so I guess you don't know that the money is not an issue. We want what we want, and what we want is salmon. We clearly understand that salmon is going to cost more than chicken, and we're prepared to pay for it.''

So now it was obvious that the interview was over. Lila was poised to make a gracious departure. Lucretia just wanted to leave, either like a lady or like a boar. Linda had other plans, which were somewhere in between, but mostly leaning toward the raw. With every mention of the cost of salmon, Larry Boxer had slowly revealed himself. It was just beneath the surface, but it was no less vile than the strange fruit once born by southern trees, or the back of the bus.

"Mr. Boxer, Larry, may I ask you something?" Linda said. Then without waiting for him to agree, she said, "Is it that salmon is not necessarily one of your specialty dishes, or is it that you're just a little bit afraid that three little colored girls won't be able to pay your bill? Because if that is your assumption, Larry Boxer, then I think this meeting is over. I know that dollar signs can't be seen in our black skin by people like you, but you are probably the worst of all the crackers I've ever run across. In fact, you are an insult to all crackers."

"What are you saying, Miss Giles?" he said, shock and dismay in his voice.

"I'm saying that if we were white, Larry Boxer, we would not be sitting here having this ridiculous conversation about chicken versus salmon because you would assume we could pay."

"I think it's time for us to go," Lila said, mostly to Linda. Then she said to Larry Boxer, "I don't think you're the right caterer for us."

"Not by a long shot," Lucretia said without looking at him.

He tried to plead innocent of all implied charges, but it was pointless. By now Lila and Lucretia had gotten to their feet to leave. Linda, though, still sat. She wasn't through.

"How long have you lived in Baltimore, Larry?" Linda asked flatly.

"About five years," he answered, equally as flat.

"Oh, well, then it all makes sense. You don't know that we are the Gileses. We have been rooted in this city since before the last millennium. We are a large part of what makes Baltimore Baltimore. So pardon us if we don't shuffle and grin while the white boy with his white boy chicken tells us about the cost of things. You have no idea." And only then did she stand and turn to leave with her sisters.

So now they sat in another storage room/office waiting on another caterer, one whose blackness gave them much comfort. Angry silence still filled the room, and Linda could not take it a second longer.

"Lila, I know you're still mad at me for what happened at that Larry Boxer's place, but I don't care. He was a racist cracker and he insulted us." Linda crossed her arms and set herself in her stubbornness.

"Linda, every white person's a racist cracker to have you tell it," Lila said through a tightened jaw. "Besides, I knew what he was implying the minute he opened his mouth about the chicken. I'm just saying there was a better way to handle him."

"Lila, he tried to sugarcoat it, and it was so clear where he was coming from. He had his mind made up about us as soon as we walked through the door. And I know for a fact he would not have done that if we had been white."

"Still, Linda, I think we had the last laugh by simply taking our business and walking out the door. We had the upper hand by doing that. We had the power. You didn't need to get in his face like that. We know who we are and what we come from. What do we care about what some pasty-faced white guy assumes about our financial situation?"

Then Lucretia, who wanted to stay safely out of Linda and Lila's argument said, "Lila, sometimes you have to let them know who you are."

"And I guess all I'm saying is that all we have to do is simply be who we are."

The conversation ended when a door opened, a different door than the one through which they'd been led by an assistant. A tall chocolate-skinned man walked in with a haste that said it was not haste at all but simply the way he moved.

"How are you? I'm John Cobb," he said, shaking each of their hands in turn.

"Mr. Cobb, if we were to tell you that we want salmon for the main course, would that be a problem?" Lucretia thought it would be wise to ask before wasting any more time.

"No, of course not. Why would it be a problem?" he said in a matter-of-fact way that allowed them all to breathe. "After all, it's your money. I'm just here to take it." And the laughter was easy and very real.

In a Place Where No One Would Think to Look for Him

It was already early evening when Lila turned onto Reisterstown Road after leaving John Cobb's Kitchen. She crept along, exhibiting the caution of a driver her age times two. The kind who know where they're going but are in no particular rush to get there. Better safe than sorry. That type. Baltimore's easy listening station was turned to a sensible volume. It was the only station in the city that didn't jumble her nerves with rap and other hip-hop nonsense after a rigorous day of teaching brainy fifth graders and choosing a caterer. She had already filed Larry Boxer away somewhere under insignificant white people, and John Cobb, who did not blink twice at the mention of salmon, made forgetting that Boxer man easy.

Cars passed when they could, their irritated drivers throwing her looks of frustration as she stared straight ahead, making herself unavailable for their lambasting glares, sometimes curses. When she stopped for the light, she caught a man out of the corner of her right eye mouthing something at her that was probably an expletive, but at that moment her attention was pulled to something she saw just ahead. Is it? Could it be? Could it be? No, not at this time of the day. She goosed her neck for a better view, but it didn't help. She couldn't be sure, but thought she saw Gil's little black sports car up ahead in the parking lot of a bar.

What to do? The light changed. Horns honked, at least three. Lila's foot went down on the accelerator and the car bounded forward in a lurch. Her driving looked erratic and out of control, but what did it matter? She made it to that parking lot.

Lila pulled her car into the space next to the black car that had caught her eye, got out and stood for several seconds, just staring at it. Then she looked inside, and right there in plain view found her proof—Gil's running shoes. The license plate! The license plate would tell her for sure, and even though she didn't remember the whole number, she knew that BRR were the first three letters. With only two quick steps she was at the back of the car. And there they were—BRR.

Lila went back to her car, grabbed her purse, shut and locked her door, and went without pause toward the bar. Then it hit her. She stopped dead in her tracks just as she reached for the door handle. Lila Giles, daughter of Eulelie and the late Judge Giles, suddenly realized that she was about to walk into a bar, of all places; and a borderline dive bar at that. It was so nondescript and side-of-the-road that it was only now, as she was about to step inside, that she'd ever noticed the roadside shack, albeit in the few times she'd driven Reisterstown Road.

All eyes turned toward her and the light she let in, and she stayed in that spotlight as she closed the door behind her. She didn't look odd, just misplaced, her suit too expensively tailored in the Brooks Brothers style the Giles women loved, her shoes too classic. She was a bit too impeccably buttoned-up for this low-down, hard liquor place. And her boniness, which showed in her gooseneck and spindly legs, made her look bookishly drab and all the more lost, as if she'd taken the wrong turnoff on her way to a librarian training course.

Once her eyes became accustomed to the dimness of the room, Lila looked around, first at the bar, then at the tables, for her brother. She didn't see him. Then, in spite of having virtually everyone's attention, she walked with uncertainty to the bar with no intention of trying to meld into this place where she did not belong.

Curtis gave her a sideways stare as he filled a glass, as if uncertain whether he was going to be petitioned for directions or asked for his liquor license. "What can I do you for?" he asked.

"I'm looking for Gilbert Giles. Do you know him?"

"Who wants to know?" Curtis said protectively. But it wasn't hard to see. She was harmless, too timid to be a woman scorned and out for revenge.

"I'm his sister," she said in a supercilious way as she pointed to herself. "I saw his car outside. I know it's his car, so I know he's here."

"Yeah, he's here. He's in the bathroom. He'll be back. Have a sit down right here on his stool so that you'll be sure not to miss him."

Lila climbed up on the stool and sat primly, holding her purse in a white-knuckled clutch on her lap. She looked down, to her left, to her right, over her shoulder, up at the ceiling, anywhere to avoid Curtis's eyes.

"So, can I get you something?" he said.

"Just a seltzer with a wedge of lemon please."

"What, you don't drink?"

"Yes, I take a drink once in a while, but I don't drink in bars."

"What you got against bars?"

"Nothing. I have nothing really against bars, but I just don't believe it's a place where ladies should take their libations. That's just how I was raised."

The two women at the other end of the bar, Curtis's regulars, sent a quick quaver of fear through her. She could see in their raised eyebrows and gaping mouths what was on their minds.

"That's just how I am, of course," Lila said. "There's nothing wrong with other ladies taking a drink here."

One of the women picked up her drained glass and tinkled the ice cubes in Curtis's direction, saying, "Hey Curtis, gimme another one. Thank God for you that I ain't a lady, otherwise you'd go broke." And they all had a laugh, mostly in Lila's face.

Gil could hear the laughter before he left the bathroom, so as soon as he stepped back into the bar he was already distracted, almost caught up, by the chortling.

"What's so funny?" he said, chuckling a bit, but at what he did not know.

"Oh nothing. Just some silliness," Curtis said. "Say, man, your sister's over there."

Gil looked across the bar as if he weren't sure it was Lila. Then his surprise turned to irritation, and he couldn't even hide it behind a strained smile. This was the one place he could go in this city where being Gilbert Giles, III didn't matter. At Jay's, nothing was expected of him for having that name. In here, he could laugh at the hinkties and the ackalacky they spoke. Out there, he was one of them. His sister Lila, just by being there, sitting so stiff-backed like a Eulelie clone, had defiled a most important part of his self. And the biggest insult of all was that she was doing it right on his own stool.

"Lila, what are you doing here?" Gil was walking toward her without a hint of a smile.

"I saw your car parked outside and came in here to ask you the very same question. What are *you* doing in here?" and she put her hand on her hip, expecting nothing but the truth.

"Lila, I come here sometimes to unwind, okay," he said, his patience threadbare.

"You never told us that you go cavorting in bars." Then she realized that she may have offended the bartender. "No offense," she said, with a quick tilt of her head in his direction.

"None taken," Curtis said with a knowing smile.

As he settled himself on the stool next to her, Gil said:

"You know, Lila, I wasn't aware that there had to be full disclosure about every single aspect of my life. Why is it important that you all know that a few nights a week I like to come in here, toss back a few and kick it with Curtis and some of the fellas?" His newfound lingo spewed out comically awkward.

"Kick it? With the fellas?" Lila said mockingly with a chortle. "Gil, please. Well anyway, it's not that it's important, Gil, it's just that, we . . . I don't know, Gil, it just surprises me to find out that my brother is one of those men who has a place—you know, a *joint*."

"And the problem here is . . . what?"

"No problem, Gil. Well, it does make you like every other man, and I've always told people that my brother is nothing like every other man on the planet. That's all. But lately you don't seem to care about that kind of thing," she said, her tone weaving in and out of sarcasm and resentment. She was just about to say something else when she saw a familiar profile on the other side of the bar. Could it be? But it couldn't be, because life couldn't be this ironic. She turned to Gil and said, "Gil, I guess it's just that things are changing so fast with you, and that's good, I guess, and it would probably be good for me too, but the name Giles set us apart at birth from everybody else. And that's bigger than change."

Gil moved in close, close, closer, even closer to his sister, until his face was nearly touching hers. The hours-old hard-liquor breath wafted past her nose with a sense-defiling stench, making her eyelids flutter. "Can I tell you a secret, dearest sister?" he finally said. "We're all just like everybody else. We eat. We sleep. We piss. We crap. There's no difference. We love our mothers and sisters and our fathers and brothers when we can't even think of a damned good reason to like them. That, dear Lila, is man's humanness at its most basic."

Gil went back to his own space and emptied his glass in the silence that fell between them. Lila's eyes blinked furiously as if trying to bring reality into focus. She cupped her hand to her mouth, then took it off because what she had to say would not be muzzled, not even by her better judgment. "Gil, why are you so angry?"

"I'm not angry. I just want you, all of you, to knock it off."

"You may not be specifically angry, but you're most definitely generally angry. You're lashing out at me, you lash out at Momma. None of us can escape it. I wouldn't be surprised if Sandra wasn't part of your anger." She looked away as if she would stop, but snapped back immediately because she knew she couldn't stop. "Is it too hard being a Giles, Gil? Is it too hard being Eulelie's son? It's all of the above, if you ask me, but we're given the life we're given. It's not as great as it could be, but it's not as bad either."

She looked away again, but this time without a hint of looking back to say more. Lila watched a miniskirted woman drop quarters into the jukebox while doing a sensual shimmy-dance. The woman mesmerized Lila and she couldn't stop staring. It wasn't necessarily her fluid movements and low-down dips. At its basic, her attraction was more about what in this woman made her feel so free, so confident that she would shake herself in the middle of a bawdy bar. There was something energizing to Lila in this kind of ease of spirit.

But before Lila could watch the woman finish her dance, two fingers tapped on her shoulder with a lightness that said it wasn't Gil. Still, in that second it took her to turn around, she prepared herself to humbly accept his apology, or at least an explanation, for his anger.

"Hey Lila," a smiling woman said, standing almost between Lila and Gil.

"Donna! What are you doing here?" Lila said, speed-blinking to make sure it was true.

"I was just about to ask you that."

"Oh, well, I'm here with my brother. We were talking." Lila was so flustered by everything—being found there, find-

ing two people there she held up to her own level of class—
that she didn't know how to answer. "And what are you
doing here?"

"I come here a lot. At least three days a week. In fact,
I've seen you here before," she said, turning to face Gil and
offering him her hand. "I'm Donna Yates. I teach at the
same school as your sisters."

"Gil Giles. Nice to meet you," and he went back to his
drink after giving her hand a clasp and one pump.

"Well, anyway, I come here to get rid of the stress of
dealing with obnoxious sixth graders with hormones on the
brink of raging, but I never thought I'd see you here after
last year," Donna said.

Lila looked at her, puzzled. "Last year? What happened
last year?"

"You don't remember? I asked you a couple of times to
have a drink with me after school and you always said that
you don't drink."

"Well, I don't. This is seltzer," Lila said, a defensive lilt
wrapping every word.

"Oh, well, anyway, you should stop in more often,"
Donna said. "This really is a fun place. I'm gonna run now.
My husband's over there waiting for me."

And as her friend walked away, Lila was left with a distant smile, and the thought of the meaningless nature of
perceptions.

Three women saunter-dallied over from the pool table
with carefree laughter and sat on the three stools next to
Gil. He glanced at them without care, gave a nervous half
smile and looked back at his drink. But there was something
intimate about his smile, to Lila. It told her that he knew
them, possibly well. Not one of them was young enough to
have been a onetime love interest. Lila could see this right
away in a woman who had the beginnings of a turkey waddle, and another with old hair—not gray, but the kind of
hair that had thinned to scraggly straw. Who were these

women? She looked expectantly at Gil, while they did the same from his other side.

Then the woman sitting closest to Gil said: "Gil, honey, we're going now. You stop by soon, you here." That, of course, was Gil's cue.

"Yeah, sure, we'll come by soon," he said, distracted. "Oh, uh, by the way, Camilla, this is my sister, Lila. Lila, this is Sandra's mother, Camilla, and Camilla's friends Margie Crawford and Dolores Willis."

"Hello," Lila said with a dumbfounded stare, despite her manners. She wasn't quite sure how she had pictured Sandra's mother, and although the picture before her was close, it wasn't quite there.

Realizing that Lila wasn't going to chat them up, they gathered their things to leave. "We'll see you, Gil," Camilla said. "It was nice to meet you," she said to Lila with an untrue smile.

"Take care," Lila said, without even attempting to look her in the face.

Once they were gone, the silence remained between Gil and Lila. She dared not, absolutely dared not, say a word about Camilla and her friends while the tension between them was this thick. Who would be the first to break the silence? Surely it would have to be him, at least the way she saw it. He owed her an apology, and she would say not another word until he groveled for her forgiveness.

"All right, Lila," Gil finally said. "Now are you going to leave or am I?"

Without dignifying his insult with an answer, Lila hopped from the bar stool and headed for the door, first with a hastened gait, then with a slower one. This was the part where he was supposed to stop her, to tell her he was sorry, that he would never darken the doorstep of this place again. But the scene, scripted so well in her mind, never played out. Before she knew it she was out on the parking lot, standing at the hood of her car, still somehow waiting for Gil to come after her. She stood there five seconds, ten more seconds. Gil wasn't coming. Hastily, she searched her purse for keys and clutched them eagerly. Then, whoops, just as quickly as things like this happen, they slipped from her grasp and fell down a sewer drain.

"Oh no! Oh no! Oh my God, no!" she cried. The keys weren't the problem—she had a spare set at home. The tragedy was that she had to swallow her pride and go back into the bar to ask Gil for a ride home. For only a split second she thought she'd rather walk, or worse, take the bus. Should she go in and be sweet, as if nothing happened and appeal to the protective big-brother side of him? No, she was too hurt to do that. Should she just take the matter-of-fact approach? *Gil, I dropped my car keys in the drainage ditch and need to get home.* That was best.

Just as she turned to go back into the bar, someone called to her. "Lila, are you all right? Is something wrong?"

Lila looked around with a start. Who in the world would know her in this neighborhood? It was Camilla and her two friends, calling to her from the car next to Gil's. "Oh, well," she said, "I just dropped my car keys in the drainage ditch here and—"

"You need a ride home?"

"Well . . ."

" 'Cause we can drop you home. Come on, get in."

"Oh, that's very kind of you, but that's okay. I can—"

"Why don't you come on? Leave Gil to his night out. He works hard. He deserves it. Come on, now."

"I ain't gonna beg her," Margie said to Camilla, but loud enough for Lila to hear.

"Cut it out, Margie," Camilla whispered, but Lila still heard. "Come on, honey, it's okay, and we don't mind."

What a choice; humble herself, or demean herself. "Thank you very much," Lila said as she walked to the car to get in. "I really appreciate this, and I hope it's not too far out of your way."

"Oh, don't you worry about that. After all, we're practically family."

Lila smiled politely as she squeezed past the pushed-up seat into the backseat. She had almost forgotten how much she hated two-door cars. So blue-collar. "I live on Hilton Street. Do you know where that is?" she asked Margie, who was driving.

"Yes, I know where Hilton Street's at," Margie answered, on just the slightest edge.

"I swear, Margie knows her way around every part of this city. Sometimes I think she moonlights as a traffic cop and just doesn't tell me," Camilla said.

"Aren't you ladies kind of far from home? I mean, I know you live in East Baltimore, don't you, Mrs. Hightower?" Lila said.

"Yes, we all live over there. But Dolores used to live over here on Park Heights, and she's the one who got us comin' over here to Jay's. It's a long way to come, but it's worth it because we always have a hell of a good time."

"When did my brother start going to Jay's?"

"Oh, I'd say about two years ago, right, Margie?"

"Yeah, about that."

"That's when we told him about it, and he's been a regular ever since."

"Oh," was all Lila said, and then nothing else until Margie turned onto Hilton Street.

"This is my house right down here."

"Wow, that's some house," Dolores said.

"Thank you."

"It looks kind of dark. Is anyone else home? Are you going to be able to get in the house?" Camilla's concern was honest.

"Oh, yes. My house keys weren't with my car keys. I keep them on separate key rings." She knew they didn't care about how she kept her keys, it was just something to say. "Besides, I'm sure Momma's home."

"Really?" Camilla said with raised eyebrows. Everyone, even Lila, knew exactly what that meant. "Well, I would love to just pop in and meet her, just to say hello." Camilla had to see her, had to look this woman square in the eyes and know her.

"Well, I don't know," Lila said. "Momma, uh . . ."

"She won't mind, will she?" But before Lila could even answer, Camilla was already out of the car heading for the house.

Lila stood at the car, dumbfounded and immobilized. She had to stop her. Lila knew that her mother was in no way prepared—socially, emotionally, the family was not ready. Just as Lila searched her mother's sack of lies for an excuse, like how her mother retired to her room, without fail, at six every evening until the next morning, Margie said: "Camilla, get back here. We gotta pick up Eustace in fifteen minutes. We don't have time for this."

"Oh, that's right," Camilla said, returning to the car. "Well, tell your mother that we'll meet some other time." Camilla folded back into the car, puffing out a breathy relief. As much as she wanted to know for sure, she didn't want to know.

"Oh yeah, and besides, I'm sure Momma would want to meet you under more formal circumstances, like having you and your family over for dinner."

"Okay, that would be nice. Just let us know."

Warped Memory

"Momma? Lucretia? Linda?" Lila yelled before shutting the door. The house seemed, at first, quiet enough to hear the quiet, but she knew someone was home because the lights in the dining room were on. When she closed the door, she could hear the faint sound of her mother's radio floating into the hall and teasing with its whispers.

"Lila, it's me. I'm in the dining room," her mother called back.

Lila walked into the room with her face dragging, but what a pleasantly distracting vision. Her mother, glowing beneath the chandelier; alone, way at the other end of the table, her radio right by her side. Eulelie wore no tiara, nor robes of silk and gold, but there was something royal to the way she sat, with her hair freed from its usual bun, hanging on her shoulders and moving ever so gracefully with every turn and tick of her head. Maybe it was the way she ate, carefree, off the fine china, and drank in the same manner from the imported crystal. Or it could have been the way she mindlessly fidgeted with her diamond ring, catching all the lights in the room in the three karats. And it could have been the symphony with its delicate melody that seemed to sing only to her mother. Whatever it was, to Lila, Eulelie looked to be one of the highborns.

"Momma, you're eating alone. I'm so sorry."

"Oh, that's okay. I waited as long as I could for you, but I was starving. What kept you so long?"

"Well, first I had a conference with the parents of my students about the spring play my class is doing. Then Lucretia, Linda, and I went to the caterers about the cotillion. Then I was going to stop by the jewelers at the plaza for Lucretia's locket, you know, the one that Daddy gave her, but then I ran into Gil. Oh, and I also dropped my keys down a sewer."

"What? What drainage ditch? Did Gil give you a ride home? Why didn't he come in?"

"No, Momma. Sandra's mother gave me a ride home. It's kind of a long story, but I was driving up Reisterstown Road going toward the plaza."

"Were they able to fix it?"

"Fix what?"

"Lucretia's locket?"

"I don't know. I wasn't able to get to the store because of my keys."

"How is that Sandra's mother gave you a ride home?"

"I'm coming to that. Anyway, I was driving up Reisterstown Road, and right around that real sleazy part I spotted Gil's car in the parking lot of this very seedy-looking bar. So

I went in to find out why my brother was in a place like that. That's when I met Sandra's mother and her two friends. She seems nice. She wanted to come in to meet you, but I stopped her."

"You did what?" Eulelie was undone. "You not only went into a bar, but you went into a bar in the worst possible part of Reisterstown Road, is that right?"

"Momma, I went in there. I had to. I think Gil's lost his mind."

"Lila, I think you've completely lost yours. God knows anything could have happened to you in that neighborhood. Those black folks over there don't even need to have a reason to kill you. They'll kill you just for bus fare. I'm really surprised at you. Someone like you does not belong in a neighborhood like that. Besides, what if someone had seen you? It just doesn't look proper, Lila, it just does not look proper."

"But Momma, Gil—"

"I don't care. Gil is a grown man and he can take care of himself. Besides, I'll deal with Gil later about this. I don't ever want you doing anything that stupid again."

"Okay, Momma, I shouldn't have gone in there, but what I'm trying to tell you is that this place is where Gil goes several times a week. He's friends with the bartender. Sandra's mother hangs out in there. Gil and I had an argument and I didn't want to ask him for a ride home and that's why she ended up bringing me home, but that's all beside the point. I'll tell you, Momma, something is going on with Gil and this new crowd of people he's hanging around with, and it's not good."

Eulelie leaned her back against the chair. A hint of a smile, knowing but not revealing, settled on her mouth, her cheeks, her eyes. Her calm, her complete lack of indignation over Gil's secret life, didn't give away the secret of a plan she kept, but it did pique Lila's curiosity. *"That was Chopin's Piano Concerto Number One in E minor,"* the soothing tenor voice from the radio said. He went on, Lila vaguely heard, about how the concerto was actually the second and not the first, but the actual first concerto was published *after* the actual second.

"Momma, didn't you hear what I said about Gil?"

"Yes, Lila. I'm not deaf. And I know that it's that girl who's leading him into the seedy life. All that's going to come to an end very soon, though."

Lila didn't have to say a word. Her mother only needed to feel those questioning eyes peering into her own to know that she wanted, needed, to hear more.

"Lila, honey, I have lived most of my life for this family, keeping up the strong tradition of pride, dignity, and class, especially in raising you children into the kind of Gileses your great-grandfather, and his father, would have been proud to call his own. I'm not about to let this girl slide her way into this family in a momentary lapse of Gil's good sense. Neither she nor her barfly mother *will* put a mark on this family line and all the excellence the Giles family name has always stood for."

"So Momma, what can we do? We can't just tell Gil that. In fact, we tried and it just made him mad."

Eulelie pulled one of the dining table chairs next to hers and patted the seat. "Come here, honey, and sit down."

This must be big, Lila thought. This was sit-down news. This was *Come here, honey, and sit down* news; the biggest kind of news.

Eulelie put her hand softly on Lila's knee, then squeezed, gently but determinedly. "What I'm going to tell you I don't want you ever to mention to your sisters—not to anyone, for that matter, but especially not your sisters. Do you understand?"

"Yes, Momma. What is it?" Lila just wanted her to get on with what she had to say. The anticipation was bound to be worse than the news itself.

"I mean it, Lila. I'm counting on you. I'm only going to tell you because you're my oldest, most responsible girl. Linda, God bless her, means well, but she couldn't keep a secret if it had handles, and Lucretia, well, this kind of thing would get her all flustered. You, though, you're steady as a rock."

"Okay, Momma, okay. You're going to trust me. Now please, just tell me."

"Lila, I've had a man find out some things about this girl Sandra."

Lila's eyebrows jumped so high they almost met and mingled with her hair. "Momma, you hired a private eye? You had her investigated?" Lila asked in a whisper.

"That's a crude term for it, honey. I'd like to think of it as doing some protective research. People like that girl always have ghosts and skeletons from their past."

"It's the same thing, Momma," Lila said, her disappointment plain as white bread and butter. "Momma, I know we don't like her for Gil, but this just seems so drastic. I mean, I thought we were going to hope for good sense to prevail in Gil, and if not, just grin and bear her, but this is pretty drastic."

"Desperate times call for desperate measures, and honey, we are desperate. Now I say the best way to avoid a disaster is to prevent it from happening in the first place. We all know that Gil's and Sandra's worlds are too different for a marriage between them to work. Gil will just end up hurt and disappointed in the long run. You know how sensitive he is. I can't bear to see that happen."

"But Momma, a private eye?"

"Lila, I'm only doing what any good mother would do— I'm protecting what's mine. Now I didn't tell you about this to discuss it—it's done. I just want you to come with me tomorrow morning when I go to hear what he's found. Will you come?"

Lila let out a long sigh. Then, talking with embarrassment to her shoes, she said, "Well, Momma, as much as I don't like this, curiosity keeps me from saying no." Suddenly, something jumped into the middle of her mind from the shadows of its rational corner. "Momma, where did you find this private eye man? Where in the world do you go to get someone like that?''

''Dottie Pettigrew-Van Dyke used him to check out that fellow her youngest girl Tina married, and you know how that turned out. That marriage was annulled.''

''Because of what her mother found out from this man?''

''That's right. Now, I want you to be ready to go at nine-thirty because I'm meeting him in the food court in the mall at ten. We'll tell your sisters that we have to help the church deliver food to the poor. They're certain not to want to come along for that.''

The front door opened and closed. Lila and Eulelie sat still, very still, and quiet, as if they were up to something. They were.

''Momma? Momma, where are you?'' Gil bellowed through the house.

''I'm in here. In the dining room.''

Out of breath, Gil ran down the hall and into the dining room. ''Momma, Lila's car was parked next to mine, but she's gone.'' Then he saw Lila, slumped into the chair behind him and put his head on the table. Still trying to catch his breath, he looked up at his sister and said: ''You had me scared half to death. Why is your car still in the parking lot at Jay's? How did you get home? *Why* did you come home without your car?''

''My car's in the parking lot at Jay's because my keys fell down the sewer and your future mother-in-law and her motley companions gave me a ride home.''

''Why didn't you just come in and get me?''

''Why would I? You can't even think of a good reason why you should even like me.''

''I never said that.''

''You implied it.''

Guilty by implication.

''Well, anyway, come on and let me take you to get your car,'' Gil said.

"No, thank you. I'll have Lucretia or Linda take me when they get home."

"Lila, now don't be silly," Eulelie said. "I don't know what's going on between you two, but you just need to forget about it and let your brother take you to get your car. You don't want to leave that car down there any longer than you have to. It'll be gone before you know it."

"Come off it, Momma," Gil said. "I park my car at Jay's for hours at a time and no one has ever stolen it."

"Well, this Jay's is something you and I have yet to discuss, but we will. Just take your sister to get her car. I'll deal with you later. Suffice it to say that I do not appreciate finding out that the son I raised into an upright gentleman is socializing with the likes of people who hang out in a common beer hall."

"Momma, for Christ's sake! I'm a grown man. I don't have any intention of 'discussing' Jay's with you or anyone else. Yes, the 'upright gentleman' you raised hangs out at a 'common beer hall,' and I hang out there frequently. That's all you need to know, and be lucky that you know that much about me. Come on, Lila."

Her mouth agape, Lila couldn't move. She sat there looking first at Gil, then at her mother, who was also in slack-jawed shock. Gil and their momma had been known to have their go-arounds. He had even been known to be definite with her will. But as she scrolled her memory, she had never known him to be downright nasty to her. Something was wrong, terribly wrong. Gil was out of sorts, and perhaps temporarily out of his mind.

"Gil, how dare you speak to me like that," Eulelie said, so calmly that it was clear her anger was beyond histrionics. "So this is how your new future family has influenced you. You're rude to me, you're rude to your sisters. Is this what you've learned?"

"If they've done anything, Momma, they've opened my eyes. They've shown me the importance of judging a person by character, not by pedigree. I've learned about the humanity of people who give everything even when they don't have anything. That's what I've learned from them, but do you want to know what I've learned from you?''

"No, Gil, I don't think I care to,'' Eulelie said, rising from the chair to leave.

"Come on Gil, let's go,'' Lila said, frightened at what might be said, what might be done.

"I'm going to tell you anyway, Momma. From you I've learned that nothing particularly matters quite as much as the right family and the right society clubs and the right part of town.'' But now Eulelie was in the kitchen and Gil was shouting to make certain he was heard. "I've learned from you to be proud of my *titled* father, the lawyer, and *prominent* judge, and his father, who was a *prominent* doctor, and still his father who had the biggest and most outstanding funeral parlor in Baltimore. Prominence. That's a big thing for you, Momma. What I didn't learn from you was to be proud of my mother who grew up in Cherry Hill, and her father, who was a train porter without a college education, and her mother, who was a maid. Why is that, Momma? Huh? Why am I proud of only half of me?'' Gil was now in the kitchen, standing face-to-face with his mother. Lila was right behind him, nervous and scared and praying it would end soon.

"Gil, I'm not having this discussion. Now for some reason you're overwrought and you want to take it out on me. Well fine, take it out on me. Just do it without me,'' and she went to walk away when Gil stopped her in her tracks.

"Momma, do you remember Lemuel Spriggs, the only friend I ever chose for myself?''

Eulelie had amnesia of the selective sort regarding Lemuel Spriggs. Gil, though, would never forget Lemuel nor would he ever get over the guilt, the sorrow of a true friendship lost. He took Eulelie back, even though she did not want to go, to the day when he found out for certain that his life was not his own.

*   *   *

It was one of those confusing fall days Baltimore claims at least once a year—too hot to be fall, with a sneaky chill hiding in the wind making it too cold to be summer. The sheer lace curtains danced on the breeze that flowed in through all the open windows, and bright light from Sunday's midday poured through the front door that sat welcomingly open. The doorbell rang, but then a knock followed. Eulelie went cautiously to the door, glaring nervously at the tall, thin, tar-black young man standing on the other side. The midday sun put a glare in the front hall, but she could see this lank of a young man who filled her heart with a galloping rhythm and her mind with ghastly imaginings; not the least was fear. She stepped to the door and held tightly to the screen door's handle.

"May I help you, son?" she said guardedly, dispassionately, desperately frightened that nothing but flimsy mesh in a metal frame was all that stood between her and her worst nightmare.

"Yes ma'am. I'm Gil's friend, Lemuel Spriggs. He invited me to dinner today."

"Oh, I see," Eulelie said, her voice rife with relief and disappointment, all at once. "Please come in. Gil never described you so I didn't know what to expect." But being a classmate of Gil's at the Anderson School, she certainly didn't expect him to be like this—shabbily dressed, black as a newly laid street, shoes as dull as dust. She knew he didn't come from a family like hers. The only questions she now had were where in the world did this boy come from and why did Gil want him as a friend.

Lemuel walked sheepishly into the living room, without being asked, and sat on the sofa. Eulelie followed, saying to him: "Please, have a seat." And the sarcasm was real.

Lucretia walked into the hallway from the kitchen and stared at Lemuel as if to wonder why he was in her home. "Momma, who's this?"

"This is Gil's friend, Lemuel Spriggs. Lemuel, this is my daughter Lucretia."

"Hello, Lucretia, it's nice to meet you."

"Hi. Momma, where's Daddy?"

"In his study, but don't disturb him. He's working on something very important and doesn't want to be disturbed until dinner. Now I want you to go and get your brother. Tell him his friend is here."

"Yes, Momma." She trotted up the stairs with the brattiest little bounce.

Eulelie sat, staring, her mere presence overwhelming the room like some Shakespearean shrew. With a motive she couldn't even fathom, she wanted him to squirm. "So, Lemuel," she finally said after watching him stare at his dusty shoes for several long, irksome seconds. He looked up, but not directly at her. "You're on the track team with my Gil, are you?"

"Yes ma'am."

"Gil says you're even faster than he is. Is that true?"

"Well, that's what the numbers say, but he's pretty fast, so it's hard to say for sure."

Just then Gil came plopping down the steps with Lucretia following close behind. "Hey, I was starting to think you weren't coming."

"Ah, I'm sorry I'm late, man. I had to catch three buses to get here, and on Sundays it's not easy to be on time when you're relying on the bus."

"Did you meet my momma?" Gil motioned to Eulelie, who had a look about her that he could not read.

"Yes, Gil, I've met your friend. I was just asking him about the track team and what you say about his speed. Either you're prone to exaggeration, Gil, or Lemuel here is a very modest young man," she said, her half smile saying more of what she truly meant than her actual words, and still Gil did not understand.

"Momma, when will dinner be ready, because I thought Lemuel and I could take a run around the reservoir before we eat."

"Yeah, man, I did like you said. I brought my running

shoes," and Lemuel lifted up a brown paper grocery bag he had sitting on the floor that Eulelie and Gil had just at that moment noticed.

"Get all hot and sweaty before dinner?" Eulelie said. "Absolutely not! You do not need to take a run around the reservoir. Sunday dinner is not a casual thing around here where you can sit there and drip your perspiration into your soup. You know that Gil. Now no more talk about that."

Lemuel put his bag back on the floor and settled into the sofa, stiff as a corpse. Instinct told him that his hands needed to be folded in his lap and he should wait to be spoken to before speaking. Sunday dinner was not a casual thing.

"Lemuel, who are your people?"

"Excuse me, ma'am?"

"Your family, your mother, your father. What are their names?"

"Oh, well, my father is Carey Spriggs and my mother is Bethel Spriggs."

She knew before asking the questions that no bells of familiarity would ring in her head, but looking into the air for effect, she said, anyway: "I see. Those names don't ring a bell with me. Where did you go before Anderson?"

"I went to Harlem Park. Harlem Park Junior High. Have you heard of it?"

"Yes, I have. Well, why didn't you go to Anderson? Gil's been there since the seventh grade. Before Anderson he was at the Country Day School."

"Yeah, Gil told me. Well, Mrs. Giles, to tell you the truth, I'm at Anderson on a scholarship. A full academic scholarship. My parents couldn't have afforded either one of those schools."

Gil interrupted, obviously proud of his friend's accomplishments, "Well, Harlem Park must have given you a real good foundation, because you know that my dad's on the board at Anderson and I know they don't give scholarships that easily. Isn't that right, Momma?"

"I suppose, Gil." Then she leaned forward, as if to share a secret, and said, in a low, empathetic tone, "It must be pretty difficult being in a school with other boys whose parents can afford certain privileges over and beyond the school program that your parents can't. That's why I've always been against these kinds of scholarships to inner-city, underprivileged kids at these exclusive private schools. I think in the long run they can do more to hurt them emotionally and psychologically than help them. You know, discourage them."

At that point all bets on modesty were off. Lemuel suddenly knew who she was, because he had seen her so many times before. She was the woman who'd help his family at Christmas just as long as they were sufficiently grateful and beholden. She was the woman who gave money to his burned-out neighbors in exchange for a photo and sycophancy in the society pages of the *Afro Gazette*. She was the woman who would not let her daughter date him because he wasn't light enough for the possibility of marriage and children. Yes, Lemuel knew Eulelie, and no matter what her real name and real face happened to be, she was the same cast back to the days of house niggers.

"Well, the way I see it, Mrs. Giles, in the long run I'll end up doing just as well in life, if not better than a lot of those so-called privileged kids you talk about. I really do believe that it's not where you come from, it's where you're going."

Eulelie glared at him, eye-to-eye, waiting for him to blink. He never blinked. Nothing could break their resolve to stare the other down, not even the heavy-heeled footsteps of the Judge approaching. *Whump. Whump. Whump.* They came closer and closer, and the standoff would not, could not, end. Eulelie's disdain was so intense she could not sense the presence of her husband, and he had a presence anyone could feel. "Eulelie!" he said, his deep, bass voice startling her from the stare-down. "Eulelie, what's going on? How long are we going to have to wait for dinner?"

"Oh, Judge, I'm sorry. Yes, right away. We were waiting for Gil's friend, here. He was a bit late." She scampered to her feet and across the room in a frantic, self-conscious way that only the Judge could induce in her. She bellowed through the hall to the cook: "Helen, the Judge wants dinner on the table now. Let's get things going." And having given her order, she was gone.

"Well, he's here now, and I would imagine he's as hungry as the rest of us," the Judge said.

"Yes dear, we'll put dinner on the table right away," she replied, already in the hallway. "Girls, your father's ready to eat," the men heard her say as she went hurriedly into the kitchen. "Let's get dinner on the table."

"Lemuel, my boy! How's it going?"

"It's going well, sir."

"I'm really glad you could join us today. How are your parents?"

"They're fine, sir. They told me to say hello to you."

"Tell them hello back. It was nice meeting them at the track meet. You have a very nice family, son. I hope you appreciate them, because that's really the only thing that matters. When you have the strength of your family behind you, there's nothing that white folks, or anybody else, can do to tear you down. Remember that, son, because that's something I've always instilled in these children. I hope it'll carry them through life."

He glanced over at Gil, who sat nervously in the corner of the sofa as if waiting for permission to speak.

"Yes sir, I will." Lemuel paused, his furrowed brow saying he had more to say. "Judge Giles, why are you on the board at Anderson?"

With squinting eyes of confusion, the Judge said: "I'm sorry, I don't understand the question."

"I mean, what made you want to be on the board? A lot of people think that you did it to make sure that more blacks are accepted into the school. You know, blacks like me, especially, who wouldn't be there without a scholarship."

"I didn't ask to be on the board over there. They asked me. Now that I'm there, though, that is my concern—getting more blacks into the school."

Lemuel fidgeted with his thumbs. Still, another curiosity burned a bubbling trail to dance on the tip of his tongue. Lemuel looked over at Gil, at first just briefly and then with a double take for several long seconds. Gil was wound tight, and deep in thought. What had he said or done, Lemuel wondered to make Gil so ill at ease?

"Dinner's ready!" a young voice called from the other room.

"Lemuel, you can sit over there next to Gil," Eulelie said the moment they entered the room. She and her daughters were moving on fast-forward, bringing in the rolls, then the iced tea. The Judge was ready to eat. They all sat in their own seats, but before Lemuel could even get settled, before the cook had even gotten the last dish on the table, Eulelie was off and running with the grace. And before his head could even bow, Eulelie was closing the grace with *Amen*.

No one said anything. Heads buried, forks moving back and forth, everyone went straight away to the business of eating. This wasn't how it was done, Lemuel thought. In practically everybody's house in the free world there was talking during dinner—with and without full mouths. Maybe it went against some particular etiquette known only to high society types. Mind your manners. No talking during dinner. But the more silent were the moments ticking by, the more anxious Lemuel became. There was something odd about a silent meal; as if perhaps there was bad blood flowing. He tried hard, very hard, not to talk. It would not work. The dinner table was the most natural and normal place in the world for him to socialize. There was no fighting it any longer. He had to talk.

"So, Judge Giles, do you ever get any flack about that?" Lemuel said.

"About what, son?"

"About looking out for poor black kids. Making sure that black kids like me get a fair shake at Anderson."

"Oh, there are some who don't like it, but that's their problem."

Eulelie said not a word, but she shot a tight-faced glare at Lemuel, as if wanting to continue the standoff.

"That's a pretty liberal attitude for you to take, sir," Lemuel said, scooping up a mound of mashed potatoes. "I mean, a lot of people in your position would look at people like me and just write us off. I mean, I wasn't born with no silver spoon in my mouth, far from it. As one of those benefiting from your liberal attitude, I thank you."

Eulelie wasn't going to let this young punk do this to her. He didn't know her if he thought he was getting the last word.

"Well, I've said it before and I'll say it again," she said, "I think there's a point where liberal generosity does more to hurt than help. I don't think any of those people are being helped by more handouts."

"I agree, Daddy," Linda added. "I think it's just like Gil said the other day. It's not fair that they get to go to Anderson free of charge while everybody else has to pay tuition. And a high tuition at that."

Not once did Gil look up from his plate, which had suddenly become more interesting than anything or anyone else in the room. His ears rang with the deafening boom of what had to be his own heart about to catapult from his chest. He could feel Lemuel's eyes pressing, sinking into him. They were eyes filled with incomprehensible hurt; eyes that had been betrayed.

The senior Gil looked first at Eulelie, then at Linda, but then back at Eulelie. He was annoyed, maybe even angry. "That will be enough, Linda," he snapped sternly, still looking at Eulelie. "And that will be enough from you too. I think we need to enjoy this meal and our guest, and leave the talk of liberal attitudes and liberal handouts to the politicians, shall we?"

"Fine, but the truth remains that these children know that they're getting the short end of the stick," and that was Eulelie's last word for the remainder of dinner. In fact, only a few other words were spoken by anyone. *Pass the potatoes, please. Would you please pass the bread. I'd like the greens, please.* It was all very polite, but painful, intensely painful for everyone there.

"Momma, do you recall ever seeing him come around to visit me again after that?" Gil said after his trip down the darkened memory lane. Only that tenor voice from the radio filled the air. *"Chopin was actually very much in love with Constanti—"* Click. Gil reached down and cut the man off in mid-discourse. Somehow it seemed inappropriate to have the details of a dead composer's love filling the room as background noise. "Do you, Momma?"

Nerves were so raw with the possibility of what might happen next that no one heard Linda and Lucretia come in the front door, nor see them come into the room.

"What are we talking about?" Lucretia whispered to Lila.

"Gil's friend from high school, that guy named Lemuel Spriggs," she whispered back.

A puzzled look overcame Lucretia's face as she tried to remember.

"Do you recall ever seeing him in this house after that, Momma?" Gil asked again. By now he sounded like a litigator, Eulelie being the adversary on the witness stand.

"No," she said in a hushed tone.

"What, Momma? I didn't hear you."

"No, Gil, I don't remember seeing him anymore after that."

"And do you know why, Momma? It's because he thought that because you were such an obnoxious snob, and my sisters were such obnoxious snobs, some of it had to be in me too. After that I could probably count on one hand the number of words he said to me for the rest of our time at Anderson. You ruined that friendship for me, Momma, and now you're trying to do the same thing with Sandra. Well, things are going to be different this time. You're not doing this to me again. If you had just learned when we were kids to stop trying to make sure all our friends fit your expectations of the people we should have in our lives, we wouldn't be going through this right now with Sandra."

"Gil, I'm sorry, but I don't remember it that way at all," Lila said timidly. "If you would just listen to your own story, you'd see that it was your own words, come back to haunt you, that ruined that friendship. If indeed that friendship ended the day he came here for dinner, it wasn't Momma who ended it, it was you."

"That's right, Gil," said Lucretia. "Besides, I remember that guy coming in here with a huge chip on his shoulder."

"And he acted like he was trying to start a family argument between Momma and Daddy, right there at the dinner table!" Linda said. "It wasn't Momma's fault at all."

Eulelie had the faintest half smile on her lips, so proud that her girls had come to her defense. Then she said, "And so now you're telling me that I'm the reason you're about to make the biggest mistake of your life by marrying that girl."

"Damn it, Momma!" Gil banged his fist down on the kitchen table so hard that the salt and pepper fell over, clinking and clanking against one another, and clinking and clanking the room into a dead quiet. Rubbing his head, Gil composed himself and said, "Hey, you know what, Momma, forget it. You are never going to get it, so I don't know why I even waste my time. All I know is that I lost Lemuel Spriggs as a friend because of you, and he was one of the finest people I've ever had the privilege of knowing. I can still say that to this day. You're not going to do the same thing with Sandra. You can accept her, or you can not accept her. It's totally up to you, but I'm going to do what I want to do."

"Gil, you are being grossly unfair," Lila said quietly.

"That's right," her sisters confirmed in unison.

Gil chuckled, then said to his sisters, "If the three of you only knew half of what was true . . ." He trailed off, thinking better of continuing. He buttoned his jacket and headed briskly out of the room and into the hall. "Come on, Lila," he snapped.

She followed Gil to the car, and followed his lead for silence. And when he went directly to the driver's side without first opening the door for her—the way his mother had taught him—she knew it would be best to wait to speak. They pulled away from the house at a furious pace, making a U-turn to put the car in the right direction. Then that car, so little, so light, hurtled so fast down the road, driven by raw anger and possibly irrational thoughts, all Lila could do was close her eyes and pray for the right thing to say that might calm her brother and possibly save their lives. When they jerked to a stop at a light, Lila took a breath and spoke. "I'm sorry about your friend, Gil."

"What?"

"Your friend, Lemuel Spriggs. I'm sorry that he's not your friend anymore. I remember how you really liked him."

"Yeah, he was the best. So real, so genuine. Would go to the wall for anybody. I really hope he's doing good now." When the light changed, Gil's foot pushed the car slower. "I don't even know if I deserved his friendship. He was the genuine article. I was a prick."

"We were all pricks, Gil. Everything from who we met at the park to who we got school notes from after a sick day was controlled by Momma. It was all we knew, so we can't gnash our teeth and whip ourselves for it. But we can do something about it now . . ."

Her voice trailed off into a silence that settled awkwardly between them. It was as if voices had to fill it before words so perfect for the moment would be lost forever in the quiet darkness of the car. As the car whizzed along Reisterstown Road, Lila bothered to see for the first time in the warm evening's scenes of people on their ramshackle porches, or standing on corners, the bliss of contentment and the way it lived upon the breasts of those she thought were the most unlikely. These people laughed, she believed. They laughed, and really felt it in a place she could not. For contentment had eluded this generation of the Giles clan.

"Earlier tonight, Gil, I accused you of being with Sandra because you're angry at Momma. Well, I just want to add something to that. I think it's just that you're with Sandra so that maybe now this family can get back to what the name Giles really does stand for."

As Gil pulled to a stop next to Lila's car, he turned and gave her a smile. It was a smile so deeply rendered with dancing eyes and invincible soul that it almost made her cry. If he had said or done nothing more, she would have still understood that his love for her ran deep. But he said simply, "I love you, sis." He laughed solidly, warmly, as if unburdened, then said, "But why the hell couldn't you have said that to Momma?"

Picking for Dirt

Lila lay in bed looking into nothingness, where her thoughts lived. There was no indication that sleep had overtaken her at all during the night—no tousled sheets, no sleepy eyes. In the quiet of the room she could hear her own heart, and her head throbbed with the dull ache of sleeplessness. Eulelie's innocent accomplice was going to go along, partly out of curiosity, partly for the thrill, but mostly because of the fear of saying no. This kind of thing goes on every day, she tried to rationalize in her mind. Every woman her mother knew had hired a private investigator at some point in their lives—some to investigate undesirable mates for their children, but most to catch their husbands' cheating hearts. They always found what they were looking to find. Eulelie was no different than all those other respectable, upright women Lila had known before she even knew she knew them. So why did she feel so dirty? Why did it feel like a dirty little secret that would leave an irreparable pock upon her unadulterated family tree?

A knock at the door made her jump like a cat. "Lila." Her mother's voice floated in a whisper through the door.

"Yes, Momma."

Eulelie opened the door, and all Lila saw was pink. Her mother was fully dressed and ready to go. She even had her purse. "Lila!" she said, amazed at what was before her. "I cannot believe you are still here in bed. It's eight-thirty and we have to meet—" She stopped herself, looked quickly over her shoulder for Linda or Lucretia, then continued in a much lower tone. "We have to meet him at nine-thirty. Now come on, get up from there. We've got to go."

"I'm sorry, Momma, but I just didn't get a lot of sleep last night." Lila sat up slowly, then put her feet on the floor.

"Well, you'll have all day to catch up on your sleep when you get back, but we have to go. I'll be waiting downstairs for you," and Eulelie left the room, closing the door behind her with a firm steadfastness that made it difficult for Lila to stare her down and say no.

Lila dragged herself, on legs that did not want to move, into the bathroom. As she was about to step into the shower, she could hear Linda giving her mother the third degree while following her down the stairs.

"Momma, where are you and Lila going?"

"She wants me to help her find an outfit for the Black Barristers' Wives luncheon next month." How easily Eulelie could lie; as if she actually believed her untruths.

"Why didn't she ask me and Lucretia?"

"Because you two have to get ready for High Tea today. Have you forgotten that we're expecting your debutantes-in-training in this house this afternoon for High Tea? I have to shop for the tea, then come back here and make those scones. You two have to get this house ready. By the way, Belva will be here at noon."

"Well, we're never too busy to go shopping. I want to go," and Linda went to gather her jacket and purse.

"No!"

Linda turned with a start. What was once a smiling face had gone to fear, to bemusement, to sulking, in all of three seconds. Before she could even ask the inevitable, Eulelie tried to salve the wound.

"What I mean is, it's so rare that I get a chance to spend time with any of you girls just one-on-one. I'll go out and do this with Lila, and then next week I'll do something special with you, and the next week with Lucretia. Is that okay?"

"Oh, sure, Momma, that's fine. I didn't know you felt that way. So what will we do?"

"Oh, I don't know. Whatever it is you want to do. Just let me know."

"Okay. Momma, are you still going down to Lexington Market to get meat and fish?"

"Yes. That's why Lila and I are taking separate cars."

"Okay, well, would you get me one of those big crab cake sandwiches from that seafood stand all the way in the back."

"Sure, honey. Do you want anything else?"

"No, thanks. Just the sandwich."

Eulelie picked up her purse from the floor next to her and got to her feet with a perky hop. "Well, I'm off. You and your sister have a good day with your activities." She planted a firm kiss on Linda's cheek and went into the hall. "Lila, let's go! Time's wasting!" she bellowed up the stairs. Then she turned and walked out, and before she had even made it to the walk, Lila was barreling down the stairs and out the door.

Eulelie and Lila pulled their cars into the parking slots side by side. Their dashboard clocks said ten exactly—the doors to the mall hadn't even been open for a solid minute. Eulelie killed a second or two by tucking a lock of hair back in place. She would have touched up her face powder had she not turned to find Lila peering at her through the window. Annoying, for both. Startled, Eulelie fumbled until she had her purse firmly in hand. Lila stepped aside to let the door swing open.

"Okay Lila, I'm coming," Eulelie said in answer to Lila's impatient lip curl. "You sure are in a big hurry considering you really don't want any part of this private investigator stuff."

"Momma, I just want to get this over with," Lila said, walking ahead of her mother toward the mall entrance.

Eulelie ran to catch up to her before Lila opened the door. Tugging her back by the crook of her arm, Eulelie said, "Now listen, you don't need to say anything. I'll do all the talking to him."

"Momma, I have no interest in talking to this man. I just want to get your information and go."

"Now, Pick is a very to-the-point man. That's why—"

"Pick! That's his name, Pick?"

"That's right, just Pick," a deep mysterious voice hissed over her shoulder.

Her head snapped around faster than her eyes could focus. He looked her squarely in the eye. He was tall, but not too tall, and thin. His skin looked less like skin than satin, and his face was perfectly balanced—no feature too big or small. In all, he was possibly the most beautiful man she'd ever seen. Not at all the smarmy, yellow-eyed, dusty-black cretin skulking around in her imagination. This was not the face, the body, the smile of a private investigator. This was the face, the body, the smile, the bearing of every Giles man in every photograph documenting her extraordinary lineage.

"*You're* Pick?" Lila finally found the voice to say.

"Yes. I'm Pick."

"Is Pick your first name or last?"

"Both."

"I see. Well, it's nice to meet you, Mr. Pick," and she extended her slender, trembling hand for only the briefest clasp and pump.

"There's no mister. It's just Pick. I prefer it that way."

But this didn't make sense. Pick, a name reserved for the streetwise, did not fit at all on this articulate, well-groomed Giles clone. Lila's mind was filled with the white noise of confusion. By all appearances, and just by those first few moments, Lila was certain that he was a man she could proudly bring home to meet her momma, if, of course, her momma hadn't already introduced her to him. Maybe his real name was John, or Gregory, or Michael, or Mark, something upstanding, something successful. Something becoming the epitome of *fine*. Pick, though, just was not a name befitting this man certain to have been bred with the culture and education of those outstanding Negroes who came before him.

This unlikely trio—the society matron, her daughter, and the private eye—strolled past stores, some of which had not yet opened for their day's business. Actually, they strolled with a trifle in their strides, as if they were there to spend a careless morning window shopping. Eulelie set the pace and the mood. It had to be this way, casual and light, as if she were out for the morning with her daughter and her daughter's dashing boyfriend. A quicker pace would arouse some suspicion. A purposeful gait would do the same. So they moved through the nearly deserted mall in silence, Pick and Lila waiting for Eulelie to get on with their reason for being there.

After passing a few stores, Eulelie stopped. Pick and Lila did the same.

"So what do you have for me?" Eulelie asked, smiling as if saying something completely banal and unimportant.

"Well, a lot," Pick said, turning away to continue the stroll. He was in control now.

"Do you have it in writing?"

"Of course, but I'm not going to give it to you right now. I just want to tell you a little bit about what I found." Pick paused long enough to check out a pair of shiny black loafers in Florsheim. "You know, she's really a decent girl. She's made some bad choices, but she's good people. Her family too."

"Yes, that's fine, now please, get on with it," Eulelie said, still smiling a charm-school smile.

"Well, her mother, Camilla, she's not from Baltimore. Neither is Eustace, her father. Her mother's from South Carolina. Charleston. Her father's from Atlanta. Her mother comes from a pretty prominent family down there in Charleston, believe it or not. I mean, she and Eustace may have raised their family hand-to-mouth, but she sure as heck didn't grow up like that."

"I don't understand," Eulelie said.

"She grew up living the way you live now. What's to understand?"

Eulelie stopped dead in her tracks. With great indignation and a trace of nervousness she said, "What do you mean by that?"

"By what?"

"She grew up living the way I live now."

"I just meant—"

"I don't know what you've *heard*, but I've always lived like this, and you insinuated otherwise. I come from one of the finest black families in all of South Carolina."

"No, Momma, he didn't say that," Lila said, mystified by her mother's paranoia. It was so strong, coming from absolutely nowhere. "He's just saying that her mother grew up like us. Why do you think he's trying to insult you?"

"I did no such thing," Pick said. "Look, Mrs. Giles, I have no idea what your life's been like, and I don't want to know because I don't care. I was paid to do a job. That's all I'm trying to do."

"I'm sorry," Eulelie said sheepishly, blushing from her self-inflicted embarrassment.

"May I finish?"

"Please."

"Okay, well, Camilla Hightower's father was a doctor and her mother didn't work, but she was *the* woman to know in black society down there. Sort of what you are here in Baltimore. Anyway, she went to Spelman, was there one semester when she met Eustace Hightower, who was a janitor at the school. Her family disapproved because he came from a family who couldn't even fathom the notion of an indoor toilet—real rural people, and poor, very poor. They got married anyway, mainly because she was pregnant, and her family cut them off. That's when they moved to Baltimore."

Pick stopped talking because it looked as if Eulelie had a question. She had the oddest expression, which neither Lila nor Pick could read. It was as if she were trying to mentally put a puzzle together and was waiting to solve it before she spoke. The corners of her mouth turned up in a half smile. Her eyes squinted, with what could have been pain, but it wasn't. Then she said, "Do you have a family name for this woman Camilla? What was her maiden name?"

"That I don't remember offhand. It's in here, though. It's all in there."

"Well, anyway, are you positive she's from Charleston?"

"Yes. I'm very thorough, Mrs. Giles. All that's not the point, though. You wanted some information on the daughter, Sandra, right?"

"Yes. Yes, of course."

"Like I said, she's made some mistakes, but she's really a good person."

"Enough of your editorial comments. Just tell me." Eulelie went over to a bench that looked all too inviting by now. She sat down, and Lila sat to her right, Pick to her left.

"Okay, well, it seems that Sandra Hightower met a boy in junior high that everybody called Dynamite. You know the type, popular but dangerous. Anyway, when she was thirteen she started hanging out with Dynamite and his crowd, and a year later she was pregnant. Pregnant and only in the eighth grade. Well, Camilla convinced Sandra that abortion wasn't the way to go, yet she didn't want Sandra to put the baby up for adoption. Said she didn't want to go through the rest of her life looking into the face of every child she saw wondering if it was her grandchild. So she and Eustace decided to send her down to Georgia to Eustace's family to have the baby. They told everybody they were sending Sandra to Georgia to get her out of the city. Said they wanted her to spend some time getting to know his family. After the baby was born—it was a girl—Eustace's sister adopted her. Sandra came back to Baltimore and went back to school as if nothing happened.''

Eulelie stared at Pick, positively nonplussed, and Lila was dazed by this unbelievable news. Eulelie was looking for something, anything, that would derail this runaway relationship. She had no idea that she would hit the jackpot with this kind of ammunition.

With a sneaky smile, she said, ''This is amazing. This is unbelievable. She doesn't even let on that she has a child.''

''Well, what do you expect? The relationship between her and that child was set up as cousins. That's just the way it is.''

''Yes, but why lie? Why all the deception? I mean, pregnant teenage girls are the rule where they live, not the exception. Who did they think would look askance at them?''

''Well, Mrs. Giles, the only thing I can tell you is that pride must be in the blood. It doesn't matter, though, because Sandra takes care of her responsibility. She's been working since she was sixteen, and from the time she started working she's been sending money and clothes to that girl, a little bit here, a little bit there. She pays for little activities the girl wants to do. She even sends her an allowance. She also started a college fund. She's determined to send her to college. She's very close to that little girl.''

''Pick, that's good work. Is there anything else?''

''Well yeah, a little bit.'' He paused, then said, ''It seems that after she got back from Georgia she became a bit obsessed with this guy, Dynamite.''

''Obsessed,'' Lila repeated.

"Obsessed. She started stalking him or anyone he dated. This went on for about eight years. He was stringing her along, though. It came to a head when he finally flat out rejected her. He embarrassed her in front of some girl he was with. They mocked her, humiliated her. Sandra snapped, pulled a knife on him and tried to kill him, though nobody really thinks she was trying to kill him. In the end he didn't press charges and the whole thing was forgotten. She got on with her life."

"Well, Pick, Dottie was right," Eulelie said. "You do not disappoint." She inconspicuously slipped her hand into the back pocket of her purse and pulled out an envelope. She passed it to him, saying, "Here's the rest of your money, plus a little extra for working so quickly. I may be in touch again. Let's go, honey."

But Lila wasn't ready to move. She looked at Pick, then at Eulelie. If she were to leave with her mother, an opportunity of some sort, she wasn't quite sure what, would be lost, maybe forever. Of that much she was certain. Her face ticked with indecision. Then, with only a second to save her chance, she lied with the precision of her mother. "I have to get some panty hose, Momma. I'll see you at home."

"Oh, now I remember, Mrs. Giles," Pick said. "I remember Camilla Hightower's maiden name. It was Perkins."

Eulelie looked at him, suddenly fearful, though she wasn't certain why. "Did you say Perkins?"

"Yeah, Perkins."

"Momma, do you know the Perkinses?"

"No, of course not. Why would I? I don't know people in Charleston. I'm from Columbia, remember. I've got to go." But the name haunted her. What was the name of that family who lived at the end of the road down in Charleston? she wondered. It was familiar, sitting right there on the tip of her memory, yet she could not summon it. And the possibility of such an odd, such an insane, coincidence of her knowing the Perkinses was what frightened her most; but it was indeed the insanity of such happenstance that allowed her to disavow its possibility. Still, in this city that moved, breathed, spoke, and smelled like a small town, and with the world shrinking daily as it was, she had to fight like anything to believe it simply could not be. Abruptly, she left with a rumbled goodbye, comforted by the thought that the family living in that big house her sisters cleaned, and that she had too much pride to clean, was the Parsons family. Or was it? Eulelie's memory would never allow her to be sure. Thus, her peace of mind was fleeting.

With Eulelie gone, Lila sat awkwardly, playing with the clasp on her purse. Pick looked around at the passersby with no reason to get up and leave, but no particular reason to stay. Lila looked over at him like a shy, prepubescent school-girl, snapping her head away when it looked as if he might see her seeing him.

"Well, I think I'll get out of here," he said.

"Oh, well wait. I wanted to ask you, are you from Baltimore?"

He looked at her with his head cocked sideways, as if she were out of line, as if the question were unreasonable. "No. No, I'm not. I'm from here and there. No place specific."

"Oh. So how long have you lived here?" she said quickly so he wouldn't leave.

"About twelve years. I like it. It's a funny city. It's like the South, yet it's not, and it's north of D.C., which is nothing like the South."

"Actually, I never thought about Baltimore like that, but I guess it is like the South."

"Okay, now, you take care," Pick said, getting to his feet.

Then Lila said, "Something tells me that you're more than this mysterious Pick."

Pick gave her a forced smile that slowly became real. He had been a private investigator long enough to know people's ulterior motives before they were even aware of them themselves. He knew what was happening. Why not play along? So he gave her a dance and a song—a lie—that he knew would befuddle her to an awful distraction. He lowered himself slowly, with the aloofness of the cool, back down onto the bench, then said: "Okay, since you just have to know, I went to Sidwell Friends from kindergarten through twelfth grade. I went to Georgetown, undergraduate and law. I graduated law school, took the bar, passed the bar, but never practiced law. When I moved here to Baltimore I started my agency, and I've been a private investigator ever since. I'm not married, although I came close once, but I pretty much like my life flying solo. Is that all you need to know?"

Though his willingness to divulge all this should have let Lila know that her mind had just been batted around like a dead mouse by a frolicsome cat, she went on to say: "I don't understand. Sidwell Friends, Georgetown Law, you're a barred attorney. Why do this gumshoe stuff?"

"Why not? I like it. It fits me."

"What does your family think?"

"The same thing your mother would think if it were your brother doing this. They don't approve. It's not acceptable. Not proper. It doesn't matter to me, though. Is there anything else?" Pick asked as he finally stood to leave.

"Yes, actually. What's your real name?"

"Lila, all you need to know is Pick."

"I know that's not the name your mother gave you. Why do you call yourself Pick?"

"Because that's what I do—I pick for information. I'll see you." Pick walked away with a swagger Lila watched until he melded into the crowd and she could no longer see him.

✒ Her Heart's Desire

Eulelie got home with just barely enough time on her side to bake the scones before the intended debutantes arrived. Time, though, was pressing down so steadily that she wasn't able to inspect Belva's work. Eulelie was quite distracted, and would be until Belva left. Lucky for Belva.

Whirling through the door burdened with bags, Eulelie passed one off to Linda, who would only carry one, and only the lightest. The rest she handed to Lila and Lucretia, as Lucretia pressed her with questions of her whereabouts. Questions, of course, she never answered.

Lila had opened the cookbook on the counter to the page that said "English Teas" in hopes to at least start the scones. "Get me the flour," Eulelie snapped at Lila, gently nudging her away from the cookbook and a mixing bowl that was far too oversized for the job at hand. Her weight shifted to one hip, Eulelie quickly read through the scones recipe, then dumped flour into the bowl.

The recipe was for the purpose of what, not how much, to put in. Eulelie was one of those cooks whose talent simply did not need measurements. Just the week before, she heard on National Public Radio that the difference between authentic English scones and scones from some pseudo-highbrow, typically American gourmet shop was that the perfect English scone was drier and not as sweet, to compliment the tea. She tried explaining this to her girls, but they didn't seem to care. Scones you found at these shops in America, she told them, were made for the American palate—loaded with sugar and far too moist. "They even said so on the radio," she said. There was no response to her attempt to educate about the scone. Eulelie had blown out a breath and shook her head in disgust as her girls tended to the tea, without the least care of something that didn't even sound like it was meant to be eaten.

"Momma, why don't you just make some sweet tea biscuits or something?" Lila asked. "Why are you so set on making these English scones?"

"Because this is High Tea, Lila," Eulelie snapped. "This is what you serve for High Tea, and we're going to do this right. If you had heard that report on NPR you would know that this is the way to do it. These girls are being presented as our future ladies of society. They need to know these things."

"Momma, we didn't have scones at our High Teas when we were presented, and we're just fine," Lila said.

"You all didn't have scones because for those three years straight Celeste Breckenridge was in charge of the spring cotillion and the debutantes. *She* never does anything the right way. I'm just grateful that she didn't have you girls washing down fried chicken and potato salad with that tea. Now Dottie Pettigrew-Van Dyke, when she took charge of the whole thing, Dottie had her High Tea the right way— with scones. We will do nothing less."

"Miss Eulelie," a voice called from the front hall, "I'm all done, so I'll be going now."

"Oh, okay, just a minute Belva." Eulelie handed the wooden spoon to Lila. "Just keep stirring this until the dough clings together, then leave it alone. I'll be right back. Eulelie rinsed her hands quickly in the sink then wiped them on her apron.

She trotted out of the kitchen and past Belva, then up the stairs. "I'll be right back, Belva dear. I have to get something for you." Upstairs, she could see the tracks of the vacuum's rollers in the nap of the carpet—evidence that Belva had really worked. When she appeared again, she came down the stairs writing out a check, with a fancy, giftlike envelope tucked against her side beneath her arm. Her contorted body, with one shoulder raised and her neck held quite stiffly, trying not to drop anything, made it look awkward, but she finished signing the check, seemingly without effort. "This is for your work today," she said, handing Belva a check. Belva glanced at it quickly, and amazingly enough, it was the right amount for her full day's work. "And this, this is for the birth of your first grandchild," and she put the envelope in Belva's hand with a bashful smile, then a self-conscious giggle. "It's just that babies are so special, and such a joy to welcome into the world, you know." She shifted her eyes down away from Belva's face, as if ashamed, then said: "One of my greatest regrets in life is that I never had—" But she reeled herself in quickly. Too much information. "Well, you don't want to hear about all that boring nonsense. Anyway, I hope you can put this to good use for the baby."

But Belva did want to hear more of all that nonsense. She wanted to hear more about this woman for whom she'd worked for so many years but had no hope of ever really knowing. She'd known for all these years that there was someone patently decent in Eulelie, wrapped up too tightly to unwind in one twirl. Eulelie had locked down again, though, and there was nothing for Belva to do but show gratitude in the way Eulelie would want her to show it. "Thank you, Mrs. Giles, this is so good of you. I really mean that. You really didn't have to do this."

"I know I didn't have to, Belva. I wanted to. Your first grandchild is a big deal, a very big deal. I just wanted to give you something to help start her life off right. It is a girl, right?"

"Yes ma'am, a little girl. Joy Nicole. She was seven pounds fourteen ounces, and twenty-three inches long. Can you believe?" Belva beamed. "But then again, her daddy's tall. My son's six-foot-five. I guess she's gonna take after him, be one of those tall girls. Not too tall, though, I hope. A real tall woman can have a hard time finding a man, you know."

Eulelie smiled at Belva wistfully. The bottom seemed to drop out of Eulelie's chest at the mere mention of a newborn baby. "Oh, don't you worry about that. I'm sure she'll do just fine. Just love the baby. And Joy Nicole, why, that's a beautiful name, and there's one hundred and fifty dollars in there for Joy Nicole. You can put it in a savings account, or buy her pretty new dresses, or do whatever you need to do with it. Of course, now-days just a few little outfits would take up the whole one hundred and fifty dollars."

"Yes, I suppose, if you go to Hecht's or Macy's or places like that. I took my daughter-in-law over to the thrift store and showed her how she could buy beautiful clothes for that little one for nowhere near the prices they charge at Hecht's or these other places."

"The thrift store? Which one? I used to go to the one over there on Belvedere Avenue when my kids were younger."

Belva stared blankly at Eulelie for several long seconds, not terribly certain she had heard her correctly. "*You*, Mrs. Giles? You used to buy your children's clothes at the thrift store? Y'all always had so much money. Why would you need to shop over there?"

"Well, of course I shopped at the secondhand store for these children's clothes." She moved in closer to Belva, then said in a hush: "Of course, they never knew. And neither did anyone else. You'd have to be crazy to pay retail prices for clothes a child is going to wear for only two minutes. That's why I went to the store down on Belvedere, because that's where you'd get the really good finds. Stuff looked like it had been worn once, maybe twice, then they'd take it to the secondhand store. And you know, down there, it's those Pikesville Jews giving the clothes away, so you know they're good quality. I say, yeah, let those Jews pay full price for these dresses, and pants, and jackets, and then I'll come to the secondhand store and get them for twenty-five cents, or forty cents, and what have you. My kids would step out of this house looking like little princesses and a little prince, and none of these people ever knew my secret. Not even the Judge. Everybody just thought we were the richest people in the world to dress three little ones as finely as we did. And the Judge, well, he just thought I was brilliant the way I could catch *sales*. That's what I told him, you know, 'Oh, I got those things on sale,' I would say." Eulelie had the sly grin and far-off gaze of someone who'd pulled off a caper quite great. Then she laughed, full-throated and quite gleefully at the thought of what she'd gotten away with for all those years.

"Well, thank you so much, Mrs. Giles, I really mean it. This means a lot to us."

"You're quite welcome, Belva, and bring pictures of that baby the next time."

Belva, struck dumb, simply turned and walked out the

door wearing a smile that she'd wear the rest of the day. Eulelie had shown sympathy when Belva's mother died, and empathy when she lost her husband, all distantly, of course. But she had never treated Belva quite so humanely as she had with something so positively ordinary as the birth of a baby.

On the front walk, Belva saw two of the first arrivals for High Tea. They looked tentative, nervous, a bit leery even, as if they didn't know if they should speak, or smile, or simply pass her by. Finally, Belva said, "Hello, girls."

"Hello. Excuse me, ma'am, but does Eulelie Giles live here?"

"Yes she does."

"Thank you."

Belva heard one of the girls whisper, "I was hoping we'd have the wrong house so we wouldn't have to go. We could just say we got lost."

"Don't worry," Belva said with a chuckle, "she's not herself today."

"Yeah?" the other young lady responded. "Well, that could be good or bad."

And all Belva could do was laugh.

$\mathscr{S}$ IX

~~Desperate Times . . .

Eulelie stood at the waist-high table at Lexington Market daintily nibbling the Polish hot dog from Pollock Johnny's that she actually wanted to devour. Decorum. She savored every nibbled morsel as those comforting smoky sausage flavors exploded in her mouth, smoothing every single frayed edge of her nerves. There was no way to even get enough of this magnificent treasure of Baltimore. Everybody else in Baltimore could have their crab cakes, but for Eulelie, no other culinary specialty in the entire state, not even black-eyed pea cakes, could compare to a Pollock Johnny's Polish hot dogs.

Taking the very last bite, Eulelie chewed and chewed, almost hating the thought of swallowing. Her few moments of bliss came to an end with that one inevitable gulp, though. She took the last few sips of lemonade and set the cup on the table. Wrapping the bag around and around, Eulelie tucked her polish hot-dog-to-go into her purse and walked away, oblivious to the scraggly man standing nearby waiting for the table.

"Hey!" he called as she headed down an aisle lined with vegetable stands. "Hey, what do you think, you have maids or somethin' 'round here? You're s'posed to clean off your own trash!" Eulelie just kept walking. She heard, but feigned deafness. She didn't even so much as look over her shoulder to acknowledge his incredulity.

Eulelie stepped up to the stand she had been going to occasionally for her fruits and vegetables for a few years— they always seemed to have the freshest. She smiled in the general direction of the people standing behind the counter without paying much attention to them at first. A husband and wife, it seemed. Maybe her eyes had gone bad. Maybe she wasn't seeing straight. She looked again, this time with purpose, then quickly looked away. Eulelie was astonished, positively stunned, but disrespectful, disapproving, she was not. Koreans? When did they move in here? "Korean Shop-owners Doing Booming Business in Mondawmin Mall,"she remembered one headline in the *Gazette* saying. Sure, she knew they were in Mondawmin. That news went through Baltimore faster than Sherman through Atlanta. It was all over the *Gazette*. But when did they move into Lexington Market? She smiled politely at them, but mostly to herself. This made Baltimore an official chunk in America's stew, she supposed.

Eulelie picked up a red plastic basket they had placed on the floor in front of their stand for their shoppers' convenience. She plucked from a pile a dozen ears of corn, two bunches of kale (the collards didn't look so good), a half-dozen plums, the same amount of peaches, and two heads of cabbages. She picked through the string beans to end up with a paltry bagful. Sitting in a pyramid pile, clearly untouched, were mangos that tempted her, drew her to them, even though she'd never tasted its delectable flesh. She plucked two from the top. "I'll try these," she said aloud to herself. Eulelie looked around, here, then over there, then way over there. Nothing else looked terribly good. This was a different stand, all right.

Eulelie stepped to the line that was longer than it should have been, considering the slim pickings of freshness. She passed the minutes looking around at all the obvious things that made the stand different from that of the last occupants, and immediately one glaring difference stood out. Behind where the merchants stood ringing up their customers pur-

chases were little wooden plaques with trite spiritual apho-
risms like, *God gives you a gift each day when He wakes you
in the morning*. What was obviously missing, at least to Eulelie, were indications of their *Koreanness*. There were none
of those watercolor pictures, mostly in pallid tones of blue,
of some tranquil lake beneath the quintessential Asian moun-
tain range dotted with skinny leafless trees and ominous clouds
on the edge of a burst. Why weren't they there, these pictures
that were the quintessence of Asia? Where were the little
plaques with Korean proverbs written in Korean? There wasn't
a trace, anywhere on the stand, of their language, those
drawings of circles, squares, and lines that give them their
special voice. It was sad. How pitiful, Eulelie thought, that
they would come all the way to Baltimore to start a new life
only to have to do away with their *Koreanness*.

Ahead of her in the line were two round boys, not more
than a decade old, and dusty, very dusty. They fidgeted in
and out of line as if something under their skin kept them
from keeping still. One held a large bag of string beans,
which he probably grabbed in chunks, Eulelie thought. The
other bounced a head of cabbage from one hand to the next,
like an incomplete juggler. And when she actually paid attention to their back and forth banter, her stupefied mouth,
which drifted open succinctly, told of her consternation. The
boys laughed and backslapped, trading witless repartee of
Your mother's so quips. The dozens. How offensive, and at
this age, no less! But it was more than offensive, it was positively humiliating, for any black person within earshot, that
these boys were carrying on this way in front of these Koreans. Maybe these Koreans' command of the language wasn't
such that they would understand, but that didn't matter to
Eulelie. Just the possibility that they could understand was
enough to make her feel as small as those pint-sized hoodlums were making themselves. That's what they were, hoodlums. And there was no way they were raised right.

She could not, would not, tolerate this insolence a second
longer. This, she believed, was how the pock of bigotry

thrived. It was how images of dysfunction made their way around the world, with black Americans stopping in the minds of many as clichéd do-nothings.

"Your mother's so black, when she wears orange lipstick she looks like a cheeseburger," the juggler said, stumbling into the aisle and cracking up.

"That's cold, nigga, but check it out. Your mother's so funky, she used Secret and it told on her." And this time they both laughed.

"Stop it! Stop it right this second, you two!" Eulelie snapped at them in that stern teacher/mother way. "You sound ridiculous. You ought to be ashamed of yourselves, talking like that. You should spend as much time on your studies as you do making up those ridiculous things you call jokes. Why don't you put that much effort into your school-work? Then maybe you'll get somewhere in life."

The boys' heads snapped around, looking for whoever had the temerity to reprimand them. The cabbage juggler reared his head back with disbelief, while the other rolled his eyes and kissed his teeth, then said: "Who you talkin' to? You ain't my muvah."

"If I were your mother you would not behave this way. Now I don't like disciplining other people's children, but you two obviously need it. What kind of way is that to carry on, saying such awful things? You're embarrassing yourself and every black person in this line. You both need to mind your manners."

And what came next made Eulelie long for the moments before, when she was only shocked by the language of their game of Dozens. Out of their mouths spewed the most hor-rendous string of expletives, most suggesting that she was at least part if not all canine. Others suggested that she make herself intimate with their bottoms. Then, in closing, they both suggested that she might want to copulate with herself. It was the foulest thing she'd ever heard from the mouth of a child. Sure, children tried out bad words to see how they felt, but what happened to the days when they tried them out on each other, and in the shadows of that secretive part of their world that said they knew it was wrong?

As if their curses weren't enough, it became clear that she was alone in her outrage.

"Why don't she just leave 'em alone," a man behind her said. "They wasn't hurtin' nobody."

"I know," came a woman's voice. "They sure wasn't."

Fear, she felt strongly. How had it come to be that two little boys—*little black boys!*—could incite in her fear for her life? Had things come to this? In her day, poor and black never seemed to matter when it came to raising respectful children. And how could it be that no one shared her vexation with these ruffians? She could do nothing but stand stark still, and silent, praying that she'd make it home with her life.

The two boys left after collecting their purchases, the boy with the cabbage backing away while saluting her with one digit on his right hand. It left her cold with fear. She watched them vanish into the throng that was Lexington Market and go who knew where. They left her with distinct imaginings that they could lay low waiting for her somewhere with their pack of hoodlums, which she was certain existed, and do God knows what to her. She prayed for home.

"Sixteen dolla-sixty," the woman said after ringing up Eulelie's purchases.

"Sixteen dollars and sixty cents?" Eulelie questioned. She really hadn't been paying attention as her purchases were added up. "That's seems a bit high for this amount of stuff."

"Sixteen dolla-sixty cents," was all the woman said without a trace of humor, her husband equally staunch.

This could turn into one of those indelicate matters that just might have her looking for succor from the last people on earth. Never. So, Eulelie paid, then took her change and the bag. She tossed them a polite and drawled-out *thank you* that slithered out through a tight smile that wasn't real. After all, she'd never invite these Korean humbuggers to brunch, but they still deserved gratitude for their service.

From two counters away Eulelie could see the rotten-toothed grin of her Lexington Market friend, as well as that T-shirt with MARY emblazoned on her chest. In most states south of Maryland, somebody like Mary would be considered white trash. In Baltimore, though, all one needed to mention was that Mary lived in Pigtown and nothing more would need to be said. That grin was for Eulelie, and Eulelie only. Two other people walking behind Eulelie returned the smile, one even waved, but Mary did not know them. She was welcoming the customer she'd been expecting all day. The customer who always spent more money at one time than any other regular. Mary threw her hand up and waved, while the pasty-white flab of her large upper arm swayed in the air, like the droopy leaves on a willow tree. She adjusted the hair net that covered her stringy blond hair, then went over to the counter to greet Eulelie.

"Lemme see whatcha wearin' today, hon," Mary said in the little-bit-country twang particular to white folks in *Bawlamoor*. Mary leaned over, craning her fat neck to see Eulelie's suit. She couldn't see much, though. Her bosom and belly, both oversized, got in her way. "You sure do wear some good clothes. Don't she, Bo?" and she looked at her nephew, who sat on a stool in the corner.

"Uh-huh, she sure do," he said with the sluggishness of someone whose parents could have been siblings.

"Mrs. G, how you doin' today, hon?"

"I'm fine, Mary, just fine. What do you have on sale today?"

"Oh, I got chicken breasts, veal chops, and pork chops. Thick and juicy pork chops. I put three pounds aside for you 'cause they're goin' fast, hon."

"Thank you, Mary. You're always looking out for me." Eulelie looked in the case at all the beautiful meats, healthy and red, which made her mouth water. For her, there were no other meat counters in Lexington Market that could compare to Mary's. She always had the best cuts of meats at the best prices. It had been a solid twenty-five years now, Mary's and Eulelie's relationship. Going anywhere else for her meat would be, well, treasonous. If Mary were to retire, Eulelie's loyalty would still lie at the counter, but Saturday-meat-day would never be the same. "Mary, you can add two more pounds to those pork chops. And give me about six of those veal chops. I'm also going to need about six lamb chops."

"I gotcha. What about the chicken breasts?"

"That's right. Give me about eight pounds of the breasts. And throw in a roaster, a turkey breast, and a roast beef. A brisket too."

"How are those beautiful daughters of yours, Lila, Lucretia, and Linda?" Mary asked while wrapping Eulelie's lamb chops.

"Oh, they're doing fine."

"They're still with you?"

"Yes, they are. Still at home, but I don't mind."

"No, that's just where they belong. Don't let them run off with some deadbeat. You keep them home where they belong till their princes come to get 'em. I swear, don't let 'em end up like my girls. I got four son-in-laws and not one of 'em is worth a damn."

"No, that won't happen to my girls. They're taking their time."

Mary stacked the wrapped lamb chops on top of the pork chops and went on to wrap the chicken breasts. "I'm gonna give you a few extra of these breasts, hon," Mary said to Eulelie in a sly whisper. Eulelie nodded and gave her a half wink.

"What about Gil? You haven't talked about him in a while."

"Oh, Mary, it's too long a story."

"He ain't sick or nothin', is he?" Mary asked with a worried mother's face.

"No, nothing like that. He just came in and informed us that he was getting married. Took all of us by complete and total surprise. I'll tell you, it almost took my breath away."

"Well, who is she? I know she must be darlin.'"

"Far from it, Mary. Far from it. She's the worst thing

that could ever happen to him, and I'm just heartsick, I tell you."

"Well, what are you gonna do?" Mary asked rhetorically as her pudgy fingers tallied Eulelie's bill on a cash register as old-fashioned as the market itself. "These chil'ren, I tell you. They go thinkin' they in love, then they make a mistake and marry 'em, then expect us to make everything okay. Well, all you can do is grin and bear it, and just be there to pick up the pieces when it all falls apart."

Eulelie said nothing, because her approach in this was going to be far from passive. She was going to do far more than grin and bear this relationship. In her hot little hands she had what she needed to do battle with the force that meant her family no good.

"Okay, Mrs. G. That'll be one-o-five fifty-seven."

Eulelie counted out the bills in Mary's hand, plus the usual ten dollars extra for Mary's time, friendliness, and good work.

"Thank you so much, Mrs. G," Mary said, as if surprised by the ten-dollar tip. "Okay now, you have two heavy shopping bags here. Can you handle them or do you want Bo to take them to your car for you?"

"Yes, actually if Bo could help me that would be just fine. I'm parked right around on Fayette Street."

"Sure enough," Mary said, putting the bags on the floor behind the counter. "Bo!" she bellowed.

"Yeah, Mary."

"Mrs. G needs help with her bags. You wanna help her."

"Okey-dokee," Bo said, lumbering over to Mary, his white, bloodstained apron too small for his overgrown body.

"Bo, I have one more stop to make for some crab cakes." She had to get the crab cake sandwich she'd promised Linda the last week.

"All-righty," Bo said. There was nothing to which he wouldn't agree. He was always at the ready to please, and that had the propensity to irritate, at times.

"You take care, Mary," Eulelie said, leading Bo to the crab cake stand.

"Awright now, hon, you do the same. I'll see you in two weeks."

They made their way through the crowd that had gathered around the produce stand. Bo took unsure baby steps, careful not to nick a knee or bump a rear end with the heavy bags. Eulelie had gotten several paces ahead of him and she turned to see how far back he had fallen. "I'm right here, Mrs. G," he said with a goofy guffaw. "I'm comin'." Eulelie finally spotted him. All she saw were teeth and gums. That's all anyone saw when they looked at Bo. Where Eulelie came from, Bo would be considered simpleminded, a half-wit; up here, most people just called him slow. Though his aunt never labeled him as such, retardation was almost a certain assumption.

When they finally reached the counter, Bo stumbled up next to Eulelie and stood right in her way, pinning her into a corner between the counter and a column.

"Bo, dear, could you stand over there," Eulelie said, pointing to the other side of the column. She tried, to no avail, to hide her perturbation with that smile that was always just right there in her face.

"Over here, ma'am?" and he took two steps sideways.

"No, Bo, there." She pointed.

"Right here?"

"No! There! There! Right here, Bo. Just stand right here," Eulelie snapped, taking him by the arm and moving him forcibly.

"Cee, can you help that lady. I gotta go in the back and finish frying these crab cakes," a woman said from behind the counter. Eulelie didn't hear her, though. She was too preoccupied with getting the simpleminded Bo to understand simple instructions.

"Sure," Camilla said. Then, just as quickly as she said that, she dropped a large vat of crab meat. *Thwat!* It fell hard to the ground and spilled out everywhere. "Damn!"

she cursed, and down she went to the floor to clean it up before the supervisor came back from break and/or somebody slipped and fell.

Eulelie stepped up to the counter but saw no one. She peeped over the counter, but saw only the top of a head covered with a green scarf. "Hello, excuse me, I need some help," she said, her tone laced with annoyance.

"Just a minute, miss. Somebody will be with you soon," Camilla said without looking up. "Roberta, I need your help over here. I just dropped some crab and we got a customer."

A woman suddenly appeared, her brow wrinkled, the rest of her deep, dark face on the verge of a scowl. "What the hell happened?" she barked.

"I dropped the crab. I'm gettin' it, just wait on the customer."

"Yes, I would like to be helped," Eulelie said, her patience growing thinner with each second she waited.

"May I help you?" This woman was anything but the service-with-a-smile type.

"I would like a crab cake sandwich with everything except onions."

The woman simply walked away. There was no *Coming right up*, or *I'll get that for you*. She simply went about the business of making the sandwich. Eulelie shook her head with incredulity. Then, turning around just to casually check on Bo, what she saw made her kiss her teeth and sigh. "Bo, you do not have to stand there holding those bags. Put them down."

"Oh, I don't mind, ma'am. I'm strong. I can hold these bags for a long time."

Camilla stood up to chuck two hands full of crab meat in the trash. She glanced briefly at the two arguing over whether to hold the bags or put them down, but went quickly back to scooping up crab meat.

When Eulelie turned back around, she saw the scarf-clad head going back down behind the counter.

"That will be three-fifty," the dour-faced woman said as

she put the sandwich in a bag. She plopped it on the counter and stared blankly at Eulelie.

Eulelie fumbled through her wallet for the exact amount. She wanted this encounter to end as quickly as possible. Taking the bag, she put the money on the counter, and turning to Bo, she said, "Let's go, Bo. I'm ready now."

Camilla stood up and dumped the last of the Chesapeake gold in the trash. She looked at Eulelie, catching a quick glimpse of her profile. Craning and squinting, she tried to get a better look, but just that quickly Eulelie's back was all she could see, and even that was getting farther and farther away. "Was that the woman who was just here?" she asked.

"Uh-huh."

"She looks familiar."

꿈 Voices of Wisdom

While Eulelie shopped for meats downtown, the sisters Giles went off to do what they did best on a Saturday afternoon. Acceptable shopping malls were moving farther and farther from the city's center. Once, long before their time, there was Mondawmin Mall, but the element changed. Then came Reisterstown Plaza, and once again that undesirable element of black folks took over. Then there was Security Mall, but again the element changed over time. So now they were left with no choice but to drive all the way out to the mall in Owings Mills, or all the way to the Town Center in Towson. Highway driving. It was worth the drive, though, just to be able to shop without the fear of that shoplifting, purse-snatching element so common to the urban malls. But it was only a matter of time, as Lucretia loved to point out, before all those bus and subway people found their way out to Owings Mills and Towson in droves, changing forever the haven where decent black folks could shop without fearing those other people who looked like them but were so unlike them.

They hadn't been in the mall an hour yet, and they already had two bags each. Eulelie's girls shopped as if it were a sporting event.

Lucretia needed shoes. Actually, need was somewhat of a misnomer, since they actually never needed anything. She wanted shoes, but in her language, need and want were interchangeable. Since their opinions held it that Hecht's had the best shoes, that's where they found themselves.

Lila picked up a pair of black shoes that in the current language of shoes were probably meant to be pumps, but to her they were nothing more than oversized clodhoppers—clown shoes. With their squared-off toes and their chunky heels, which were flattering to no woman's legs, these shoes were just variations on all the others on display. "What in the world do people see in these ugly shoes?" she asked her sisters.

"Aren't they just awful?" Lucretia said.

Linda took the shoe from Lila to study it. "I don't think they're so bad. I mean, it's a fashion trend, I guess."

"Would you wear them?" Lila asked.

"No, I didn't say that, I'm just saying it's a trend. It'll be over with before you know it."

"Well, just give me a classic pump any day over these big old things," Lila said, walking away from her sisters to find her conservative pumps, Eulelie shoes. Then she heard someone call her name. It was a vaguely familiar voice that her mind could not identify without turning around.

"Hello, Lila." It was Sandra.

Of all the faces she expected to see, Sandra's would not have been the one. "Oh, hello, Sandra," she said awkwardly. "Um, how are you?" She looked over in her sisters' general direction, and they were looking directly at her—still as a humid night. Lila was lost for all words after the salutational niceties. Oh God, and to make matters worse, here they come.

"Hello, Sandra," Lucretia said as she and Linda approached. "This is our youngest sister, Linda. You didn't meet her when you came to visit."

"Hello," was all Sandra said, meaning it for both of them.

"I'm sorry our last meeting had to end so abruptly," Lucretia said. "But that's Gil for you, overly sensitive and a bit paranoid."

"I see." Sandra smiled in a droll way. "Well, I don't know. I guess he had his reasons."

"Listen, Sandra, I don't want you to get the wrong idea about our family," Lila said. "I know it seemed as if we were less than . . . well, welcoming when Gil brought you by, but you have to understand that it was a shock. It was a shock, and it hurt just a little. I know for myself, I always envisioned meeting the woman Gil would marry long before they would decide to marry. I always saw us becoming close friends and going to the mall together, and having lunch together. I personally feel cheated out of all that. But I guess it's still not too late." She laughed nervously and louder than her usual.

"And let's be honest too," Lucretia added. "You're just different from the type of woman we expected Gil to marry."

Lila drew in an audible breath and held it, unable to believe her sister's candor. Even the plain-spoken Linda would have found another way to put it, or she wouldn't have put it at all.

"Oh, I didn't mean that as an insult," Lucretia said apologetically and as sincerely as it sounded, as sincerely as her rounded eyes pleaded Sandra would find it. "What I mean is that Gil hasn't dated a lot of women, but the women he's dated have all been from families that we've known, or at least heard of." As she stumbled awkwardly over her words, she was hoping to make them less cutting. She failed. "We've just always dated who we know. It doesn't make us bad people, it just makes us who we are."

"I can respect that. You'd like me to stay in my place," Sandra said. "But don't you all know that if black people had always stayed in their place, we'd—and I include the

Gileses in that *we*—we'd still be drinking the same but different water, and we sure wouldn't be drinking it here in Hecht's."

"Nobody's talking about staying in anybody's place," Linda said, laughing nervously. "All my sister's trying to say is that the social ties of our family have set it so that the natural course of things is that we'd most likely marry someone from families in the same social circle. It's been this way for generations. It's nobody's fault, and like my sister said, it doesn't make us bad people, it's simply a fact of our lives."

"What are you saying? That my family's not the type of family your family would want to have ties to? You know nothing about what kind of family I come from," Sandra said with a half smile, her eyes bearing down hard on Linda.

Lila's face had grown so ashen with embarrassment she almost looked as if she were about to be sick. Then she said, almost obsequiously: "The shortcoming is ours, not yours."

"Well, that's probably the truest thing I've heard any of you say. You three have a nice day," and Sandra went on her way, leaving the Giles sisters in the middle of the Hecht Company shoe department pondering her impudence.

≈ Game, Set . . .

Gil was in Frederick taking a deposition. That's the only reason Eulelie took the risk of showing up at Sandra's office at Monday's lunchtime, uninvited. She had only one of two days to seize, and she chose this day, which was a perfect sunny one for a stroll and ambush. Eulelie was hunting with one bullet, and she finally had a clear shot. In her mind, she had it all planned. They would walk-dawdle and talk about nothing in particular—the weather, clothes in store windows, maybe even a yay or nay talk about the football stadium for downtown. It didn't much matter. All that mattered to Eulelie was lowering the boom, and oh what a boom she had to lower.

Standing at the receptionist's desk, Eulelie clutched her purse tightly; not out of fear or nervousness—it was just her way. Even though the receptionist was giving Eulelie a cue with her eyes, if not her entire face, to speak, she waited patiently for the woman to hang up the phone before addressing her with, "Good afternoon, young lady. I'm here to see Sandra Hightower."

"Is she expecting you?"

"No, she is not, but I'm certain she'll see me. My name is Eulelie Giles," and Eulelie stood straight-backed and full of pride, staring at the piercing blue eyes staring back at her.

"Just one minute. I'll get her." She picked up the phone and pushed several buttons. "Gil's mother is here to see you, Sandra . . . Okay," and she hung up. "She'll be right with you, Mrs. Giles. You can have a seat."

"How did you know I was Gil's mother?"

"Sandra has mentioned you once or twice," the woman said with a protective stone face.

Eulelie smiled affably, taking several long seconds to let her mind synopsize this box blonde with scorched roots. She was someone Eulelie would have spotted at twenty paces as a receptionist—not even a secretary. First of all, the home-colored hair was a dead giveaway. Then there were the clothes that screamed discount store—K mart, possibly Value City. She couldn't see the woman's shoes—they would have given the ultimate answer. Eulelie was certain, though, they were nondescript pumps with chewed-up heels made of a lesser grade of leather, if leather at all. And they would be red to match her red, synthetic knit oversized sweater that had only two more washings, at best, before becoming a stretched-out blob of yarn. Deciding she didn't want to waste much more time on this dead-end-job clock puncher, Eulelie wiped off her smile and headed for one of the comfortable-looking armchairs. Before she could even get to it, a door opened with such force and fury that the receptionist nearly jumped from her seat.

"Mrs. Giles, what happened? Is it Gil? Did something

happen to Gil?'' Sandra was so frightened and so sure that something must have happened to Gil that tears had already pooled in her eyes, just waiting for the bad news to fall.

Stunned, Eulelie's eyes grew so wide they looked as if they might never close again. "No, no, Sandra. Nothing has happened to Gil. Calm down.''

Sandra sank into the chair beside her. With her elbows on her knees, she put her head in her hands, trying to pull back the reins on her racing heart.

"I'm sorry, dear. I didn't mean to frighten you. I just stopped by because I was downtown. I thought maybe we could have lunch.''

Sandra slowly raised her head, and on her face was the most indescribable look of perplexity. She couldn't speak. There were so many words spinning and swirling in her head, but she couldn't seem to grab one long enough to put it on her tongue. Maybe she heard wrong, she thought. Maybe with the rush of adrenaline pulsing through her body, she only *thought* she heard Eulelie Giles ask her to lunch. "I'm sorry, what did you say?''

"I thought you and I could have lunch.''

"You want to have lunch with me?'' Sandra asked, pointing first at Eulelie, then at herself.

"Yes, I do. Are you free?''

"Well, yes,'' she said with a shy giggle. "Let me get my purse and I'll be right back.''

Eulelie continued to sit, looking around at the typical office artwork hung on the walls. A framed poster announcing a long-gone exhibit at the Met in New York of "Van Gogh in Arles." A poster announcing an exhibit of Manet, and so on. This could have been any office of any business anywhere in America. They were interesting to look at, though, as they inspired a reflection on a Diego exhibit she and her art club went to New York to see. What a time they had. Not only did they take in the Diego at the Met, and everything else the magnificent gem of Fifth Avenue had to offer, they also walked up the street to the Guggenheim.

The next day every gallery in SoHo was honored by the patronage of the six-member Good Friends Arts Club of Greater Baltimore. And the restaurants; they ate some of the best food New York had to offer. Just taking that short trip back to New York in her mind brought a shadowy smile to Eulelie's face, until she suddenly felt self-conscious—watched. She felt the eyes of someone piercing into her. She looked at the door through which Sandra disappeared, but no eyes were there. Then she looked over at the receptionist's desk, and there they were. Those Windex-blue eyes were watching her as if she were common riffraff up to something. Eulelie stared back at her with haughty indignation and attitude, lots of attitude. It was clear to her that Sandra had this woman thinking awful things about her. Not that she gave two hoots and a holler about what some common white-girl reception-ist thought of her. It was just the absolute temerity of this girl to look at *her* with anything less than respect. The *click-thwack* of the door opening broke their concentration on one another.

"I'm ready, Mrs. Giles."

"Good. Do you have a favorite place around here at which you like to eat?" Eulelie asked as they left the office under the suspicious eye of the receptionist.

"Well, there's a place down on Charles Street called Bud's. It's a bit of a hike, but Gil and I like to go there."

"All right, that sounds fine," Eulelie said through a forced smile.

The doors to the elevator opened as soon as they stepped into the hall. Sandra ran to catch it, and Eulelie walked with the short, dainty steps of a lady not pressed for time and got on after Sandra. Two raven-haired women who could have been sisters were the only ones on the elevator, one as chatty as the other in their Baltimore accent, which had the ten-dency to be irksome and crude when spoken as loudly as these women were speaking. Their voices were simply too blaring, too grating for their accents to impart the folksy charm so unique to Baltimore-speak. They were in mid-

conversation when Sandra and Eulelie joined them, but they
continued, unfettered, about the *bastard of a husband* one
of them had the misfortune of being married to for twenty
years. He had cheated, he had lied, and as near as Eulelie
could tell, he wiped out the family's savings to keep his
paramour in a downtown apartment. Eulelie felt as lewd as
a Peeping Tom, standing there listening to a conversation far
too private for a public elevator. They twittered on, one
trying to outtalk the other, in a way that seemed as if they
could have been mocking two cackling hens. Then, without
any warning, the one with the most to say, the one who
wasn't married to the *bastard of a husband*, changed the subject. "What on earth is that lovely piece of music? Do you
hear that?" she said to the other woman about the music
that filled the elevator. "It is simply beautiful. I wonder who
it is. It's obviously classical music," she said, as if enlight-
ening someone with the obvious.

Then, Eulelie said, mostly to her shoulder, but in the
woman's general direction: "It's the second movement of
Mozart's Clarinet Concerto." Answering the woman was automatic and certainly not intentional; neither was the arrogance, but oh, the airs with which she said *Mozart*. How
incredibly self-satisfied she felt proving to this know-it-all
white woman that, yes, she was a black woman intimate
with the classics.

"Oh, Mozart," the woman said, surprised either by the
answer or that someone even bothered to answer her. Then
she gave a polite thank-you to Eulelie, to which Eulelie
didn't respond verbally, but simply gave a nod of her head
so slight it was barely detectable.

When the doors opened in the lobby, Sandra stepped out
and to the side, waiting for Eulelie, who followed her. The
two women stepped out last and walked past offering a stiff
smile, not directly to but in the general direction of Eulelie.
Then they were gone and forgotten, as far as Eulelie was
concerned.

Sandra and Eulelie left the building without a word between them. Walking to the corner, silence prevailed. Sandra looked around her, ill at ease. Suddenly, the ordinary comings and goings on Saratoga Street became fascinating. The shoe-repair shop had shoes in the window as if it were actually a shoe *store*. She'd never noticed that before. And that office building that she walked past every day was now as empty as a ghost town. It was amazing to her what she could see just by walking with someone she did not want to be with or talk to. Before either of them knew it, they were six blocks from where they started.

"Bud's is just one more block this way," Sandra said, turning the corner.

"So you say you and Gil eat at this place often?"

"Yeah. Almost every day."

"Hmmm, that's funny. Gil never mentioned a place called Bud's. Then again, there's so much Gil doesn't tell us about his life these days. He keeps a lot of secrets."

"I guess you're talking about me," Sandra said defensively.

"No, no, not just you. I wasn't talking about that. It's also some place called Jay's, where I understand he spends time drinking."

"Yeah, I know Jay's. Actually, my mother told him about Jay's."

"Yes, that's what I've heard." Then, without missing a beat, she said, "Well, the most important thing is that Gil doesn't keep secrets from you. Then again, Gil has had a very clean life, he doesn't have any dark secrets from his past to keep."

"How do you know?" Sandra asked, with all due respect.

"Excuse me, dear?"

"How would you know he doesn't have a dark secret to keep? I mean, if he did, you probably wouldn't know because it would be a secret."

"I know because I know how I've raised my son. He didn't live the kind of life conducive to secrets, dear."

"All I'm saying is that you never know."

Eulelie took a deep breath, not out of exasperation, but for energy, for confidence. "In fact, as a mother, you do know. For instance, your mother knows about your daughter down in Georgia. In fact, she helped you with the secret, didn't she?" Eulelie was as matter-of-fact as was humanly possible, given what she was doing.

Sandra stopped as if she had run into an immovable force. Eulelie stopped a few paces ahead. Sandra's eyes squinted, not from anger, but confusion.

"Gil told you?" she said, though she couldn't imagine it.

"You mean, Gil knows?" Eulelie said, astounded by the thought.

"Oh, of course Gil knows, but how do *you* know? If Gil didn't tell you, who did?"

"That's not important. What *is* important is what will happen to my son if he decides you're not the woman for him. Will *he* be stalked like that boy Dynamite and maybe even stabbed?"

Sandra began to sweat. All of a sudden the already surreal had turned nightmarish. It was clear to her, for the first time, that she was not merely looking into the face of a boyfriend's protective mother. She was standing face-to-face, eyeball-to-eyeball, with the devil.

"Mrs. Giles, that was a very bad time in my life. Not that I need to explain it to you, of all people, who will never understand, but having a baby at fourteen was traumatizing for me. All of a sudden I had this baby that was born from me but could never be mine. The only thing that made it all make sense was her father, and he kept me around only when it was convenient for him, then dumped me like a bag of stinking garbage. So I acted out of emotion. I apologized a long time ago for it, but I won't keep apologizing and I won't apologize to you."

Sandra stormed off so fast Eulelie could feel a *pwoof* of a breeze as she went past. Her gait gave her rear a little switch it didn't normally have.

"Sandra, where are you going? Don't rush off. Wait."

Why Eulelie said this, not even she knew. It just seemed like the right thing to do.

Sandra did come back, though, but only to deliver the one rock she'd been saving to hurl. It was time. "You know, Mrs. Giles, Mrs. Eulelie Giles, yes, I have made mistakes in my youth. So have a lot of people. But there is one thing I don't know, and maybe you can help me out since you seem to be such a pro at it." She was bitterly sarcastic, and it was dripping in venomous globs from her voice. "What exactly is the proper etiquette for hurling bricks through the window of another woman's home, competing for the same last name? Now you stand there and figure out how I know about that." Then she turned and walked off, and this time there was no going back.

Eulelie was left standing alone on Charles Street, only paces from Bud's, slackjawed and mad—mad as a hornet with a poked nest.

SEVEN

~ Defending the Wretched

Lucretia rushed through the doors of the movie theater, looking around the lobby, just beginning to panic that perhaps she'd been left. Haste was not good for her, since she'd never managed to move her girth gracefully when speed was involved. Everything, even her legs and face, seemed to jiggle. It all settled back into place when she saw, off in the distance, behind the ropes of the concession, someone frantically waving a hand in her direction. There she is, Lucretia seemed to say as she let out a long breath. So she shifted into her careless, cutesy sashay and headed over to where Deliah Borders stood buying popcorn and soda.

Deliah and Lucretia had been friends since Deliah's parents made it halfway into Eulelie's void when Eulelie needed to sell one more table to the Black Barristers' Wives Christmas Ball, nearly twenty years ago. The Borderses were "project people" who opened taverns on the east and west sides of Baltimore and became well-to-do. But she was a shrill-voiced harpy, and he was a crude loudmouth, and so far as Eulelie was concerned, money did not change these facts. If Eulelie had known that Lucretia had any kind of connection to Deliah, she would have told her of the Borderses' lowdown ways—even more than Lucretia already knew—in an effort to end the girls' friendship. Lucretia herself didn't think Deliah Borders was so bad. Though pretentious and mostly ill-bred around the edges, she was a sincere friend, if a bit pathetic. Deliah always seemed to be looking for where she belonged, and always trying to belong in the places she was least likely to fit—the Gileses' world, thinking her parents' ill-gotten financial security was all that was needed for entrance. And then there was that bleak period when Deliah dyed her hair blond and started talking like a Valley girl, trying to fit herself into the world of any white person who would have her. Deliah was clearly confused.

"Girl, why are you so out of breath?" Deliah asked with a twang that just might make one believe she was less than educated.

"Well, I ran here from the car. I had to park all the way across the parking lot. I didn't remember if the movie started at twelve-fifteen, or twelve forty-five."

"It's not until twelve forty-five. Remember, though, we said we'd meet at twelve-fifteen to decide if we wanted to see the Angela Bassett movie at twelve-fifteen."

"Oh yeah, that's right," Lucretia said.

"It's sold-out, so we just have to wait for the other one."

Lucretia followed Deliah to a bench near the window, but before they got there Deliah started in on Laura Ballard. Surely, Lucretia had heard. Laura Ballard, Dr. and Mrs. Ballard's youngest, had gone and gotten herself pregnant from an afternoon sofa tryst with the sixteen-year-old boy next door, whose face and body had conspired to make that thirty-year-old woman forget he was a mere child. And the sofa of conception sat right in the Ballard's living room. Deliah knew the whole story of how the public version of the pregnancy was going to claim rape with a moral pro-life high road, since Laura wanted to keep her baby.

"I swear," Deliah said, plopping down on the bench and holding out the tub of popcorn for Lucretia to help herself, "I don't know how it is people can live in such a delusional world."

Lucretia plucked a few kernels off the top and nibbled them one by one. She carefully smoothed her dress to her bottom as she sat, just the way her mother had drilled into her, then said, "Yeah, I guess, but think about how awful it would be for them to admit what really happened. Everybody would be talking. People would lose respect for Dr. Ballard and their family name. I don't think what they're doing is delusional at all, but even if it is, they're not hurting anybody." She turned and looked at Deliah with a Cheshire cat grin that said she had a secret of her own. Then, in a whisper she said, "To tell you the truth, Deliah, I would do the same thing, and I'm pretty sure my mother would insist on it. If Baltimore weren't so gossipy, nobody would even have to keep secrets like that."

"What about Lila and Linda? Would they do the same thing?" Deliah asked as if asking for a reason.

"Lila, no, never. But then again, Lila would never be in a situation like that. She's too level-headed. Too responsible. As for Linda, sure, she'd do it. In a heartbeat she'd do it, and then she'd come to believe that it really did happen like that. I don't know what happened with Laura and that boy, you know, how they came to end up messing around, but I can't judge her." Lucretia gazed off across the lobby, searching for the moral truth. It was somewhere between what she might do and what she should do. The gap was enormous. "That boy is gorgeous, Deliah, and I can imagine losing my head and going too far, letting my passion tell me that age is just a number. I would hope that I wouldn't, but hey, who knows. None of us is perfect." Lucretia was talking not so much to Deliah but to her conscience. Deliah was the eavesdropper.

"So, what's going on with Gil and that girl Sandra? Are they still getting married?" Deliah asked, her intention to change the subject obvious.

"Yes, of course," Lucretia said without emotion.

"Linda told my brother that she can't stand her. She said nobody likes her," Deliah said with a mouthful of popcorn. "So what, is your mother cool with it now?"

"She's the same as always," Lucretia said blandly, hoping

Deliah would figure out that she didn't want to talk about Sandra.

"Well, I don't know what's wrong with your brother. I've heard some pretty raunchy stuff about that girl, you know, through the grapevine."

Lucretia's head turned toward Deliah so slowly it looked as if someone might have been operating it from across the room. Her eyes squinted to slits before she found herself saying, "Deliah, what the hell are you talking about?"

"I'm talking about Sandra, honey. She's a skank, Lucretia. Let's just say that Gil is far from being the first. Girl, she's from East Baltimore, what do you think? And for your brother to be with her, I don't know. What's wrong with him that he'd want somebody like that? Who's going to respect him now?"

Lucretia was staring straight ahead now. She'd hoped Deliah would have known when to stop, but she went too far. In the seconds it took Lucretia to decide whether to say anything at all, whether to insult only Deliah, only her parents, or the entire low-life Borders clan, Lucretia simply said the first thing her mind poured into her mouth. "Deliah, you want to know something? You're a pig. You are a stinking, hypocritical, low-life pig. In fact, to call you a pig is a deep insult to all pigs everywhere." Then she shifted and resettled herself a few inches away.

Deliah's jaw dropped. She held a handful of popcorn in midair between the bucket and her mouth. That handful of popcorn was right there, in perfect launching position to throw it right in Lucretia's face. But Deliah was struck too deeply dumb to have the presence of mind for that kind of spontaneous anger.

"Don't act so shocked. I should have told you this years before and been done with you, but I felt too sorry for you, being the social climber you are, always there with your nose pressed against the window but rarely invited in. Don't you ever wonder why, Deliah? Anyway, I don't know what you've heard about Sandra or what you *think* is the truth, but you are misinformed. You do it all the time. You spread lies that you know are lies as if they're the truth. You even make up some of the lies that you spread. Well that's it. You've gone too far this time. And if you keep spreading this lie, I'll put Gil himself on your rather large tail, and then you'll have him to deal with.''

Lucretia stopped pummeling Deliah only long enough to take a breath. Then she said, ''You know, you talk about Sandra, and fine, she may not be a lot of things; she may be from East Baltimore and her family might not make it onto the A,B,C, or D list for us, but big deal. None of that makes her a skank. And who are you to judge, anyway? Look at that motley clan you come from, with your father running numbers out of his so-called business and your mother selling hot clothes from the garage. Give me a break, will you!'' Lucretia was so angry she stood for a dramatic exit and dropped her purse, spilling enough from it so that she had to get to her knees to collect it. But when she stood, she went right back to what she had to tell Deliah. ''I'll tell you another thing. When you run a vacuum cleaner through that family of yours and your own life, then maybe you'll be able to put down my brother, or Sandra, or anybody else. I'm gone.'' And she burned a furious path to the door.

Deliah hollered across the lobby to her: ''Hey, what about this ticket? I bought this ticket for you! You owe me seven-fifty!''

''Eat it, you pig!'' Lucretia yelled, almost screamed, over her shoulder. All eyes were on her exit.

Lucretia made her way across the parking lot with a walk that told strangers her path was anger, leaving them to search behind her for what or who could have stirred such obvious rage. She got in her car, but was too mad to drive, so she sat staring at the shiny car staring back at her, as if something in its sleek grill would make things make sense. She had defended Sandra against Deliah in the same way a knee jumps when hit in just the right place, and there was something about this that felt so right, yet so wrong.

An Inconvenient Relation

Eulelie had managed to put the incident with Sandra from the top of the week in a place where it wouldn't bother her. She put on her favorite earrings, dabbed on too much of her favorite perfume, and went downstairs. It was the second Saturday of the month, the day she met with her knitting club. Most clubs to which she belonged were comprised of clusters of women from the Black Barristers' Wives. The four members of the Reservoir Knitting Club (the name being Eulelie's creation) were the exception. They were just four socialites with a common hobby.

Standing in the middle of the living room, she had no memory of where she'd put the week's knitting pattern. It was her turn to bring it, and it had taken her nearly a week to come up with the pattern and then make copies. For that reason alone, she was not about to walk out of the house without them. She checked the drawer of her writing table, but they weren't there. She leafed through the pages of her knitting magazines, but she still couldn't find them. In the corner was her basket—her knitting basket she called it—where she kept her needles and yarn. She pushed aside the ball of white cotton and the ball of plum wool and found nothing. But the edge of a white piece of paper was peeking out from underneath the new skein of green wool. Pushing the yarn aside, she spotted the copies folded up together, unfolded them to make sure, and confirmed that they were indeed the directions for the cable knit sweater and matching beret.

As Eulelie's eyes peered over the top of the page, she saw something she hadn't noticed earlier. It was a lovely mint-colored envelope that had fallen underneath her chair; only a corner peered out. The subtle color that could mean an invitation or an announcement of sorts made it scream at her to open it. She figured it had fallen days ago, when Belva brought in the mail. In one quick hop she had the envelope in hand. Dust had settled on it—it had been there weeks, not days, she thought. The postmark made it official—this elegant green envelope had been sent nearly two weeks ago. It was addressed to her. In one quick rip Eulelie opened it. She stopped only for a second to read the return address stamped in printed letters on the envelope flap. Her anticipation and curiosity had her immobilized. It simply read:

Hightower
3014 B Culcourt Way
Baltimore, Maryland 21212

Her eyes browsed over the entire note that seemed simple and to the point. The handwriting was beautiful, almost like art. It was steady and easy to read, and made her think of love letters in the time of powdered wigs and corsets.

Dear Mrs. Giles,

Thank you so much for the lovely evening at your home. I found it to be an honor to be in your company as well as that of your lovely daughters. You all are everything Gil says you are, and he has spoken highly of you all. Your home is so beautiful. In my wildest immagination this is the home I would love to have. Gil is very lucky to have such a wonderfull family. Thank you again, and I hope we will have another occassion to be together, and the next time we will be on time.

Sincerely,
Sandra Hightower

"Momma, will you be back for supper?" Lucretia called from upstairs.

"What? Oh, yes, we're just meeting for lunch," Eulelie answered, distracted and bewildered. "I should be back well before suppertime."

"Okay, well, have fun."

"Have fun," Linda said, "and don't forget to bring home some of that homemade ice cream."

"Yes, fine," Eulelie said, tucking the letter into her purse. "Goodbye."

Eulelie's car crept away from the curb like a new driver—or an old one. Turning onto Gwynns Falls, she tooled along in the right lane all the way across, because eventually she'd have to make that right turn. Better to be ready. Cars on line for the Exxon filling station brought her to a complete stop. The ones turning into the Crown station simply slowed her down, but changing lanes was out of the question. That's who Eulelie was on the road. She believed stability on the road was the mark of sanity. By her definition, she'd be about the only one on the planet not in need of an asylum.

On the radio was a story on Norwegian folk dancing that had her hooked since the Crown station on Gwynns Falls. It was almost mystifying, to her, the way her radio could relay a story about something as visual as folk dancing in a way that made her feel she was there—and dancing! The folksy music, the shuffle of shoes against floor, the colorful descriptions of those native Norwegian costumes, came together to make Eulelie feel that she could go home and actually replicate those dancing Scandinavians in her living room. Oh, the places this radio took her in the world, she thought with a smile.

When she finally made her way downtown to Stouffers, she saw Celeste's car pulling into the parking garage just ahead of her. She rounded the corner and pulled up right behind. She honked and waved, but Celeste didn't see well in the dim light of the garage, and if Eulelie had not known better, she'd have thought her friend had just turned a cold shoulder. They pulled into spaces, one right next to the other. The folk dancing story had just ended. Thankfully, she'd miss none of it. Otherwise, she would have had to sit in the car till the end. It had spun her up just that tightly in its charm.

Eulelie gathered her purse and sweater and got out of the car, grunting as she stood from a growing-older pain in her hip that made standing a slower process than she'd wished. Finally on her feet, Eulelie said, "Hi there. Great timing, isn't it?"

"It certainly is great timing," Celeste said.

"I'm just glad the parking lot wasn't full. I really didn't want to have to walk three blocks like I had to the last time."

The ladies got into the elevator, which was right near their cars. Just before the doors closed, Eulelie said, "Look, there's Dottie's car. She must be in the restaurant already."

So they got off the elevator and walked directly into the restaurant. The hostess tried calling them back so she could do her job, but they didn't need her. They didn't know her. She was too new to know who they were—that they were regular enough to know where they were going.

Dottie Pettigrew-Van Dyke and Agnes Jenkins were huddled together, Agnes listening from the edge of her seat to every word from Dottie's mouth. When Eulelie and Celeste walked up on them, Celeste could hear Dottie saying, ". . . and don't you know that Gil is planning to marry this girl . . ." All Eulelie heard was Agnes saying, "No! You've got to be kidding." Celeste knew exactly what they were talking about, so she gave them a smooth out. "Don't tell me you've started already with the Augustine story. I thought you'd wait for Eulelie."

"Oh, hi, girls," Dottie said, with the canary's tail feather between her teeth.

"Dottie, dear, how are you?" Eulelie said.

"Oh, just fine. I've already started without you. They've already brought my usual." An old-fashioned, that was her usual, and though it sounded like a sweet, gentlewoman's drink, after her usual two Dottie always spoke a little louder and laughed a lot harder. Of course, she had that luxury. She was the heiress to the *Afro Gazette*.

The waitress, as though she'd been summoned through the spirits, showed up with a round of all their usuals. A vodka stinger for Agnes. For Celeste, it was gin and bitters. But for Eulelie there was none of the hard stuff to muddy her senses and loosen her tongue. She had one glass of chardonnay; never two, under any circumstances. Loose lips, you know. They gave the waitress their orders and got down to their real reason for being there.

"So did you hear about Augustine's daughter, Eulelie?" Dottie asked.

Eulelie had a swallow of wine in her mouth, but she shook her head no and raised her eyebrows to signal Dottie to tell.

"Come on, don't we have better things to do than talk about that lost child?" Celeste said after a swallow of drink.

"Oh, just be quiet, Celeste," Dottie said. "You're always trying to act so high and mighty. Don't listen if you don't want to hear, but Eulelie wants to hear."

"Fine, I won't listen," and she didn't, turning her attention to equally uninteresting events around the restaurant—a table of elderly blue-haired ladies, the couple at the next table, the middle-aged white man at the bar still trying to be as tanned and trim as the twenty-two-year-old version of himself.

"Well, I'll tell you," and Dottie pulled up closer to the table, lowering her voice. "Augustine came home and found that girl on the living room sofa having relations with a sixteen-year-old boy. And he lives right next door to them."

"That doesn't make sense," Eulelie said.

"Isn't it a shame," Agnes said. "She ought to be ashamed of herself." She sighed, then sipped her vodka stinger slowly.

"Now, this was two months ago, and now they've found out she's pregnant," Dottie went on, spitting out the word *pregnant* like it was too filthy to remain on her tongue.

"How old is that girl?" Eulelie asked.

"She's the same age as your Linda."

"Umf umf umf." Eulelie's lips were pressed together in judgment.

Then Agnes asked, "So what are they going to do?"

"Well, she's going to have that baby and live right up there with Augustine and the doctor."

"Well, you know that's how it always goes," Eulelie said. "They acted like that girl was the queen bee. She even walked around acting like she was so much better than everybody else. She is one stuck-up girl, I tell you. Always has been. Lila, Linda, and Lucretia never could stand her. They knew back in junior high that she was headed for trashy ways, even with her uppity attitude."

"Yeah, well, we'll see how they'll handle it," Agnes said.

"I can tell you right now how they're going to handle it," Dottie said.

The two women leaned in closer to the table. Not one word would get away. Celeste was still looking around for something, anything, more interesting than their gossip.

"Augustine is going to say that that girl was raped."

"Raped!" Eulelie said loud enough for the people at the next table to hear. "So what, did she have that boy arrested or something?"

"No. Augustine is saying that she was raped by some man in the park."

"Augustine told you this?" Eulelie asked.

"Yes she did. She said she'll just say that they didn't want to put her through the trauma of having to report it to the police. She sat on the phone and told me all this last night."

"Why didn't she just go and . . . you know . . . get an abortion?" Agnes said, embarrassed at having said the horrible word.

"Get this. She wanted to keep the baby, and Augustine doesn't believe in it. I'll tell you another thing. I'll bet you anything they're going to want me to give it a write-up in the *Gazette* that'll make it sound upright. You know, spin it in a way that makes it seem like this courageous young woman wanted a child and so *chose* to have one without the benefit of a husband. They'll want me to do a big spread on the christening and everything."

"Well, will you?" Agnes said.

Dottie took a sip of her drink, then said, "Oh, I don't know." And it was said in such an offhanded way, there was no doubt that she most likely would.

"At this point, what does it matter?" Eulelie asked. "Having a baby out of wedlock by a child father is only keeping in line with her other ways. I swear, this whole thing sounds like we're talking about some hillbilly trailer park trash. *White* hillbilly trailer park trash." Eulelie was unforgiving. "It's such a shame too. She comes from such a good family." Eulelie paused only briefly, then looked at Dottie pleadingly. "Well, you know, my problem is still not solved."

"You mean Gil and his intended," Dottie said.

"Yes, exactly. This girl is just not going away."

Celeste put her empty glass on the table with such a determined thud, the aftershock jingled the silverware, which was ever so lightly touching each other. "Eulelie, please. What is it about this girl? So what, she comes from East Baltimore. So what, her father's a machinist and her mother hawks seafood at Lexington Market. Big deal. I think your problem is that you don't want to lose control of Gil. Those children have been under your thumb for too long, and it's time for you to let go of them and all your preconceived notions of who they should be as a *Giles*." Her emphasis on Giles was said mockingly.

With eyes rolling and teeth clenched, Eulelie turned so slowly, it seemed for a moment that she would slap Celeste. Then she said: "Celeste, as usual, you don't know what you're talking about. I just want the best for all my children. I'm just trying to raise them the way their father, and grandfather, and great-grandfather would have wanted it."

"Eulelie, in case you haven't noticed, they're raised. They're grown, honey," Celeste replied.

"Look, let me show you what I'm talking about." Eulelie plucked out Sandra's thank-you note and held it up for show-and-tell. "She sends me this thank-you note, but doesn't even bother to check it for spelling. It's filled with misspelled words.''

No one said anything for several long seconds as they stared with blank, befuddled eyes that waited for more. Celeste turned away and shook her head. Dottie looked down at her empty plate. She was the one who had to end up speaking their collective minds. "Eulelie, I really do think that the fact that she was polite enough to send a thank-you note says a lot more about who she is than a few misspelled words. I mean, is it possible that you're being a bit harsh on her? Besides, a lot of people can't spell. Heck, I'm in the newspaper business and I can misspell too.''

"You know what, forget it. I shouldn't have expected you all to understand. It's not your son, so none of you have any right to judge me.''

The food arrived. It sat untouched for almost a full half a minute while they stewed on Eulelie's last words. The truth was, they all judged each other. It was just the nature of the beast of which they were a part. After all, Eulelie and Agnes Jenkins wanted to reign supreme in Baltimore's black society, where Dottie ruled. Still, each would stab the other square in the back to be queen, if necessary. As for Celeste, their blues weren't exactly hers; she was the classic *in it, but not of it* woman.

"Well, Eulelie honey, it could be worse. She could be a white girl,'' Dottie said with a lighter tone the moment needed.

"Oh my,'' Eulelie said with a chuckle, throwing her head back in mock despair. "Don't even joke about something like that. I don't even know what I could do if *that* happened.''

After the meal was finished and all libations swallowed, they settled the check. It was Celeste's turn to pay for lunch, and she always paid with cash. Eulelie silently believed that Celeste and her husband had bad credit, and that's why she never paid with a credit card. Celeste never said so, and Eulelie would never ask. She sat there watching the bills land on the table, *twenty, forty, sixty.* . . as the corners of her

mouth, instinctively and unknowingly, turned up just enough
to keep her lips quiet so as not to reveal a full smile. Then
she remembered. Quickly, Eulelie went in her purse and
took out the copies of her sweater and beret pattern and
passed them out. With that, the meeting of the Reservoir
Knitting Club was adjourned.

Ghost of Charleston Past

Dottie had to meet her husband, who was dawdling over
at Harbor Place. *He's so henpecked he's got holes in him* her
friends had been known to say about him. Since it was one
of those days that went well with water and a stroll, they
all walked over with Dottie. In the plaza between the two
pavilions, a clown juggled bowling pins while a captivated
audience of clapping children gaped in awe and their parents
temporarily relaxed. Passersby munched on crab cakes, or
cotton candy, or ice cream. A group of ten rollerbladers
whizzed by, turning the four women into dodging jackrab-
bits. The skaters were in control, the ladies weren't.

"Look, you all, I'm going to go on," Eulelie said, overwhelmed by trying to maneuver through the crowd and keep
out of the roller path, all in a group. "I want to get some
of that homemade ice cream to take home to the girls."

"Okay, Eulelie," Dottie said.

"And if you don't completely understand the pattern,
just let me know," Eulelie said, throwing her hand up in a
half wave.

They said their goodbyes and Eulelie went on, making
her way through the throngs of people taking advantage of
the Baltimore spring weather that would, in a matter of
weeks, become oppressively hot and heavy as wet wool. Just
as she was about to start up the steps to the Light Street
pavilion, she heard someone, albeit faintly, say, "Doralee
Washington?" Eulelie hadn't heard that name in years, thirty
years, to be exact. Surely it had nothing to do with her.

"Doralee, is that you?" She whipped her head around to see who had called the name. It was a familiar face that had aged but was still recognizable, if not really known. It was the face of a stranger she knew.

"You're Doralee Washington, aren't you? From Charleston?"

Eulelie still didn't respond. She just looked blankly with questioning eyes. As if she were looking into the eyes of the ghost of Charleston past.

"It's Pepper. Do you remember me from Charleston?" And Pepper was all she felt she needed to say. If Doralee was going to remember her at all, it would be as Pepper. "Don't you remember? We went to school together."

"No, I'm sorry, I don't. I mean, I remember the name slightly, but nothing else terribly specific," Eulelie said, barely audible, but finally finding the words from somewhere to speak. She knew she should have remembered her. In her day, every colored child in Charleston went to school together.

"How are you?" the woman said with diffidence, not knowing if she should give a hug or keep her distance. She kept her distance since Doralee had a mulish amnesia.

"Just fine," Eulelie said, discomfited by the face of a woman who could have been anyone wanting something. What was most unsettling was the essence of its mystery. It had aged, this face. That much was clear. And its slenderness may or may not have been a part of its appearance forty years ago. It was hard to say, since she didn't remember. Perhaps her entire memory of South Carolina had melted into oblivion.

"Doralee, your sisters don't even know where you are. They say they haven't seen you since your momma and daddy died, and that was almost thirty years ago, right? I had no idea you were here in Baltimore."

Eulelie looked at the woman with a haughty defensiveness that was determined to defy the truth. "I don't know what you've heard, Pepper, but my sisters don't need to know where I am. As far as I'm concerned they're the past and that's where they need to stay. It's the same for them too, I'm sure. It's messy family feuding, and I'd like it if you'd just leave it that way."

Out of shock, Pepper said, just barely above a whisper, "Of course, Doralee. Besides, it's not my problem to fix."

"It's not a problem at all. It's just the nature of family, that's all."

"I guess you're right," Pepper said, gazing past Doralee. "As close as my family was I only see them at funerals because the man I married came from a family that was spit-poor. My mother and father rejected my husband because his people weren't educated and professional. They weren't society people like my parents, even like my grandparents. You know, the last thing my father said to me on his death bed was that he had never been more disappointed in me than he was the day I married my husband. And he was dyin'." She paused to look into Doralee's eyes only to have Doralee look away nervously.

"Anyway, I can tell you're livin' a good life up here just by the way you talk. And just look at your clothes! This suit is just . . . well, so elegant." Pepper stood there for a few seconds. "Why did you do it, Doralee?" she finally asked. "Why did you leave Charleston without a trace like that?"

Eulelie let out a laugh that no one could have known was laced with her soul's consternation, then said, "You know something, Pepper, it really doesn't matter why I did things the way I did them. The truth is, I'm so far from that place, I don't even remember anything about it, quite honestly not even you. I've got to run now," and she pulled her purse closer to her and stepped back as if about to bolt away. She didn't want to give the woman the chance to ask to keep in touch. Inching closer to the steps, she said, "And remember your own words, Pepper, it's not your problem to set right." Then Eulelie made it up the steps faster than she ever thought her age would allow. She took them two at one time.

"Of course, but . . . Doralee. Doralee?" the woman yelled. The young woman once known as Pepper, who was now Camilla Hightower, only wanted to tell Eulelie that she knew all about *Eulelie*, and about what fate had done to them.

Eulelie pretended not to hear over the sounds of Harbor Place. She waved and mouthed *'bye* just before vanishing through the doors of the pavilion and out of sight. Camilla just watched her leave, realizing it was somehow better this way, and knowing that Doralee, that poor little girl from Charleston who always wanted more than she had, would never stop running.

Eulelie didn't stop for ice cream. She didn't even pick up the fried chicken gizzards she so loved. Ice cream and gizzards meant nothing to her now. She zigzagged hurriedly past all the strolling bodies, making her way with bumps and brushes and an occasional *excuse me* through the pavilion, coming out at the other end. And by the time she got to her car, she was like a drunk the morning after; with no recollection of her path. She got in with the swiftness of someone being chased, and locked the door. Her heart, which was running at a breakneck pace, only gave her the strength to slump over the steering wheel and try to figure out why Charleston had to come slithering out of the past like a snake from the creek.

Thinking She's Pulling One Over

Lila had stolen away to the sunroom without her sisters ever missing her. She dug into the pocket of her dress with an eagerness that said she was trying to get away with something, searching for the tiny slip of paper on which she'd written the phone number she had been trying for weeks to pry from Dottie Pettigrew-Van Dyke, who just had to know

every detail of why she wanted it. The last thing Lila wanted
was to have to call that woman again, even though the lie
she told was a simple one about a friend whose marriage
could benefit from a private eye. Not complicated at all. It
was in the excess, unnecessary details Lila added, being such
a poor excuse for a liar, that made the lie too difficult to
remember. Lips pressed together, forehead crinkled, she
moved through the room, the small space made vast by a
tiny slip of paper. It had to be there, otherwise she'd have
to call Mrs. Pettigrew-Van Dyke again and remember the
entire lie, and she just didn't want to lie again. It turns out
that lying lips do have a conscience, she thought. Finally, she
found it, sliding it out of her pocket with two fingers.

Her heart beat insanely as she dialed. What if he answered? What would she say? So she hung up, realizing she
hadn't devised a plan. She couldn't just call up, *Hello Pick,
this is Lila Giles, I was wondering if you'd like to have dinner
with me.* She was certain he'd think her a fool, and then he'd
most likely decline. She picked up the phone again and dialed, this time prepared. The phone rang twice before an
anxious-sounding woman answered.

"Hello, I'd like to—" she started with a crackle of a
voice. She cleared her throat, then began again. "Hello, I'd
like to set up an appointment to meet with Mister . . .
uh, Pick."

"Yes," the woman said, and asked who was on the
phone. And in one of those seconds that she could never
take back, one of those seconds that set everything on the
wrong path, Lila said: "My name is Gloria Jenkins and I'd
like an appointment, please." As soon as she said it, she
wished she hadn't. There was no questioning herself as to
why she did it, because there were no answers. And even if
there were some sort of odd opportunity to take it back, it
still would have been too late, because before she knew it,
the woman had her on hold, only for Pick himself to pick
up next.

"Yes, Mrs. Jenkins, this is Pick. What can I do for you?"

"Well, I'm interested in having you investigate someone for me," she said in a voice deeper and slower than her natural one. It sounded so fake, almost as if she wanted him to know it wasn't real. But she thought it gave her the sound of wisdom, that it would make him believe he was talking to an older woman. "I got your name from Dot—" She almost said it, but then remembered that he might check it out and then find out that Gloria Jenkins had been dead for years. After that it would just be a matter of seconds before he'd know the truth. So she said: "I got your name from one of the ladies in my club. I'd rather wait to see you to tell you the details of the assignment."

"Yeah, sure, Mrs. Jenkins. Okay, so I'm looking at my schedule and I can meet you on Wednesday around seven in the evening."

"Seven, oh that's perfect," she said, the lilt of excitement nearly betraying her fake older woman attitude. "There's a restaurant on Charles Street, Café One. It's right near the conservatory. Why don't we meet there over drinks and that way we can talk without interruption."

"That'll be fine," he said with a laugh that gave her heart a start. What did it mean? It was filled with so much. And when the laughter trailed off, he said: "I'll see you then." The line fell silent and Lila was left holding an empty phone.

By the time she found her mother in the front hall coming in from her knitting club meeting, Lila had no memory of hanging up the phone or even leaving the sunroom. Her nerves were a jangle of jitters. Now she'd done it. Her fascination with this man who went against everything that appeared to be his grain had drawn her into a lie she knew she had to face.

"Momma, how was your meeting?" she managed to say.

"It was just fine." Eulelie said no more, climbing the stairs to her room, leaving Lila to watch, stupefied, as her mother walked in a distracted trance into the dim light upstairs.

~~ She Could Lie to the World, But . . .

Running, running, running, running. Eulelie was off and
running, again. It was back, the dream from which she could
not run. She went along the reservoir, running, running, cars
whizzing by, their occupants staring at the odd sight of
twins, one queenly, the other oafish. They ran along Hilton
Street all the way to Gwynns Falls Parkway. In this version,
the neighbors all along Hilton Street waved and cheered
from their porches that Eulelie the pursued would be victor
over the pursuer. As she turned onto the parkway, her lead
over Doralee was considerable. There were some with dumb-
struck gawks who clearly had never seen the relay. They
stopped and stared with gaping mouths. What the hell are
they doing? Others who were familiar with their run smiled,
some outright laughed, others yelled out, *Run, girl. You've
got it.* There were others, still who gossiped among themselves. *That old girl can run. I hear she's chasin' her 'cause she
stole her man.* They ran all the way to the parkway and then
across it and over into the park. And just as always, there
was the fall from out of nowhere and the deserted Reptile
House. And the two women were there also in the shadows
coming out of the Reptile House, except this time they
spoke to each other: *I pray for her eternal soul. If I don't, it'll
be damned forever,* and then the other said, *You're so right.
Let's go.* Then they walked off into the town, still shrouded
in the shadow from nowhere. She awoke. This time, though,
she was nervous, yes, but also angry, very angry, and ready
to do whatever she had to do to stop this madness her
mind controlled.

Later in the morning the Giles sisters, Lila, Lucretia, and
Linda, ambled through the door from church looking very
much like church women; like they might have been the
models for a Bearden painting that would have been called
Sunday, After Church. Linda closed the door and locked it,
then turned to the mirror to take off her hat and straighten

her mashed hat hair. Lila and Lucretia went farther into the house, Lila to the kitchen, Lucretia into the dining room. Lucretia scoured the dining room for clues, then went into the kitchen. Her eyes met Lila's and they spoke to one another in the language of bewildered faces.

There was not a hint, anywhere throughout the two rooms, that Eulelie had left her room. The silver tea service still sat undisturbed on the butler's pantry. On her alone days, Eulelie always served herself, in her bedroom, tea and biscuits on that old silver tea service that had been in the Giles family going back two greats. But there was no sign of water having been boiled, and the brand-new box of tea biscuits sat unopened on the counter.

"Reverend Popper sure did preach today, didn't he?" Linda said, sauntering into the kitchen.

It wasn't her sisters' silence that made her realize something was wrong. It was their scrunched foreheads and worried eyes.

"What? Didn't you think he gave a good sermon?"she asked again, pouring herself a cool drink from the refrigerator. She took one small sip, then: "Oh yuck! What in the world is this? Whatever it is, somebody forgot to put sugar in it."

"Linda, what are you doing? That's my diet drink. Don't—" But before Lucretia could reach Linda to salvage what was left of her precious, boiled orange-rind drink, Linda had tossed it down the sink. "Linda, you just wasted an entire glass of my drink. Aw, shoot!"

"Well, I'm sorry. I didn't know. God, you get so upset." She opened a cream soda and sat at the kitchen table, slipping out of her shoes. "So, what about Reverend Popper's sermon? It was good, huh?"

"We're not thinking about Reverend Popper's sermon, Linda," Lila said. "Look around, don't you notice anything?"

Linda looked to her left, to her right, straight ahead, then down along the sideboards. "No, what are you all talking about?"

"Momma, little miss self-absorbed," Lila said while landing a soft pluck to Linda's head.

"Stop it! And what about Momma?"

"Haven't you noticed that Momma has not been out of her room since she got home from her club meeting yesterday?"

"She hasn't?" Linda really hadn't noticed.

"No, and something obviously happened that really shook Momma up," Lucretia said.

"It's just probably this whole thing with Gil and Sandra, that's all," Linda said. "It's enough to make you want to lock yourself in your room and never come out. I did."

"Well, Momma's not like that, Linda," Lucretia said. "She handles things in a much more stoic and *grown-up* way than that."

"Yeah, you fool," Lila said. "I'm going up there to see what's the matter."

Lila went off down the hall with her sisters, who, too cowardly to lead the way, trailed behind. Linda lagged the farthest, dawdling like a five-year-old at bedtime. None of it made much sense to her, checking up on and fretting over their mother, who just wanted to be left alone.

"Lila, why don't you leave Momma alone. There's nothing wrong with her," Linda finally said.

"Linda, how can you say that?" Lila asked. "Have you ever seen Momma act like this, locking herself in her room, missing church?"

"No, but that doesn't mean there's something wrong. Look, if you'd stop being so doggone bossy and stop trying to run everything, then you'd see that Momma doesn't need you, or us, pestering her. She probably just needs some time to think about this whole thing with Gil. Please, who hasn't felt like holing up in their room over this thing? God knows I have." Determinedly, though, Lila led them down the hallway to Eulelie's room, Lucretia and Linda lagging so far behind now they might as well have been walking backward. Lila landed one soft knuckled tap on the door. No response.

Through the door they could hear the radio filling the room softly in a way that gave Linda a chill. Something just might be wrong. "See, Lila, she's just in there listening to her radio programs on NPR. She's okay. Let's go."

But Lila knocked harder, three taps in succession. "Momma," she called. There was some rustling in the room of a mysterious nature. It could have been a plastic bag or a plastic wrapper. They looked at each other, puzzled.

"Momma," Lila said again, louder. "Momma, can we come in? We're awfully worried about you. Is something wrong?"

"Girls, I'm fine," Eulelie said from the other side. She was not at all convincing. "I'm a little under the weather, but I'll be just fine. I'll be downstairs in a little while."

"Momma, can I bring you some tea, chamomile or mint?" Lila said, her lips less than an inch from the door's frame.

"No, honey, you all just go on. I'll be okay."

"Momma, you know Gil's coming for dinner today. It *is* Sunday, you know," Linda said, with seemingly no compassion for her mother's malaise.

"I have not forgotten, Linda, now you all just go on and leave me be so that I can get ready for dinner. I'll be down in a while. You three go ahead and start dinner. If you really want to help me, just start dinner."

Leave me be. What had come to possess her? they all wondered silently. Eulelie Giles had never spoken with such backwater southernisms. She was too old to be going through the change, and too young to be senile. Maybe it was some sort of thing that happened between the change and senility; some sort of phase where you forget proper language. They didn't know. Eulelie was simply not herself, and it was anyone's guess why.

Lila and Lucretia sat without words in the living room sipping lemon iced tea when Eulelie finally came downstairs. Linda was in the kitchen, checking on dinner. "Girls, I want to talk to you," was all Eulelie had to say, and Linda did not trifle with haste. She scampered to the sofa next to her sisters. Eulelie was serious, in her tone, her somber face, her straight back, so they knew it wasn't a trivial matter; probably something related to her imitation of a hermit in the last twenty-four hours. Nonetheless, she had her daughters' undivided attention as they waited for their momma to tell whatever news; good or bad—it had to be an extreme.

"Momma, what's wrong?" Lucretia said.

"Yeah, Momma, you look so serious," Lila said.

"It is serious, girls. I have been giving this whole thing with Gil and Sandra a lot of thought."

"Really, Momma? We haven't," Lucretia said without letting her mother finish.

"Yeah, we just figure he'll come to his senses soon. He knows we don't like this, and he would never choose somebody like her over us." Linda was certain of this. She was the one who most believed in her brother's ability to see the light, even at the eleventh hour.

"Maybe, Linda. But he just *may* choose her over us and we could lose him forever," Eulelie said.

"Momma, that would never happen," Lucretia said.

"No way," Linda said. "He's not stupid."

"It has nothing at all to do with being stupid. It's choosing one kind of love over another," Eulelie said.

Then Linda said: "Yeah, but our love will always be there. Our love is special. We'd never turn our backs on *him*. It's *her* we don't want."

"And if our love is indeed unconditional, Linda, honey, he has nothing to lose by choosing her, does he?" It was something not one of them had considered.

In all the banter, in all the back and forth, no one noticed that Lila had nothing to say. No one noticed the way she nervously picked at the hem of her skirt. She couldn't be sure of anything anymore, except her brother's love—his love for her, her love for him. The rest of this fell someplace else in her mind in sharp tiny pieces, like a puzzle she simply couldn't put together. Before Sandra entered their lives, everything was so comfortable, so sure. Nothing was hazy, everything had clear and defined edges; clear and defined colors. Even Gil had a clearly defined place not just in the family, but in her life. Things were no longer the same. What confused her was whether this altered state of the natural order of things was good or bad. Instead of watching their lips move, she decided to pay attention.

"Momma, what's all this about?" Lucretia said. "Are you having a change of heart about Sandra?" She wanted to cut right to the bottom line. It was a most futile exercise, to her, to talk about Gil's choice, which in her mind came down to only one.

"I don't know. I just know that he's my only son and your only brother, and to lose him because we think his choice for a wife is not a good one is just ridiculous. I could never forgive myself."

"And I'm telling you, Momma, it'll never happen," Linda said. "Gil would just never do that to us." She was holding on to every bit of faith she had in her brother. Where was their faith?

"Look, girls, I just ran into a girl I knew from South Carolina, and she only sees her family at funerals because they have never accepted her husband. They were a very close family too, very close, just like us, but they had money and influence and this man she married came from less than nothing. When she eloped with him, she gave up the kind of privilege that black people in those days hardly ever had, because her family cut her off. She's been living here in Baltimore all these years hand-to-mouth, and you know what? She says she never once regretted her choice. I'm not going to force my son to make that choice because he just may not choose us."

No one said a word. What was there to say? There was no way to counter their mother's logic. Eulelie had been profoundly affected by her chance meeting, it was clear. Either because of Pepper's story of snobbery and rejection, or because of the fact that there was now someone in Baltimore

who knew her true beginnings, Eulelie had to hurry and find
a way to tolerate Sandra. Eulelie's house, whether made of
glass or cards, was quite fragile. One wrong move in this
most delicate situation and she could lose her son, and that,
to her, would be like a death, slowly.

Eulelie had been so good at it—pretending. She had even
begun to really believe the stories she told over and over
again of having a lineage of doctors and ministers and merchants and landowners. The air of black lineage, she had
studied all her life. She watched the way her mother was
treated by the real wives of doctors and ministers and merchants when they'd bring by bags of old clothes and food.
They were maternal and patronizing, yet sweet as sugar, and
gracious and humble all at the same time. It was all put on,
but when you're poor and in need, you don't care. They had
a certain way of walking, straight-backed, head high, and
they took small steps with a slow gait, because they were
never in much of a hurry to get anywhere. And though she
never practiced it, she knew that when the day came that
she'd have to use it, it would envelop her as if she were
born to it. That's exactly how it happened too, because in
Baltimore, among the black folks she wanted, needed to
know, knowing the right way to act was as important as
where you learned the right way to act.

"Lila, why haven't you said anything?" Lucretia asked.
"What do you think about this?" She wanted to know if
they all thought their mother had surrendered too soon.

Lila looked at her sisters with pleading eyes that were
begging for advanced forgiveness. Then she looked at Eulelie,
while still nervously picking at her hem, and said: "Well, I'm
sorry, but I agree with Momma. I mean, what difference
does it make? Okay, we think Sandra is all wrong for Gil,
and she may be, according to who we have in mind for him
to marry. But isn't the most important thing that Gil get to
marry who he loves? I don't know, I met Sandra's mother
and—"

"You did what?" an incredulous Linda said. Lucretia's mouth was agape, but Linda said it all.

"I met Sandra's mother. It's a long story, but I saw Gil's car outside a bar on Reisterstown Road, I went in, Gil and I had words, I lost my keys and Mrs. Hightower and her friends, who were there, gave me a ride home. She's very nice. You know, she's a mother. She loves her children just like Momma. And as for Sandra, well, if you think about it, she's no different than our own mother—our mother Gloria. There's no shame in being poor, you all."

Eulelie stood up slowly and walked into the hallway. Just as she was about to turn and go upstairs, she looked back over her shoulders and said: "I'm going up to take a nap. Lucretia, I want you to call your brother and tell him that I would like him and Sandra to come over tonight for dinner."

"What?" Lucretia said.

"You heard what I said. Tell them to come to dinner. Oh, and try not to have that snotty little attitude that I know all too well. On second thought, Lila, you call," and Eulelie went back up to her room.

The next sound heard through the house was Eulelie's door closing with a soft but determined thud. The hand that pushed it was final. Lucretia stared up at the top of the stairs for close to a full minute. When she turned around, she saw her sisters still sitting on the sofa, Lila staring off in space, Linda as nonplussed as herself.

"I think Momma has just completely lost her mind," Lucretia said, going off to the kitchen in a huff.

"Momma hasn't lost her mind. If anything, she's come to her senses," Lila said, more to herself than her sister as she went into the hall to make the call her sisters would find an unforgivable betrayal. Her heart was pounding so hard she could feel it in her shaking hands. What would Gil say? Would he flatly refuse to subject Sandra to the sharks? Probably. "Oh, this is so hard," she whispered to herself as she listened to Gil's phone ring.

Finally, he answered. She said, "Hi, Gil, this is Lila.

Momma wanted me to tell you to bring Sandra to dinner tonight . . . Yes, I'm serious . . . Momma? Well, she's taking a nap now . . . Okay good, you can come . . . Seven is fine. I'll tell Momma. 'Bye.''

The house was as quiet as a mortuary in the dead of night. The somber faces of Linda and Lucretia were that of women who had just experienced a mortal loss. Lila had left them to their brooding while she tended to the dinner. The two straightened up, tucking stray pieces of mail in drawers, fluffing up throw pillows, straightening the pictures on the piano and even giving a halfhearted unnecessary polish to the furniture and mirrors. They did all of this for the rest of the afternoon without saying a word to each other. There were myriad words to express their anger for the tragedy that had fallen on their home. What good were words? Words would merely add darkness to their already embittered hearts.

The click and faint creak of Eulelie's bedroom door opening wafted through the silence of the house. Her footsteps down the stairs seemed unusually loud, even menacing. They didn't know what to expect this time.

Eulelie stood at the threshold of the living room and smiled. "Thank you for straightening up," she said.

"You're welcome," they said in a monotone, scarcely above a whisper. Then they went off to help Lila.

Eulelie slowly made her way to her chair and sat, staring straight ahead at nothing but her thoughts. Thoughts about South Carolina. Thoughts about Doralee, the girl she used to be. Doralee was unsophisticated, uncomplicated. Doralee didn't know about luncheons and formal balls and cotillions. She didn't know about playing host to a house full of lawyers and their wives, much less how to make small talk about nothing. Young Doralee dreamed about Paris and Rome, but never of preparing to go. And now Eulelie, who'd never been, rested in the comfort of knowing she could.

Now, Eulelie, the woman with the beautiful southern name that had the lilting sound of class, knew it all. Eulelie

knew about finger sandwiches and bridge. Eulelie knew how
to have a housekeeper; the right tone and posture to take,
letting her know in whose charge she was kept, and that
while in charge she'd expect nothing but deference. She was
a woman with the right kind of lineage. The kind that in-
cluded important Negro men and women who were educated and didn't know about such things as picking beans
and bales of cotton. She, unlike Doralee, lived on and was
from the right side of the tracks. Eulelie was a barrister's
wife.

The motor of Gil's sports car, which could be heard a
block away if you listened carefully, announced their arrival.

"Girls," Eulelie called out, "your brother's here."

The three of them walked into the front hall, two of
them moping all the way. Eulelie met them.

"I'm going to say this once and I'm not going to say it
again: I want you to judge this girl by what's in her heart,
not by anything else. She seems like a sweet girl and I want
you all to give us a chance to get to know her and find out
what kind of person she is. Do you understand?"

"Yes, Momma," Linda and Lucretia said, since they knew
she was speaking only to them.

Lila said nothing. She looked straight ahead at the door,
knowing not what lay ahead, and fearing the unknown.

Gil and Sandra were just about to step onto the porch
when Linda looked into her mother's eyes and saw that she
was not in the mood for foolishness.

"Linda, do you understand me?" Eulelie would have no
part of Linda's tantrums tonight.

"Yes, Momma, I understand."

Lucretia opened the screen door for the couple. "Come
in," she said with cheer too sweet to be sincere.

Lila touched Sandra's arm as she stepped over the threshold. It was gentle and obliging. An obsequious apology. "Sandra, it's good to see you again."

"Thank you. It's good to see all of you again too." She

looked at Linda blandly. This was the one who *really* didn't accept her. This was the sister who protested the loudest and strongest. But at least she was the most honest.

Then Gil said, "Sandra, this is my sister Linda. You didn't meet her the last time. She was busy." He gave his sister a complex look impossible for her to read. It was one of forgiveness and anger—his smile forgave, his darting eyes were angry.

"We met at the mall a few weeks ago," was all Sandra said, giving Linda a peculiar smile.

"Say, I love your haircut," Sandra said to Linda. "It's so becoming to your face, and you have the right kind of hair for that style."

"Thank you," Linda said with a bashful smile she tried to hold back but couldn't.

"And of course, here's Momma," Gil said, stepping out of the way to give access for a kiss, a hug, a handshake, or maybe a slap-fight, whatever they were going to do to each other.

"Hello, Sandra. I'm so glad you could come for dinner at the last minute like this. Come on in and sit down." Eulelie smiled what was the warmest, most sincere smile she'd ever given Sandra, and Gil could tell it was sincere because her gums didn't show. The only thing was, she never once looked directly at Sandra. She led the way into the living room and sat in her chair. Then, in nervous chitchat speak, Eulelie said, "Linda's haircut has had to grow on me. I didn't like it at first. I thought it looked too . . . well, I don't know. She just looked so regular. The one difference, though, between her and most of these other girls with that haircut is what you pointed out. She does have the perfect hair for that style. All these girls have that good . . . what I mean is pretty hair that doesn't need perms."

Sandra didn't respond. What was there to say? She plopped down so close against Gil on the sofa that the crack of dawn couldn't slide between them. It was survival of the fittest in this sea of socially registered barracudas, and Gil was her lifeline.

"So Sandra, how are the wedding plans coming along?" Eulelie asked, really wanting to know.

"Oh, just fine, Mrs. Giles. I've got my dress and head piece. The biggest thing we have to do now is decide on what hors d' oeuvres we're going to have."

"Where's the reception going to be?" Lucretia asked.

Sandra lowered her head a bit, unconsciously. "Well, it'll be in the church hall," she said quietly, embarrassed, knowing that this was not a family to host affairs in church halls. "It's not much, but it's all my parents can afford. They insist on following tradition and paying for everything."

"How many people are we talking about?" Eulelie asked, with an obvious purpose.

But Gil answered for Sandra. "About seventy-five or so, Momma. Why do you ask?" How could he possibly trust her motives? She was up to something, but what, he didn't know. He just knew it couldn't be good.

"I ask because if your mother and father won't mind, I would like to host the wedding reception. We could have it right here. You haven't seen my garden out in the back. It should be in glorious bloom by late June. Come, let me show you." And excitedly, Eulelie led a stunned Sandra through the house by the hand and into the backyard. Eulelie had come to life with the hope of being able to host a formal party.

"Wow!" was all Sandra could find to say. She had never seen this much land attached to someone's house she actually knew. "Mrs. Giles, this is beautiful. I would be honored . . . I would love to have the reception here. I'm sure Ma and Daddy won't mind."

"Yes, and I'll order tables to go around the sides on the grass, and your parents are not to worry about the expense. We can do away with tradition for this. Why, I heard on the radio just a few months ago how a lot of families are throwing away all that tradition of the bride's family paying for everything. Grooms' families are now paying for as much as half, and depending on the situation, sometimes they pay for everything. It's perfectly acceptable nowadays, they say." Then she trotted way out to the back of the yard and spread out her arms as far as they could go. "The wedding party table could be right here, and right up there where you're standing, we could have the bar with a bartender." Then she speed-walked excitedly to another corner of her yard. "Right here, right over here in this spot, we can put a little string quartet. Oh, that's right. I'm sorry, I don't know what kind of music *you* would want played."

"Well, at the church hall, we were going to have dancing, but a string quartet sounds nice. Classy. I've never heard a string quartet. They would play classical music, right?"

"Yes, but you can't dance to that." Eulelie didn't mean it the way it sounded, and the second after she said it, she hoped Sandra, and especially Gil, didn't hear it the way it sounded. Her snobbery had a life all its own.

"So we don't have to have dancing," Sandra said, just happy that she was going to have a wedding reception that was too good to have ever been a part of her dreams.

"Well, if you want dancing, there's no reason why we can't have the string quartet playing while the bridal party enters and through the meal. Then, after dessert and coffee's been served, we can have your dance music. That would work."

"How would we get dance music out here?" Sandra asked, turning to Gil with wide eyes.

She was looking to Gil for an answer, but Gil just stood over near the rosebushes, too amazed to say a word, much less hear her question. This was simply all too surreal for him. His mother just a week earlier had ambushed his fiancée with information she got from God knows where; she had made a shotgun attempt to blackmail, sabotage, run her out of town, who knew what? But now she was ready to throw Sandra a wedding reception that in Sandra's eyes would be fit for royalty. What gives? he wanted to know.

"Sandra, would you excuse me and Momma for a minute. There's something I need to ask her. Something personal." He paused to look into her quizzical eyes. "It won't take long. Just go in the kitchen and help my sisters with dinner."

"All right," she said, walking away with lead in her bottom, hoping to catch a hint of what they would talk about; her, or maybe Eulelie's mean mission the week before. Or he just might let her have it for the whole situation. At least she hoped she'd catch one word. But Gil wouldn't let that happen. He followed her out of the corner of his eye until she was well inside.

"Okay, Momma, what's up here?"

"*What's up?* I don't understand what you mean." Coy was her best game.

"Well, it was only a week ago that you launched your commando raid on Sandra, dredging up something from her past that was, *is*, quite painful for her. Now you're tripping all over yourself out here to offer her your sacred garden for the wedding reception. Can you see how these things are . . ." He balanced his hands like the scales of justice, searching for the right word. ". . . just a bit, oh, I don't know, maybe psychotic?"

"Psychotic? Oh Gil," she said with a belly-chuckle, "you are so naive."

"*Naive?* Momma, you found out something so personal, that was such a deeply hidden secret, that many of her family members don't know about it. Now how did you find out?"

"Gil honey, one day you'll learn that the only thing secret about a secret is how many people know."

"No Momma, I don't buy that. You and that Dottie Van stab-her-mother-in-the-back,   get-any-dirt-on-anybody-as-long-as-she-gets-what-she-wants, have conspired on this somehow. This just smacks of something that rag peddler would be involved with. She put you on to one of her private detectives, didn't she?"

"Gil, I don't know where you get this stuff."

"Come on, Momma. Dottie Pettigrew-Van Dyke gets discounts from private detectives vying for her business, she uses them so often. So are you going to tell me the truth about how you found out, or am I going to have to do my own private eye work?"

Eulelie was caught. Trapped like a laggard animal. There was no point in lying, she thought. He would eventually find out, that was just his nature—to seek until he found. Eventually she would have to tell him the truth, so why not put off the agonizing, not to mention humiliating, moment when she would have no choice but to come clean?

"Okay, Gil honey, you're right," she said. "I did hire a detective to check her out, but honey, I'm only trying to protect you, protect what this family name has always represented."

"Would that include my mother, Momma? Did my mother represent this family well? I mean, she grew up in Cherry Hill, in the projects, really no different from Sandra."

His mother. Their mother. My mother. No matter how it was put, that word was caustic to her ear. She didn't know who they meant. To her, *Mother* always meant *Momma*, and she was *Momma*. Were they deliberate with such heart-breakingly cruel comments? There were many ways to kill, and this had to be the most inexorable way of all. She had to address it; there was no getting around it. *Mother* did once exist. But why did she have to haunt so steadfastly?

"Your mother was different, Gil. She may not have come from much, but she knew how to be a Giles. Sandra is a little ragged around the edges, your mother was not. Your father always said that when she married into this family it was as if she had been born to be a Giles."

"So why was her name never mentioned? Never. Why didn't you and Daddy make sure we would always know her?"

Eulelie hung her head. She could not look pain in the face. "At the time, Gil honey, we thought it was best for you kids to become attached to the mother who would raise you. Not faded pictures and faint, barely existent memories of a mother. We were only doing what we thought best."

But Eulelie was lying, or rather, editing the story. What she left out was the tantrum. What she selectively forgot to speak of was the night she argued so fiercely with the Judge that her temper led her to break every single frame in the living room holding a picture of Gloria Giles. And when the violence of shattering glass woke Gil from a child's sleep, and he called to his father from the top of the stairs, Eulelie's face appeared, telling what a clumsy oaf she was to drop those glasses. That was the night when the elder Gilbert Giles, the Judge, caught hell from Eulelie, who would not play second, neither in his life nor the childrens', to a woman in the ground.

Gil didn't say anything for several long and arduous seconds, picking at leaves on a bush and staring at his shoes. He dropped the few leaves he had in his hands and looked up from his shoes. He took his mother's tiny soft face in his large hands and kissed her cheek. "Just don't do it again." And he walked off toward the house, leaving his mother alone in her garden, relieved, unburdened from a lie, but afraid, very afraid, of what would come.

Soon after Gil disappeared into the house, he reappeared with the others, Eulelie lost in her plans. She was placing the setup of tables in her mind, unaware that her hands were pointing around·the garden.

"Momma, what are you doing?" Lila asked.

"Oh, I'm just situating the table in my mind. I think the mayor and his wife should sit with me in the front, don't you?"

"The mayor!" Sandra shouted, louder than she thought. "The mayor's going to be at *our* wedding?"

"No," Gil said, looking at his mother for an explanation. The offhanded assumption was ludicrous.

"Of course," Eulelie said, puzzled by Gil's adamant no and the question on his face. "Of course the mayor will be here. Your father was his mentor, and he has always thought highly of you, Gil."

"Momma, it's going to be a small wedding. There's no need to turn this into a society wedding."

Laughing at her brother's seeming innocence to the way things were, Lucretia said: "Gil, wake up. No matter what, when any of us get married, it's always going to be a society wedding. That's just who we are. We are the Gileses, and that's just what it would become."

"Not our wedding. Not this wedding," Gil said defiantly.

"Gil, I am not about to insult the mayor of Baltimore because of some ridiculous need you have to prove something. What you're trying to prove, I do not know."

Gil reared back. "*Prove something?* The only thing I have to prove is that I love Sandra, and I don't need Baltimore's social elite to make that official."

"If that's how you see it, Gil," Eulelie said, seemingly hurt. "But you know that this family has always had its social obligations to invite certain families and certain dignitaries to everything. Your great-great grandparents even knew and socialized with Frederick Douglass. Frederick Douglass! Can you imagine that? This family has always been a part of who to know. That's just the way it has always been. That was decided long before I was even born. To do otherwise would just be bad manners, Gil, bad manners."

Gil walked in a circle, rubbing his head. "Momma, Sandra's family are simply people. None of this matters to them, whether Mrs. Pettigrew-Van Dyke will be here or the mayor, or Doctor and Missus Whoever. They wouldn't even care if Frederick Douglass himself were to walk in here from the grave. They're just simple folks who want to see their daughter get married and then have a good time afterward."

Sandra wasn't sure what Gil was trying to say, she just knew it wasn't setting right in her mind or on her heart. She was sure there was a compliment skulking around in those words somehow, but at the moment it eluded her. He knew nothing about what her parents would want, the elbows they'd like to rub. For the briefest second her mind landed on a thought she was ashamed to have: Could Gil be secretly beset by what tormented his mother and sisters? This could not be. She would have surely known by now, or so she silently and ceaselessly prayed.

"Excuse me, Gil," Sandra finally said, "but I don't think you're qualified to speak for my family, for my parents. How do you know they don't care about whether the mayor is going to be there? How do you know that that wouldn't be a good time for them? I think—no, I *know*—that my parents, my whole family, would be proud to have the mayor at our wedding. Right now, at this moment, you're the only one who has a problem with this. Oh, and just so you'll know, if Frederick Douglass, or any other dead man, were to walk up in here from the grave, that's something my parents probably wouldn't want to miss."

Looking from Gil to Sandra then back at Gil, Eulelie wondered what she'd just done. Had she started an argument? Was this the beginning of a rift? Could this be the first of many irreconcilable differences to come? Or would this be *the* argument? "Okay, then, it's settled," she said.

Eulelie went into the house ahead of the rest. She had something for Sandra that would change her life and her expectations of her life forever. In the den, she hurriedly shuffled through stacks of record albums that were older than her children until she found it. The excitement welled in her until her fumbling fingers dropped the stack, causing a noise that sounded like a falling body. "Momma, are you all right?" Gil yelled from the dining room. She assured him everything was fine and told them all to gather around the table without her. When she got the record she'd been looking for on the turntable, finally, she didn't move from the stereo until she heard those two transporting chords. She had been hearing those two chords practically every day for nearly twenty years, and they never failed to take her all the way back to the very first time she heard them. It was at the home of Eulelie Parker, the daughter of a wealthy white, old-line society family in Charleston. They lived high. Their house was a landmark of sorts in town. Massive, blindingly white, and conjuring nothing but images of the days when men, women, and children far darker than the house and its inhabitants scampered about in fear, and slaving for the pursuit of a privileged life only Eulelie Parker's greats and great-greats would ever know. People, black and white, passed by that house just to see for themselves, and dream of what it would be like to live so well. The Parker's house was the center—or at least one of the centers—of high society in the South in those days.

Eulelie Parker went off to travel around Europe once she turned eighteen. While she was gone, the Parkers vanished into the darkness of one muggy Charleston night, and to this day no one knew why, but their mysterious departure remained on every tongue in town. There was talk that Eulelie's father had been embezzling money from the bank where he'd been chairman for thirty years (as if he weren't born into enough wealth), but no one knew for sure. Not even a month after they left, Eulelie Parker came back and took over the house, answering no questions. Once again Charleston's showpiece was restored to its rightful place in Charleston's high society. She hosted parties even grander than her parents, playing host to famed musicians and writers she'd met on the continent, and not a few politicians enthralled by the glamorous life.

With the Parker house having a revolving party door, Eulelie Parker needed help. She needed servants, colored servants. White servants wanted too much money. Doralee's mother had worked in the Parkers' kitchen for years, but Eulelie Parker didn't want her. She had been to Europe and had come back enlightened, progressive in her views about coloreds and such. She didn't want servants looking like worn-out cotton pickers. She wanted servants looking like Doralee—fair of skin, smooth hair, features finer than the

wide-nosed, juicy-lipped coloreds who had served her family
in previous years. She wanted coloreds who would not stand-
out in such an obvious way that would put folks in mind of
slavery. She wanted house Negroes.

So Doralee began working for Eulelie Parker when she
was only twelve. This rich white woman indelibly marked
the life of a young Doralee in search of an image to emulate,
in search of anyone's wealthy life to dream of for herself.
Eulelie Parker had culture and grace and class. She knew
things that even the women in Charleston's colored bour-
geoisie didn't know, and they were educated Negroes; they
knew everything.

Eulelie Parker had seen a world outside of Charleston.
She told a swooning Doralee about things that were too unbelievable to be true. Eulelie Parker said it was so, but Doralee could not believe there were Negroes actually socializing
with white folks in a place like Paris, writing books and playing jazz. Eulelie Parker actually met these people and sipped
wine and cognac with them, right in the same *café*. Right at
the same table, even. Doralee tried, but her mind, narrowed
by life, just would not let her picture such scenes and see
these places in Europe where coloreds and whites were allowed to know each other in such a way. But it gave her
wanderlust. It was with Eulelie Parker that Doralee first
began to know that she wanted a life far away from Charleston. It was from Eulelie Parker that Doralee took her name
when she stepped off that bus in Baltimore. But the most
special part of Eulelie Parker was that, for a wealthy Charleston white woman in those days, she was particularly kind
to Negroes.

The day she started working for Eulelie Parker was a day
permanently etched in Doralee's memory, alongside the day
she left Charleston and the day her name came to be part
of a legend. It was a Saturday in May that God blew on and
made simply glorious. Eulelie Parker was having a garden
party in honor of some important French actor friend she'd
met in Paris. He was tall, very tall, some would even say too

tall, but still he moved with the grace of sex in his three-piece suit. A suit that was certain to have cost him more money than Doralee would make in a month of days serving Eulelie Parker. She had never thought much about white men—handsome or homely—but this man was certainly the finest looking white man Doralee had ever noticed. He even called Doralee "dear" and threw her a sideways smile that made her heart leap when he asked for more champagne.

Eulelie Parker had hired a string quartet to play for her party. There had been a rumor for years that this was standard for Parker parties, but who among ordinary folks would know? Certainly not Doralee nor anyone in her family. Live music! And with instruments Doralee had only seen in pictures. She was so mesmerized by the ease with which they were able to get music out of them, it was a wonder she could even serve properly. Her eye was always on the musicians. Everything they played was as pleasing to her virgin ear as the next. She had never heard this kind of music. Never! Then they played something that wasn't terribly special, but for some reason reached down and stroked the heart of her soul. As soon as it began, it claimed her. Thank God everyone had been served and no one needed anything, because she could not move. How could they eat? Didn't they hear this beauty? Everyone went about eating, laughing, toasting, guzzling champagne, as if the most beautiful piece of music ever written was not wafting through the splendid summer air. Even the other servants just stood around blank-faced, unmoved. Bored. It was as if Doralee had found a glittering jewel that no one else could see.

Eulelie Parker walked up to the group of colored maids standing there, ready for their next command. "You can start cleaning the dinner plates, I think everybody's finished and ready for dessert," she said in passing, on her way into the house.

But Doralee stopped her. She had to know. "Excuse me, Miss Eulelie," she said. "But can you tell me the name of that song they just played? It was real pretty."

Eulelie Parker smiled, seemingly pleased to give a colored a bit of her culture, which would probably never make a bit of difference in her life.

"Honey, it's not a song, it's called a *piece* of music, and I believe it's Beethoven's String Quartet Number Two. Can you remember that?" she said in a manner a bit too fawning to be sincere.

And Doralee said, "Yes ma'am, I sure can." And she did. She wrote it down and kept that scrap of paper in a special place for years, until she was able to replace it with the recording not even a day after she married Gilbert Giles, II.

Once unsophisticated Doralee, now Eulelie Giles, sat on the edge of an ottoman thinking about Eulelie Parker when she heard her son say: "Momma, we're waiting for you before we say grace."

"I'm coming," she said, jolted from her reverie.

They were all sitting in front of full plates, waiting, but waiting with impatient hunger. Eulelie took her matriarch's seat—at the head of the table. Gil, sitting at the other end where his father once sat, said grace.

"Sandra, do you hear this?" Eulelie said. "It's Beethoven. This is my favorite piece of music, and I thought it would be one of the pieces the quartet will play at the reception, perhaps when the bridal party is being introduced."

"This is really nice. I think that would be good," Sandra said politely, trying to be as excited as Eulelie expected her to be. She liked the music well enough, but it was nothing spectacular. It really didn't sound, to her, any different than the other centuries-old music written by dead Germans whose names she couldn't pronounce.

"Of course I'm going to have to get a program together of what I want them to play after this. There's no way I would leave it to them to create their own program."

"Well that's fine, because I don't know classical music. Where do you find a string quartet, anyway?" Sandra asked.

"You go to Peabody," Linda said, her impatient tone intimating that everyone knew the obvious.

"How would she know that, Linda?" Gil retorted. "It's not like hiring string quartets is a part of people's everyday life."

"Sorry," Linda said, without her heart.

"By the way, Lila, Lucretia, Linda, would you three like to be my bridesmaids?" Sandra asked as she nervously pushed the parslied potatoes around the plate with her fork.

"Well, of course they would," Eulelie said with delightful surprise, setting her fork down with a clink on her plate. "Isn't this wonderful, your keeping with proper etiquette in asking the groom's sisters to be in the wedding party. This is just so very nice, and they would love to. So, how is it that you know about this tradition?" Eulelie asked.

With a question in her eyes, Sandra looked at Gil, then at his sisters, then at Eulelie, and she still didn't understand. Did they all think that she wouldn't, shouldn't, know something so simple? "I don't know, Mrs. Giles, it's just something I know."

"For goodness sake, Momma," Linda said, "it's not like it's some secret ritual kept by some exclusive girls' club. It's common knowledge in wedding planning." Unsmilingly, she looked in all the faces that were looking into hers, Sandra's showing the greatest awe. Then, still without a trace of good humor, Linda's eyes went into her plate and she ate as if nothing terribly unusual had happened.

"Yes, Linda, I suppose you're right," Eulelie said with a chuckle. "Anyway, this will make it such a family affair. That's what makes the custom so nice."

Everyone agreed with a smile, but Lila's seemed a dubious one. But then she said: "Well, yes, I would love to be in the wedding."

"Yeah, I'll be in it too," Lucretia said, "just as long as you don't pick some tangerine, puffy-sleeved hillbilly prom gown for us to wear." Then she laughed at her joke, throwing her head back with a pretense she'd perfected.

The room filled with layers of silence. No one, not a soul, was smiling. Sandra's scowl was most intense.

All Gil managed to get out was, "Lucretia . . ."

"It's a joke," Lucretia said. "Don't you get it? You know how nobody ever picks pretty bridesmaids dresses because no bride ever wants to be outshined on her big day. So you end up seeing this beautiful bride after these dumpy bridesmaids in frumpy dresses walk down the aisle. Don't you get it?" she asked again, hoping they would, otherwise her clumsy joke, certainly not meant in the way it was being received, would surely light an ugly family war.

An easy laughter broke out in the room. Even Gil laughed with abandon, and with relief.

"Yeah, you're right," Sandra said, still chuckling. "But to get around that, why don't I show you my dress and then you can pick your own dresses to match the style of mine. That way it'll be what you all like and can agree on."

"Oooh, that sounds like fun, doesn't it?" Lila said to her sisters.

Lucretia smiled in agreement, but Linda only smiled when her mother's face told her that she must. And she did, and it even looked sincere to the eye not trained in Linda's ways, but her brother frowned with annoyance.

"Well, that will work out fine," Gil said to all of them. "Momma, in a few weeks, we're going to pick up Sandra's gown. We thought maybe you'd like to see it."

"I would like you to see it," Sandra said quietly, not wanting to impose herself on this woman who had seemed to put ill-will behind her. *Please say yes*, she silently prayed. If Eulelie said yes and really meant it, she would feel, somehow, fully accepted, like she was really going to be a Giles.

"Well fine, that would be fine. Bring it by. That will be just fine," Eulelie said without taking her eyes off the kale at the end of her fork. She looked at the china closet, even at the painting on the wall over the buffet, but she still could not look at Sandra, and definitely not at Gil, because her eyes would give away the secrets of her heart.

≈ Here's to the Ladies Who Knit

After dinner was eaten, dishes cleared away, Gil and Sandra long gone, and Eulelie retired to her room, the Giles sisters were in the den, tending to evening activities. Lila sat by the window at the round, heavy oak table that most often served as Eulelie's games table, and graded papers she'd give back to her students in the morning. Linda was reading a romance novel whose cover showed a bare-chested black man coveting a heaving-breasted, cocoa-colored woman weakened by his passion. "How can you read that trash?" Lila asked, looking up from her papers. Linda didn't answer. She merely shifted, settling deeper into the sofa, drawing the book closer as if to shut out her sister's judgment. She looked up only when Lucretia let out a frustrated *"Damn it!"* from where she sat knitting in the chair in the corner.

"What happened?" Lila said.

"I just don't get this pattern. I don't see how people do this knitting stuff. Momma makes it look so easy."

"Well, why don't yo go up and ask Momma to help you?" Lila asked.

"No, I don't want to bother her. Besides, I know she's tired after today." She let out a sigh of disappointment. "I'll just work at it again tomorrow."

Lila went back to grading her papers, only to be jarred seconds later by a better idea. "Hey, you know what? Why don't you ask Sandra?"

"Ask Sandra what?" Lucretia said, looking at her sister as if she were completely insane.

"Gil said that Sandra knits beautifully, and sews too. Why don't you call Gil and get her number and ask her about it? Maybe she can help you over the phone."

That brought Linda out of her book. She looked at Lucretia, then at Lila suspiciously. "So now you and Gil are sitting around talking about all of Sandra's hobbies and talents? Please give me a break."

Lila looked just as suspiciously at her sister in return,

then shook her head and gave her an exasperated smile, her eyes rolling up to the ceiling. "Linda, you were sitting right there at the table when he was talking about it. Don't you remember, when we were all waiting for Momma to come to the table for dinner? Anyway, Gil said that Sandra had knitted the sweater she was wearing and that she made most of her clothes. You were sitting right there! I even saw you looking right in Sandra's face! How could you not have heard that?"

"I just didn't hear it, okay? I don't know, maybe I wasn't paying attention. So shoot me!" and Linda was pulled back into the tale of lust.

"So why don't you call her?" Lila said to Lucretia.

"No, I don't think that's something I'll do," Lucretia replied in a happy-go-lucky, singsong voice. She was hoping it would end there.

"Why? You know she would help you. And maybe you could get to know her a little better in the process. Then maybe you won't be so aloof toward her."

"Oh yeah, I'm aloof toward her, and I guess the two of you are just like old girlfriends, huh?" Lucretia's sarcasm was raw and right on the surface.

"I didn't say that, Lucretia. We all need to look for some common ground with her, including myself, but at least I'm trying. Here you have the perfect opportunity to get to know her, and you won't. Why won't you call her?" Lila said, shaking her head in frustration. "Come on, will you? Gil *is* going to marry Sandra, that is a fact that's not going to change. You can either accept that Sandra will soon be a Giles or you can rail against it for the rest of your life. And if you do rail against it forever, what will that accomplish? The sun will still rise every day to find Gil and Sandra happy and married. And you . . ." She paused long enough to point her face toward Linda. ". . . *and* you, will be stewing in your funks and drowning in your schemes to alienate her and break them up, and you'd be pushing Gil further away in the process. Is that what you want?"

"Don't you worry about what I want," Lucretia said without looking at her sister.

"Lucretia, Linda, have you two thought of what would happen if you made her feel so unwanted in this family that she and Gil really did split? Could you live with yourselves? Wouldn't you feel the least bit guilty?"

Neither sister answered her. Instead, Lucretia stood, moving slowly, deliberately, gathering the yarn and her knitting in one armload. She went to where Lila sat grading her papers, and standing over her sister, said, "Stop pushing her on everybody, Lila. If you want to have a love fest with Sandra, well then you go right ahead, but leave us out of it. Whether I love her or hate her will be *my* decision." Then she dumped the knitting, yarn, needles, pattern, everything, on top of Lila's papers. "Here, it's all yours. You finish the sweater. Now you have a reason to *bond* with Sandra." She was about to leave the room in a storm, then, as if a change of heart had taken her over, she turned and said: "Listen, whatever relationship I'll end up having with Sandra will be on my own terms, not dictated by you or anyone else. Just don't force me and I'll do what I need to do," and then in a tempestuous haste she left the den.

Lila sat seething as Lucretia left the room. She recalled when her mind was closed as tightly as Lucretia's and her world was defined by being a Giles, but she didn't remember possessing the anger, or the anger possessing her. "Can you believe her?" she asked Linda, not necessarily expecting an answer.

Linda lifted her eyes just long enough to say: "That's what you get. You need to leave Lucretia alone and stop trying to make everybody get along. It's just not going to happen that way, Lila."

Lila tossed the knitting across the room onto the sofa and missed. It fell on the floor, where she left it. Linda looked down at it without expression, then went back to her book. Lila gathered her papers from the table and left as piqued as Lucretia had just moments before.

"Good night, Lila," Linda said in a mocking voice.

But Lila said nothing, the patter of her slippers fading down the hall and up the stairs with an angry expedience she wore comfortably well.

EIGHT

Lila sat in Café One a full half hour before Pick was due to show up. They seated her at a table, instead of having her wait at the bar, and for that she was most grateful, and relieved. It seemed to her that she would not be able to survive the awkwardness of having to climb down off a bar stool only to have to explain why she was there to greet him in the first place. Yes, this was much better. To sit at a table with time to collect herself, and stop herself from picking unconsciously, nervously, at the corner of the napkin she had prematurely spread across her lap.

The hostess walked past, and Lila offered her another thankful smile. It was part of the woman's job to return it, Lila knew, but she still had to let the hostess know how she'd saved her.

"Can I have your waitress bring you a cocktail?" the hostess asked.

Suddenly Lila was aware of her emptiness, or rather, her empty hands with too much nervous energy. She looked at the woman, wide-eyed, stricken. "Oh, well, I don't . . . well, anyway, I suppose she could bring me a . . ." She had to get a drink. The plan was to meet Pick over drinks, so what would she look like sitting there without one? But Lila's mind wouldn't work to remember any of the potent libations she'd heard her mother's friends talk about. She didn't want to drink, but she felt she had to drink. It was either that or end up with a lap full of shredded linen napkin. "You know what, you can have the waitress bring me an old-fashioned."

"I sure will. Do you want that made with bourbon, brandy, gin, rum, rye, or vodka?" The woman rattled the choices off as if she were talking to an experienced woman.

"Oh, I don't know. I guess with bourbon," Lila said, asking for the only liquor she could remember from her choices.

"And you don't have bread yet. I'll have her bring that as well," the hostess said.

"Thank you so much." It occurred to her then that eating, even bread, while drinking spirits somehow looked better.

When the hostess left, Lila found herself enthralled by an older couple eating their meal in absolute silence. She had noticed them before, but thought she had witnessed a lull in the conversation. Now it was clear—they simply were not talking. Like two strangers doing nothing more than sharing a table in a crowded eatery; except this was not a mere eatery, and there were so many empty tables the place looked closed. Why weren't they talking? Was he mad? Was she mad? There was nothing, and this baffled Lila as she squinted, not to see better, but to try to understand. Didn't the woman want to comment on her steak? Didn't the man want to say something about the wine? They were so intent on not talking to one another, it seemed, that neither one so much as looked up, or around to find her gawking at them. It made Lila melancholy, because she remembered meals, particularly near the end of her father's life, where he spoke only to his children, and if it weren't for her mother's incessant chatter, to which he was forced to respond, the two of them would have eaten their meals the same way as this couple before her—without a word between them.

A basket covered with a white napkin broke her stare as it came into her line of vision, attached to a thin, white arm, and was placed in the middle of the table. On the tray, which the waitress balanced with her other thin arm, was a lone highball glass filled with a golden liquid surrounding perfectly square ice cubes. "One old-fashioned with bourbon," the waitress said pleasantly.

"This is an old-fashioned?" Lila asked, her eyes rounded with shock.

"Yes ma'am. This is what you ordered, isn't it?"

"Yes, yes it is. I'm sorry, it's just that I've never had an old-fashioned before and I didn't expect it to look like this. This looks like scotch, or something hard." In all the years she had pictured this drink, she saw it as pale yellow with a delicate slice of lemon straddling the lip of the glass; something that would take her imagination back to the days of genteel ladies in fragile lace and bustles.

"Yeah, I know. I can take it back if you want to order something else."

But Lila was curious about this drink that her mother's friends made sound like the liquid of the gods. Besides, she needed something, right away, to mellow her in those anxious moments that would pass before Pick arrived. "No, no, that's all right. This is fine. I'd like to see what this tastes like."

"Well, good luck. The only people we get in here ordering this drink are usually old-lady socialites at lunchtime." The waitress smiled and left Lila to her drink.

Lila took one sip that was barely a drop. Her face twisted, of its own will, into a grimace too ugly to belong to her sweet face, and her eyes watered. Just that small drop sent a trail of fire into her belly, and she thought it would never go out. She wouldn't give up, though. She picked up the glass again, and this time drank enough to make a decent swallow, and the second time around wasn't so bad. She immediately felt a tingle all over her body that rushed to her head with a quiet murmur that made her smile. But she nearly choked on her pleasure when she looked up to see Pick walking through the door. Quickly, she dropped her head to look into the napkin in her lap, suddenly struck with the paralyzing thought that she had made the hugest of mistakes. Slowly, she raised her head just level enough to see where he was, and saw him looking in her direction and obviously telling the hostess he knew where he was going, then breezing past her. Lila quietly invoked the help of God. How could he know she was Gloria Jenkins? This was horrible. This was a nightmare, and she had brought it on herself. In a last desperate attempt to deny the truth, Lila thought that maybe he would think running into her was just a simple coincidence.

Before he even reached the table however, before he even passed the table in front of her, Pick said, "Lila Giles, or should I call you Gloria Jenkins?" She knew his smile was meant to put her somewhat at ease about her ruse. He didn't want her to think it was as bad as her humiliated face said it was. After all, he did show up.

Still, Lila knew she had to explain, and quickly. "I, um . . . Well, you see Pick, I . . ." What could she say? At first it seemed best to play on the coincidence, since that was, after all, her original plan, but good judgment told her not to. Besides, that might backfire too. Her only choice was to admit to the lie as innocently as possible. "Pick, how did you know?"

Slowly, moving with a fluidity that told of his control over every muscle in his body, Pick pulled the chair from the table and took his time sitting in it. He looked past her and summoned the waitress with his eyes, then slid his eyes into hers, saying, "Lila, I knew it was you the day you called."

"You knew my voice?" she said with quiet excitement.

"No, I can't say that it was your voice that gave you away. But I know that the woman who gave birth to you is Gloria Jenkins. So I figured I'd show up here today to see if it was really you, or to see if I had a story of resurrection from the dead to sell to the tabloids." He laughed in a light way meant to put her at ease. No harm done. "What I do want to know, though, Lila, is what you really want with me.''

Lila took another swig of the old-fashioned. What did she want with him? She wasn't sure in any specific way, but she was certain she wanted something. "Pick, I don't really know what I want, at least not exactly. All I know is that I was really drawn to you after I met you," but she immediately realized what she'd said, or at least how it sounded. "Oh, but no, you know. I'm not drawn to you or interested in you in *that* way. I mean, I'm sure a lot of women are drawn to you in that way, you know. I know that a lot of women would want to be romantically involved with you because you seem, you know, nice.'' She stopped herself from babbling, realizing if she'd kept going she would have dug herself deeper, and made herself an immense fool. So she concluded, "It's just that I'm not.''

"Understood, and no offense taken,'' Pick said with a shadowy smile.

The waitress had come to the table at the tail end of Lila's babbling, but waited for them to finish before she asked, "What can I get for you this evening?''

"You can bring me a Bombay Sapphire martini, shaken with a twist.''

"Coming right up,'' she said, leaving with a waitress's speed.

"So, you were saying you were interested in me, but not in *that* way. So go on,'' Pick said.

His intention was to make her blush, and he succeeded.

"I suppose I'm just intrigued by what made you go against everything you were raised to be,'' Lila said, her face contorting into a question mark. "I mean you had the best education, you're a barred attorney. And then you give all of that up to sneak around in dark alleys to catch people doing God knows what; at the very least doing what they're not supposed to be doing.''

"Is that what you think I do? You think I lurk around in dark alleys? Lila, I think you've seen too many bad movies.

Much of what I do is research—on the computer, through agencies, whatever. I know how to find out just about anything on anybody."

"So you don't follow people?" Lila said skeptically.

"I didn't say that. I'm just saying that's not all I do. It's not as seedy as you make it sound."

"Oh, I didn't mean to imply that what you do is seedy. I'm just saying that you went to some of the finest schools in the country. You got an excellent education, and I'm sorry, it all just doesn't fit with what you do now."

"Oh that. Well, I'll tell you. I don't think my time at Andover and Princeton was a waste of time at all. I just—"

"Wait. Andover? Princeton? That's not what you told me. You told me you went to Sidwell Friends and Georgetown."

Pick accepted his drink with a sideways smile from the waitress. He took a long sip, set it down on the napkin, then said, "Is that what I told you? Oh, well then, I guess what I mean to say is that I don't think my time at Sidwell Friends and Georgetown was a waste of time at all."

Lila looked at him with a blank face that somehow spoke of her disapproval. This required another swig, and as she turned the glass up to her lips, her eyes did not move from his. She set her glass down, still staring into his face for answers. "You lied to me," and it was clear she was insulted.

"You lied to me. Now we're even." He didn't gloat with an arrogant smile the way a lesser man might. There was no need. He simply sat, waiting for her lead since this was her dance. "So now what?"

"So what's the truth? Did you go to Friends or did you go to Andover? Did you go to Princeton or did you go to Georgetown?"

"You should ask yourself—and really think about this, Lila—but just ask yourself, does it really matter?"

Lila looked past Pick's head to see the silent couple about to leave. She had looked over at them just in time to see the husband give his wife a polite smile. That was at least something, she thought. "It matters. I just don't really know why it matters. I guess it matters because it helps people know who you are, you know. It finishes the picture."

Pick laughed ironically, then took another swallow of his martini. "I'm going to tell you something. If I wanted to, I could make up a past, complete with family history and everything, and make my way into your mother's social circle without a problem."

"No you couldn't," Lila said assuredly, and with a smile that had a twinge of arrogance to it, confident that *his* confidence was overstated.

"Sure I could. I've spent enough time lurking around, as you call it, in your world to know all your little likes and dislikes, what impresses you, what you scoff at. All of that stuff I know, and I can wear it just as comfortably as anyone, if I wanted to. If anybody wanted to, they could do it. You just have to want it badly enough. So for that reason, Lila, for that possibility, you should always question why that superficial stuff like where somebody went to school, or what social clubs they belong to, or if they're on the social registry, or what their family background might be, is important. And always question what you *think* you know is true."

"I'm sorry, Pick, but I have to disagree with you. I know you think you're pretty good at this undercover stuff, but this world, this clique here in Baltimore, of which my mother is at least co-president, is impossible to make your way into as an imposter. It's too small. Everybody is connected in a complete circle. Do you know what I mean?"

"Yeah, of course I know what you mean. All I'm saying to you is that everybody is connected in ways that don't mean anything. They might as well exchange résumés, you know, just give each other a sheet of paper with their histories printed on it, because all they're doing is talking, and none of them really know the truth about each other's lives. They lie to themselves and they lie to each other. And everybody lies on their résumé."

Lila drank the last bit of old-fashioned, looking with stern eyes at Pick over the lip of the glass. She put the glass down determinedly then fidgeted with the triangles and circles cut into the thick tumbler. Without smiling, she said to Pick: "If you think you know so much, then answer this: Why is it that everybody's secrets always somehow seem to make it around as gossip? Like Laura . . . Well, never mind. You don't know her. Anyway, I just don't think they would lie to each other about, you know, important things."

"Important things like what, Lila? College degrees, or maybe about who's the real father of a bastard baby?" Pick said blandly and without expression.

Lila's eyes grew round. "So you know about Laura Ballard?"

But Pick said nothing. He motioned for the waitress again with his eyes. Holding his empty glass in midair as a prop in his sign language, he ordered another martini. "What are you drinking?" he asked Lila.

"An old-fashioned. But I don't want another," Lila said, her last two words practically slurred into one.

"Ah, Dottie Pettigrew-Van Dyke's drink. I guess you look up to her, huh?"

"Of course. I think her whole family's incredible. Just think, the *Afro Gazette* has been in the Pettigrew family for more than a hundred years. That's some legacy," Lila said, with something just shy of gushing admiration.

"Yeah, it's something to be proud of, all right." But there was sarcasm in his tone. "Lila, do you ever wonder what happened to Dottie's son, Roger Pettigrew-Van Dyke?"

"I don't have to wonder. I know where he is, he lives in California. Los Angeles, I believe. He's an investment broker."

"You're sure about that?" Pick asked.

"I'm as sure of that as I am that you're sitting there."

"Uh-huh. Well, you know, I came to know Mrs. Pettigrew-Van Dyke because Roger and I were friends." And then, to keep Lila from straying from the subject, he said, "Don't try to figure out how we know each other. It's not important. Roger *is* out in Los Angeles. That much is true. But he's not an investment banker. He's a pimp. He's my buddy, but he's a pimp. That's a fact."

Lila wanted to believe that the liquor had made her miss something. Was there such a thing as slurred hearing? She thought that maybe he had said pip. Maybe Pick meant to say that Roger was a pipsqueak. Roger had been a bit of a whiner as a child, she remembered, certain that this is what Pick meant. Maybe Roger still whined. She had to know what Pick actually said, what he really meant. "Excuse me, Pick, but I don't think I heard you," she said, and by now most of her words were sliding into one another.

The waitress had brought Pick a fresh martini, and he took a sip before saying, "You heard me, Lila. Roger is a pimp. A rather successful one, I might add. He lives quite well."

Lila felt she'd have to put her chin in a sling to get her mouth to close. The news was as shocking as if she had heard it about her own brother. "So you mean . . . so what . . ." She stammered and stuttered, the words, the questions, thrashing around in her mind too furiously to settle into one solid question. She looked away from Pick, away from everything, then turned back with a closed-lip smile and said, "How could this be? Are you sure you have your information right? Pick, Roger was valedictorian of his class from Morehouse. I know he dropped out of the MBA program out at Stanford, but still, his future was solid. He's a Pettigrew. He's a Van Dyke."

"Lila, first of all, it is most definitely so. My source is none other than the man himself. He's quite candid about it. All of that other stuff, Morehouse, Stanford, Pettigrew, Van Dyke, I hope you can see now that none of that matters."

"So does his mother know?"

"Yep, she sure does. She's known for a few years now. Like I said, he's up front with it, but his mother's the one who lies and double-speaks and changes the subject when it comes to the issue of Roger. She took it real hard. Remember that heart attack she had about three years ago?"

"Yeah, that was awful. But you don't mean . . . ?"

"Yeah, that's when she found out. Her husband thought it would just about kill her." Pick cocked his head sideways, shielding the distress in his eyes from Lila. He said quietly, "Yeah, that was a real shame. A real shame."

Lila was in mourning for something that had suddenly been lost. It could have been innocence, Roger's innocence, or it could have been truth. Most likely, though, it was her faith in everything that had always made her ground solid. She sat staring catatonically at the flickering candle in the middle of the table. It lured her deeper into its entrancing flame, where she could question and maybe find answers to why everything she had believed in for as long as she knew how to trust was no longer as it had always been.

"Lila, are you okay," Pick inquired.

She heard him not as if he were across the table from her, but as if he lived only in her mind. Then reality jostled her. "What?" she said.

"Are you okay?"

"Oh, yeah." She rubbed her head as if she'd just awakened from a nap. "Wow, you know that drink has really gone to my head. I should get going," and she dug through her purse for her wallet.

"Listen Lila," Pick said, hoping to stop her frantic purse-rummaging, which had put him on edge. "I didn't tell you what I told you about Roger to upset you, or depress you. I don't know, I just think you're a good person. There's something in you that seems different from everything you seem to be." Pick's face slid into a sly grin that could have meant anything, but then he surprised himself when he confessed, "Look, I admit I've done a lot of messing with your mind, but I feel a little bit protective of you, which is weird to me, and I don't want to see you gradually turn into . . . Well, I just think you have it in you to be more than . . ."

"Who, my mother?" Lila said, with a no-nonsense look

that said she would have agreed with him if that had been what he meant.

"I didn't say that. I suppose I mean that you have a chance to save yourself, and you should do it, Lila. That day I met you with your mother at the mall, I could tell just in the way you held yourself that you were embarrassed. You didn't want to be there, and you shouldn't have wanted to be there, regardless of how wrong you think that girl is for your brother. Nobody should live with the kind of hellish paranoia that makes people like your mother and all of her friends hire somebody like me. Don't get caught up. At the end of the day, Lila, and at the end of your life, you've got to decide for yourself what's important."

Lila smiled with her entire face, especially her eyes. "You're a nice man, Pick, and I really thank you for trying to make me feel better. But this is something that's going to take a while to set in for me."

"That's understandable. In the meantime, let's blow this stuffy joint and go somewhere to get you some coffee. Old-fashioned, huh? Wrong drink for your first time drinking alcohol."

"Oh, you're so sure I've never had alcohol before, are you?" Lila said playfully, giddily distracted from her melancholy with the thought of making Pick's instincts wrong.

"Of course it's your first time drinking alcohol. Mimosas at Sunday brunch don't count."

"And just how do you know so much about me?"

"Lila Giles, your mother would be proud. You wear her breeding well." And Pick laughed at the irony. But when he looked into Lila's stone face, he could see that she didn't think Eulelie's imprint, her will, was even the tiniest bit clever in its all-consuming power.

⊸ Miracles Are Meant for the Souls of Believers

It was the holiday, above Thanksgiving and ranking even higher than Christmas, that filled up Sandra's soul to overflowing. In it she celebrated her faith, her steadfast belief in miracles. What could be more miraculous than death and resurrection? Hope. It gave her hope for something and someplace more blessed, and second chances, both on earth and beyond. On that Easter Sunday morning when she gave to the world a new life, which was her daughter, whose love would always shine on her like the bright light of eternity, she was blinded by the revelation of the depth of Jesus' sacrifice. Death gave the birth meaning. Easter was the time her faith came together to give her a clear understanding of why she, or anyone, bothered to pray.

Sandra bubbled around her mother's kitchen, helping prepare dinner for the next day. Everyone would be there for Easter Sunday dinner. Even her brother and sister from New York got to town on Maundy Thursday—no way would they incite their sister's wrath by missing Easter. And Margie wouldn't miss dinner with the Hightowers. Neither would her husband and children—all four of them—not to mention three other families from the neighborhood, and five people from the church with no family in Baltimore, who would follow them home after services. This was the extended family who'd been given unspoken invitations for Easter Sunday dinner for the last fifteen years. Camilla was getting ready for her fullest house of the year—fuller, even, than Christmas—and she couldn't do it without Sandra, whose magic with yams and lamb were matched only by her exuberance for the holiday.

Camilla stepped behind Sandra and hugged her around the waist. "I don't know what I would do without you here to help me," she said, and kissed Sandra on the back of her head. Only a mother could find the same comfort and tingling warmth in kissing a hard-haired adult head as a downy soft baby head.

"Oh, Momma, you know I love this. I wouldn't want to be anywhere else doing anything else."

"I just hope we're gonna have enough food."

"I think we will, even with all these mouths to feed." She pushed a strand of hair off her forehead like a woman slaving to please.

"Well, all these people are your doing, you know."

"Me? Ma, what are you talking about?"

"You started all this back when you were sixteen. Invited all these people and didn't tell me till Good Friday morning. You said you wanted a big family to celebrate God's holiest day. Said you wanted aunts and uncles and cousins, and if you couldn't have real ones, you'd borrow some. That's just what you did too." Camilla was laughing so hard Sandra could barely understand her.

"Well, there's just something special about a home with a lot of family."

"What are you gonna do about goin' to Gil's mother's? I'm sure she's expectin' you two for dinner." Camilla felt odd just mentioning her, the oddest part was just bringing herself to say that name that didn't belong to the woman— Eulelie. It was too much lying, to call her Eulelie; and then there was the fear of slipping and calling her Doralee.

"Yeah, we've got to go over there for brunch. Gil and I will be back here in time for dinner." Sandra paused, then contorted her face as if she'd just bitten into a sour onion. "I don't know, Easter just doesn't mean the same to them as it does to us. I mean, they believe that Jesus died on the cross for our sins and everything, but it just doesn't seem like . . . I don't know, I can't explain it. It just doesn't seem to be about religion and faith."

"People keep God in their own way, Sandra, you know that." Camilla knew the rage she was about to stir up, but she had to say this: "Besides, I think you're too hard on her."

The words were barely out of Camilla's mouth when Sandra slammed the knife down on the counter with great force. It was a blue-moon occurrence for her to feel anger toward her mother. Angrily, defensively, quietly, she said, "How can you say that, Ma? Have you completely forgotten the way she's treated me in the month that I've known her?"

"Sandra, just listen to me," Camilla said, taking her daughter's hand and squeezing it, both for comfort and to capture attention. "I know how she's been, but you have to understand that somebody like her has a lot of pain in her soul. Somewhere, a long time ago, somebody didn't tell her she was okay just the way she was. It can happen in the richest and the poorest families. Sandra, this woman is afraid of not measuring up herself, that's why she's so fast to let people know when they don't, or when she *thinks* they don't." Now she was hugging Sandra, close and tight. Her words would somehow sink in this way. "Baby, this whole family has always let you know that you were loved no matter what you ever did or said. We let you know that you were just fine being Sandra. Don't keep bad feelings in your heart for her, honey. Feel sorry for her and try to understand. She don't like herself enough to see that what she's doin' is wrong. You understand?"

Her mother had such a way of breaking the most complex things down to their least common denominator. "You're right, Ma," Sandra said. "I need to remember the reason for this holiday. I would be a bigger hypocrite than she if I can't forgive her, especially at this time."

"That's right, Sandra," Camilla said, so happy that her words fell on clear ears. "Don't ever forget that none of us are bigger than Jesus, and if he can forgive *us*, then we can forgive each other."

The coarseness of the ringing phone blasted in their ears. Startled and nervous, Sandra wiped her hands and took a giant step to the phone, but it still rang twice more before she could answer with an agitated "Hello?"

It was Gil, and her mother could tell by Sandra's suddenly softened, puppy-love, "Oh, hi." She told him what she was doing—chopping onions for the collards. He had to hear the entire menu for the next day's dinner before getting to his reason for calling. Would she like to attend church with his family tomorrow? Sandra said *umm* and *ah*, meanwhile shifting from one leg to the other, a dance she danced when nervousness jiggled her body.

Attending church with his family would require breaking a tradition that went back farther than she could remember. Church with her family and then back home to talk and laugh through a din of other talking and laughing all going on in one small room. This was an Easter tradition. Had she not acquiesced enough on her tradition by having Eulelie's brunch slice up her day? As it stood, there would be no scream-talking just to hear herself, like there would be back at the homestead for her. There would be polite conversation spoken in something just above a whisper, and champagne, and haughty food; food that somehow would not be enough to completely fill a stomach, but still left it without an appetite. Sandra wanted to be at her mother's holding off her hunger with just snacks and Coca-Cola till dinner, her mother's dinner, with real food—the kind that would leave her incapable of doing anything but sitting, stupefied and fooddrunk on the sofa, maybe with her skirt open at the top.

"Do I have to let you know right this minute?" Sandra wanted to know. "Only because my sister and brother are here and Daddy really looks forward to all of us attending church as a family, and to tell you the truth, I'm looking forward to it too." She could not have been more honest with him. No excuses, no tiny lies that God would understand even on the day before the celebration of His most sacred gift. "I'll call you later and let you know for sure." She told him she loved him, not bashful at all about displaying such personal emotion for her mother to hear.

"How's Gil doin'?" Camilla asked when her daughter hung up.

"He's fine, but he wants me to go to church with his family tomorrow. Before you even start in, Ma, I'm telling you now that I don't want to go, and it has nothing to do with his mother or forgiveness. It's about tradition. The Gileses aren't the only ones with family tradition, you know."

Camilla went to the refrigerator, opened it and searched till she found what she wanted. As the can of cola hissed and plopped, she shut the door with a light push, took two sips and said: "Sandra, it's your decision."

"I know, Ma, and I've already made it."

✍ The Lady Doth Protest Way Too Much

Gil and Sandra walked into his mother's living room and found no place to sit. Their hands were not linked, their smiles nowhere to be found. The tension between them was hauled in from the car and set smack in the middle of the room. The ride to Eulelie's was rife with disconsolation—each having their own reason. Gil was still stinging from Sandra's rejection of his family's invitation to church. He didn't know why it meant so much to him, since he was just a Christmas and Easter churchgoer. What did it matter to him that Sandra chose her own church, the church she attended, maybe not every Sunday, but certainly more frequently than Christmas and Easter? In fact, he didn't care. What did matter to him was that she did not accept his mother's invitation, which was so graciously and stunningly put out there. There had to have been a way for Sandra to have accepted and still go to her own church. She could have gone to both services; she could have gone to his mother's church for the coffee and doughnut hour. He didn't know—he hadn't figured it all out. Somehow, though, he felt Sandra could have been more flexible. More willing to compromise. Couldn't she see that his mother was coming around?

"Gil, go get some chairs from the dining room for you and Sandra," Eulelie said, looking back and forth between the two, trying to study what was already clear. Gil went off obediently, without saying a word, and still without a smile.

Sandra stood alone, boring a hole into the carpet with her eyes while the voices drifted around her. She waited for what seemed an eternity for one chair. Then she heard her name. She looked up to see the only face in the room she could see. He smiled, warmly and with effulgence, as if he'd been waiting forever to see her. The smile she returned was similar, because she felt she knew him as well as he seemed to know her, though of course he didn't. Forcing her eyes from his would be like forcing her eyes from the magic of the pink metallic glow brought with a new day's dawn. Reeling in her smile, her subtle radiance at the sight of him, would be like telling the darkest lie to her soul. Then she realized that it hadn't been him who called out her name, and she came quickly back from the place they had gone together.

"Sandra, dear. Hello? Sandra," Eulelie said, trying to get her attention. "My goodness, dear, that must have been some daydream you were lost in. I'd like to introduce you to Dr. and Mrs. Breckenridge. . . ."

"Celeste," said Mrs. Breckenridge.

"Celeste," Eulelie said. "This is Dr. Van Dyke and his wife, Mrs. Pettigrew-Van Dyke, and their daughter Missy. And over there are the Doctors Crenshaw and their sons, Doctors Joseph and Lawrence Crenshaw."

"It's a pleasure to meet you all," Sandra said quietly as she sat in the chair Gil had just set down next to Missy Van Dyke. Missy was friendly, but quiet, with a big toothy smile that made her seem uninteresting and probably friendless. Her teeth were so long, her lips looked strained in their work to cover them. She was certainly not pretty, though she could have been considered cute. She was a plain girl with potential for more, and Sandra almost felt sorry for how unknowingly close she was to her potential. She returned Missy's smile, which made her appear as nothing but teeth, saying: "Hi, how are you?"

"I'm okay," Missy said. "This is your first brunch here, huh?"

"Yes. Last year Gil hadn't told . . . Well, anyway, I didn't make it around here last year. This seems nice, though."

"Yeah, nice," Missy said, on the border of sarcasm. They sat close enough that no one else could hear them. With tightened lips, as tight as her teeth would let them be, Missy went on: "You should know that it doesn't get much better than this. The only good thing about it is that I get to go home. You, on the other hand, are stuck with them all for the rest of the year. For the rest of your life, even."

Missy's smile now was pitiless and empathetic all at once, which gave Sandra a clammy feeling on the back of her neck. Sandra's head-turn ended their conversation. What could she say to this, anyway?

Her eyes landed on Missy's mother, Dottie, who had come back into the parlor from the dining room. She sat across from Sandra with a plate of food, looking like one of those women from a prosperous family line whose affluence survived through all the names Negroes were called. It was in the way she lowered herself into the chair, slow and man-nered, smoothing her dress underneath her, then crossing her legs beneath her at the ankles. She was refined, and without the pretense some tended to bring to that quality. Sandra didn't know that this woman was the heiress of the *Gazette*, but she was clearly someone important. Not that Dottie was trying to appear important; she wasn't. Old money simply announces itself. She held herself with such ease, knowing, even, how to eat a meal without a table. Sandra's awe began wearing thin, though, as she noticed Dottie had a perplexed look. Had she offended this elegant woman in some way? Was it her mere presence? It would bother her until Dottie said what was on her mind.

"Eulelie, where are the blinis with caviar?" Dottie said, pushing food around her plate as if expecting the blinis with caviar to be hidden there somewhere.

"I didn't make them this year," Eulelie said.

"Oh, Eulelie girl, I was looking forward to those blinis with caviar. You always serve them at Easter brunch. Why not this year?"

"Oh no, I don't bother with caviar anymore after I heard

this piece on NPR a few months ago about the caviar mafia. They say so much of that stuff is illegally poached, and when it gets here you think you're paying top dollar for top quality caviar, but most of the time it's low-grade stuff. And people are getting killed in these caviar rings. Can you believe that?''

"Eulelie, I tell you, you and your National Public Radio," and Dottie let out a good-natured laugh she managed through quiet lips at her friend's radio obsession.

"That's right. It takes me around the world and back."

"So you two are planning to get married," Celeste said.

Sandra held her breath, waiting for . . . well, judgment, put-downs, something that wouldn't be obvious to the naked ear. It would be vile, hanging in the air like the stench of five-day-old garbage in the middle of a Baltimore July. "Yes ma'am," was all she said.

"I love weddings. They're always full of so much hope." Celeste paused, clearly not through, then said: "But I've been married long enough to tell you the truth. Marriage is just like flies at a screen—half of them are waiting to get in and the other half are waiting to get out."

The whole room broke out in hysterical laughter, the kind of laughter Sandra never expected to hear in Eulelie's home. She studied Eulelie with an open-mouthed gawk, as her to-be mother-in-law laughed to near crying. Who knew she was capable of cracking up like this? This kind of unabashed display of hilarity seemed like it would not be the proper way for a Giles to laugh at anything, regardless of how rolling-around-on-the floor funny it might be.

"Celeste, I'll tell you, you will just say anything," Eulelie said, dabbing the funny-tears from the corners of her eyes with the tissue she had leaned over and plucked from the box on the coffee table. "Where in the world did you come up with something like that?"

"Girl, you are so crazy," someone, maybe Dottie, said.

"Now you know I'm telling the truth. It's been around since the beginning of time. Every woman just dies to be married from the time she's old enough to tell the difference between boys and girls. And why? Because we see that beautiful white dress and that day of being a princess and we want marriage more than anything else in the world. Who we marry is not important because we just know he's going to be wonderful and romantic and we'll be their princess forever." The room was roaring with laughter, until everyone, basically at the same time, realized that there was something else going on other than a humorous anecdote.

Somewhere in the middle of her funny tale of truth, Celeste began to lose her connection with the laughter. She spoke with the dead calm of a wounded woman who had checked her emotions out of her marriage ages ago. And she took on a blank daze, talking to no one, but merely thinking aloud. She continued: "We see those flies on the other side of the screen, but we just never think, no matter what they tell us, that we will be one of them. Then we get the white dress and the princess-day, and little by little, as time goes by, we find ourselves moving closer and closer to the screen, without even knowing it. Oh, and then we want the baby because we fall for the myth of the pampered pregnant princess and we foolheartedly believe it will make the lure of that screen go away. And we have that baby, and with each baby we get we want the other side of that screen so badly we just might give up everything for it. What's the most thankless job a woman can do?" She paused not long enough to get an answer, then said: "Well, it's not a waitress. It's wife and mother, which is one in the same." And she was not smiling when she said this.

This window into her personal angst surprised everyone, especially her husband, who looked at her through squinty eyes that were trying to make out the face of a stranger. Suddenly, Gil and Sandra's tension had been trumped by something bigger, and no one saw it coming. A thin polite laughter scattered around the room, but most merely squirmed in their seats while finding interest in their hands, the floor, the walls, anything filled up time until the moment passed. But Joseph Crenshaw threw Celeste the line with which she could save herself from her own anguish.

"Ain't that the truth," he said. "I'm probably the only man on the face of the earth ever to be stung by a fly." Perhaps they thought it was funny; perhaps it was because everyone empathized with Joseph during his divorce; perhaps they needed the release; or perhaps it was everything coming together at the perfect time. Nonetheless, Joseph got a bigger laugh than Celeste, and it saved the moment for her. She was grateful, tossing a thankful smile at him, which he returned.

"You see what I'm talking about?" Celeste said. "Joseph knows. That child he married was just triflin', I don't care if she is Judge Cranfeld's daughter. She wanted the gown and the wedding." She laughed, relieved to have a way out.

"Well,I don't know about that," Sandra said defensively. Nobody was going to think she was one of those flies at the screen with questionable motives. After all, it was talk of her wedding that gave Celeste's story its impetus. "It may be that way for some women, but that would never happen to me." To the carefully trained ear, which they all were, Sandra's protest was terribly obtuse. Perhaps she was saying she wasn't one of those flies at the screen. She could have also meant that she would never *become* one of those miserable flies on the other side of marriage. Or was she simply saying that she would never be at an Easter Sunday brunch telling anyone who'd listen that she was a married fly waiting for freedom day? She felt the need, and only she knew why, to go on for clarity's sake. "I mean, Gil and I *both* want to be on the other side of that screen, and for the rest of our lives."

The room suddenly became pregnant with awkwardness, confusion, even more so than with Celeste's rambling confession. Sandra's protestation was simply too much. Gil shot her a look as if she were mad. Then his eyes rolled and his forehead wrinkled with the horror of embarrassment. What was she talking about? And who did she think cared? Shy and retiring, Sandra was not—this he knew. Today, though, he wished she were, partly because he was still mad at her for her earlier transgression, partly because there was no need to keep the conversation going by way of their business. She did not need to open her mouth to prove anything to anybody. The thought never entered his mind that she may have been trying to prove something to herself. He left the room without a word.

"Well, would anyone like a mimosa?" Eulelie asked, as if Sandra had not just desperately defended her love.

Lucretia and Linda stood at the portal with trays of tall, inviting glasses of mimosa. Sandra looked behind her, as did the others. Her hackles were smoothed. Eulelie wasn't rendering her contribution to the conversation insignificant. She was just trying to be a good hostess; or maybe the timing was just extremely good to her.

Missy Van Dyke, who sat between Sandra and Joseph, got up, leaving the space awkwardly empty, as far as Sandra was concerned. As long as Missy sat there in her painful shyness, she didn't have to think about Joseph Crenshaw. But there he was, affable, talkative, with a face more beautiful than the one every woman leaves when she awakes in the morning. What was it that made him eerily familiar? He would haunt her every thought until she knew. Something, politeness, a channeled spirit with coy female wiles, forced her eyes demurely back into his. She smiled nervously and nodded. He smiled, nodded. And then those eyes tried to speak, but just that quickly her eyes darted away, unable to take the intense intimacy with eyes that she imagined by candlelight.

Joseph waited until he knew he was right there in the corner of her eye. "Congratulations to you and Gil," he finally said. "I wish you two all the best."

She looked for just a second into the face of an angel, and then at the wall. She believed no woman could look for long into those deep pits filled to the brim with his soul, and at that perfect-toothed, perfect-lipped smile, without losing a part of her heart to them. Or maybe it was just what he did

to her. "Oh thank you," Sandra said after swallowing a sip
of mimosa.

"It's nice to meet you. I can see that Gil is a very
lucky guy."

"Thank you again." There was so much more she wanted
to say. She wanted to hint to him that Gil's family didn't
think so; something like: *I'm glad to see someone approves of
me.* Or: *Well, you're the only one who thinks so.* She thought
better of it, though. He was a total stranger, albeit a stranger
with whom she shared an unspoken connection. He had
more reason for loyalty to the Gileses than to her. It was
best just to let his compliment lie. Besides, there was no
reason for her to believe that his compliment was meant to
make Eulelie and her daughters wrong for their judgments.
It was safest to assume that it was a compliment meant for
the sake of politeness. Then again, his eyes had been saying
things to her that were more real than imagined.

Silence, maladroit and painful, fell between them once
again. On her left was the memory of Gil, still pouting like
Eulelie's big baby boy, making Sandra wish she were in a
place where she'd be wrapped in love. Then to the right,
was that face in which she could lose herself and her virtue.
Just as she was wondering if Gil would hate her forever, and
if they were at the end of their road, she felt someone sit
down in the vacant chair beside her. It was him.

"That sweater you're wearing is very unusual. I mean,
unusual in a good way. I like it. Where did you get it?"
Perhaps Joseph sensed that she felt like a fish among fowl,
just as he and everyone else knew things were not quite right
with her and Gil. Her blatant defense gave it away, but more
obvious than that was Gil's reticence. Joseph had never
known Gil to come into one of his mother's social gatherings
without loquaciously treating the room to his personal ruminations on either city politics or the law; unless he was flat
out mad about something, and then he could be as moody
as a rapacious lion without a kill in sight. After five years in

a bad marriage, spotting rocky relationships was as easy as finding a beacon in the blackness of night.

"This sweater? You like this sweater?" Sandra asked, giggling shyly. In fact she knew it really was a stunning sweater. It was the palest green ever made, with flecks of even paler shades of yellow, pink, and blue. It clung softly to every curve and mound of her figure. No one noticed except Joseph, but she was a classic fetching beauty in her Easter sweater.

"It's beautiful."

"Well, I made it."

"You knitted that sweater?"

"I sure did. I knit all the time."

"That sweater is unbelievable. It's the stitching that makes it so unusual. The stitching and of course the . . . you know, what do you call it?" He was rubbing his thumb against his four fingers, the universal sign for money, but Sandra knew what he meant.

"Yarn."

"Yes, the yarn. What is that, cotton?"

"Yes it is."

"Do you knit for other people? Because I would pay you. I'd like to have a nice sweater for the fall. A cardigan. How much would you charge me?"

"Generally, I don't knit for other people. I mean, I've never really done that except for close friends and family, and I don't charge them. I wouldn't even know how much to charge."

Their deal was hanging in the air when Sandra heard Gil's voice, flat and steady: "Sandra, we should probably be going to your mother's now."

"Oh, okay. Uh, yeah you're right." Sandra was flustered and flushed with the prickly heat of . . . could it have been the guilt of lust? "Oh, it was nice talking to you," she said to Joseph as she got up to leave.

"It was great talking to you too. And I hope you'll consider my request." And when Joseph looked up at Sandra, the sun, filtered through lace curtains, cast a ray across his face that made his light brown eyes appear golden. Then he turned his head ever so slightly toward Gil and the illusion was gone. None of that mattered to Gil. Some explaining was called for. "I was admiring Sandra's sweater, and when I found out that she made it, I asked if she'd make me a cardigan. It's so unusual, and I like sweaters you can't find anywhere else." He stopped just short of the threshold of overexplaining.

"Yeah, and she makes all her clothes too. They're sort of good enough to sell, but she won't make that next move." That's as close as Gil would ever come to praise of her, she thought.

"That's impressive. Well, okay, you guys have a great rest of the day," Joseph said as he got up and went toward the dining room. No need to prolong uneasiness.

"Momma, we've got to go," Gil called across the room.

"Oh, so soon?" Eulelie said, coming over and taking Sandra's hand.

Sandra gave it, hesitantly, as if she weren't going to get it back. The impromptu show of affection was stunning. "Yes, my mother's having dinner and I cooked most of it, so I feel obligated—"

"You don't have to explain. I understand. You're very lucky to have such a close and loving family. If you don't have family, you don't have anything."

"Well, I do want to apologize for not attending church with you this morning. It's just that my brother and sister are here from New York, and my father likes us to worship as a family when we can."

"Oh no, I'm sorry to have given you such short notice. Besides, you didn't miss anything. Reverend Popper was boring as can be this morning. Anyway, did you two get something to eat? Lila made some stuffed eggs that were just out of this world."

"No, we didn't get anything." Sandra looked at Gil for

a bail-out. There was no time to eat, but she did not want to insult by declining.

"Momma, can you just put a couple of plates aside for us and we'll get them later?"

"Oh sure, that's fine. I'll do that. I'm glad you two came." She squeezed Sandra's hand, then let it go to hug Gil. "Have a wonderful dinner. We'll miss you tonight for dinner at Dottie's, but I'll see you two next week."

And just past Eulelie, Sandra saw that smile, saying all that she felt.

⟋⟍ Outside the Comfort Zone

Gil puffed and grunted to get the car into a space barely big enough, just so it could be in front of the Hightowers' door.

"There's a spot down the street. Why don't you park down there?"

"I want to park here. I want it to be in front of the door to keep an eye on it."

Sandra's mouth twisted in aggravation.

It was being fine-tuned in Gil's mind, but he was finally going to say something after the silent treatment the entire way across town. The words, the tone, had to be just right. He didn't want to look petty, he didn't want to look nosy, he didn't want to seem jealous. It had to be a simple, uncomplicated question with untainted motives. The answer it elicited had to leave no room for more questions. Gil turned off the car and turned to Sandra, confident he had the perfect question to find out what he wanted to know without looking like an invidious Neanderthal. "I can tell that Joseph really wants you to make him a sweater. He loves high quality stuff, and your knitting looks like it comes right out of Hecht's. So, are you going to make him one?" That should have done it. A question with a compliment twist thrown in was always the way to go.

"Oh, well, he sat next to me after . . . what's her name? Missy, I think, got up. Then he complimented my sweater, and when I told him that I had made it, he started talking about me making one for him. I never told him I would, because I just don't like knitting for people I don't know. I just have this feeling that if I start doing that, knitting won't be fun anymore, it'll be work."

"Uh-huh, yeah, you've said that before." Gil's eyes went shamefully to some out-of-focus point past Sandra. "Listen, I want to apologize for the silent treatment. I do understand that you wanted to be in church with your family, especially with your sister and brother being here." His apology sounded sincere, and for the most part it was genuine. But what he understood clearer than anything was that other men could be drawn to Sandra's sweetness, and toughness, and honesty, and faint beauty. It would not leave his mind—that perfect-toothed smile, the piercing eye-to-eye stare, the clutch to her every word. Gil knew the feeling behind the look. It was the same way he felt the moment he and Sandra first met. Joseph Crenshaw was smitten by his plain-spoken lovely, and Gil saw the unmistakable attraction the moment he saw Joseph's eyes fall on her.

His apology would have been more effective had her mind been in the present. As she stepped out of the car, waving to Nicki, who bounced around in the doorway like an overstimulated puppy, Sandra couldn't shake those eyes, dark and stuck on her, from possessing her every thought. Walking up the walk, stepping into the house, hugging her sister and her brother, all she could think of were those eyes watching her.

Gil stepped in the house behind Sandra, to be slapped by the frenzied pitch of too many voices trying to be heard. His eyes went back and forth, scanning the room, and he tried to make sense of the pandemonium that was too much for his mind, and the tiny room, to absorb.

"Happy Easter, Gil honey," Aunt Margie said.

"Gil, come on in here, baby," Camilla said, grabbing his

hand. "Find anyplace to sit and claim it 'cause if you move you lose 'round here today." She belted out a giddy laugh that came straight from her soul. There were more people in her house than she had house. The smiles, though, and the laughs, and the mere ease of this bread-breaking fellowship, made the toil worth every ache in her puffed-up feet.

Sandra headed for the kitchen while Gil made his way across the room and sat on the stairs. It was the only spot in the room that no one had claimed. Though there was nothing but a white banister separating him from the throng, sitting there kept him isolated, cut-off. He preferred it that way. Sitting unnoticed and disengaged, he could observe rather than participate in this love fest of which he'd never feel a part. There were the three women and man over by the window talking about a singer in the church choir. Nothing in common. There were the three men on the other side of the banister talking about last week's Bible study. Nothing in common. Everywhere he looked this larger than life family were all connected to each other in a way that transcended blood, and transcended his ability to understand.

As he eavesdropped on the men's Bible study debate, he spotted two older women in his peripheral vision, one with blue hair, walking toward him, grinning from ear to ear. He prayed they would simply continue past him and head upstairs, but he could tell that he was their destination.

"Hi, how're you doin'?" the blue-haired lady said. "I'm Ida and this is Reetha. You're Sandra's boyfriend, aren't you?"

"Yes ma'am. I'm Gil Giles."

"Nice to meet you. Camilla just talks about you like you're her son, and now I see why." Her head bobbed gaily around like a ball of blue cotton candy.

"Sandra's a good girl and she's gonna make you a good wife," the other one said.

"Yes ma'am, she will."

"We'll be at that wedding for sure. Nothing could keep us away," she said, her blue head still bobbing with every word. She grabbed Gil's hand, gave it an old-lady squeeze, and said: "God bless you, baby." They left him sitting alone again and went toward the kitchen, probably to tell Sandra they'd just talked to her handsome boyfriend.

"Hey, you Sandra's boyfriend?" one of the Bible study men said through the spokes of the banister.

"It's nice to meet you, man. I'm Mel, this is Grady, and this here is Joe."

"It's nice to meet you all too." Gil didn't know what else to say, and even though the banister was less than conducive to a civilized conversation, he just did not want to engage them badly enough to take away the barrier by standing up. And just who were all these people, anyway? No one used last names, no one gave explanations of connections. There was no telling who was family, who were neighbors, who were church people. Everybody just melded together into a village, with the villagers snatched from here and there.

For some reason, Gil decided to focus on a worn-away spot of carpet on the stairs. That should discourage conversation. When he looked up, Sandra's brother Paul had showed up with a can of Coke, saving Gil from the moment. Paul let out a long sigh then sat down next to Gil on the steps. "Coca-Cola?" he asked, handing Gil the can. On his face, Gil wore the chagrin from their first and last encounter as he thanked him for the Coke. The last time went less than well. They were sitting, right there in that same room, when Gil, well-meaning but naively got a good taste of his size twelve Johnston and Murphy's when he said: *So, how does a photographer like you live? The work can't be that steady.* Paul had heard it before, especially from his family, and everyone in the neighborhood. In Baltimore, sensible living was about going someplace at nine in the morning and leaving there at five, and at the end of the week taking a check from someone called *boss.* You were considered particularly sensible if, in the morning, you went off to the post office, or Social Security, or some other part of government service that would employ you for the rest of your life, no matter what. That was life in Baltimore, but some escape it. Some moved on to chase their heart's desire without the pressure of judgment for not being the same. Paul escaped to New York.

"So, how you doin', Gil?"

"I'm all right, and yourself?" Gil still couldn't look him in the eye.

"I'm cool, man. I'm doin' okay."

"How's New York?"

"Still nuts, man, still nuts. Up there, you sort of exist to conquer the city, you know, try to keep one step ahead of everything."

"I couldn't do it, you know. I couldn't live in a crazy city like New York. Give me Baltimore any day, where life is predictable."

"Well, that's one thing New York is not. By definition, life in New York is unpredictable." Paul took a sip of Coke, then grimaced as the rush of fizzle burned up through his sinuses. He squeezed his eyes shut, as if in ceaseless prayer, until it wore off. When it was over and he could see without looking through the glare of Coke tears, he followed Gil's gaze, which was transfixed on Nicki and her friends. What was so fascinating about this group of giggling, cackling teenage girls? They were just doing what was most natural.

Gil sensed Paul watching him. Lest his motives be mistaken for something lewd and ungodly, Gil explained: "You know my sisters and I never had friends like that."

"Y'all didn't have friends?"

"Of course we had friends, it's just that we never just sat around laughing and talking. All of our friends were pretty much our friends because their parents were friends with our parents. I guess it was easier for our parents to keep track of what we were doing."

"Well, all those girls' parents are friends with my parents. I guess what you're saying is that your parents chose your friends and you and your sisters didn't click with your parents' choice."

"It's not that we didn't click with them, it's just that we didn't, I guess, interact like that. We were always doing something, either playing cards, or Monopoly, or Scrabble."

"So, you've always been pretty buttoned up, huh?"

"I guess if you separate people into buttoned up and unbuttoned, I'd be considered buttoned up."

"Yeah, I can tell. You seem like you feel a little bit out of place with all these folks runnin' 'round here, talkin' too loud and eatin' too much. I guess you're not used to this kind of madness, huh?"

"I don't feel out of place. I just don't know most of them." Gil looked down at his shoes, which were neurotically shined to Annapolis regulation. Then he looked into a face that was trying to find answers, only Gil wasn't sure of the question. "So what, you think I'm snubbing everybody?"

"I'm not saying that, man. I'm saying you sit all the way over here all by yourself. It's like you're afraid to talk to people. Body language, man. Your body is saying that you don't want to be bothered."

"I sat here because there was no place else to sit. So I don't want to be bothered because there was nowhere for me to sit?" He was warm and getting warmer by the minute.

"Look around you, man. Not everybody has a place to sit. People are walkin' around, talkin', laughin', sharin' the day with each other. Look around. That's what this is all about."

Sandra could feel it in the pit of her gut, just by seeing them from across the room, that she was about to walk up on bad blood. Gil only stabbed the air with one rigidly pointed finger when he was angry. Paul only gestured with his hands when he was hot under the collar. What could have happened? Paul didn't carry grudges around like so much burdensome baggage, so it couldn't have been what Gil said about being a photographer. Gil may have said something else without thinking. That was possibly, probably, what happened.

"What in the world is going on between you two?" she said. "You look like you're ready to tear into each other."

"Oh nothing, Sandra," Gil said sarcastically. "Your brother just thinks that maybe I think I'm too *highfalutin* to be here. Well, somebody here is trippin' hard about class, and I don't think it's me." Gil brushed past Sandra and went toward the kitchen.

Sandra gave Paul a scolding sideways glare. "Paul, what did you say to him?"

Paul stood and sidled up to her. He put his head close to her ear so there'd be no mistaking what he was about to say. "I ain't say nothin' that wasn't the truth, and you'd better check it out."

Sandra's face contorted with bewilderment. Of all of her mother's children, Paul was most like Camilla. He had vision where most saw haze. That's what kept him working in a place like New York—he didn't just photograph people, he knew how to capture the unknown. With only one encounter, Paul could have someone simplified to two, no more than three, adjectives. As long as she'd been his sister, Paul had had this gift, and he was never wrong. Moreover, and more troubling to Sandra, he never lied.

A Change of Heart, or a Glimpse into Their Own

The sky was sunless by now, but still not dark enough to be called night. Lucretia and Linda had left their mother and sister at the Van Dykes—Eulelie ensnared in a game of bridge, Lila ensnared in an equally tiresome game of Scrabble with Missy and her cousins on the Van Dyke side of the family. Neither were for Lucretia and Linda. Surely there were more interesting pursuits for them.

"Let's ride out to Gil's," Linda said to Lucretia, who was in the driver's seat. "Momma and Lila won't need us to pick them up for a few hours yet. Let's go."

"He's probably not home from Sandra's mother's house

yet. He won't be home," Lucretia said. "Besides, *she* might be there."

"Oh, so what. We're his sisters. We have the right to drop by, so she'll just have to deal with it and get used to it." She buckled her seat belt, then stopped, before starting the car, to think about what she'd just said. "That sounded awfully territorial, didn't it?"

"Oh, who cares. Gil is our territory, and she's the trespasser," Linda said, prepared not to give it another thought.

"Well, I care, Linda," Lucretia said, starting the car, then adjusting the mirrors to suit her, since she sat slightly lower behind the wheel than her mother. Driving away from the Van Dykes' house, she continued, "Think about it, Linda. Like Lila said, Gil marrying Sandra is more than a probability, it's a reality. He's going to marry her. At some point we're all going to have to find a way to get along with her, and let's face it, us putting our claims on Gil will do nothing to help the blood that started out bad between us." She waited for a response from Linda, but none came, so she said: "So what do you think?"

"I don't think, Lucretia. Look, the way I see it is that, yes, he'll marry this girl, and their marriage may last for fifty years, but that doesn't mean that I, or you, or any of us will have to love her and accept her with open arms into the family. She doesn't fit, Lucretia, plain and simple. And I have no problem with maintaining a certain civility toward her as my brother's wife, but she will never, at least in my mind, be the *sister-in-law*. Things happen like this in families all the time, and people manage to work out a life that's quite livable. You'll never find us shopping at the mall, or having lunch downtown, or calling each other to share our lives, but we will exchange Christmas gifts, and perhaps a compliment or two every now and again, and maybe you'll find our banter going just slightly beyond the cordial hellos, but that's where it all will end. I'm quite fine with that, and that's what I'm planning to do."

"You've actually thought about this, haven't you?"

"Of course I have. I had to. I had to find a way to accept this on my terms, and that's what I'm doing." Linda had a plan, she was prepared for this marriage, and quite possibly she was the only one.

Lucretia blew out a sigh, then pressed her lips together. "I don't know. We've always been such a close family. I just think it would be so nice if she could be more than just our brother's wife to us, and if we start now, maybe she can be."

Linda said nothing, staring straight ahead at the rear of the other cars moving up Liberty Heights.

Lucretia shot a look at her sister, then quickly looked back to the traffic. She shook her head confusedly and said, "I don't know, maybe you're right. Who knows?"

"Hey, turn here," Linda said suddenly. "Stop me past Jeffrey Borders's house. He hasn't called me since that night Momma almost caught us."

Lucretia looked at her for a second, then said, "Linda, you take some ridiculous chances with him. Momma's going to catch him one night, *or* one morning."

"Oh stop it, Mother Superior. Besides, what am I supposed to do? I can't stay at his house."

"I guess you can't, Linda," Lucretia said with an unstoppable laugh, "since he lives with his parents too."

"Anyway, it's just easier to do it this way, besides, Momma's so out of it. She actually thinks we're all still virgins. She thinks she knows our every move, and as long as she thinks that, then who am I to ruin the illusion?"

"Well, why don't the two of you opt for the classier solution to your trysts like the backseat of your car, or a seedy motel," Lucretia said sarcastically.

"I don't care what you think, Lucretia. All I know is that I have needs just the same as everybody else."

"Let's just hope your needs don't destroy your reputation. Jeffrey Borders is a louse and a loser, and his family is tacky. Especially that sister of his, Deliah," Lucretia said. "He's just low-life enough to go telling about it all over town."

"I don't know about that, Lucretia. You don't know him like I do. Besides," Linda said with a mischievous grin, the canary feathers practically dangling from her pouting lips, "he's good at a few things. What's with you, anyway? God, you're sounding more and more like Lila-two-shoes."

Lucretia simply drove, staring intensely at the road and trying to decide if what Linda had just said was an insult or a compliment. Lila had the tendency to be the irritating do-right big sister, but Lucretia also knew that Lila often made sense. Still, Linda's words hit her in that part of her gut that fluttered with confusion. She pulled the car in front of the plain brown and tan rectangular box of a house that once passed for modern, the house where new money and little taste lived.

Without looking at Linda, Lucretia said, "We're here."

But Linda didn't move to get out of the car. Then, as if it pained her, she said to her sister: "Look, I'm sorry if I hurt your feelings by saying you're acting like Lila."

"Hurt my feelings? What are you talking about? If you had told me I was acting more and more like you, *then* I'd be insulted." And she turned away to look out her window.

"Fine, Lucretia. You got me back. Now, are you coming?"

"Please, I wouldn't set one foot inside the Borderses' house. I had to tell Deliah off over something she said about Gil. I'm not speaking to that sow."

Linda lowered her head and gave her sister an under-eyed glare. "What did she say about Gil?"

"Oh, it's not important enough to repeat, but don't worry, I put her in her place."

"All right, well, I'll be right back. I just want to make sure we're still . . . well, close." Linda opened the door, closed it with a weak-armed push, then did a dainty trot up the path to the house.

Before Linda could even ring the bell, she heard someone on the other side of the door mockingly call out, "Jeffrey, you've got company." And then the door swung open. It was Deliah, looking as if she was itching to start trouble.

"Come on in, Linda. I'm pretty sure Jeffrey wasn't expecting you, but come on in, anyway."

Yeah, Linda thought, without a doubt, Deliah's trying to start something, or waiting for something to start. It was hard to tell. Linda could hear the din of company—voices wafting in from the kitchen. The smell of the Chesapeake hit her hard in the face; most likely steamed crabs. The house looked to her like it probably had its own peculiar, probably unpleasant smell, but no home should smell like the sea. She prayed that those crabs would keep Mr. and Mrs. Borders, and anyone else, in the kitchen, as they would never know she was there. She had already begun thinking of a lie she'd tell her mother if it were to get back to her that she was at the Borderses' house to see Jeffrey. It wasn't complete yet, but it had something to do with Jeffrey wanting some information on a car loan. But besides her not wanting it to get back to her mother, she just didn't want to have to see those awful Borderses. Their sycophancy was unbearable when it was meant for Eulelie, but when they became the sycophants of her or her sisters, it was nothing less than pathetic.

Jeffrey came through the swinging saloon doors that led to the kitchen with a feline thin woman on his heels. She was desperately trendy, Linda thought, in a ghetto goddess sort of way—every hair plastered to her head, a swatch of fabric that served as a skirt worn with an even skimpier top, high clodhopper heels, earrings nearly the size of her head dangling from her ears. She had the hippest of everything swathing every part of her. Upon seeing Linda, the woman draped herself, in one territorial motion, over Jeffrey's shoulder. It was so obvious that even Linda was embarrassed for her.

"Hey Linda," Jeffrey said. "What's up? Happy Easter." He didn't know what to say.

"Happy Easter. Who's your friend?" she said flatly.

"Oh, this is Myra. Myra, that's Linda. I've told you about my friend Linda."

"Yeah, I remember," Myra said in a way that meant she'd heard something naughty.

It didn't faze Linda. She dismissed Myra with an eye roll that was too slight to be seen, but it was felt. "Anyway, I thought I'd drop in to say hi. I haven't talked to you in a while. So, now I'm going to run. Lucretia's waiting in the car and we're on our way out to Gil's."

"Lucretia's in the car?" Deliah said. "I'm not speaking to her."

"Well, I guess it works out all the way around, Deliah, because she's not speaking to you," Linda said without looking at Deliah.

Linda went to the door, and just as she was about to open it, she said to Jeffrey, "Can we talk outside?" Then, without so much as a second's glance at Myra, she added, "Alone."

Jeffrey turned to Myra, who was still making herself an appendage on his shoulder, and said, "I'll be right back. Why don't you go down to the den and pick out a movie." He headed for the door while Myra just stood there watching him as if what was happening was too brazen to believe. But he slid out the door and closed it behind him in spite of Myra's shock.

Linda stepped off the stoop and walked slowly, like a courting tease, to the middle of the path. She struck a pose that had one hand tethered to the other wrist behind her back—like the guilty trying to appear without fault. Then she cocked her head to one side while her lips slid into a coquettish grin. Linda was well aware of herself. Still, she was aware of his distance, and somehow she knew what was coming.

"So, you've been a stranger," Linda said, her lips moving mockingly.

"I've been hangin' out with Myra a lot."

"Myra," Linda said, more to herself than Jeffrey. It's just

that he said her name in such an even way, as if she should have known. "Well, it's funny how Myra seems to know all about me, yet this is the first time I've heard her name."

"I've known her awhile."

"What's a while?" Linda said, unable to even know herself why jealousy had wrapped itself around every word.

"A while is about a year or so. I don't know specifically." Jeffrey looked nervously past Linda to find Lucretia's eyes pasted on him.

"Um-hmm," Linda said with a purpose. Then she shrugged her shoulder with a false nonchalance and said, "Well, she's tall." It was something to say.

"She models."

"Oh, right, a model. Well, what halfway decent-looking girl in Baltimore isn't a model, Jeffrey?"

"Linda, what does it matter?"

"It matters because you've been dating me the same time you've been dating that *model* who supposedly struts up and down the runways of *Baltimore*." And with the way her voice dropped with *Baltimore*, it was clear that Linda intended condescension. But she just wouldn't let it go. "You know, I've read all about it in the fashion pages. Paris, Milan, New York, Baltimore." And just when it seemed her scathing attack of Myra the stranger was over, she added, "Oh, and let me guess, the model has her own apartment."

"Linda, you know what, you and I are not dating. We never have been. We have sex. We're sex buddies, that's what we are. That's what we do. You set that up when you didn't want your mother to know anything about our involvement. So all we've ever been about is sex. That's not a relationship, Linda. And yes, Myra does have her own place, but that has nothing to do with anything."

"So what? You're saying you have a relationship with Myra the model?"

"That's right, and it's getting more serious." Jeffrey stepped back as if to take in all of her. Then, just to distance himself even more, he slid his hands in his pockets, rocked back and forth on his heel, toe, heel, toe, then said, "When your mother almost caught us in bed, Linda, that was not cool. That whole scene made me lose a little bit of my manhood. I felt like a stupid teenager with nothing but hormones. I shouldn't have been there and you shouldn't have had me there."

Linda's eyes grew very round, both with surprise and tears at the brink. Mostly tears. She fought them back, though. Why should he be handed the opportunity to gloat on a silver tray covered with her tears?

Linda had turned to walk away when Jeffrey said, "Linda, I don't mean to hurt your feelings, but we just can't do this anymore. I'm twenty-eight years old and I'm sneaking into your bedroom just to have sex and spend some time with you. I need something more."

Linda looked back at Jeffrey over her shoulder and said, "Jeffrey, please reel in your ego. It is not that serious. It's not as if you have the tiniest ability to break *my* heart. Enjoy the ride with your model."

And Jeffrey watched her go to the car with a proud strut. The kind of walk where her back stiffened with a rod and her head cocked sideways with a sassy indifference that really wasn't indifference at all, but something just shy of humiliation. Still, he stood shock still, watching her fold herself into the car and slump back into the seat. And everything about her said that she wished she had never come. He would not move until they drove away, because then it would be final, her contempt would be set in that stone part of her heart, and the possibility of taking back his words would become an impossibility. No one humiliates a Giles.

The car would not move until Lucretia knew everything. "What just happened over there?" she asked.

"I just broke up with him. He's got somebody else he's been sleeping with for I don't know how long. Some sad excuse for a so-called model with a face like a racehorse. She's in there right now. They should make quite a menagerie in that house with him being a weasel, her looking like a horse and that pig-faced sister of his, Deliah."

Lucretia simply could not take her eyes off Linda. If she stared at her long enough, she thought, maybe she'd understand. She broke her gaze only long enough to shoot a nanosecond of a glance at Jeffrey, who was still a statue on the front lawn. Finally, she spoke: "Linda, there was nothing to break off. I mean, the two of you were never dating. You two are not a couple. You sneak him in the house to have sex with him, and it's never been more than that."

Linda looked at her sister with a face flattened by aggravation. She stared squarely into the place where truths are usually shared and said, "It seems to me that I've heard this before, and if I wanted a replay I would go back over there to the source. Anyway, I'm not going to bicker over semantics. The bottom line is that he'll come around. He'll come to his senses and climb down off that seven-foot-tall horse. In the meantime, though, I'm going to make him suffer. Drive."

And as Lucretia pulled the car away from the curb, Linda did all she could to keep her eyes from what so tempted them.

So they drove on to Gil's house. Since it was only the two of them, and since the previous subject needed to die a death of natural or unnatural origin, they had nothing but time, place, and opportunity to talk about the sister who wasn't there; the sister who seemed to lose all sense of pride and loyalty when it came to the matter of Sandra.

"So what do you think is going on with Lila?" Linda asked Lucretia.

"What do you mean? Are you talking about the way she's always acting like a self-appointed United Nations ambassador whenever anybody mentions Sandra's name?"

"That's exactly what I'm talking about. You know, honestly speaking, I don't absolutely hate Sandra. I suppose I can admit that there must be something virtuous about her that made Gil fall for her. It's just that I don't see it. I think she has no class, and on top of that she seems to have a big old chip on her shoulder," Linda said impassively. Then she shook her head sideways and said: "But Lila, for crying out loud! She's so busy being the voice of reason that she can't see the reality of how wrong this girl is for Gil."

They were stopped at a red light, and Linda looked out the window at a man and woman standing at a bus stop, he dressed from head to toe, from hat to shoes, in white, with the exception of a red shirt, and she dressed in a too tight dress cut too high up on her massive thighs. And her shoes had the nerve to be gold, bright gold, perching her thickset legs at least six inches off the ground. "Look at that," she said, pointing with a slight movement of her head. After all, she didn't want them to know she was talking about them. "These two fools done up in their Easter duds, I suppose. What in the world makes a woman that fat squeeze her big behind into a dress that tight and that short and still think she looks good? What, is she supposed to look sexy?"

"Yeah, well look who she's with. Somebody needs to tell him that Superfly lives no more and Shaft is probably dead in Africa somewhere." They both laughed uncontrollably. Lucretia power-locked all the doors.

Then Linda said: "Yeah, Supershaft, huh. And to make matters worse, they're getting on the bus looking like that. It just doesn't make sense," she said, wiping her laughing-tears from the corners of her eyes.

When the light changed, their moment of comic relief was over. Back to Lila. "Anyway," Linda said, "I think Lila's one of those people who just wants everybody to like her."

"So she'd be willing to let Gil ruin his life just because she wants Sandra to like her? I don't know about that."

"Then how do you explain her, Lucretia?"

"I don't know, maybe she's just more open to accepting something new than we are," Lucretia said, rounding the corner into Gil's cul-de-sac. She brought the car to a stop right behind Gil's little black sports car parked in the drive-way, turned off the engine, and slumped back in a sulky heap. She said: "I know that's what scares me the most about this whole thing. Having to get to know a new kind of people, having to get to know the way they live and the things they like to do. Feeling uncomfortable every time they come into our world, a world that's so doggone foreign to them that to explain it all would put them and me so ill at ease that we'd all just want to retreat back to our own worlds that make so much more sense. I don't know. Maybe it is like Lila said. Maybe it is more our problem than hers."

Linda sat staring blankly and without blinking at Gil's house. Her face was solemn with her thoughts. "I guess I've never thought about it before—you know, why I don't like this whole thing. That makes so much sense it scares me to talk about it." And so she didn't, she just got out of the car, went to the door, and rang Gil's bell.

"Hi girls," bellowed Gil's neighbor from across the cul-de-sac, a Mrs. Something-or-other who always seemed to have something to do outside, no matter the weather, whenever any of the neighbors were receiving company.

"What is that woman's name?" Lucretia said just as she was catching up to Linda.

"I have no idea. Just smile and wave," and so they did.

"Where's your other sister?" the woman inquired.

Linda said nothing, but simply looked at Lucretia with a moping exasperation.

"She's visiting friends," was all Lucretia said, politely.

"Oh, that's nice. Happy Easter to you and your family, or what's left of it."

Together, they gave her a quiet *thank you* before Gil opened the door and saved them from more forced chitchat.

"Hey, you two," Gil said, his widened eyes showing his surprise at seeing them. He looked past them expectantly.

"Momma and Lila are still at the Van Dykes," Linda said, somehow knowing he was at least halfway expecting to see them. "We have to go back and get them in a few hours."

"Yeah, so we drove out here to kill some time. To tell

you the truth, I didn't expect you to be home," Lucretia said, crossing the living room to plop on the sofa.

"Well, I left Sandra's mother's a little early. Say, you didn't by any chance bring me that plate of food from the brunch that Momma put aside for me, did you?"

"No," Lucretia said, puzzled by the question. "Didn't you have dinner with Sandra's family?"

"That was the plan. It didn't work out that way. I got into a little thing with her brother. He pissed me off, so I left. It's no big thing."

"So you don't have anything to eat?" Linda asked, as if he were some poor wretch.

"No, nothing here. I was just about to order something from Orioles' Pizza. You all want anything?"

They both declined.

Linda sat down next to her sister on the sofa and picked up a magazine that sat on the edge of the coffee table. Thumbing through its pages benignly, she said, "Momma would just have a fit if she knew that you were ordering your Easter Sunday dinner from a pizza and sub shop."

"Well, what Momma doesn't know won't give her a conniption, now will it?" he replied with a furtive smile, an unmistakable sarcasm wrapping his every word. He continued to dial.

Linda shot a sideways smirk at her sister, nonplussed by what seemed to be a most unprovoked acrimony toward her mother. She kicked off her shoes, letting them plop loudly to the floor without any regard to the startling double clunks they made. She studied Gil as he finished ordering his Easter dinner. Thirty minutes, she heard him say, the cheese-steak sub and small pepperoni pizza would take to get there. Her face was bland as she stared at her brother, thinking of the hypocrisy Gil shared with Jeffrey Borders. Jeffrey Borders, who wanted to be a part of her world as much as Gil once took comfort in his place and privilege in the world as a Giles. Look at him, she sat thinking as she clicked her nails as if picking them clean, just so superior now that he's tasted temptation. He has his *real world*, and she wanted no part of it. She just didn't want his smugness to push her patience too far.

Gil sat in a chair in the corner, the pained look on his face from a growling stomach saying his hunger could not wait. He'd try to put it out of his mind. Leaning forward, he asked, "So, how was dinner with the Van Dykes?" His acridity toward his momma and the slow food seemingly vanished in the way that fogs will inevitably fade.

"It was nice," Lucretia said. "It was really no different than any other year."

"Yeah, it never is," Gil said flatly.

Linda looked at her brother, annoyed, and prepared to take no more of his elusive yet uppity put-downs, of what, she did not know. But of one thing she was certain—they were, indeed, meant to put down. "What do you mean by that? You've always been more than happy, all these years before Sandra, to go to the Van Dykes' Easter dinner that was 'no different than any other year.' Why are you all of a sudden acting so snotty?"

But Gil didn't answer. Instead, he had a question of his own. "Have either of you ever had the least bit of curiosity about Cherry Hill, where our mother was raised? It's part of our heritage too, you know."

"Gil, I've never been to Cherry Hill," Linda said. "I don't want to go to Cherry Hill, I will *never* go to Cherry Hill, is that clear enough?"

"You've never been to Cherry Hill, you say," Gil said in that way that made him seem much the barrister.

"That's right, I've never been there."

"Well, maybe you'd be interested to know that you have, indeed, been in Cherry Hill. When mother was still alive, and our grandparents too, we used to go down there every Sunday for dinner. That's right, Momma did not invent the concept of Sunday dinner for this family. Before she came along we were having Sunday dinner at our grandparents in—that's right—Cherry Hill."

Linda could think of nothing to rebuke what he'd said. This was something of which she clearly had no conscious memory, so it wasn't her fault. At once, she had the perfect comeback: "Well, should I say that I have never willfully gone to Cherry Hill?"

"Why?" He looked equally at Linda and Lucretia, knowing that Linda's sentiments were meant for both of them. "Let me tell you something about Cherry Hill. If you think it's nothing but projects and a run-down ghetto down there, you're wrong. People own homes down there, nice homes. There are families who have been living in some of those homes right down there on the water for forty and fifty years now."

"There's water down near Cherry Hill?" Lucretia asked.

"Of course there is," Gil said, saying with his tone that she should have known this. "You don't even have any idea where Cherry Hill is, do you?"

They both thought for a second, but each looked painfully blank. Then Lucretia said: "I think you pass it on the Baltimore-Washington Parkway, don't you?"

"Yeah, you do."

"And I do know that Dottie Pettigrew-Van Dyke's brother owned a home down there that his son and his family still live in," Lucretia said, proud that she knew that much.

But Linda, unable to believe, said: "Who?"

"Dottie's nephew Sam Pettigrew. You know, he's a dentist."

"Oh yeah. Geez, I didn't know he lived in Cherry Hill."

Gil shook his head in despair, then chuckled. "Linda, there's so much you don't know because you all don't leave Momma's house long enough to learn it. Did you even know that those homes in Cherry Hill were developed after the war with the idea that black veterans could be able to afford a house for their families?"

They shook their heads in the negative.

"That's right, the men and women who bought their

homes down there were no less honorable in their desires to raise their families up in a beautiful home than the men and women in the Giles family. In fact, Granddaddy Giles once said that he had thought about buying one of those houses in Cherry Hill because they were so affordable at the time. He didn't, though, because he said the concept of it seemed too much like apartheid.''

"So why do people always talk about the projects in Cherry Hill?'' Lucretia asked skeptically.

"Because projects are there, Lucretia. Projects are everywhere. Matter of fact, they've probably got more projects down there now than houses. It's kind of sad, to tell you the truth, because you go through there and you see nothing but rows and rows of those low-rising projects that look as drab and depressing as army barracks.'' Gil stopped short, thinking he heard the car that would be bringing his food. He craned his neck to look through the window past his sisters' heads, but he quickly found that his stomach had played a trick on his ears. He continued: "Anyway, instead of holding so fast to your opinion of the place, you all should know that our grandfather was simply a hardworking man who came home from the war and bought his family a home in a place where he could afford one. The only difference between our two grandfathers, the only real difference, was just a couple of thousand dollars in the bank.''

"And family lineage,'' Linda said curtly.

Lucretia looked at her sister, her lips pressed impatiently, then said: "Every family has lineage, Linda. And you're right, Gil. I mean, should the fact that our mother's family lived in Cherry Hill mean that we shouldn't know anything about them? Is that *why* we don't ever talk about her, about Grandmommy and Granddaddy—just because they lived in Cherry Hill?''

"I don't know,'' Gil said, looking again out the window and finally seeing someone just unfamiliar enough to the cul-de-sac to be a delivery person. "I'll be right back.''

Gil opened the door before the man even rang. It all took

less than a minute. That's all it ever takes for a hungry man. Pushing the door shut with his foot, Gil came back into the room plopping the pizza down on the coffee table. "Have some, if you want." And back in his seat in the corner, he un-wrapped his sub, spreading the wrapping over his lap like a napkin, then chomped into his sandwich, the sweet smell of fried onions and green peppers, mingling with meat brought barely to the birth of charred, bursting into the room all at once.

With a mouth full of cheese-steak sub, Gil picked up his thought, talking, then chewing, then swallowing. "Tell me something. What if Momma had grown up poor, I mean really poor, and she had been raised in some backwater place worse even then Cherry Hill?"

After swallowing her bite of pizza, Lucretia said: "That's a ridiculous what-if, Gil, because we all know that Momma grew up as privileged as Daddy."

"That's right, Gil. That's why she and Daddy were so perfect for each other. They were from the same world." Linda said.

"Maybe," Gil said, chewing another bite of sub, "but Daddy married our mother long before he married Momma, so she had to be just as perfect for him too, at least in some way. What I'm saying is, suppose Momma wasn't what we've always thought she was. . . ." He knew that didn't come out just right, so he rephrased it: "I mean, what if her family's circumstances had been different than they were? What if, let's say on paper with all that family lineage stuff you all always like to talk about, she didn't really fit into the Gileses world. Would we not accept her as our momma? Would she be less deserving of our love after having raised us?"

"Of course not, Gil," Lucretia snapped at him. "That just sounds stupid. Why would you even suggest something like that."

"I'm just asking, that's all. Just asking," and he chomped heartily and happily on his sub while his sisters looked on in bewilderment. And he was satisfied, quite satisfied.

$\mathcal{N}$INE

Gil and Sandra had circled the block three times already. People waiting at the bus stop were beginning to notice them and stare each time they approached. This was the worst time of day to collect anyone from Eutaw Street, even if that someone was your mother. With all the cars trying to make their way out of downtown, and big lumbering buses picking up commuters, that block of the street had Gil right on the edge. He honked, called anyone in his way an idiot, yelled a few expletives, and drove right up on bumpers, only stopping inches short of a collision. "Where is your mother?" he snapped at Sandra.

"She said she'd be done at six. It's already ten past. I don't know where she is."

They were approaching the front of the market for the fourth time now. The people at the bus stop were gone. The bus up ahead must have just taken them away, because a new crop hadn't begun to sprout. Then they noticed a familiar waiflike figure looking in both directions, looking for someone.

"There she is," they said together.

Gil honked the horn. Sandra rolled down the window. "Ma, over here!" she yelled.

Camilla trotted to the car and got quickly into the backseat. "I was hopin' you two wouldn't be pullin up here with that little two-seater of yours, Gil," she said with a throaty chuckle.

"What's wrong, you wouldn't have appreciated sitting between us on the brake?" Gil ribbed. Camilla had an amazing affect on him. There was something about her way of being—the ease with which she lived life, the way she laughed, the way she didn't apologize for herself, the contented way she settled back for the ride after being on her feet all day selling fish and shrimp and scallops and crabs—that erased all the unpleasantness of going around in circles and sitting in traffic behind exhaust-belching buses. Something had obviously held her up, but she didn't offer an excuse, and neither Gil nor Sandra asked for one.

Gil drove like a race-car driver over to Eastern Avenue. The bridal shop was closing at seven, and if they didn't get there on time, he knew Sandra just might have been disappointed enough to cry. But they pulled up in front of the store with twenty minutes to spare. Gil parked after Sandra jumped out excitedly and ran in. He and Camilla waited in the car.

"She's so excited," Camilla said.

"Yeah, she is. I guess this is what every woman lives to do," Gil said.

"Not every woman. Just the lucky ones like me and Sandra." They both laughed. Camilla laughed the hardest and loudest. She slapped him on the shoulder and fell back on the seat, still cracking herself up.

"Hey, did Sandra tell you that we're going to swing by my mother's? Sandra wants to try the dress on for all of us at the same time. Even me!"

"No, she didn't tell me that," Camilla said, her laughter turning abruptly off.

"I didn't have a chance to tell Momma either, but I'm sure she won't mind. At the last minute, Sandra decided we would come get you."

"Gil, I'm just comin' from work and all. I look a mess. I can't meet your momma lookin' like this," Camilla said pleadingly, looking for any excuse to hold off the inevitable. In a way, it would be as embarrassing for her as it would be for Eulelie. This was as good a reason as any.

"Relax, we're just dropping by. It's not like we're staying for dinner."

"Oh, but still, the way I look will offend her, I'm sure. Sandra told me . . ." Camilla was trying to find the most delicate way to say it. ". . . well, what she and your sisters think about us."

"Oh yeah, well, that's all in the past now. Momma has come around and so have my sisters, pretty much. I think a lot of it had to do with the suddenness of it all. They didn't even know I was serious about anybody. Besides, Momma wants us to have the reception in the garden. Did Sandra tell you?" And Gil knew, even as he spoke of his mother's change of heart, that there was something about it even he couldn't believe. He and Sandra had spent a pleasant enough evening together having dinner with his mother, caught up in wedding talk. She played the string quartets for Sandra and made her really feel like she was about to become a part of their line. As long as he didn't think about it, he could believe that his mother did have an awakening of sorts, but when he sat quietly and listened to that part of his heart that really knew what was in his mother's heart, there was no way it could be real without a miracle.

"Sandra told me all about the reception, and that's very nice of your mother. It's just that I look and smell like I just came off a fishin' trawler on the Chesapeake, and I just think that we should do this another time, when we can plan for it. A lot of people don't like people just droppin' by, you know."

"Momma's not like that. She loves for people to drop by. This is Baltimore, remember."

Sandra got in the car and they took off, headed to something for which neither could ever be prepared. Gil didn't give Camilla's worries a second thought, focusing on the traffic and the music on the radio. Something about love being strange. Sandra was in her own, contented world of day-dreams about her wedding day. But Camilla was vexed. She could not imagine what would happen once they met again. Would Eulelie panic and admit everything, right there? Or would she be so good in her role as Eulelie that she would simply not skip a beat, greeting her with the subtle shades of snobbery and innuendo Sandra had come to know so well? Then, it was possible that Eulelie could break down and tell on herself. Camilla didn't know. Things could go smoothly in their own way, or everything in Eulelie's world could simply fall apart right there for everyone to see, and Camilla did not want to bear witness to such personal pain. All she could do was hang on to whatever shred of hope she had for the best.

That shred of hope was slipping away fast. By the time Camilla pulled herself out of her troubled thoughts, they were close to the Giles home. She could tell. In all her years in Baltimore, she had never known anyone in this part of town. Pretty fancy. Some parts were not as fancy—like the row houses they passed on Gwynns Falls. Row houses were nothing special. She and Eustace lived in a row house. Of course, the row houses on Gwynns Falls had porches. Where she lived, the houses just had steps and a door. But porches were nothing special either. Some of those people living in those porch-fronted row houses were just like she and Eustace. She assumed that for fact. Camilla knew they were near Eulelie Giles's house, though, when they turned off Gwynns Falls and the houses started getting larger—and farther apart. Big stone houses, big brick houses, some with a porch on the front, some with a porch on the side. More than a few had porches top and bottom, and some even had a porch that wrapped around the house. Porches, porches, porches. These were impressive porches. No one like her or Eustace lived in these houses or sat on these porches.

They parked. Camilla looked up to see the biggest house on the whole street. Her heart was pounding harder than the day she and Eustace sat before her mother and father to say they were in love. For some reason, at that moment, her father's words were haunting her mind. They echoed. They echoed. They echoed. *What the hell kind of life can he give you? He's poor. He's black as the night, and he don't come from spit.* She couldn't stop the echo, because she knew she was about to walk into the circle that was about to come full around for Eulelie/Doralee.

They went single file up the walk. Gil was in front, with Sandra close behind clutching her pristine white garment bag. Unaware. Behind her, several paces, Camilla dragged her feet. Her heart was a loud bass drum in her ears, and she heard nothing but the boom.

"Momma, we're here," Gil said, walking in the house.

In the living room, Eulelie sat in her chair, and her three daughters sat like obedient ducks in a row on the sofa. A woman who seemed to talk through her nose prattled on about the invisible life of London's Jews. Eulelie turned it off as soon as she heard her son's voice in the house. She didn't want to be torn between the story and Gil's visit.

"Hello, honey. We're waiting to see this gown, Sandra," Eulelie said.

"Okay, but first I want you to meet someone. We brought along my mother so everybody could see the dress at the same time." And Sandra took Camilla by the arm, pulling her from against the wall next to the door, where she had tried to plant herself permanently, and into the living room. "This is my mother, Camilla Hightower. Ma, this is Eulelie Giles, Gil's mother."

Suddenly, for Eulelie, everything and nothing made sense. Fate was more than cruel. It was downright evil and sadistic. How could it be that in this time, at this place, this could happen? It could not be that in all her years of living with another name, with another past, it would catch up to her—and in this way. How could it? She was so far away from what made her Doralee Washington that there was never a need to even keep it in the quietest corner of her heart. But if her worst nightmare were to come true, it would still be less horrifying than what was happening now. Suddenly, everything about Pepper Perkins was as clear as if they were each still in the past, living lives as disparate as the present. And as if she had never forgotten, the picture of a wide-brimmed, proper-lady hat ducking into a shiny black car blinked in Eulelie's mind.

Poor Eulelie, trapped by her past, her future up for grabs, nearly had her heart completely stop. The veil of horror slid over her face, first with her eyes, which were catatonically fixed on Camilla, and then her lips, like those of a mute, which moved as if trying to speak but emitted only silence. Eulelie had never passed out a day in her life, but right now, had she been standing, with her head full of feathers and her heart tethered to a stone sinking in her own sea of lies, she knew she would have fainted dead away.

She knew it had to happen. Eventually the time for truth had to come. She knew that one day, something big or small would force it out of her. But of all the ways she had imagined her children learning the truth about her, Sandra had never entered her mind as the unwitting bearer. And now Eulelie was forced to decide which was more important, truth or image, in the few seconds she had to think of what she could possibly do, now that she was trapped.

Then, just when Eulelie thought she would lose everything, something happened in those same seconds that baffled both Eulelie and Camilla. It was an act of compassion that only another mother could find in her heart to give.

"Eulelie, is it?" Camilla said, walking over and extending her hand, which smelled of lemons.

"Yes," was all Eulelie could say as she took Camilla's hand with her own, which seemed its own force, pulling Camilla toward her.

"What a beautiful old southern name. You don't hear names like that the farther north you get. I haven't heard that name since I left the South."

"Neither have I," Eulelie said, smiling quizzically but graciously. "Neither have I." And the two women stood, hands clutched in not so much a handshake as a lifeline. In her eyes, Camilla could see Eulelie's humility and gratitude and unalloyed terror. It was then, Camilla knew, that she was in it, initiated, a part of Eulelie's deceit in a way she had never intended to be.

"So where can I change into my dress?" Sandra said. "I can't wait for you all to see it."

"You can change in my room," Lila said, jumping up excitedly to lead the way. She may not have been thrilled with the idea of her brother getting married, but there was something about seeing a wedding dress that filled her head with pansies and doves.

"Wait! Wait! Wait! You mean Gil's staying?" Lucretia said. "No, Gil can't stay. It's just not done. You're not supposed to see her in her dress until the wedding day. That's tradition. You've got to go. Sandra, tell him he's got to go. It's bad luck if you stay, if you see her!"

"Let him stay," Linda said, almost under her breath, but everyone heard. She picked at a fingernail then looked into space.

"Aw, Lucretia, we don't believe in all that nonsense," Gil said. "It's jut a dress."

"Okay, well, it's your bad luck."

"Oh, I believe luck is what you make it," Camilla said, making herself comfortable in the chair across the room.

"You're absolutely right," Eulelie said. "I say the fact that two people can come together in this crazy world at all is all the luck they need."

"Isn't that the truth," Camilla said.

"Can we get you a cool drink, Mrs. Hightower?" Eulelie asked, her nervousness only slightly beneath the surface of obvious.

"Yes, thank you, and please, call me Camilla."

Gil left to get the glass of iced tea, while Eulelie and Camilla chattered excitedly about the wedding, still with a formality as if they'd never met. Was this the same woman who not so long ago would have just as soon had tea with the devil than bless this marriage? Now, here she was talking so fast and furiously about the wedding that her thoughts were barely formed before they came tumbling off her tongue. Their conversation was like a manic relay race. Camilla would scarcely finish a sentence when Eulelie would take the baton and was off and running. Lucretia and Linda sat as still as daybreak trying to imagine what could have come over their mother.

"Are you ready?" Lila called down the stairs.

Gil came back into the living room carrying a tall glass of iced tea and some sweet biscuits on a tray. "Yeah, come on down," he said.

Lila came down first with a da-dum-dum-dum rendition of "Here Comes the Bride." When Sandra got to the bottom, Lila said, "Here she is." She stepped aside and gave Sandra the floor.

Sandra rushing into the living room with a swish. "Ooooh!" she exclaimed with the giddiness of a little girl playing princess in a grown-up dress. "What do you think?" she asked, twirling and spinning, giggling and grinning from ear to ear.

"Oh Sandra, it's just lovely," Eulelie said.

"Yes it is, honey," Camilla said. "I thought so the day we bought it, and I still think so now."

"It's nice. It's really nice," Lucretia said, and that was quite a compliment coming from her, considering she had planned to observe in silence, along with Linda.

Sandra turned to Gil. His was the most important opinion in the room. "What do you think?"

"I think it's pretty," Gil said flatly. "It's pretty and I think you look very elegant." Sandra didn't expect much more from him. When it came to matters such as this, he was a man who only knew a few words.

"You know what it is, honey," Camilla said, scooting to the edge of her chair. "You're wearing the dress, the dress is not wearing you. You see that so often, you know, women overwhelmed by their clothes."

"That's absolutely right," Eulelie said.

With a blinding smile, Sandra twirled in the middle of the room, lace and tuille and taffeta whispering in a whirl of white. And with each revolution that smile, if only perceptible to her mother, became more and more feigned, her eyes ever more distant as they secretly envisioned another.

With her legs having returned beneath her, Eulelie stood and moved past Sandra, who was still twirling, lost in her own world of white. Eulelie motioned with her head to Camilla in the direction of the garden. "Camilla, why don't you come out to the garden with me so you can see where the ceremony will be?"

"I'd love to," Camilla said with enthusiasm, but moving with trepidation. She followed Eulelie down the hall, through the kitchen and the sunroom and into the garden. And when she saw it, her face said it all. "Oh, my! This is just beautiful."

"It's my little oasis," Eulelie said, realizing the pretense as soon as she said it, so she came to her point. "So, you're Pepper Perkins."

"Yes, I am. When did you figure it out?"

Eulelie laughed heartily, because it was impossible for Camilla not to have known. "When did I figure it out? Just now, in the living room, Camilla."

"No!" Camilla said, putting her hand to her mouth to stifle a large guffaw. "You mean you didn't know that day we ran into each other at Harbor Place? Because I knew who you were. I thought with the way you ran off so fast that you knew."

"No, Camilla. That day I was just running from the past." Eulelie paused. They were almost way over at the farthest edge of the garden, and Eulelie didn't want to say another word until they were well away from the house. When they reached the garden's end, she said, "You must wonder who I am. What kind of person I am. It's very complicated, Camilla, but there's not much I can say in defense of myself except to say that I wanted more. More than

Charleston could offer me, so I came here and got myself educated and married the life I always knew I wanted. Who I was born to had already dictated what my life would be if I had stayed there. I wanted more than a nothing-special life stuck in the poverty I was born to and letting that life suck the life out of me way before my years." Eulelie looked at the ground for a few seconds, then over at her roses. She smiled. They were starting to bloom. How easily she could be distracted from the pain of truth. Then she looked up at Camilla and said, "You know, it's funny. We were always considered to be from the other side of the tracks, and I guess we were. The ironic thing is that we were so poor our house might as well have been on the tracks. But I'm telling you, Camilla, there wasn't a little black girl like me in that town who didn't want to grow up to be like your mother."

Pepper chuckled, first under her breath, then loud enough for Eulelie to hear. "Life is funny the way it goes around, Doralee. My family wrote me off because I married an uneducated man who came from the wrong side of the tracks, and Sandra is going through the same thing with you acting like she's not good enough for Gil. It's funny how things go around, isn't it?" Camilla said nothing more about that. There was really no need for more words.

Eulelie could not look at Camilla. It was clear that their hearts were so different. "Camilla, there's nothing I can say to you that will justify the way I treated Sandra. She frightened me. Do you know what I mean? She was Doralee."

"My daddy's dead now. Did you know that?" Camilla asked, as if it had some bearing.

"Yes, you told me that day we met."

"Well, till the day he died he still didn't accept Eustace, that's my husband. On his deathbed he told me that the day I married Eustace Hightower was the darkest day of his life and the most disappointed he'd ever been in anybody. He said I was doin' nothin' to make the race better by stayin' married to him. And he was dyin', Doralee . . . I mean Eulelie. I'm sorry, I don't know what to call you."

Eulelie couldn't help her. At that moment she didn't know who she was or what she should be called. She was like a woman who had just had the memory of herself snatched by trauma. It was gone, but she stared, wide-eyed, into Camilla's eyes, hoping she'd find her name, herself, there.

"You know somethin'?" Camilla continued. "I think it's gonna be the same way with Momma. You say you and every other little black girl like you down there wanted to be like Momma. You have no idea what kind of bitterness you're wishing for. I have wondered, over the years, what that kind of bitterness does to the eternal soul."

Eulelie looked away from Camilla, then in a whisper that Camilla had to strain to hear, said: "It makes it very dark, Camilla, and very sad."

Flirting with the Apple

Less than twenty-four hours after she swayed and swirled around her future mother-in-law's parlor wearing a gown intended for marrying another, Sandra stood on the corner of Charles and Pratt wondering if what actually beat inside her chest was indeed a heart. In her mind she was Hester Prynne. Her head darted like a ravenous chicken pecking for feed, north, south, east, west. She had no idea from where he'd come. Sandra cursed herself for not insisting they meet at a restaurant, or someplace less public. City Lights, Phillips, any restaurant at Harbor Place would do, or even in her car, though that would have given it a low-down twang. Even so, they had to meet right in the open for everyone and anyone to see. She was changing her drawers on the front porch, as her grandmother used to say. But she wasn't, actually. This was so innocent. This was just a meeting about a sweater; business, so to speak. It was like having dinner with one of the lawyers in the office to discuss a case, she reasoned; except that never happened. Still, dinner would be like sitting across from an inconsequential stranger . . . in whose arms she imaged getting lost. An inconsequential stranger whose smile could melt the chastity belt off a Nubian virgin. No! No! *No!* From where did these thoughts come? These thoughts could not be. She loved Gil. She wanted to marry Gil. Gil was the one. And Joseph was a fleeting distraction. Fleeting distraction. Fleeting distraction. Repeat the mantra, she told herself. Fleeting distraction.

But one doesn't talk to a fleeting distraction for hours and hours. Night after night, from the day they met, Joseph called her under the guise of getting her to knit his sweater. And somehow they ended up talking into the next day about everything and nothing at all. They listened to each other's facts of life, and love, and family. They laughed until near tears at stories both embarrassing and simply funny for the sake of humor. And when Sandra gave to Joseph the secret of the moment when she had to give her baby, fresh from her womb, to someone else to love and raise, she put part of her soul in his hands. And in all those phone chats in the quiet of the night, not once was Gil mentioned. Never, in the history of sweater-making, had the process been so convoluted.

Softly, sensually, a hand that gave a lover's touch fell on her shoulder. When she turned, she fell immediately under the spell of the most resplendent smile.

"Hi," she said with a flustered hop. "Okay, so let's go. Let's get out of here."

"Hold on. Where's the fire?" Joseph said with confused laughter. "Where are we going? Where do you want to go?"

"Phillips, anywhere, it doesn't matter. It's just that I can't stay long."

"All right. Well, are you hungry?"

"I guess I could eat something."

"Great. Let's just go over here to the top of the Hyatt. We should be able to get a nice table with a view before it gets too crowded."

So they headed down Pratt Street. From somewhere, she

did not know where, the oddest thought came to her. *Somebody with a P Chased Carroll with a Stone*—Maryland signers of the Declaration of Independence. In a fifth grade history lesson this was how they were taught to remember the Maryland signers. Chase, Carroll, and Stone, but was the other one *Pratt* or *Paca*? She couldn't remember, and for some reason, at that moment she had to remember. It was an eccentric tidbit of nothing particularly important that jumped her from nowhere, but her failed memory was vexing.

Without looking at him, she said to Joseph: "Was it Pratt or Paca who signed the Declaration of Independence?"

Joseph looked at her, puzzled by the question. "I'm sorry, what was that?"

"Pratt or Paca? One of them signed the Declaration of Independence with Chase, Carroll, and Stone. When I was in the fifth grade, my teacher gave us a way to remember the Maryland signers: 'Pratt or Paca Chased Carroll with a Stone.' Only I can't remember if it was Pratt or Paca."

"That's pretty clever," Joseph said with a chuckle, not condescending, but charmed. This was truly an odd conversation, he thought, but he knew she wasn't just trying to impress him with her knowledge of Maryland history. "To tell you the truth, I don't know. I guess I don't know my Maryland history as well as I should."

"I don't know why I can't remember. I don't even know why I thought about it."

"Probably because of Pratt Street. We were just on Pratt Street."

"Yeah, I guess."

"Well, for the sake of where we are, and to feel a part of history, let's just say that it was Pratt who signed, *and* Chased Carroll with a Stone."

"Okay," she laughed, not the least self-conscious. "That's fair enough."

Before she knew it they were walking into the Hyatt. He put his hand gently on the small of her back as she went through the door. Probably out of gentlemen's habit. It sent a warm wave of comfort through her that she tried not to study because there was no understanding it. They rode up on the elevator that looked out over the harbor. For years, many years, she had driven past this hotel, watching the lights of the elevators slide up and down and wondering what it was like inside, up at the top. Soon she would find out.

They stepped out of the elevator and into a dimly lit hallway that was also somewhat of an entrance into the restaurant. The crowd was just beginning to swell.

"Two for dinner," Joseph said to the hostess.

She led them past the bar and lounge area to an even dimmer area where every seat at every table gave a perfect view of the harbor.

"This is really very nice," Sandra said.

"You've never been here before?" Joseph asked, sounding surprised.

"No. Should I have been here before? I mean, is this some kind of *in* place to be?"

"No, not really. It's just that this is probably one of the most romantic spots in the city, and I thought that maybe Gil would have brought you here."

"No, Gil has never brought me here. But if it's so romantic, why are *we* here?"

He had a lot of explaining to do. "Well," he started, with a reasoned tone that would attempt to save him from his own subconscious, "romance is about more than ambience and a beautiful view. When two people feel a certain way about each other, the circus could be romantic."

"That's true," Sandra said, her suspicion, for some strange reason, at rest. She opened her menu, found what she wanted, then closed it.

"You know what you want already?" Joseph said in disbelief. That one simple act, he thought, told him a lot about her, about the decisions and choices she made.

"Yes. I know what I had a taste for and I found it on the menu. Salmon. I wanted salmon, so that's what I'll get."

"Very impressive. It takes me forever to decide on something on a menu. I guess I just always have a taste for every-thing,'' Joseph said as he continued to peruse the list, frustrated by all the choices.

Then the waitress showed up only to heap more choices on his appetite. She rattled off a list of specials, one sounding more delectable than the other.

"I'll have the blackened salmon," Sandra said without missing a beat once the woman finished her recitation.

"The same for me," Joseph said, closing the menu and giving up on finding something he was absolutely dying to have. "Would you like wine?" he asked Sandra.

"Yes, I'll have a glass of white wine."

"Why don't you make that a bottle of Cabernet Sauvig-non Blanc."

The waitress left, leaving them in their easeful silence. Sandra was mesmerized by the view, and Joseph by her. He studied, as if committing to memory, every part of her—her eyes, which slanted ever so slightly at the outer corners; her quite substantial nose, which jutted down at a sharp angle then flared quietly; her lips, which, when held together in repose, resembled some sort of exotic tropical fruit filled with the sweet temptations of worldly sensuality. Then there was her, and all that her physical person emitted about the inner workings of her mind and soul. He knew so much about her just by sitting there and watching her simply be. It was clear that there was a peace deep within her that no one could disturb, and he had a sick feeling in the pit of his gut that Gil had no idea what a precious gem he'd found.

"So," she said after taking a sip of water and pulling herself away from the view. "You really do want this sweater."

"Yes, I do, ma'am. All I need to hear from you is that you'll make it for me."

"Yeah, I'll make it, otherwise I wouldn't be here."

"So you have to tell me how much you'll charge me."

"I told you, I'm not used to charging people, so I wouldn't know how much to charge you. This isn't some-thing I do for a living. It's just for fun."

"How about a hundred dollars?"

"For a hundred dollars you could go to Hecht's and buy yourself a sweater."

"That's not the point, Sandra. I couldn't buy a handmade sweater in Hecht's. I couldn't buy a sweater made by you, now could I?"

"No, I guess not. But I'm not comfortable taking a hundred dollars from you or anyone. So why don't we do this: Why don't we just let this dinner call it even. You're taking me to dinner, I'm making you a sweater. How's that?"

"Well, if that's how you want it, but I'm telling you, you're selling your talents way too cheaply."

The waitress returned with the wine, and a sparkling silver ice bucket. She opened it, poured a few drops in Joseph's glass. He tasted it, really tasted it, using his senses to experience the full flavor. "This is fine," he told the waitress. She poured both glasses then left. When she was completely out of earshot, he said: "I went to a few wine tastings and I act like I know what I'm doing."

"Well, you had me convinced."

"Really? That's funny. You know, I know that there are subtle flavors you're supposed to taste at the beginning of a sip and at the finish, but I'll tell you, I've never been able to do it. Like this Cabernet Sauvignon, you're supposed to be able to taste green pepper on the finish. It just tastes like wine to me. All wine just tastes like wine to me."

"To me too. Here's to wine. May it always taste like wine," and Sandra raised her glass with a lilting giggle.

Joseph laughed, loudly and almost beyond control. "That's really funny," he said, clicking his glass to hers. He took a sip, then put his glass down. "I really like the way your mind works."

"Oh really, and what do you know about my mind and how it works?"

"Well, I know it's quick, and I know it's creative and a little bit eccentric."

"Nope, not at all. It's just that . . . well, look at the way you just brought up, out of the blue, Pratt and Paca. That's pretty interesting. A lot of people hold themselves too tightly to wonder out loud about something like that—something so wacky. Most people don't wonder about those kinds of things at all. I know I don't. Yet, not only do you think about it, you think out loud about it. That's pretty cool. It shows that you're a thinker.''

"Everybody's a thinker. If you have a brain, then you're a thinker."

"No, that's not true. There're a lot of good minds going to waste because people don't bother to think. Many people just live by rote, you know. They get up in the morning, they do this, they do that, they go to work, they come home, they do this, they do that, then the next day they do it all over again without ever stopping to think about what they're doing, or who they are, or if Pratt or Paca signed the Declaration of Independence."

They laughed intimately, leaning into one another across the table, eyes locking in a familiar gaze. It was then that Joseph had to remind himself that in just about a month he would be sitting in Eulelie's garden witnessing her promise her love, her life, herself, to another man. And she had to remind herself of the same thing. They were flirting with the apple. They couldn't make it stop, they couldn't ignore it. At this point it was of an incorporeal nature, and fighting it was as futile as rejecting God's will.

"May I ask you something personal?" he said.

"Sure, as long as I'm not expected to answer it if I don't want."

"Do you love Gil in a way that fills you to the top?"

Sandra's head reared back. Her eyes grew round like tunnel eyes, trying to take in as much as they could in the dark. "That's an unusual question."

"But valid."

"Well, I didn't say it wasn't valid. I just didn't expect anything like that. Do I love Gil in a way that fills me to the top? Honestly, no, it doesn't fill me to the top, but I love him, and it's a love that's enough for a lifetime. I don't think you run out of love, you know, Besides, love's not something you just fall into like tripping over your shoes and falling into a pool or something."

"Yeah, I agree with that, except that I believe there's another level of love that goes beyond that. The kind where your life becomes a complete and perfect circle because that person is in it. I don't mean depending on that other person for a part of yourself or to be happy with yourself, and I don't mean that 'in love' business because that's nothing but infatuation. I don't know if I'm making any sense."

"I know what you mean. What you're talking about is a once in a lifetime love, and most people never find that. Most of the people out here who're married don't have that, but sometimes you have to take whatever love you find in this world. What you're talking about is the Rolls-Royce of love, and that's darn near impossible to find."

"I think people just don't take the time to find it. People are too busy deciding to settle on, as you say, whatever love they find, that they don't wait to see if that other metaphysical love will even happen to them."

"And what if it never does? What if people go through an entire lifetime searching for this love you're talking about and they end up dying single and ninety-five years old without ever finding it? Then what?"

"Well, it would be no different than dying married and ninety-five years old, having settled on whatever love they could find. It's the same level of emptiness."

At that moment their food arrived, which was a good thing, because Sandra could say nothing. The conversation had agitated her, but she didn't know why. Quietly she said grace, then ate her food without saying another word to Joseph. He had irritated her with his reasoning. It was stupid reasoning that made sense. What business was it of his if people wanted to get married with whatever love they found in this world? People made all sorts of bad love decisions every second of the day, and never had it ever come to be the end of the world.

"So Sandra, how does this work? Do I just tell you my size and then you can make it?"

"No, I have to measure you, or maybe you can take your own measurements and tell me what they are," Sandra said, figuring it best to lead herself not into temptation.

"That seems like it would be difficult. I'd rather you take them. Say, did you drive in today?"

"No, I take the Light Rail in to work. It's easier."

"Well, how about I give you a ride to your car, and then I can run by your place real quick so you can measure me?" Joseph said, innocently enough.

Sandra hesitated. "Okay," she finally said timidly. "That's fine. It won't take but a second."

By the time they reached Sandra's apartment, the day's light was almost a memory. The vague warmth of the sun's day-long work had blanketed the city with a gentle radiance Sandra wished would last forever. But even this moment with Joseph and the setting sun could not eclipse the guilt; the kind that made for indescribable restlessness. Then, as only fate would have it, her nosiest neighbors, a spinster duo of mother and daughter, were also on their way into the building. Fortunate for them they had their topic of discussion for the evening as they watched Sandra bring a man other than the usual—her father, brother, or Gil—into her apartment, with the setting sun. "Hello," was all Sandra said. They spoke politely, as Joseph stepped aside to let them on the elevator first. Providence stepped in when the other elevator opened. Sandra shot fast as lightning onto it. "Come on, Joseph," she said. "We can take this one."

Joseph stepped into the elevator and stood flat against the wall next to Sandra. "Is it my imagination, or were you trying to avoid those two women?"

"No, it's not your imagination. They're so darned nosy. Before the doors would be closed good they would have been asking me who you were, expecting an introduction."

"And what would you have told them?"

"What? I don't know," Sandra said, flustered by the question.

When they stepped off the elevator, her apartment was right there. She opened the door and let Joseph go in ahead of her. Pretty risky, he thought. "What if Gil were sitting here waiting for you to come home?" he said aloud.

"Well, first of all, Gil wouldn't be sitting here waiting for me to come home because Gil doesn't have a key to my apartment. So if he were sitting here, I suppose it would be breaking and entering."

Strange, Joseph thought, mighty strange. By all he could see—and he'd only seen a bit—there was no reasonable explanation as to why these two people were even together, much less about to marry.

"Okay," she said, "let me get my measuring tape so you can be on your way."

"Well, that's rude. Just put me out. Just tell me you don't want me around here."

"I didn't mean it like that," she said, her voice muffled by the closet as she searched for her measuring tape. "It's just that I would think you'd want to get on your way, having so many teeth to see tomorrow," she said, closing the closet door.

"It's nice of you to be concerned, but I don't work on Fridays. Since my brother and I are practicing together, each of us only works four days a week."

"Well, excuse me. It must be nice to have it like that."

"It's not bad."

"Okay, just lift your arms for me," she said, stretching the tape out. "I need to measure your chest, your arms, your hips, and the length of your back."

"Good enough. Do I need to take off my shirt?"

"No!" she said frantically. Then, in an attempt to recover, she said: "I mean, it's for a cardigan that will be worn over a shirt anyway, so there's no need for you to, uh, disrobe."

"There you go, talking dirty," and he laughed at his own joke. Sandra did not.

She stood in the middle of the floor waiting for him to stand up to be measured. Instead, he asked for a cool drink. She had Coke, ginger ale, and orange juice. He accepted the Coke. He watched her clink the ice cubes in the glass and pour the Coke from where he sat in the living room.

"Do you sit at that breakfast counter in the morning and drink your coffee?" he asked, genuinely wondering if people actually used them as they were intended, or if they merely added an interesting touch to a room.

"I don't drink coffee."

"Well, whatever you eat or drink in the morning. Do you sit there?"

"Sometimes. Why?"

"Just curious. Helps give me a picture."

Sandra handed him the glass then sat across the room on the sofa.

"So, tell me about your work. Do you think law is fascinating enough for you to want to become a lawyer?"

"Not you too. Everybody wants to make me into a lawyer. Yes, I find law fascinating, but do I want to be a lawyer—no, I don't."

"Hey, I don't want you to be anything you don't want to be. I was just asking."

She looked, in a bashful schoolgirl way, down at the rug. "Do you think it makes me a nonambitious nothing to want to just keep doing what I do?"

Joseph didn't know how to answer such a question. This was the first hint of vulnerability he'd seen her reveal. It made his heart smile for her to have let him see her in this way. "No, I would never say that. Who said you lacked ambition?"

"Well, in so many words, Gil and his mother. Gil has told me, a couple of times, that I should go on to law school and become a lawyer. He even told his mother that that's what I was planning to do."

"Why does he want you to be a lawyer?"

"Why do you think? You should know. You're a part of that black high society here in this town where what you do and what pedigree you come from is more important than the person you are. It's just prestige, I guess. It would be very prestigious for Gil to be able to say that his wife's a lawyer too. And I guess if I were a lawyer, maybe Eulelie Giles would be able to forgive my sin of being born on the wrong side of town."

Joseph sat for a few seconds sipping his cola, not certain of what to say next; trying to fathom, rather, the best way to put what he had to say next. "You know, there's always been something a bit odd, over-the-top, maybe, about Eulelie Giles. It's as if she's on some sort of self-appointed mission to rid Baltimore, maybe even the entire race, of people not born into money or a *fine* black lineage. It's like she's got some sort of personal vendetta against black folks without money and without a fine family tree. Personally, I think she'd be an interesting study for the psychiatric community. Believe it or not, though, her way of thinking is really kind of the exception as opposed to the rule for the people you call black high society people. Unfortunately, though, she's bred a whole new generation to think the way she thinks about their own people."

"Not all of her children. Gil's not like that, and Lila's kind of nice. She's not as bad as her sisters."

"No, Lila's not as bad as her sisters. She's okay." He swallowed the last gulp of cola. "So, let's get at this," he said, setting the glass, empty of everything but tinkling ice cubes, on the coffee table. "But just for the record, I think whatever you want your life to be should matter to no one but you, and anyone who bases your worthiness to be loved on something like that is a fool."

"I didn't say Gil was doing that."

"And I didn't mention Gil's name, but since you brought his name up, I'd like to ask you another personal question."

"That's fine, but the same rules apply."

"Fine. What do you want from a life with Gil?"

"I want what, I think, a lot of women want when they get married. I want to love him until I die. I want to be a good mother to our children, if we're so blessed, and I want to be the best wife I can possibly be. That's all I want out of life."

"And what if you don't love him until you die?"

Sandra gave him that smile, that smile that let this world know that she got its joke. "I don't even think in those terms, Joseph."

There was nothing else he could say. He was certainly not going to tell her that she was making a mistake. After all, women fooled themselves on a daily basis by marrying the wrong man. Why should he try to be her savior? He got up from the chair and stood in the middle of the floor, waiting for her to do what she needed to do.

Sandra stepped up to him, for the first time realizing his true height, his impressive chest. Is it hairy? She let herself wonder for the barest second. He peeled off his jacket and flung it onto the chair. A scarcely audible sigh and gasp rumbled up from deep within her, but Joseph heard. He asked her what was wrong. She claimed it was nothing. She put the measuring tape around his back, much like an embrace. It couldn't be helped. This was business. Before she could even take her arms back to read the measurement on the tape, lips, his lips, were pressed softly, moistly, against her lips. She didn't run from them. She didn't pull back or hesitate in the least. Sandra melted into that kiss that could have possibly been the longest kiss ever given and received. She pressed into him, feeling his desire, feeling her own. The kiss, with a passion not of this world, was finished off with tiny, affectionate pecks and a soulful gaze.

"I just kissed another man's intended bride," Joseph said, with two long blinks that brought him back to the present showing his chagrin over such a trespassing, such disrespect.

"That's not what bothers me, Joseph. What bothers me is that I kissed you back."

TEN

Eulelie's room had become something far more than the place where she slept. It was now the place where she lived with memories and fading photos of a slipping-down life. And the silence. It was filled with an overwhelming silence. Not the kind that brings peace or calm. Not even the kind that brings sleep, and certainly not the kind that induces coherent thoughts. That room's silence had become something of an albatross, but more than that, it was something she feared, something descending, like never-ending darkness, or death. At one time only she and the Judge lived in the wallpaper, the drapes, the carpeting, every single corner, and especially the wainscoting at which they stared every night while discussing life matters in what was left of the day's remains. Even in death he lived there with her. Now, though, the room had become invaded by the apparitional presences of Sandra, and Camilla, and Doralee, especially Doralee.

Suddenly, an overpowering, almost paralyzing thought came to mind—Christian fear. Most times she didn't believe in Christian fear. It was the bane of life and one's ability to live it. On this day, in her room, she believed in it as strongly as she believed the Judge knew all about her. The moment he fell into eternal sleep and gained omniscient vision, he knew she was Doralee. How did this work, this Godly forgiveness of heavenly life? she wondered. Did he forgive, and if not, would he ever? And did he know only from the day he died, or did God's vision allow him to see back into her past to the scratch and claw poverty? For the first time since the day she watched his black casket lowered in the grave, Eulelie did not want to meet him on the other side. God would forgive her her sins, but facing the Judge, even in the unconditional love of eternal life, was far too humiliating to imagine, at least on this side of heaven. Even in prayer, Eulelie was afraid to talk to the Judge. There was so much to explain, so much he would have to understand. First, he had to know that she truly loved him. The world from which he came, the world in which he lived, made it easier to love him, but the love was no less true. Maybe, just maybe, clear sight would let him hear that her deception was not as much about becoming someone else as it was about leaving someone else, everybody and everything else, behind.

Camilla, with an inconspicuous wink and nod, made a promise to hold tight to her knowledge of Doralee's passing. Why, Eulelie did not know. Was she being set up for a later blackmail? Was Camilla ensconcing her daughter's position in the family with the power of truth held hostage? Or could it be that her heart was kind enough, pure enough, and light enough to find a common ground with Eulelie's pain? Could it be possible, in the world that jades the soul, for someone to see past assumed malice to empathize with a soul in pain, a heart filled with the hatred of what's real?

Eulelie got up from the side of her bed and went to her chair in front of the window, the rocker that was once the Judge's mother's. If she could suspend any moment in time, it would be this time of every day. There was something about the way the sun crept into the room and lay on everything with just the right illumination that drew her here, to this room and this chair, every day. She slid open the drawer of the slender table that stood next to her chair. Something crinkled under the manipulation of her thin fingers. It was a bag of pretzels, from which she plucked one and began to

munch and crunch. She rocked once, then twice, then picking up speed, she rocked furiously, clutching one arm of the
chair, perhaps to keep from flinging herself across the room.
With the other hand she held tightly to the pretzel on which
she crunched with tiny bites, savoring every one. But she
kept rocking. It was as if she were trying to get somewhere,
or leave someplace. It was all those people in the room, all
those people draping her with guilt and making her wrong
with nothing more than their presence. They had to leave,
one by one or in a group, it did not matter; but they had to
get the hell out of there. That rocker had to gallop right
over them, Eulelie's weight and will crushing them into an
unrecognizable heap that would no longer distract her from
digging for words and strength.

Her children. There was no way to avoid telling them,
and they had to hear it from her. The pain, the betrayal, the
confusion they would likely feel would be enough insult. She
played it all out in her mind, as if it would take place right
there in the middle of her bedroom. She could see Camilla
in a fit of anguish over her daughter having been socially
wronged or slighted in some way, real or imagined, blurting
it out, her children hearing what they would not believe.
Besides, Camilla would say, *Eulelie, you're nothing but a fraud
yourself. That's right. Your mother's real name is Doralee and
in the real world she grew up so far on the other side of the
tracks they couldn't even see the train. Don't believe all that
crap about her coming from a family of Negro doctors and ministers and merchants. I knew her and her family, and her father
did this-and-that jobs around town and her mother was a
scrubwoman and a mammy to white kids.*

Her insides churned with the fury of a winter tornado.
She could take her chances, watch her step and her mouth
and her snobbery, hoping and praying that Camilla would
take it to the grave. And even if Camilla were to lay bare
the truth, she could zealously deny it all and deem Camilla
non compos mentis. *Gil, are you going to allow this woman
to revile your mother in this way?* Eulelie the innocent would

declare with just the right amount of righteous indignation. It would never work. Only the truth, and nothing but the truth, so help her God, would work.

Several knocks had fallen on her door before she finally answered. "Yes, Lila, what is it?"

Lila opened the door and stepped in with trepidation, holding a newspaper. "Momma, I know you're resting, but I had to show you this. It's Gil and Sandra's wedding announcement." She held it out for Eulelie to see. "Momma, is this a misprint?"

Eulelie skimmed it, and handing it back to Lila, said: "No, this is just how I wrote it."

Lila looked at her mother with plaintive eyes and drooping mouth. Disappointed. "Momma, Gil *and* Sandra are going to be very upset."

"Lila, dear, just get ready for tonight. I don't want to talk about this wedding announcement."

Lila left, leaving her mother to her solitude and her demons. Closing the door, she glanced at Eulelie's gown laid out perfectly on the bed and wondered how her mother, who'd be the picture of perfect beauty in that dress, would be able to explain the ugliness of twisting the truth with her typical ease.

She Flat-Out Lied

Camilla sat on the sofa with the weariness of her day throbbing in her feet. She plopped them, swollen and red, on the coffee table. What they needed, her feet, was warm, sudsy water. They needed to float, free of leather lace-ups and the gravity that kept them penned beneath 120 pounds of woman. She longed for that tub of water as she waited for her feet to deflate. Rubbing her aching shoulders, she could not wait for Eustace's magic sensual touch, which would do other arousing things to her. Slumping sideways onto a pillow, Camilla drifted into a swift, shallow sleep.

From head to foot, she was at rest. A soft snore whispered from her barely parted lips. She was floating and flying on feathers. Then a click and thwack snatched her cold from the reverie. It was Margie letting herself in.

With her heart just about in her throat, Camilla said: "Margie, you nearly scared me half to death, girl."

"I'm sorry, baby. I wasn't sure if you was cookin' and I didn't want you to have to stop what you was doin' just to let these old bones in." Margie sat down next to Camilla, slouching back as if to commiserate with her friend's weariness.

"Girl, I'm so tired. I know I *need* to be in there cookin', but I had to rest my feet. They hurt like nobody's business." She noticed the newspaper in Margie's hands. "What you got there?"

Like a bearer of bad news, Margie lowered her eyes and pressed her lips, then said: "It's the *Afro Gazette*. It just came out today and it has some . . . Well, I just thought you should see it 'cause Sandra's sure gonna be mad."

"What is it?" Camilla asked, taking the paper as Margie handed it to her. Margie had folded it to what she wanted Camilla to see.

"It's the kids' wedding announcement."

The picture of Sandra and Gil was quite flattering. Sandra was smiling, happy, at ease; he was serious, with a hint of a smile—difficult to read, but the essence of Gil. It was a short write-up, too short, Camilla thought, to possibly have enough words to make anyone mad.

Gilbert Horatio Harding Giles, III, son of the late Honorable Gilbert Horatio Harding Giles, II and Eulelie Antonia Giles will wed Sandra Camilla Hightower in mid-June. The ceremony and reception will be held in the garden of the groom's mother, Eulelie Giles, and will be officiated by the Reverend Albert Popper and the Reverend Warren Coles. Gilbert Horatio Harding Giles, III is a partner in the prestigious legal firm of Carmi-

chael, Cunningham and Giles. Ms. Hightower is an at-
torney as well with the firm Putney, Gaines, Woods and
Coombs. They will honeymoon in the Caribbean.

Camilla stared quizzically at the paper, then read it again. It was possible she had misread it, or missed something altogether, she thought. Her eyes were not misted over with the remnants of a heavy sleep, though. They were not playing tricks on her, nor were they blurring words. She looked up at Margie with wide-eyed confusion. "Why do they say in here that Sandra's a lawyer?"

"That's what I'm sayin', honey. They tryin' to make her out to be somethin' she ain't. Now, it ain't too bad bein' called a lawyer if that's what you do. But what they did was downright lie, and you know Sandra ain't gonna like that. Not one little bit."

"You right, Margie. Not one little bit." Camilla put her head in her hands, letting the paper fall into her lap then tumble onto the floor. "What in the world am I gonna do with that woman, Margie?"

The Beginning, the End

Across town and dangling from Gil's arm, Sandra was entering a ballroom that had been stunned by her brilliance, walking a walk that had no traces whatsoever of her natural gait. It was regal, tall, stiff-backed, yet fluid, as if she were hydroplaning across the floor. It seemed natural, but mostly elegant, even to those who knew she did not walk this way. There were eyes on her she could feel. Not every eye in the room—she was breathtaking, but she wasn't so filled up with herself to imagine turning every head in the room. No, this was not imagined, she could feel eyes, admiring eyes, longing eyes, aching eyes. Seeing them was unimportant. She knew they were there. She knew he was there. They reached the table, finally, where all the faces of society sat—Eulelie, her daughters, their dates (who stood for her), three miscellaneous well-put-together women and their husbands (who also stood for her).

"Sandra, you look positively . . ." Eulelie could not decide between stunning, beautiful or gorgeous. She went with: ". . . beautiful, and very glamorous."

"Yeah, you look great," Lila and Lucretia said in unison. Linda said nothing.

Stunning. That dress is stunning. She looks beautiful, the rest murmured.

She couldn't avoid them all night. Eventually she would have to look into those caressing eyes across the table and face the truth that was told in her own. Get it over with, she told herself. Only by looking into the face of the man who, just the night before, ravished her with a splendrous kiss that transcended her to places she'd never known, would she believe that it was all very real, and quite possibly, quite probably, really love. When she saw his face, she knew beyond reason that every single soul at that table knew what was happening to those two.

"Sandra, I'd like you to meet my parents," Joseph said. "This is my mother, Marie Crenshaw," he said, pointing to a buxom woman seated on the other side of Gil, who looked younger than her obvious years, "and my father Vincent." He pointed to the man next to her. Quite impressive. Joseph attached no titles to either of their names. She knew his father was a dentist, and his mother a college professor. He could have said, *These are my parents, Doctor, and Doctor*, but he didn't.

"Sandra, it's a pleasure to meet you," his mother said, extending her hand across Gil to clasp Sandra's. "Joseph has talked about nothing else but your incredible knitting since he met you at Eulelie's Easter Sunday. I'm sorry we didn't get a chance to talk then. Joseph, though, was quite impressed with you. He's just dying for you to make him a cardigan."

Linda shifted uncomfortably, then gave Marie Crenshaw

an imperceptible eye-roll. Linda laid a feathery touch on Joseph's shoulder, like a cat peeing to mark its territory. With exaggerated hand and head movements, she proceeded to draw the Crenshaws, including a distracted Joseph, into listening to inane anecdotes of how hard she worked putting this cotillion together. Sandra at least tried to give the polite perception of interest in Linda's chatter, fidgeting compulsively with the handle of her purse. It was studded with rhinestones, and the tiny bumps were the perfect playground for nervous fingers in distress. Quietly, her nails clicked over the gemlike stones. Compunction had her strong in its grip. She longed for the days when Eulelie and her girls were the only complicated element in her life. Now, sitting next to her future husband and across from her soul's lover, she had to face the intricate question of love's nature. Cursed the day she laid eyes on a Giles. Cursed the day she heard the name Giles. Cursed the day she took takeout to Hopkins Plaza instead of going to Bud's with the office gang. Cursed! Cursed! Cursed! Cursed, especially, Gil and the way he sat there fast in his claim to her. It all made her mind scream.

Joseph's brother Mark had tired, from her very first word, of listening to Linda. He turned to his date, Lucretia, and placed his hand over hers, which she had rested without thought on the table near his plate. Through a frozen smile that was meant to camouflage words, he said to Lucretia, "Your sister is indefatigable."

"If that's a nice way of saying she talks too darned much, I agree," Lucretia said outright without a grin to camouflage. She just wanted Linda to shut up. Lucretia's crooked mouth of exasperation said Linda was embarrassing herself and anyone who knew her.

When Mark turned himself so that she could take in all of Lucretia, she blushed like a child. His smile, pleasant and embracing, set off a tingle in the back of her neck that almost made her shoulders wriggle. She sat up straighter in her chair, but then was suddenly lost for anything to say.

"My ex-wife was a lot like Linda, talked a lot, you

know," he said softly, so as not to be overheard. "Mostly about herself, just like Linda. It was too much, sometimes. You're nothing like your sister."

Or his wife, Lucretia thought. This observation had to be a point in her favor, but she merely smiled and raised her eyebrows with a modesty far too innocent-looking to be anything but feigned. She wanted to say more in her own favor, but she chose to say nothing. Why chance becoming like Linda and the ex-wife? Instead she asked, "Can you waltz?"

"I know the steps," Mark said, laughing. "Putting them all together fluidly, well, that's another story."

"Yeah, it's the same for me. I don't even remember how I made it through my cotillion. Probably with a lot of stumbling over my escort's feet."

"Roger Pettigrew-Van Dyke was your escort, wasn't he?" Mark asked as if he wasn't sure. He was quite sure.

"Yes, that's right. Geez, that was so long ago." Lucretia gazed at nothing, thinking back on her night in white all those years ago. She thought back on how Roger was so handsome and tall and polite that night, but wished the whole while that he were elsewhere; and even now she remembered his distraction so well. "Wow, I haven't thought about Roger in ages."

"I wonder where he is these days? I don't hear anything about him," Mark said.

"Well, Mark, he was one of the lucky ones. He got out of Baltimore. Went as far away as he could, way out West. I don't think he wanted any part of his piece of the *Afro Gazette*."

Mark moved a little closer to Lucretia, in a way that said he wanted to gossip. "It's funny, you know. Dottie Pettigrew-Van Dyke talks about her son only when she's asked, and then without much elaboration."

Lucretia gave him a distant smile, as if she knew something. Then, without even thinking about whether she should say it or not, without editing it in her mind first, she said, "That's what you do when you're Dottie Pettigrew-Van Dyke or Eulelie Giles. You talk about unpleasant things only when they're forced on you, and then you don't elaborate." And she just kept staring at nothing, with glassy eyes that said she was thinking about everything.

But Mark wasn't going to let something that provocative get away without explanation. What was troubling Lucretia, he wondered, that would make her say something so acerbic? "Well, that was pretty telling," he said. "Would *you* care to elaborate?"

"No, Mark. It's not important. I'm just spouting off." Then she looked across the table at Lila. Desperately wanting to find her way out of her conversation with Mark, Lucretia tried with her eyes to pry Lila from what seemed to be a deeply intimate discussion with her date, Lionel Breckendridge, who, right now, appeared to be more than an escort; quite possibly a flame. Eye contact was not working, since Lila's eyes were fixed on another, so Lucretia said, "We were just talking about waltzing, Lila. Do you remember how hard it was for me?"

Lila turned to her sister with puzzled, almost agitated eyes. It was only when she happened to notice Mark looking at her expectantly as well that she said, "You were awful. Your biggest problem was knowing left from right. I remember how you and Daddy had a time practicing in the living room." She chuckled, and it swelled into a full laugh. Then, to Mark she said: "Yeah, Daddy used to say to her, 'Whatever you do, little girl, don't become a dancer unless you get a transplant for that other left foot.' "

By now Lucretia was laughing too. "That's right! He sure did say that. I tell you, Daddy sure could come up with them," and she just couldn't reel in the laughter.

Lila turned back to Lionel, who had caught the laugh attack. Then, laying her hand on the top of his thigh in a way that could have meant everything, but also could have meant nothing, she said to him, "I wish you could have known Daddy. You would have really liked him, and he would have liked you."

"He sounds like a great guy, from everything you've told me," Lionel said with a tone and an eye-locking stare that was far too intimate to have been pal talk. "I wish I could have known him too." Then he lowered his voice to a level seemingly meant only for Lila's ears and said, "And I wish I could have known your mother."

What was this between them? Lucretia wondered. When did this happen? She knew of dates, here and there, that Lila had gone on with Lionel. Lucretia had assumed those dates were just two people going to dinner, or to the movies. . . . *from everything you've told me . . .* And *I wish I could have known your mother.* There was far more than mere companionship going on between Lila and Lionel. Then, from nowhere, Lucretia gave herself an invisible smile and thought, *Lila and Lionel,* that's just so cute. She could just imagine the monogrammed napkins, and hand towels, bath towels with washcloths. And those two *L* names sang to-gether so mellifluously. *Lucretia.* How could she ever hope to find a man with a name that would sing so amiably with *Lucretia?* And then, in the second it would take her to shoot a pouting glare at Lila, Lucretia remembered that she was hurt. Because even though they never did, these were the kinds of things sisters should share.

"I'll be right back," Lila said, pushing her chair from the table with a haste that said she had just read Lucretia's mind. "It's time for Momma's opening remarks so they can start serving dinner." She got to her feet, then reached past Lionel to touch her mother's shoulder, at the same time noticing that Linda was still going. "Momma, it's time to get things started."

Lionel was left to fend for himself, so he stood as well, as if he had a job to do. "I'll be right back. I should go to the men's room before things get started." He was nervous, giving more information than anyone needed.

Mark and Lucretia watched Lionel speed-walk to the

door of the ballroom, and once he had disappeared to who knew where, Mark said, almost mockingly, "I guess they're pretty serious, huh? You can always tell a couple on the brink of falling in love."

Lucretia didn't answer right away. She fixed her sad eyes on Lila, who, she knew, had really done nothing wrong. And something that was not her will made her look at Sandra, then Gil, only to be reminded of how any of them had come to know Sandra. This is just who we are, Lucretia thought, we're strangers playing the role of a perfectly close family.

The lights brightened. Eulelie stood in the center of the room. Thanks to the Linda Show, Eulelie had not even been missed by that end of the table. She commanded everyone's attention with a haughty, high-headed stance and a strong, sharp, "May I have everyone's attention, please." She said more than a few words about the Black Barristers' Wives and the good they did and their purpose for sponsoring the debutantes. She might as well have been saying *blah-blah-blah*, *yakety-yakety-yak* for all the attention she received at her own table, especially from Sandra, who tried harder than anyone to listen but couldn't. How could she? No matter where she looked, she saw Joseph's face.

"I'll be right back," Gil said, scooping up his camera from the floor.

Sandra's head spun with the suddenness of his departure.

Then, like some sort of fabulous Hollywood photographer, Gil was snapping pictures, one after the other, of his glamorous mother as she gave her speech. He caught her from every angle, in varying stages of animation. That camera clicked and clicked until finally Eulelie gave him the look that said *enough*. Actually, she'd allowed it to go on longer than usual. For someone who was in the *Afro Gazette* practically every week, she always displayed an unmistakably pained discomfort at having her picture taken. She said it had something to do with stealing her soul. Gil never bought such old-wives-tale nonsense, but nonetheless respected her distaste for photographs.

Now that whatever it was Eulelie had to say had been said, Sandra's appetizer was put in front of her, but with Linda still talking, Sandra didn't even notice the food. She stared at Linda, stupefied by Linda's need to keep going, and her eyes narrowed with empathy and compassion that Linda seemed to be at the edge of compulsion by now; as if stopping were beyond her power. Sandra believed that Linda was actually trying to avoid the silence, awkward and thick, that would hang between her and Joseph if she stopped talking, and that if she talked without ceasing, somehow she wouldn't see Joseph's distraction. Sandra felt Linda's pain every time she looked to Joseph as if she were seeking something—an inkling of approval, or a hint that she was impressive enough to inspire infatuation. He was anything but forthcoming, and Sandra was convinced it was her fault. It was her fault because Joseph couldn't help himself, desperately stealing glances of her across the table; trying not to stare too long, trying not to get caught. And she felt immensely guilty about that.

Sandra saw Lucretia mouth to Gil, *I wish she'd shut up!* and she almost laughed out loud. How does she do it? Sandra wondered. Most people don't have as much to say about themselves even when asked. Without prompting, without anyone showing the tiniest bit of interest in anything about her, Linda spat and spewed out the kind of self-praise particular to only the pathologically self-involved. The oddest thing was that most of it involved insignificant details of the most pathetically uninteresting kind. And the poor Crenshaws, Sandra thought, stuck at that end of the table with Linda and her ego, looked desperately, hopelessly, trapped in interminable boredom.

The main course was brought to the Gileses' table by John Cobb himself. It was poached salmon, and when he put the first plate on the table for Eulelie, John and Lila shared a knowing smile that was so brief no one noticed. And the same subtle wink-and-nod smile happened between them when he brought out the cheeses after the main course—a subtle brie, a bleu, and Gouda.

When everyone had barely been able to finish the raspberry cheesecake drizzled with thin lines of a chocolate raspberry sauce, it was time for the debutantes. Lucretia had made her way to the podium to introduce the new inductees into Baltimore's black society. She knew she looked plumper than usual in a gown too wide for her generous hips, and with Gil right on her heels with his camera, knowing what she looked like from behind, all she could do was pray that he wouldn't snap that camera from back there.

At the podium, Lucretia's nervous fingers fumbled through the pages with all the debutantes' important information. They were in order, but she just needed to check and double check. Her worst fear was that with one mispronunciation, or announcing one name that actually belonged to another, she would single-handedly turn this elegant affair with years of tradition into one of those middle-class affairs where black folks made an attempt at class and culture but only succeeded at buffoonery. But those fears were never realized, as she took her time presenting the eight young girls, one by one, all dressed in white gowns that harkened back to the sweetness and innocence of another time. They were escorted by equally virtuous-looking young men with a clean-cut bearing that typified them as ones who wore their trousers snugly above the line of partition. In no time at all the debutantes' moments in the sun, their fifteen minutes of microcosmic fame, were over. The band struck up a waltz, and the couples glided as if they'd been born to this dance. It was unspoken, but nonetheless true, that no one else would be invited to the floor while it belonged to the couples. It was just as well. How beautiful all that black and white looked in motion.

"I would like to have the first spin around the floor with the bride-to-be, if you don't mind," Joseph said to Gil, in a way that was completely and amazingly without the longing he actually felt.

"Well, I was hoping to have the first dance with my fiancée, but considering I have the rest of my life to dance with her, I suppose it would be okay for you to dance with her."

Sandra's brow furrowed with shock, or confusion, or annoyance, or all of the above. There were more than a few facets to Gil's personality, but maudlin was not one of them. "Excuse me, but what is this, 1899 or 1999? I think I can decide who I want to dance with," she said to Gil with a demure smile that indicated she was both serious and kidding. Then she turned to Joseph with a coquettish flit that she could attribute only to the vamping powers of her dress and said: "Yes, Joseph, I would like to dance with you." She got up, Gil pulling her chair back, and went to the dance floor under the dagger-eyed glare of Linda.

Joseph slipped his arm around her waist and took her hand, gently putting their bodies together. That warmth, once again, went through Sandra from head to foot in less time than a heartbeat.

"So," she said, her tone sapped with jealousy, "Linda seems happy to be with you, and downright pissed off that I'm dancing with you right now. And that's an understatement."

"If you're trying to ask me if there's anything going on between me and Linda, the answer is no. She asked me to come to this thing, and my family has been supporting the Black Barristers' Wives Spring Cotillion for years. That's why I'm here."

"So she was coming and you were coming, so why not be each other's date."

"Something like that. Remember, though, *she* asked *me*." He paused for a beat, looking past her hair to see Gil watching their every step. "You didn't tell Gil, did you?"

"Tell Gil what?" she said, snapping her head back to look in his face.

"Tell him about making the sweater."

"Oh, that. No, not yet. I thought you were talking about . . . you know, the other thing."

"You are many things, Miss Hightower, but a fool, you are not."

He rubbed, gently, his hand up and down her back, then drew her even closer. The crack of dawn couldn't come between them.

"Joseph," Sandra said softly.

"Yes, Sandra," he answered in a low, sensuous tone.

"What do you think happened last night? What do you think that kiss was about? Why did it happen?"

"Sandra, why ask me that question? You know perfectly well what happened last night. We're falling for each other without a prayer of being able to get back up. At least be honest enough with yourself to admit that."

Sandra didn't respond right away to his adamantine tone and words. She just thought about what he'd said for a minute or so, then said: "So we don't have a prayer, huh?"

"Not a one in heaven," and he looked at her with a smile too beautiful to belong to a mortal man.

Sandra returned one, and it was then that they knew the point of turning back had long passed.

Poor Gil. He was not blind. He knew. When he saw Joseph pull Sandra just a little closer, hold her a little tighter, press his body into hers, he knew that this was not their second time. More importantly, though, Gil was certain that this was bigger than just the chemistry of attraction; they desired one another, and he was at a complete loss as to how or even if it would play itself out. Gil was certain, if Joseph had not already been with Sandra, he would be, and soon. The entire room had to know, but he was the one with his heart pounding in his throat as he watched, from across the room, his fiancée and an old childhood friend fall deeper, harder for each other. What was worse, all he could do was wait to hear the inevitable from her.

Gil and Sandra left in haste after she and he danced an antiseptic dance of one step, two step—two bodies awk-

wardly trying to flow as one but never achieving synchrony;
as if their souls were strangers. Nothing like the fluid movements that she and Joseph shared, their bodies content together. Gil drove her home without saying a word. She
didn't think twice about the silence. There was no counting
the number of moody, silent car rides she'd taken with him.
Who knew what set off this bout? It could have been almost
anything, or absolutely nothing, or something that made
sense only in his mind. She'd come not to care anymore.

"I'm really tired tonight, Gil, and I want to get up early
and go to the Farmer's Market with my mother."

Gil gave her a veiled response that said he didn't believe
her—one of those *uh-huh*s with the distracted intonation of
a question. Then irritated, he growled: "Don't worry, I have
no intention of staying the night. I have some things to do
in the morning myself."

He pulled into the semicircle that was the driveway to
her apartment building. Usually, when dropping her off, he'd
pull aside in the driveway and park. He'd say, *I'll see you
upstairs*. Not on this night, when something was gnawing
away, churning like mad in his gut.

"Aren't you going to see me to my door?"

"Sandra, won't you be okay? I mean, I'm tired. I've had
a long day and an even longer night. I just want to get home.
Besides, you have a doorman."

"Fine," she said, the insult evident in her every movement as she gathered her purse and adjusted her wrap on
her shoulders. "I'll see you." She gave him a quick peck on
the lips, her mouth barely lighting on his. She got out of the
car, still not believing that he would not see her upstairs.
Sandra didn't know if it was more appropriate to be mad,
or hurt, or maybe both, or maybe neither.

She got into her apartment, of course, without incident.
She walked past the very spot where she and Joseph had
kissed. The thought of him went through her like a curling
wave carrying off all that was pernicious, leaving nothing but
the chaste. She thought of his hands caressing with a touch

like no other. She thought of his arms as safe and warm as love itself. Falling onto the sofa to think more about him, Sandra kicked off her shoes, then inspiration, like a storm cloud parting the skies, struck. She pulled out a writing tablet and pen from a table drawer beside the sofa. Clearing her mind for an unblemished thought to form was nearly impossible. Her mind kept going back to that kiss. His lips, softly, gently, pressing against hers, his tongue shyly probing a place it had never been. His hands, one placed with only the slightest firmness on her bottom, the other exploring her back. It was a kiss that she wished had lasted forever—a kiss that made her want more. Another thought came to her. If this were a hundred years ago, their love would have taken years to grow to this point. But Sandra and Joseph fell in love at once with all the conveniences of contemporary customs. What they had was a modern love. Suddenly, she had her first line. Just as she was about to put the pen to the paper, knocks fell on the door. Soft knocks, but unnerving ones no less. A burglar or a murderer wouldn't knock quite so softly, she thought. Then she remembered that a burglar or murderer probably wouldn't knock at all. It was Gil coming back to finally say what was on his mind. He was the only man, besides her father, the doorman would let up without buzzing her.

"Who is it?" she said guardedly.

"It's Joseph."

Sandra opened the door with great haste. Her face said it all. On her list of the very last people she'd expect to knock on her door at midnight, Joseph's name would have been right there at the top. Or would it be the bottom? Well, he'd be on the list, for sure.

"What are you doing here? Why didn't the doorman buzz me?"

"The doorman was asleep," Joseph said, waiting for her to invite him in.

"So much for twenty-four-hour security. Come on in." Sandra closed the door and followed him into the living room. In a flash it hit her from nowhere. "Joseph, what if Gil had been here? That's quite a reasonable possibility, you know."

"Relax, will you. I saw Gil drive off. I would have looked for his car, and on top of that, I would have awakened the doorman and had him buzz you if I wasn't sure. But I saw him drive off, so . . ." He smiled so gloriously with his entire self while teasing her with a playful lift of his brows. "Anyway, what were you doing?"

"Well, to tell you the truth, I was about to write a poem."

"A poem? What else don't I know about your talents?"

"Who said anything about talent? All I said was that I was going to write a poem. Whether or not it's good or bad or if I'm talented at it is anybody's guess. I just like writing poetry."

"What are you going to write about?"

"I don't know. Life, its ironies, things like that. Nothing all that specific." She wasn't about to tell him the truth.

Joseph went across the room and sat in the same chair as the night before. Actually, the night before was his reason for being there. He had to know how that kiss was to play in his life. It was large, too large a kiss to ignore or pass off as lust or passion out of control. He had been struck by lust and passion before, and this was not it. He had also known sheer animal attraction of the one-night duration, and this was not the same. This kiss had to be a prelude to something more than what could become a longing for what might have been. And it was certainly larger, he believed for sure, than whatever it was she had with Gil.

"Sandra, listen, I want to tell you why I came all the way over here tonight. Last night something more than a kiss went on between us."

"Joseph, that's already been established."

"Yeah, okay, so where do we go now?"

"What do you mean? Joseph, I'm going to marry Gil. That hasn't changed, it just complicates things."

"Sandra, you could be so untrue to yourself?"

"It's either that or be untrue to Gil. Why should he be hurt because I fell for you? I'll marry Gil, and eventually you and I will become fond, hazy memories of one another."

"Or tortured fantasies of what could have happened between us."

"Look, all we did was kiss, and I'm not saying that it didn't mean anything. I'm just saying that it was a kiss that happened once, and if we're careful with ourselves it will never happen again." Sandra looked away. What she had to say next would be impossible to say with his eyes inside her—either because of guilt, or fear of seeing the truth. Somehow, she found her way to his face and said: "Joseph, I'm not going to break it off with Gil. So . . ."

"And I would never ask you to do that. Listen, before you walked into Eulelie Giles's house Easter Sunday and we smiled at one another like two old friends—no, like two old lovers—you had no idea this would happen. I had no idea this would happen, but it happened. I don't know what all this means in terms of all that spiritual, metaphysical mumbo-jumbo, but I want to see this through to whatever it will be. We owe each other that much."

"And what if it ends up being nothing, Joseph? What if we end up in a good, solid, buddy-buddy friendship?"

"Well . . ." He looked confused How could they ever be less than eternal lovers? How could she defile what was happening between them with such a thought? Anything in this world was possible, though. "Sandra, do you really think that's a possibility, or even a probability? I know I don't. You know, my father always told me and my brother that when we met the one woman that our heart and soul would recognize as a life partner, we would know it *immediately*. Well, all I can say is that I knew it that day in Mrs. Giles's living room, and I still know it today. I didn't know it with my ex-wife, but I married her anyway. I lied to myself, but worst of all I lied to her. We both lied to ourselves and to each other." Joseph was feeling desperate, knowing he was fighting a losing battle with Sandra's integrity, loyalty, pride. But he had to give it one last try. "My father told me that when a man is ready to make a lifetime commitment he will do it right away and without hesitation. It took me three years to decide to marry my ex-wife. I'm telling you right now, Sandra, that I want to be the one standing there next to you in Eulelie's garden. Well, maybe not in Eulelie's garden, but in some garden promising my love and my life to you."

Sandra laughed and laughed at the thought of the two of them in Eulelie's garden. Not because she couldn't fathom the two of them mating for life—when she allowed it, that picture was sharper in her mind than the actual picture that was always there simply by the virtue of the nature of things. She laughed because of the preposterousness of the two of them standing before a minister in *Eulelie's* garden, Eulelie flitting here and there playing the hostess, too mannered to tell them that their wedding in her garden was in poor taste, but still loving the fact that her son was nowhere near the bride. When she regained her composure, she said: "So why did you marry her?"

"Because I loved her enough. I didn't love her with my life, but I loved her enough."

"It happens. So I guess in a way, you were a fly at the screen yourself."

"I suppose I was, Sandra, but that just means I made a big mistake, because when the love's not big, Sandra, it's a big mistake, and a big mistake like that will make a bad marriage. I just thank God there were no children to complicate matters even more."

Sandra just stared at the wall, knowing that he was staring at her. "So, would you like to read some of my poetry?"

She'd shifted the gears of the conversation so fast, the question took him off guard. There was no way he would say no. "Sure, of course. I would be honored." He had no idea he was walking into an inquest of sorts.

"Okay, I'll be right back," and excitedly she skittered

down the hall and disappeared into the back of the apartment.

"May I help myself to a soda?" Joseph asked.

"Sure. Please do," she hollered.

Joseph clinked three ice cubes in a glass, *clink, splink, clinkle,* and poured ginger ale from an oversized bottle that had already been opened. Remembering Gil's fondness for ginger ale in that long-ago lifetime called childhood, he smiled ironically to himself before stepping to the refrigerator to return the soda. Joseph closed the door with a solid push that rattled the empty crystal cake plate that sat atop the refrigerator. He returned to the living room, thinking Sandra probably should have been back from wherever she'd gone by now. How long could it take to find poetry in her own home?

"What are you doing back here?" he said, walking slowly to the back, looking for a den or some other such space. "What are you doing, plagiarizing Nikki Giovanni?" Walking farther, he realized there was no den or office, only a bathroom, and across from that a bedroom, where he found her on her knees rummaging through a box she'd obviously slid out from underneath the bed. Not just any bed. This was a centerpiece of a bed, high, four-posted, and something he had only read about in nineteenth-century British novels—a feather mattress that promised to envelop weary bodies in a comfort akin to a mother's hug. It stopped Joseph dead in his tracks.

"My God, that is some bed! Where in the world did you find something like that?"

"It was my grandmother's. I begged and begged and begged my father for it when she died. It was the most valuable thing his family owned, and they only had it because my grandfather got it from this rich white family he used to work for. Daddy said they were just going to throw it out, but old granddaddy asked them for it. Can you imagine throwing out something this grand?" She told him all this while rustling through papers.

"May I sit on it?" he asked. "I just want to see how it feels. I've never actually seen one of these beds." Joseph wasn't making an untoward move. He was genuinely intrigued by this relic that had come from another century. "You're a truly fascinating woman, Sandra Hightower," he said, sinking ever so slightly into the depths of the bed. He lay back, because once on it he could not help himself.

"Why do you say that? Just because I have this old bed?"

"Not just that. It's everything. Around every corner there's something more interesting than the last thing. You're a real eclectic, and no one would know that about you. It's like, somebody could know you their whole life and still find out new and different things about you every day. Does Gil appreciate that about you?"

"Gil doesn't necessarily call it that, or pay attention to it. He just considers this stuff to be my way. In a way, that's all it is—just my way. Sometimes, though, I think he thinks I need to settle myself down, you know, like I'm a little bit flighty. Although," she added, so Joseph wouldn't get the wrong idea about Gil, "he does tell other people about the things I do in a way that says they're interesting . . . you know, like they're special. It's just that he doesn't really tell me."

"Ah, I see," Joseph said, coming somewhere close to sarcasm. "If a tree falls in the woods and no one's there to hear it . . ." Joseph didn't finish.

"What? What does that mean?"

"You know that trite question all those Philosophy 101 students are given—'If a tree falls in the woods and no one's there to hear it, does it make a sound?' I guess, in other words, if he tells his friends how special you are but never tells you, does he make a sound? You don't have to answer that. In fact, I would prefer it if you didn't. It's just something I thought of when you said that. Anyway, you're anything but flighty. And you know something? I admire your modesty. There are people far less interesting than you who're more impressed with themselves than you are with yourself."

"You mean like Linda?"

"Well," Joseph chuckled, "I wasn't thinking about her, but now that you mention it, yes, exactly like Linda."

Sorting out the good ones was taking longer than Sandra expected, so she had to keep the conversation going. She shot a corner-eyed glance at him, then said: "So, tell me something. Why a dentist? What made you become a dentist?"

"Lack of imagination, I guess. It was sort of the family business. It was the easiest way to get a job, I suppose. And anyway, my parents are from the *be safe* school, and what would have been more safe for me, and I guess my brother too, than dentistry?"

Sandra closed the box and slid it back under the bed. She stood up, smoothing her dress, and climbed onto the side of the bed. "Okay, here we go. These are the poems you can read. I had to find the ones I think are the best. The rest are not so hot."

Joseph sat up, picking up the one on top.

"Love Tears," the title read. "Hmmm, this looks interesting."

Joseph read eagerly, awaiting the moment when he'd see clearly into the window of Sandra's soul. *I lay it bare for you, my love. My Love.* He read with hunger from there on, only to get to the middle and understand that the first line had a completely different meaning than he thought was obvious. It was a love poem but not a love poem simply for love's sake. It was about love as ethereal faith. It was about the platitudinous nature of *I love you*'s and ruminations on love. The poem, above all else, was about the spiritual orgasmic heights a pure love can continually reach throughout a lifetime, the beauty being that it will transcend this world. This poem made him wish he'd read more poetry after reading the bare minimum that he, and most everyone else, read for that required English literature class.

As Joseph read her most special poem, with the transported look she'd always hoped Gil would get, Sandra waited impatiently. He read and read and drifted further up, or out, or somewhere. He was not there with her, or at least that's what she thought. Sandra shifted nervously, wanting to know where he'd gone and if it was to a good place. All she had to go on were his eyes, which danced across each word with anticipation of the next, and his hand, which tenderly stroked his chin, then rubbed his thigh. She knew when he'd reached the end. His opinion would, for a reason she did not know, mean everything. She knew it would be more than the passive *It's nice* that Gil gave her.

Joseph looked at her as if for the first time. There was a sadness about him. "This is just . . . I don't know, beautiful, fantastic. I know what I want to say, but nothing could relay the sincerity of how incredible this poem is to me. I don't know how much my opinion counts because I know nothing, really, about poetry."

"Thanks." Sandra blushed. "Your opinion counts, and it means a lot."

"The inspiration was, what? The love you have with Gil, or the love you had with someone else?" He hoped it would be neither. "You write of an ethereal love that's too pure for this world, you know."

"It's about my parents. The poem is about my parents and their love, I guess, as I see it. I wrote just about their love, not their story. Their story is not as much of a true love story as their love itself is."

"I guess I know what you mean. I mean, I don't know anything about your parents, but based on this poem, I sure would love to meet them."

"You're right, though. Their love doesn't seem like anything this world could ever know, and that's what I wanted the poem to say. Man, their love seems like too much to hope for and way too much to pray for." Sandra's eyes went to the floor, where the words she'd just spoken, the intensity of her parents' love, wrestled their way out of her subconscious, and sparred with all that was present in her mind. Those words had meaning for now and for then. There was power in their truth. Her head turned slowly, not by her will, but by something that had decided destiny long before. Her eyes lifted and fell, helplessly and unashamedly, into the two deep pools of his soul. The same deep pools that her mind, without being able to stop itself, had dipped into from time to time since Easter Sunday. There was no looking away, no pulling back. Their hearts had found their way to this place. What sacrilege not to follow.

What had metamorphosed from an incorporeal familiarity, to the earthliness of attraction and sexual tension, to an unfailing admiration, had extended up and out to a new and higher place of intangible intimacy that encompassed all that had come before. They knew that if there were no words in this world to speak, they would still hear each other, still feel each other. When their lips met softly, quietly, they surrendered to what had to happen. He lowered her back on the bed with ease, as if she were as fragile as fresh-blown glass. They smothered each other with an abandoned desire, not of two creatures in sex-crazed heat, but with a God-sent passion. Like a sculptor revealing what he prized most, Joseph slid Sandra's dress from her body so tenderly she didn't realize it was gone. With the lightness of a gosling's down, he ran four fingers over skin soft and richly colored to the warmth of nutmeg. She unbuttoned his shirt slowly, one by one, her passion mounting in anticipation of what she'd find. And then she saw all that she'd imagined, the thickest mound of dark curls on a chest that seemed as broad as a steed's. Then Joseph entered a place that, it seemed, no one had ever fully gone before.

The bed, old and full of creaks and moans, groaned with the weight of their desire and squeaked with the delight of their love. On this bed, this old twittering bed that could tell more stories than all of history, one more story was begun. Joseph and Sandra made love with a devotion that made every kiss, every touch, every embrace, every move of their conjoined bodies fuse their souls to one. Her body felt the peak of a pleasure she'd never known, just as intensely as it had once felt the worst pain. She was taken to a place within herself where the purest tranquility lived. And at the very moment when he became a part of her, and she of him, Sandra shed the tears of love she always believed were too much to hope for and way too much to ask for in prayer.

What's in a Sign?

She woke with a start, springing straight up on the bed to her knees with petrified, wild-woman hair, like someone had set her underpants on fire. Her heart was frantic in the blackness of a new day; her hair drenched in perspiration, her pillow no different. Eulelie panted like an overworked plow horse, or a woman taken over the brink by earth-shattering sex. She was desperately trying to get back the breath that fear had snatched out of her. It was more like a foretelling nightmare than a dream. It was real, too real, far too real, to be a dream.

Everyone was there—Gil, the girls, Sandra, her mother, and those same two strange, yet troublingly familiar women, who this time sat muted in the corner, their faces still shrouded like a secret, while the others gamboled round and round and round, like ring-around-the-rosy, singing something just as jaunty. In the dream they all surrounded her, except, of course, the women in the corner. She couldn't hear what they were singing, but their smiles were like bright beacons, their eyes like dancing stars. Skipping and tripping, some fell into each other, some kept in perfect step. She must have done something really wonderful to deserve such adulation. Oh, she was so happy in her glory. Then, like a distant parade moving closer and closer, she began to catch snatches of their song that was, clearly to her, one of praise. It was faint, so faint, too faint to make out the words completely, but they were happy words, she just knew. Slowly it came to her as the revelers yelled louder. *Eeee-eeee-eeee* was all she could make out.

Then, as fast as lightning can send the streak of death, the words of their chant weren't so important. Their faces, they were different. Their smiles, all at once, faded, faded, faded until she saw nothing but teeth, sinister teeth, devouring teeth. And eyes, their eyes of daggers, were as malevolent as pure hatred. Maybe it was the smiles, or it could have been all those spiteful eyes, but something opened up her ears, making the words to their singsong chant as clear as a bell. *Doralee go away, go away Doralee. If you can lie, you can steal, go away Doralee. You're not real all these years, go away Doralee.* The women in the corner held their purses and nodded their heads, as if sending silent amens to a pulpit. Eulelie didn't care about them, though. She didn't even know them in spite of their mumbled chants of *You know who we are*, over and over again as if their brains had short-circuited on that one thought. Still, they didn't matter to her, and neither did Sandra and Camilla. Their menacing faces counted for nothing. Her children, they were the ones who mattered. In the dream, it was their hurtful and hurt-filled glares that put a heaviness on her heart, which made her feel as though she were dying. As jolting as it was, that's not when she woke up. She woke up when a lizard, a chameleon, walked into the circle of ridiculers and began taunting her with its long scaly tail, its poking devilish tongue, all the while changing into every color of the world.

Eulelie got up from the warmth of her bed and went, shivering, to her dresser. Opening the drawer, she pulled from it a nightgown, it's whiteness seeming to glow in the dark of the room. As she peeled the gown she was wearing from its sweat-soaked cling to her body, she could not shake the terror of that dream from her mind. Her dry gown notwithstanding, Eulelie was chilled to her bones by the cool night air. She hopped back to the bed in three steps and settled herself under the comforter. The wildest thoughts raced through labyrinthine paths in her mind, finding no end, no conclusion. Eulelie had always been too practical a woman to believe in signs. Signs were better left to star-gazers and hippie-dippie artists waiting on some supernatural force to guide them through a life without purpose. On this night, however, the world of signs and fate made more sense than ever before.

In the blink of an eye, better yet, the waking of an eye, Eulelie Giles—widow of His Honor, Gilbert Horatio Harding Giles, II, highly regarded member of Black Barristers' Wives as well as the very proper Reservoir Knitting Club, and many, many other socially elite organizations that kept her neatly ensconced in the thick of the black socialite circuit—suddenly had more in common with the useless hippie-dippies of the world than she'd ever dreamed possible. On this night the world of signs and fate made more sense than ever before. This dream had just given her a sign of the Poe kind, and she knew it was best to take heed. It took her no time to drift back into a slumber, albeit restless, but at least she could sleep knowing what had to be done.

✐ Lives Change with the Sun's Rising

Sandra and Joseph were lying in the light of a new day. The breaking sun slid into the room, bringing the world and all its complications along. They had slept entangled in a lover's embrace and they awoke the same way. Sandra woke first, with a placid smile. Her smile was like her soul's re-flex—she really didn't even know it was there. Her thoughts were immediately of the most sublime night—the night out of which she'd just awakened after making a perfect love far too lofty even for dreams. It was the little things about it—the way he kissed her gently after she climbed to the summit of their passion, the way he looked through her eyes and into her. The way he loved her all night. The way his smile said everything. And his voice when he spoke to her, or simply said her name, made the heat of their love that much more intense. It was a new and unusual experience, talking during lovemaking. Making love was always silent, with only the moans and grunts of physical pleasure. But a stream of Joseph's conscious mind flowed from his mouth, sharing with her every emotion as he became aware of it. He laid his soul bare before her, and she her soul to him. Their love-talk connected them in a larger way than their bodies ever could, because when she spoke to him and he to her, having him inside her took on a rare form that separated them from all other lovers in the world. There was no doubt—they were making love to each other.

True lovemaking was clearer to her now than it had ever been. The truest of lovemaking was not about those few seconds of intensely explosive pleasure, delighting every cell in the body. No, it was about two bodies, two minds, two souls speaking to one another in the intimate and exclusive language of love. And because true lovemaking is never about a mad dash to the peak, it can be eternal. So they took their time, because the only thing that mattered was that their bodies were together, and she felt physically as one with his. She thought of all those people who called simple sex lovemaking, and how cavalierly they could simply say *make love*, but actually mean have sex. Even she had been known for such blasphemy, but never again. Loving Joseph gave her the clear-sighted understanding that to have a man enter her body with deep affectionate love, respect, spiritual intimacy, and ethereal passion was second to nothing earthbound copulation had to offer.

Sandra flexed her foot and yawned with a quiet, contented sigh, waking Joseph.

"Good morning," he said, kissing her on the top of her head.

"Hi." She giggled like a virgin. "I mean, good morning."

"How do you feel?"

"I feel loved," Sandra said, without having to give it a second's thought.

"You are loved," he said, kissing her head again. Joseph

closed his eyes and replayed their lovemaking. Thinking about the way her body uncontrollably quivered with the pleasure of their bodies moving as one, the way her touch aroused him to even higher peaks, the way she loved him all night, made his heart quicken just as it had when they made love. When reality floated rudely into the midst of his musings, his lightness of being changed to something too heavy, too painful to bear alone. "Sandra, you know that what happened last night changes everything. I made love to another man's fiancée."

Sandra said nothing for several uneasy seconds. She snuggled closer to him and tugged nervously at the sheet. "Well, Joseph, that's not what bothers me. What bothers me is that I don't feel guilty. I just feel loved. Gil will never understand something so complicated as this." She paused, then sat straight up. Turning to face Joseph, she said: "Maybe he doesn't have to understand it. But he has to accept it."

The phone rang and they both stared at it like frightened deer staring down the muzzle of a rifle. It was clear to both of them who was calling. Who else would it be? And why would fate have played this scene any less clichéd? Reaching past Joseph, Sandra picked up the phone. "Hello," she said in her usual cheery, morning voice, trying to sound as natural as possible.

The voice on the other end, her mother, was apologetic for calling so early after Sandra's late night out, but she had news Sandra would not like. Sandra had to know, she would want to know, Camilla told her. She read the wedding announcement over the phone while Sandra listened with rapt attention, feeling compelled to do so by her mother's troubled voice.

"Ma, say that again, the part about me being a lawyer."

Camilla read it again, while Sandra sat in stilled silence.

"Oh my God, the woman just plain-out lied. Why would she do something like that? She's sick! And this is just about the sickest thing I've ever heard of!" Then Sandra looked over at Joseph, who was watching her with confusion. He stroked her head, her back, her shoulders, not knowing why she was in need, just knowing that she needed it, needed him. Sandra reached up and touched his face with feathery fingertips. A blanket of calm enveloped her. Smiling, she said to her mother: "You know what, Ma, don't even worry about it. There's something I want to talk to you about anyway, and it has to do with this very situation. I'll be over later." She hung up and laid her head on Joseph's chest.

"What's up? What's going on?" Joseph asked.

"Well, Eulelie Giles is at it again. She put the wedding announcement in the paper, and in it it says that I'm a *lawyer* with the firm I work at."

"Sandra, if you had told me that it was anybody other than Eulelie Giles, I would be surprised, but nothing she does surprises me, and it shouldn't surprise you either. On the other hand, I don't think this is something you should let go. She needs to be called on this."

As Sandra lay there thinking about the shame that would drive a woman to such lies, the fog in her mind lifted. What had to happen became clearer. Everything had changed, nothing would be the same, and Gil had to know, sooner rather than later.

What she didn't know was that Gil was already up to speed. As she lay there, moments away from making morning love with Joseph, pulling away from the curb down on the street was Gil, who had sat there all night while she and Joseph took each other to a place Gil had never, ever tried to reach.

ELEVEN

~ You Think You've Got Problems

Lila pulled into the parking lot alongside Gil's car. The scene was uncomfortably familiar as she prepared herself, once again, to step inside the bar. This time, though, she didn't just happen on Gil's car. Lila went there looking for her brother. He was the only one she could trust with her problem. She couldn't talk to her sisters. How could they understand with their heads in the sand? Talking to her mother would not only be useless, it would be self-destructive. Gil would understand. He lived in the world. Only her brother would know exactly how she felt.

She walked through the lot, looking around in a halting way. Paranoid. As badly as she needed her brother, she did not want to be seen going into this bar twice in her life. Opening the door, she stepped inside, the din of the crowd, the smell of the smoke, the dimness of the room hitting her all at once. When her eyes became accustomed to the gloom, she looked around for Gil, but she didn't have to look far. He was there, where he always sat, at the bar, third seat from the end.

Lila went up to him with slight trepidation. Gil looked as if he had been deprived of sleep, maybe even food, and in all probability a bath. "Gil," she said timidly, gently touching his shoulder.

Startled, Gil turned with a jittery jerk. "Oh, you. What are you doing here?" he asked matter-of-factly.

"I need to talk to you about something, but you look as if you have your own problems. Gil, you look awful. What's wrong?"

"Look, Lila, I'm okay, and if you've come here to put Sandra down, believe me—"

"That's not why I'm here, Gil. Besides, that train has moved on. Momma knows now that you love Sandra and you're determined to marry her. Whether she likes it or not doesn't matter. At least she knows that she has to accept it."

"Then why *are* you here?"

"Because I have something I need to talk to you about." Lila paused, took a deep breath, and for the first time actually gave voice to what had been only in her mind for far too long. "Gil, I want to move out. I want my own apartment."

"Well, move out, Lila." Gil chuckled, thinking about the irony of her bringing to him, on the worst day of his life, a solvable problem.

"Gil, now you know it's not that simple. You remember how Momma carried on when you came back to Baltimore from law school and moved into your own place. She ran every guilt trip in the book on you. You were leaving four women without a man in the house, she said. You were going to cause her to worry herself into an early grave, she said. The guilt was awful, Gil, don't you remember?"

"Yeah, Lila, I remember, but that was six years ago. Almost seven. Momma, I'm sure, will be more reasonable now. Tell me this, though, why do you want to move out now? I mean, what took you so long?"

"I can't say it's one thing. It's a lot of things, but mainly it's just that I'm twenty-eight years old. I don't need to still be living with my mother. On the rare occasion that I meet a man I wouldn't mind dating, they're turned off because I still live at home. I want to get married, Gil, but first I've got to get a life for myself, you know."

"I thought your life was already full. I thought all of your lives were full," Gil said facetiously. "I thought all any of you needed were each other. This family."

"Gil, don't act like that. I know that we're like spoiled little princesses, but in the real world men don't marry spoiled little princesses, at least not anymore. They also don't marry women who lean on family lineage for their self-identity—a pedigree that's larger than herself, larger than all of us, Gil."

Lila took off her suit jacket and ordered a drink. Actually, just a seltzer—with a twist. In its way, it was a drink. She looked over at Gil while she waited for her fizzy water. He was drinking like a man who wanted to get drunk fast. Her brother, her always impeccable, never-seen-without-a-crisp-shirt, never-went-a-day-without-shaving brother, looked as if the last twenty-four hours had not been very kind to him.

"Gil, forgive me for stating the obvious, but you look like crap. What's going on? What in the world is wrong?"

"Lila, have you ever wondered how we would have turned out if our mother hadn't died?"

"No, not really, Gil. I don't think about that stuff. I don't really think about our mother." Lila looked away from Gil because she knew she had to offer an explanation for such heartlessness. She had a reason, all right, a good reason for not thinking about her mother; she just never set the actual words free into the universe. Turning back to Gil with bashful eyes that looked past his rather than in them, she told him a truth she'd kept since childhood. "I don't think about our mother because Momma always made me feel like I was doing something dirty by talking about her. Momma made me feel like if I even thought about our mother, I would be betraying *her* in some way."

"You think you're alone with that?" he said with an ironic chuckle. "Wake up, Lila. All of us probably feel that way. I know I do. I've never asked Momma about Mother, I rarely even mention her at all, except when I want to make a point, you know, get her goat. I just think about what I remember about her."

"You remember Mother? I never knew that."

There was no reason for Lila to know about Gil's memo-

ries of their mother. They didn't talk to Eulelie about their
mother, true, but they never talked to each other about her
either. Gil was shocked by his sister's shock. After all, he
was six when his mother died. Of course he'd remember
her. Lila sat completely under the spell of Gil's stories as he
told her of the way their mother made up songs with their
names and sang those homemade songs to them whenever
they were sad. In fact, she sang not only when they were
sad. She would make up songs for any reason, or no reason
at all. He remembered one of his songs she'd sing whenever
he'd act silly: *Silly Gilly, my boy Gilly is acting like a silly
billy goat. Yay!* Lila laughed along with Gil, but she wanted
to hear one of the songs made up about her. She bounced
in her seat like a child begging for sweet treats.

"Please, Gil, think hard. Try to remember something she
would sing to me."

Gil thought hard, and it showed on his creased face.
There was one that was coming to him slowly. It was something about lilies. He had it, finally: *Lila Lily, Lila Lily, my
Lila makes me think of lilies. Lila Lily, Lila Lily, my Lila is a
sweet little lily.*

"That's a beautiful song," Lila said. Bouncing again, she
excitedly asked, "What else? What else about Mother?"

Gil told her how he remembered that their mother loved
lavender, the scent, that is, and she wore it all the time.
When he was fifteen and on a class trip to the Smithsonian,
he remembered leaving the class to follow an older black
woman who breezed past him smelling of lavender. He
caught her just as she was about to enter the ladies' room,
and that's when he knew the name of the scent that had
haunted him since his mother's death. For that whole year
he was obsessed with lavender. In the market with Eulelie,
he would sneak off and buy lavender soap with his allowance. Whenever he found anything that smelled of lavender,
he'd get it and squirrel it away in the red shoe box he kept
with other boxes on his bookshelf, or under his bed, or on
the shelf of his windowsill, or on the corner shelf of his

closet, wherever it could be the least conspicuous. He would take it out and smell its contents whenever he wanted to remember his mother.

"You know, I still have that box of lavender stuff, and I still take it out and smell it whenever I want to think about her." Gil took a sip of his fourth drink. Staring down into the sparkling glass of golden liquid, he remembered something else Lila would like to know. "You know, on Sunday afternoons, after church and after dinner at our grandparents'—at least I think it was dinner, it was a big meal—anyway, us kids would be so hyper, running around and making noise, so she would put us all in the car and drive us out to BWI—of course back then it was called Friendship Airport—and we would watch the planes take off."

"I sort of remember doing that."

"Yeah, that was fun. She would watch those planes take off, and you could just tell that she wanted to be on one. I remember the last Sunday she took us out there. She told us that she had never been on a plane in her whole life, but always wanted to. Then she said that we would be so much luckier than she ever was because we would take so many plane rides. When I think back on that day, it makes me think that she knew she was dying. She was so small and frail, and I think she was weak. I think she knew she wasn't going to live long enough to ever take a ride on an airplane."

Lila stared off as if in a daze, with Gil's memories floating in her mind. Then she said: "Yeah, I wonder what we would have been like, what life would have been like, if Mother hadn't died."

Then Lila came up with a memory of her own. Not of their mother, but of their momma. It was the first week of summer and the first of many, many more Sundays that the Crenshaws would join them for dinner. After church, Eulelie dressed the children in their play clothes—Gil in a pair of navy-blue, Little Lord Fauntleroy suspendered short pants and a blindingly white shirt, the girls in the same pale pink eyelet sundresses. Gil, Joseph, and Mark traded baseball cards and marbles on the porch. The three girls played with dolls in the yard. Lila was always the mother. So when it came time to fix dinner for her husband (Lucretia) and her daughters (Linda and three dolls), she went around to the side of the house, dug some of the earth in Eulelie's garden, turned on the hose and made mud pies. When she returned to her family with the pies, her dress was covered with the ingredients—mud. All over the skirt of her dress was mud, caked in some spots, thinner in others. But she continued to play, oblivious to her messy dress until she heard: "Lila Maria Giles, you come in this house right now." Lila turned with a frightened jerk, her face flattened with fear. She figured she'd done something wrong, but what, she wouldn't know until she reached a tight-faced Eulelie.

Eulelie stood on the porch, hands held in hard fists at her sides. She fussed in a high pitch, almost loud enough for the neighbors to hear, but Lila could not seem to catch a word of her diatribe. She was deaf from fright. When Lila reached the porch, she was in tears, knowing she was in trouble, knowing she was going to get her legs smacked, but not knowing why. The smack was stinging, the words were too: "Why can't you ever play without looking like a little pig that's been rolling around in slop?" Then she was dragged, crying, into the house by her bony little arm. Eulelie stood her in the hall, in full view of every grown-up in the parlor, and continued to chastise her. "I buy you such beautiful clothes, and what do you do? You go out and smear dirt all over them. Now you go upstairs and change into something else. And you stop that crying too."

Lila remembered climbing the stairs with the heaviness of humiliation dragging her down. Not only did Eulelie embarrass her in front of Joseph and Mark, but also in front of their parents. She heard her father's voice challenge Eulelie's reprimand: "She's just a little girl who wants to play, Eulelie. If you didn't want her to get the dress dirty, you shouldn't have put it on her and sent her out to play."

Eulelie, unwilling to accept his challenge to her mothering, rebuked with: "Gilbert, if you're not going to support me as their mother, then I might as well just give up. I'm trying to get that girl to be more responsible so that the other two can learn from her. I'm just trying to teach her how to appreciate and take care of her clothes. What will people think if they come here to find our children covered with mud like common street urchins?"

When Lila heard her father say, "Fine Eulelie," in a tone that bespoke total surrender, she knew then and there that life with Momma Eulelie would not be easy. She closed her door and shook with big sobs until her clothes were changed, then went back downstairs with the perfect little girl smile.

When Lila finished her turn on memory lane, she saw Gil grinning. Actually, it was more of a mocking smirk that could have been influenced by almost anything from that awful day in Lila's life. Before she could even ask, Gil stood up, tossed a twenty and a five on the bar, and gestured to Curtis that he was leaving.

"All right man, you stay cool. I'll see you again," Curtis said.

"Yeah, you bet," he said to Curtis. Then to Lila, he said: "Well, speaking of Joseph Crenshaw, I've got to go and meet Sandra. I'll see you."

She tried to ask him why Joseph and Sandra had anything to do with one another, why their names were in the same breath, but the words could not make it out of her gaping mouth in time. Her head spun with possibilities. Before she knew it, though, Gil was gone and her moment for clarity was lost. Just as she was about to settle up, a familiar figure appeared in her eye's corner. Her head snapped around, only to find him staring directly at her. It was Pick, alone in a corner, sipping on some sort of frothy drink with a floating umbrella. She waved. He nodded, then smiled. Somehow Pick, sitting there in the corner of a bar, no one with him, no one around him, fit the stereotype of a private eye. The corner wasn't smoky, nor was it any more dimly lit than the rest of the bar, as so many spy movies would have it. Still, the cliché of the image could not have been more perfect.

She paid her check, leaving Curtis a tip so generous it was on the border of gauche. For some reason it was important that Curtis not think that she, Gil's sister, had no respect for his services. She walked, but wanted to run, over to Pick.

"This is a surprise, albeit a pleasant one," she said.

"Well, I have to say, of all the places I would expect to see you, this would be about the last one on the list. I know your brother hangs out here a lot."

"How do you know my brother? Oh, that's right, I forgot." She tapped her finger on the table with the anxiety of the attraction she felt, a little bit sexual but mostly plain old curiosity, still as fresh as the day she walked through the mall with him, an unwilling player in her mother's spying game; the same attraction that compelled her to lure him, falsely, to a downtown restaurant. Lila had put her jacket on at the bar, but her pounding heart was sending a rush of heat through her that made the jacket, lightweight and cotton, unbearable. She took it off.

"So, what are you doing here?" Pick asked.

"I needed to talk to my brother and I figured I could find him here."

"Still trying to get Sandra out of his life, huh?"

"Oh, no, that's happening, you know, the wedding. We've all pretty much accepted that. I had to talk to him about something else. I'm going to move out and get my own place." Lila looked away at nothing in particular. Shame would not let her look him in the eye. "You're probably thinking, 'Why is she still living at home with her mother, as old as she is?' "

"No, I'm not thinking anything like that. And, by the way, I have no idea how old you are, and before you ask, don't ask me to guess. I don't pass judgment so easily."

"But in your line of work, isn't it your business to pass judgment?"

"If I just looked at the surface of what I find about people, sure, but I don't. If a man cheats on his wife or a woman cheats on her husband, infidelity is just the surface issue. There are generally layers of circumstances that lead to it. To just say this guy's a bastard or this woman's a two-bit tramp for cheating is making a value judgment no one has the right to make."

Lila could only wrap her mind part of the way around such liberal generosity. Day used to be only day and night used to be only night. And now there was dawn and there was dusk, sort of wrong and almost right; except when it came to certain unforgivables like lying and cheating and treachery. She didn't think Roger Pettigrew-Van Dyke abominable for being a pimp, but she thought his mother abominable for lying about it. Pick had to know that life made sense only within the stark parameters of her closed mind when it came to such matters, so she said, "But when anybody cheats on anybody, that's just wrong, I'm sorry."

"Look, when a man cheats, it's usually about sex, rarely for love, but still, sex is a very basic human need, especially for men. If his wife does not want him in bed, he either lives a celibate life for the sake of staying true to his vows, or he satisfies a human appetite that God gave us. Same with women. When a woman cheats, it's usually about love, rarely for sex. Who doesn't need to be loved? If her husband does not give her love, or even if she thinks that she's not loved, she either spends her life in a loveless marriage or satisfies a very human and important appetite that God also gave us."

None of this made sense to her. The words, of course, she understood, but not their point of origin. "How can you say that everybody needs love when you said yourself, that time in the mall, that you're better off being alone? Well, nobody can truly love you if they're not with you."

"Yeah, well, I suppose what I should have told you is that I'm wise enough to wait until everything is right—you know, the right time, the right woman. That way, no mistakes are made and no one gets hurt."

"So, you believe in soul mates?"

"I believe in something like that. I guess I believe that there's only one right person for everybody. Sometimes you find that person, sometimes you don't. Most of these folks out here who hire me because their husband or wife is cheating just didn't find that right person. The only mistake they made is not waiting. You can't judge a person, or make them wrong for jumping the gun out of desperation or loneliness or social pressure, or whatever. Everybody's got a story, that's the most important fact of life to remember."

"Okay, well, what about people who don't tell the truth about themselves? That surely is abominable."

Pick took a swallow of his drink and set it, in a slow, deliberate way, back on the table. He looked squarely, piercingly, and without question into Lila's eyes and simply said, "Everybody, Lila Giles, has a story," and that was all he needed to say.

Trapped in the Claws of Tradition

Gil stopped by his mother's house on his way to meet Sandra. He had no particular reason, he really didn't even know why he was there. It was as if his car was on an automatic pilot, guiding him to a place in search of answers. Before he knew it, he was walking through Eulelie's door. At first he thought no one was there. The house had the quiet stillness of untroubled water. Closing the door behind him, he didn't call through the house for signs of life, he just walked slowly, pensively, around the corner and into the living room. It was a shocking sight to see Eulelie in her chair with that worried-mother faced he knew so well.

"Hi, Momma. I didn't think anybody was home. Why didn't you say anything?"

"Oh, I just thought you were one of the girls. Lucretia is out to dinner with Mark, and Linda took my car to the mall. Her car's in the shop. I don't know where Lila is. I waited dinner for her.''

"Lila's fine, I just left her.'' Then Gil remembered that it would make life, not quite like hell, but more like purgatory, for Lila by telling Eulelie where he'd left her. He decided to lie. "I had dinner with her tonight and I left her just a few minutes ago. She should be home soon.''

"I'm not worried. Lila's a good girl. She'll be okay.''

"Momma, you look worried. Is there something wrong?''

"It's not worry, honey. I'm just a little melancholy, that's all. I've been thinking about your father. I hope you know how good a man he was.''

Gil leaned forward and fidgeted with a crystal bird on the coffee table. "I do, Momma, and I miss him more than you could know. He was a big part of what made this family strong, even—''

He was about to say *even after my mother died*, but thought better of it. "It just seems like it's all up to me now, with Uncle Horatio living down in Annapolis and Aunt Lucretia living who knows where. I don't even remember the last time we saw them. I feel like there's a torch to be carried on with the Giles name on it, and I'm the only one who can carry it. You know, that's a lot of pressure.'' Gil twirled the fat little bird on its side. He had done this for as long as he could remember. It had kept him busy and out of trouble while waiting on his mother and sisters for church, or brunch, or dinner, almost anything for which they either had to prepare themselves, or food, or both. It was so perfunctory he was barely aware of what he was doing. His angst-ridden fingers were drawn to that bird like a pigeon to home.

"Gil, your father would only want you to fulfill your potential. Your uncle Horatio and your aunt Lucretia were weak. They didn't appreciate this family's history and the duties of that history that were given to them at birth. They took it all for granted. But you're something different. Your father would be proud that you followed in his footsteps of law. But you know, his dream was that you would one day be the mayor, and you will, it's just a shame the Judge won't get to see it."

"Momma, why . . ." Gil set the bird right on the coffee table and sat back on the sofa. He had to compose himself before he could say another word to her. "Momma, what has ever made you think that I *want* to be mayor of Baltimore?"

"Well, because you can. You have the name, we have the money. You are the Giles golden child, Gil."

"Yeah, but Momma, if I really wanted to be mayor, don't you think I would have worked my career, early on, to make that happen? Don't you think I would have shown some interest in running for something in the city council, or something, anything?"

"Gil, honey, you are a Giles. You don't *have* to make it happen. With your name, you just say you want it to happen and it happens. You're not just some ordinary man off the street who says 'Oh, I have great plans for this city.' You are Gilbert Horatio Harding Giles the Third, and people know what that name stands for—it stands for pride. It stands for a family that's hardly ordinary. Gilbert, are you aware of the fact that after slavery, not one generation of the Giles family lived in poverty, or the projects, for that matter? They believed in education. They believed in getting their own. It's a proud thing for a black man in America to say that he doesn't need a white man for anything. So, it's okay to take your time, but you have to know that your destiny is waiting for you."

"Momma, I'm not taking my time. I'm just trying to live my life for myself, and not for some family tradition or what's proper that was set in motion by a bunch of dead men that I never even knew." He was firm of voice. "Why can't you see that?"

Eulelie's eyes widened, then narrowed, as if trying to focus the picture. She looked at him, then across the room, then back at Gil. "You mean to tell me that all this time I was thinking you were going to fulfill your father's dream and the incredible heritage you've been blessed with and you were no more interested in it than the man in the moon?"

"Momma, the man in the moon could have told you I wasn't interested. Everyone knew, somehow you didn't. Why haven't you ever put this kind of pressure on Lila, or Lucretia, or Linda? Why don't you *groom* one of them to be mayor? They're Gileses too."

"Gil, you know as well as I do that your sisters don't have what you have. They're good girls, but let's face it, they'd make better mayors' wives than mayors."

"Then groom them to find some unsuspecting prospect that you can designate for mayor. That should be just as impressive. All I want is for you to lay off of me. It's just too much."

"Was it too much for your father, or your grandfather, or your great-grandfather and his brothers? You know, the Gileses don't breed ordinary men. They have always bred me to do great things." Eulelie's chest was stuck out so far one would think she had been the one to do the breeding throughout the family line.

Gil soon deflated her, though. With a stinging tone to reflect his tight-lipped anger, he said: "Would you stop it, Momma? Just stop it! What do you care, anyway? It's not like you had anything to do with my breeding. Everything I am, I am because I have my father's *and* my mother's blood, not yours. So, if I'm an ordinary man, it's because underneath all this shit you call breeding and lineage and heritage beat the hearts of ordinary men, oh, and at least one ordinary woman—my mother."

Eulelie was struck mute, not by his tone with her, not even by the way he flaunted his mother in her face, but by the absolute irreverence he displayed in using that s-word not only in her presence, but in actually addressing her. Things were now very serious. Everything was in a downward spiral, and moving at a breakneck pace in ways that involved disdain, disloyalty, but most of all, ingratitude.

"Gil," she said meekly as she watched him walk toward the door.

"Yes, Momma?" He was angry, and that was the mildest of what he felt.

"Is there anything I could ever do to make you stop loving me, to make you hate me and never want to see me again?"

Gil turned to her. "Momma, what kind of question is that? I would never stop loving you, no matter what you do, or how you act." He paused, then said guardedly, "Or what you have done. I just want you to give me a break." He turned to leave again, then said: "I'll see you soon, Momma."

"Gil, wait. I want you to come over next Saturday. Not for dinner. There's something I need to tell you and your sisters, and I'd rather tell all of you at the same time."

"Sure Momma," he said, his back turned to her now. Her words were serious sounding, with meanings that could conjure thoughts of impending death, impending out-of-wedlock birth, almost anything. But it all passed by Gil without him reflecting on her mysteriously somber request. Then he said to her: "I have a feeling my Saturdays are going to be free from now on." He said nothing more before he disappeared around the corner into the hall and out the door.

Eulelie heard the door close, its clack echoing through the empty house. She thought hard about that sound as metaphor, before the tears fell. She closed her eyes then and prayed for one chance to make her life make sense again.

Making Right What Was Wrong

Gil sat in the restaurant waiting for Sandra. It was her decision to meet at this out-of-the-way place. He'd never been there before. How did she know about it, so far out on Reisterstown Road? It was way past the Beltway. Why would she ever need to be this far out of town? She lived on the east side. To Gil, it seemed like he was almost in

Westminster, it was so far out. It was Joseph, he just knew. It had to be Joseph. This was where they rendezvoused. Now cruelly, spitefully, maliciously, she was arranging to meet him there to rub his nose in their affair. He pictured them, over in the corner, kissing, rubbing, feeding each other, panting with anticipation of the love they would later make. How could she be so heartless? Then he thought about it, and his pictures faded. Suddenly, he didn't see them there, he didn't see them in the corner. Sandra was not heartless. She may have been to this place before, out of the way though it was, but he was certain it was not with Joseph. Sandra had far more class than to do something quite so tacky.

While deep in his thoughts, he didn't see her standing in front of him.

"Gil, hi," she said in a strange, distant, almost cool way—a way he'd never before heard from her.

"Oh hi, I didn't see you come up."

"Yeah, I could tell. You were lost in thought." She pulled out the chair and sat down. The waitress appeared seemingly from the air, asking if they wanted a drink. "I'll just have a white wine," Sandra said.

Gil wanted nothing. He just shook his head. When she left, he said to Sandra: "So, you wanted to talk." There was no way he would waste time with superficial small talk about how lovely the cotillion was the night before. The point was the only place he wanted to get to, and quickly.

"Yes, I do. First, I need to talk to you about something you may not even know about. In fact, I'm sure you don't, otherwise I hope you would have been as upset as I was. Anyway, I read our wedding announcement in the *Afro Gazette*, and your mother actually wrote in there that I'm a lawyer with the firm. Now, it upset me to know that your mother doesn't think I'm good enough just because of who I am. What I do has to factor into my worthiness to be a Giles. But her making that up is the least of what makes me mad. She didn't even think about that fact that it could cause problems for me with the firm. I mean, they could think I told her to put it in there, and I could lose my job. What are they going to think when they read that flat-out lie?''

Gil looked across the room, then down at the table. When he mustered enough calm to look at her, he said: ''Is that why you slept with Joseph? Was it because you were mad at my mother, my family, me?''

''What? How . . . How . . . How in the world did you know about that?'' Sandra was flushed with disbelief, with consternation, with embarrassment.

Gil shifted in his seat. ''Well Sandra, I didn't really know, I just assumed because I know he spent the night with you after the cotillion, but you just admitted that you did.''

''And why do you know that he spent the night?''

''Because I spent the night in my car outside of your building. I saw him driving toward your apartment after I dropped you off, and I thought to myself, 'What would Joseph Crenshaw be doing on this side of town?' So I turned around to see if he was going where I thought he was going, and surprise, he was going to see you, just as I thought.''

''Whether you believe it or not, Gil, I came here tonight to tell you about it. I've always been honest with you, and I was not going to chicken out with this.''

''Oh sure, you're honest. You've screwed him how many times, and now your conscience is telling you that you have to be honest. There's nothing you can tell me about honesty, Sandra, because while I degraded myself by sitting all night outside your building, Joseph was warmly ensconced between those long luscious legs of yours, and all I could do was sit there and imagine when it might be over.''

The waitress walked up on their conversation, heard everything from *ensconced* on, and had a look that wondered what in the world they were discussing. Sandra thanked her for the wine with a polite yet abashed smile, then went back to her straight-faced business. ''You know it doesn't really matter how many times it happened because everything has changed now. Just for the record, though, it only happened that once, and that's the God's honest truth."

Sandra talked in a layman's language of metaphysics, trying to give believability to the unbelievable. She knew this was all very unbelievable for Gil. There was a tiny part of herself that couldn't believe it. She talked incessantly, though, waiting for the moment when Gil would get it. What she couldn't accept was that Gil would never get it.

Besides, he already knew everything. He saw the attraction when they met at his mother's. He knew it was an attraction, a connection that wouldn't simply die. He knew that Joseph desired her, but the rest, all this talk of soul lovers and soul mates and soul this and soul that—by Gil's standards it was just an excuse for her lack of self-control. Gil at least patiently tolerated all her talk about knowing each other's soul, but when she started talking about looking into Joseph's eyes and seeing the part of herself that would complete her, he'd had just about enough. In the realm of Gil's staid, straight-and-narrow world, life was to be lived in only two shades—black and white. There was no gray, there was no off-white, and he resented Sandra, almost hated her, for trying to force the colors of her world on him. He was vexed, and hexed, and perplexed by this woman he loved, but did not know why he loved.

"Sandra, I really wish I could buy all this crap you're trying to sell," he finally said. "The truth is, all I can see is that you and Joseph had been screwing each other long before you climbed into bed together. Do you think I'm blind *and* stupid? I saw the way he looked at you, the way you looked at him. I watched the two of you dance the other night, and I knew there was something more intimate going on than just a slow dance."

"Okay, Gil, if you want to turn this into something dirty and disgusting, you do that, but God knows what's in my heart."

Sandra took an angry gulp of her wine. She stared at a hanging fern that was full, lush, and fake-looking, while trying to steady her internal rage. Screaming would not have been enough to make him understand, neither would shaking him until his bobbing peanut-head would nearly snap from his neck and bounce along the hard, tiled floor. Some old-time song wafted to her from a distant speaker. Something about the broken-hearted and love that's now departed. She knew the song well, but the words eluded her. That was best for now, she thought, as she sat there breaking someone's heart.

"So, what does all of this mean for us, Sandra? Am I supposed to just chock this up to a big mistake and put this all behind us?" The words within the question seemed sincere, but the truth of his intention was right there in his tone, and it was clear—there was no way Gil would ever forgive her and Joseph, so the possibility of forgetting was nowhere in the cards.

"No, Gil I don't expect you to put this behind us, and I know that you won't and can't. And so I think you know that we can't get married. It would be a lie. It wouldn't be fair to you or me. I would be forcing myself to be defined by everything other than the things that makes me *me*."

"What's that supposed to mean, Sandra?"

Sandra took another gulp of wine, probably for courage, then said: "It means, Gil, that I'm not a lawyer, I don't want to be a lawyer, I'm never *going* to be a lawyer. I'm a woman who writes poetry, loves to knit and sew, and only wants to one day be a loving wife and loving mother. When I die, that's what I want people to say about me, that's what I want people to be impressed with and remember about me. Not what I did for a living."

"Sandra, what are we talking about here? That's the quality I fell in love with about you."

Sandra laughed ironically. He simply did not get it, which meant that he didn't even understand his own basic, eternal nature. "Gil," she said, "that might have been the quality you fell in love with, but in the bigger picture of your family, that's the quality about me you despise the most. It's not good enough and it never will be."

"So that's what it's going to come down to, huh? This is all my fault because I suggested something I thought you'd be good at that would enhance your life."

"Gil, your mother lying about what I did in the paper is more than a suggestion, it's a command, and if you can't see that what she did was wrong, then you're just as clueless as she is."

"Sandra, the bottom line is that you screwed Joseph, yet I'm the wrong one."

Sandra slammed her hand on the table so hard, palm down, heads snapped to her attention. One of the intensely blond women at the next table gasped and jumped with fright. The woman stared Gil down with the disdain of sister-hood faced with the horror of a wronged woman. Sandra smiled, Eulelie style, as if everything was just fine. In the lowest, calmest tone she could muster, she said: "You know what, Joseph is not the issue here. If you could pull your head out of your ass long enough to see the truth you'd be able to admit that this is a conversation we needed to have a long time ago. I admit that a lot of the reason why we didn't talk about this is my fault. I should have listened to that little voice telling me that something was not right when you didn't let me meet your family until we were just about to walk down the aisle, but I was just as blinded by the idea of love as you were." She reached for his hand, but stopped just short of touching him. It seemed inappropriate. It no longer felt natural. "Gil, I love you, just not in the way that we both deserve."

Gil got up, digging in his pants pocket for something. He pulled out some crumpled bills, studied them for a second, then threw them on the table. He leaned over the table toward her face, just shy of Sandra's comfort zone, and said, loud enough for the two women at the next table to hear, "Just for the record, Sandra, I think Joseph is one hell of a good man, and he's nothing if not a gentleman. Right now, though, considering he just fucked my fiancée, I think he's a son of a bitch." And though that f-word was most appropriate for the intensity of the moment and the fire of his anger, he did not wear it as naturally as some other man might. It pushed off his tongue as it would off a cherubic choir boy's—somewhat comical, ineffectual, and at its essence innocent.

Even with his laughably foul mouth, Gil walked righteously off and out of the door, leaving Sandra alone with her wine and two disapproving faces staring into her own. The skittish woman and her friend eyed Sandra's engagement ring and smirked sideways at her with judgmental scorn. It was as if they'd reassessed the situation, deciding that Sandra had no right to any anger in light of what she'd just done. She had some nerve, their faces said.

Sandra wanted to tell them to mind their business, to judge lest not ye be judged, to kiss her round rear, but she didn't. Had she heard what these women just heard, she knew she would have the same judgment, and her scorn would be equally as fierce.

TWELVE

Rain fell on the windows with noisy taps, thwacks, and sputters, a noise too big for the house's soundless rooms. The sunless sky cast a hue of deep gray over the Giles home that was at once comforting and homey, yet disquieting and unearthly. The stillness of everything was chilling—even the inanimate, especially the inanimate. Eulelie walked into the living room, the darkest room. In one hand she carried a cup of tea on a saucer, in the other an old, tattered photo album where she balanced her radio, which played a dour piece of music that could have been Mahler—she couldn't be sure. Those musers of the melancholy all sounded the same to her.

Only two steps in the room, Eulelie was stopped cold in her tracks from the chill that rushed through her. She squinted her eyes, craned her neck, hoping her sight had been corrupted by the room's gloom. Never before had she noticed it, even though it sat on the fireplace mantel for at least two decades. It was the picture of the Judge in his robe, regal, standing guard over the room and anyone in it, larger, more prominent, than the other framed pictures of Gileses that adorned the mantel. For all these years Eulelie would have bet her furs that the Judge was smiling approvingly down on the room and his family. On this day, this day of all days, she saw through gray shadows a smileless Judge, a humorless Judge, a Judge with the slightest upturn on the right side of his mouth, which hinted at a smile but actually looked more like an ironic, disapproving smirk. After she got over the shock, she continued on to the chair, where she sat staring at the picture. Had someone replaced the smiling picture of her Judge with this one? And if that were not enough to keep her internal angst churning, as she flipped through the old photo album in her lap the Judge was smiling in not one of the pictures. Eulelie was looking to these photographs for comfort as she was about to tell her children the truth about herself. Instead, what she found was fate's cruel way of revealing to her that she'd never actually seen what was before her eyes. Her life as a Giles had been one long exercise in deception.

Eulelie closed the album of photos and unclear memories. There was some commotion on the front porch. It had to be her girls, because she wasn't expecting anyone, and no one in their right mind would drop by on a day like this. A key turned in the door and the muffled voices floated in to her as if on a rain cloud. The next thing she heard was Lucretia's startled question.

"Momma, why are you sitting in here in the dark?"

"The dark is good for reflection, Lucretia. I'm just sitting here enjoying my tea."

"It's really coming down out there, Momma. You're in the best place," Lila said, taking off her rain shoes before walking on the living room carpet. "But it is awful dark in here, Momma. Why don't you turn on a light?" And Lila flipped the switch to the wall lamps.

"What did you girls get at the mall?"

"Shoes," Linda said. "We all just got shoes. Lucretia got two pair. Oh, and Lila got some makeup and nail polish."

Linda went off to fix lunch for everyone. Lila and Lucretia, like overindulged children at Christmas, tore into their shoe boxes, eager to try on their new shoes. Lila was first on the floor. She stepped left and then right. Then she walked as naturally as she could while bending this way and that, trying to get the best angle on how her new shoes looked in mid-stride. She pulled up the hem of her mid-calf skirt to reveal her full, shapely calf. "How do my legs look in these shoes, Lucretia?" she asked, and her sister nodded her approval, only half paying attention. Then Lila turned to her mother, asking if she liked the shoes, but she could see that Eulelie's mind was elsewhere as she gazed off into a vacant space in the corner. For the last month, maybe longer, Lila had noticed the way Eulelie would periodically check out. Sometimes it happened right in the middle of a conversation. She'd heard about this kind of thing. Sort of a premature dementia—not quite senility, definitely not Alzheimer's. Whatever it was, she could no longer pretend that something very serious was not happening to her momma's mind.

"Momma, what is it?" she said now. "For weeks you've been like this. We talk to you, but you don't even hear us. I just asked you how you liked my shoes, and it was like you didn't even hear me. Is everything okay?"

But Eulelie didn't even hear that until a few seconds later, when she could feel that her deep thoughts were no longer floating on the empty chatter that filled the room. "What? What was that, honey? I'm sorry, I didn't hear you," Eulelie said, startled from her mind's cocoon.

"Momma, I want to know what's wrong with you. For weeks now you've seemed preoccupied with something. You space out and don't even hear us half the time. Is it Gil and Sandra?"

"No, honey, it's not them. I've just been thinking about our life, looking at these pictures. You know, reflecting on old times."

"Are you sure that's all it is, Momma, that you've just been a little melancholy?"

"Yes, that's all it is." Eulelie looked up at the Judge's picture on the mantel again. In the light of the room, there was still no smile. It had gone away, Eulelie thought, through the influence of some sort of house spirit. People in the South believed in these things, that hovered in the shadows

of old homes; some were good, but some had the malevo-
lence of the archfiend. Eulelie never believed in them, until
now. She was sure there was some insolent force living in
her home, going around changing picture faces. She couldn't
imagine how it came to live there. No one would have invited such evil into the midst of their bliss. These evil spirits
had been blamed for everything from making cats and dogs
lose their minds to stealing pies. If they could actually make
a pie disappear, it wasn't so implausible to Eulelie that they
could have the supernatural power to change a picture.

"Do you girls notice anything strange about that picture
of your father?"

Lila and Lucretia looked up at the same time. They studied the picture, first looking for something obvious, then for
something not so obvious. Actually, they tried to see things
that weren't necessarily there. Was it his robe? Lila asked.
Was his robe hiked up more in the front than it should have
been? Lucretia thought maybe it was his shoes. His shoes
didn't seem to match. But his robe hung perfectly, and his
shoes matched with equal perfection. Just then Linda came
back to the room with a pitcher of iced tea and glasses on
a tray.

"What's everybody looking at?" she asked.

"That picture of Daddy. Do you see anything strange
about it?"

Linda set the tray on the coffee table and looked, squinty-
eyed, at the picture. Her head cocked first to the left, then
to the right. Her expression was rife with bewilderment.
Then she said, to everyone's, even Eulelie's, astonishment:
"Did somebody change that picture? I could have sworn, all
these years, that Daddy had a big old smile on his face. That
was a proud day for him. That was the day he was appointed
to the bench. The same day as the anniversary of the day
you and Daddy met, Momma. Don't you remember?"

"Yes, honey, I remember."

All of their heads turned toward the hallway when they
heard a key turn in the door.

"Gil?" Eulelie called out. "Gil, is that you, dear?"

"No, ma'am, it's me," Belva said as she stepped into the parlor.

"Oh, hello. I almost forgot that you were coming today. You can start upstairs. We're expecting Gil soon, and we'll all be down here for quite a while."

"Yes ma'am," the woman said, moving quickly to get on her way upstairs.

"Oh, by the way, did you happen to take the other picture of the Judge away and replace it with this one?" Finally, Eulelie had a reasonable explanation as to exactly what happened to her smiling Judge.

"What? Replace a picture? No, of course not. I don't bother your pictures, Miss Eulelie. I just dust them. I would never have done that!" The accusation was actually too bizarre for Belva to even be outraged, but she was puzzled.

"Okay, that's fine. I just thought I'd ask."

Belva had disappeared up the stairs when Gil's key turned in the door not two minutes after hers. He stepped in, plopping his umbrella in the stand behind the door. When they heard the door slam shut, Eulelie called to him, just to confirm, even though she knew it could be no one but him.

"Yes, it's me, Momma. Who else would it be?" he said with irritation. He rounded the corner into the living room, and his face said the rest. Something had him awfully cross.

"What's eating you?" Lucretia asked.

"Nothing. I just have a lot to do today. I have to prepare for a case that could drag on for months, and I want to get to the point of why Momma wants to see all of us together. What is it you need to say to us? The sooner we get this over with, the sooner I can get back to my work."

"Lila, close those doors for me, please," Eulelie said, pointing to the white, windowpaned French doors.

Gil sat down on the piano bench with a glass of iced tea. He looked over at Linda and asked: "Have you heard from Joseph Crenshaw lately?"

"No, he hasn't called me since the cotillion," Linda said, "and I'm really pissed with him. It's like he doesn't even care about this relationship."

Lila gave Linda a slackjawed stare, then said: "Linda, honey, you don't have a relationship with Joseph."

"Be quiet, Lila," she said. "You don't know everything."

"You went out with him once and suddenly that qualifies as a relationship? Grow up, Linda."

"I'm not even listening to you, Lila."

"Yeah, well, he's been busy," Gil said.

"Really?" Linda asked. "How do you know? Did you talk to him? Did he tell you to tell me that?" She was hopeful for any news, any little hint of interest from Joseph.

"No, I haven't seen Joseph. Listen, everyone, I might as well tell you now because you'll find out sooner or later." He took a few gulps of iced tea, set the glass down on top of the piano, then looked at Eulelie. "I didn't come to dinner last Sunday because I just didn't want to talk about it, but Sandra and I are not getting married. Sandra and Joseph Crenshaw met here on Easter Sunday, and I'm sure you all will be glad to hear on Sandra is more likely to become a Crenshaw than a Giles. She and Joseph have been seeing each other, actually more than seeing each other. Actually, seeing a lot of each other."

"What is that supposed to mean?" Linda said, still not believing.

"It means, Linda, that Joseph and Sandra are sleeping together, screwing each other, having sex, making love, however you want to put it," Gil said, trying to get it through the thickest skull ever.

"I don't believe you, Gil. I just don't believe you," Linda said.

"Linda, why would I lie about this? Do you think I want to believe it?"

Eulelie was positively nonplussed. Of all the ways she could have thought of eliminating Sandra from her life and her family, this would not have come to mind. It was so simple—temptation. Who would have thought that the mere enticement of another man would take her away forever? This changed everything.

"Gil, are you absolutely certain about this?" Eulelie asked when she was able to speak.

"Momma, I'm not hallucinating. It really happened."

"How do you know?" Lila asked. "I mean, are you just assuming, you know, putting two and two together and coming up with six?"

"No, but I wish I were. It happened the night of the cotillion, after he dropped you off, Linda. I was leaving Sandra's place after dropping her off, and as I was driving away I saw him drive by. I watched them dance that night, you know. I knew, when I saw their bodies together in such a comfortable way, that he had either been with her, or he was going to be with her. I could tell they wanted one another. So I turned my car around and followed him, and sure enough, he was headed to Sandra's. I parked outside of her building, waited for him to come out, but the sun came out before he did."

"Well, okay, all that says is that he might have fallen asleep on her couch talking," Linda said.

Everyone gave her the same lowered-eyed look one would give a beloved relative with mind slippage. Then, with questions of what to do, Lila looked at Lucretia, Lucretia looked at her, then at Gil. Gil looked back and forth between the two of them, then at Linda. Gil was the one with the most reason to hurt, but as always when dealing with Linda and her mind full of dreams and fantasies, they had to lay out a featherbed of emotions to cushion her fall from the loftiness of blissful love that was real only in her mind.

"Linda, I'm sorry you had to hear it this way, but Joseph wasn't right for you anyway," Gil said as tenderly as he could.

"That's right," Lucretia said, putting her arm around her sister for comfort.

But Linda, mad enough to spit nails, swatted her sister

away. "She is a soulless pig and a rotten slut, and I hate you, Gil Giles, for bringing her into our lives. None of this would have happened if it hadn't been for you."

Gil looked wounded, but he wasn't. If he knew absolutely nothing about his sister, he knew of her intense and all consuming self-involvement. So he simply sat there, taking her biting insults and venomous jabs. That's when Lila had had just about enough. Somebody had to stop her. She'd already gone too far. Lila had to stop her before she went too far ever to turn back. "Now just wait a minute, Linda. First of all, Joseph and you were never a couple. He never, ever showed any kind of interest in you, so the only one in this room who was hurt by what he did is Gil."

"You don't know anything, Lila," she spat at her sister.

"Oh, I don't? I don't know anything? Well, I do know that you accuse Sandra of being a slut and a whore, but your behavior hasn't exactly been golden, you know. And you know what I'm talking about."

"I don't. I have no idea what you're talking about."

"Oh you don't. Well, this should ring a bell: "Oh, fuck me, Jeffrey. Fuck me like I've never been fucked before. Oh, Oh, Oh God, Jeffrey, it feels so good.' That went on right upstairs in your bedroom not even six months ago. You were down at Lexington Market, Momma. You don't even have the decency to respect Momma's home and take care of your sexual needs elsewhere. Momma, she was actually delusional enough to think that I couldn't hear her from the next room. Shoot, you could hear that racket all over the house. And her squeaking bed in the middle of the night is not due to cramps, Momma. She screws Jeffrey Borders up there in her room all the time, Momma, all the time."

"Lila, you lie so much," Linda retorted, too flustered to give her sister a more ardent response.

"Lila, that wasn't right," Lucretia said. "What if Linda told Momma about your sexual exploits?"

"What is there to tell? Yes, I have had sex, lots of it, but not once have I had it right here under Momma's roof. I have more respect for her and for myself, unlike you. Do you think, Lucretia, honey, that I didn't know what you and Mark Crenshaw were doing that night when you were straddling his lap wearing that long full skirt? That skirt didn't cover everything. I could see that his pants were down around his knees. And, might I add, this was when Mark was still married to and living with his wife. So go ahead, you tell all you want about the sex I've had, but you will never be able to say that I did anything sexually in this house."

Eulelie's face was ashen with disbelief. Was she actually hearing these awful things about her daughters? They could not have possibly had sex. There never seemed to be a time when their whereabouts were not accountable. When did they have the time? When did they have the opportunity? In her mind, she was never out of the house long enough for anything wanton to take place. Her home was pure, and so too were her daughters. If she took comfort in nothing else for her entire life, she took comfort in these two convictions. Something was amiss. Suddenly, her house was made of cards, and someone was pulling each one, slowly, gently, meticulously away, forcing her to end her life as she and everyone else had come to know it; causing her only son's heart to be broken; causing her girls to turn on and snipe at one another. Someone, something, perhaps the archfiend, had cast a curse on her hearth, and she had no idea how to reverse it. The bickering did not stop.

Linda said: "Lila, you just kill me. You have some nerve acting so sanctimonious about this, like Lucretia and I are such harlots because we had sex here and not in the backseat of some car. I think I do recall that that's where you've had sex before, right in the backseat of a car."

"Well, Linda, it doesn't surprise me that you would recall that, after all, you do have total recall of all things imaginary."

"That's enough, all of you!" Eulelie snapped. "Now, I'm shocked at what I've heard here today, but it's done, and there's no sense in going on about it. But you all should know that from now on there will be none of that. I have no control over what you girls do outside of this house, but I merely ask that you respect my home by not bringing men in here and having relations. From now on, this house will be about truth and honesty. A pure home."

Lila lowered her head, her jaw clenched, her fingers transformed into white-knuckled fists, her eyes pasted to the floor. Something down there had to stop her. But that thing, that agitating thing she'd always been able to beat down, would no longer keep quiet—it would have its say. It scolded her and branded her a pretender, because she had once accused her brother of coveting it, when she was the one who pretended not to know the rage that had painted her completely red, slowly, inch by inch, until she was coated in the layers of its years. She wanted to control it, more than anything. Her mind told her, as it had in the past, that she was larger, stronger, smarter, better than it; but rage, having its own will, its own destiny, told her that her mind was no match for its power. It was rage that now guided her across the room to the mantel without her mind knowing how it got there, or even why it was there. From what seemed to be some distant corner of the universe, she could hear Eulelie's voice droning on about family honor and family pride, and this and that and the other about family. And then her rage, raw and red and complete, guided one lone finger, like a precise missile, to catapult every one of her dead elders from their perch, crashing the framed pictures to the floor with a thunder more violent than anything nature could create in her heavens.

"You want truth and honesty, huh, Momma?" Lila said with a spine-tingling calm that juxtaposed the storm of breaking glass, but that calm rose, slowly and steadily, with her anger. "Well, why don't you burn this house to the ground and build another one, because truth, honesty, and purity could never live here, Momma!" By now the foot of the fireplace was strewn with generations of Gileses, and they were covered by the jagged shards of glass that were one Giles's wrath.

Eulelie called out for Lila in that panicked way mothers do when danger is descending. "My God!" Eulelie screamed, falling to her knees without fear of being cut or hit by falling glass. "My God, Lila, what's gotten into you? Gil, stop her!"

Then Lila took the photo of her father the Judge in one hand. She was ready. She would do it. It was right there, high in the air, ready to go smashing to the floor in one last moment of defiance, one last declaration of anger. But she was stopped by her mother's shrieking pleas.

"Lila please, no!! Please don't! Not the Judge! Gil, stop her! Do something, please!"

But Gil just sat there, shocked enough by his sister's wrath, but somehow knowing that she wouldn't do it.

And she didn't. Lila gave him a reprieve, propping him politely back in the center of the mantel. The Judge had to see, he had to hear, because she wasn't through.

In a moment that gave the room a chilling aura, a moment more frightening than all those frames soaring from the mantel, Lila laughed hysterically, disturbingly, as if in the grip of something demonic. It was a disconnected laugh—separate, of course, from anything rational, but separate also from her. She plopped without care down on the coffee table, right in front of her mother, who was still on her knees as if praying for a resurrection.

"Oh my God, oh my God, oh my God!" Eulelie moaned in disbelief. "What has this child done? What has gotten into her?" She wailed on to herself as if Lila, as if no one, were there. Slowly, she turned to reveal a tear-streaked faced to the daughter she'd never met. "Lila," Eulelie said with a voice that was drowning in tears that seemed to well from deep within, but her iron will was still clear just in the way she said her daughter's name. "I have not put my hand to your bottom since you were eight years old, but I swear to you that I will slap you where you sit if you don't stop this nonsense."

"Slap me, Momma! Beat me! Do whatever you need to do to keep the truth away, but I will always come back talking, and *you will listen!*"

Lila listened to the rain outside magnify the silence of everyone waiting for her to speak. When she began again with her voice lower, her eyes less crazed, she seemed more rational, like the Lila everyone knew; except this Lila had an ax to grind on her own edge. "Family lineage, Momma, has only been your obsession, except we were all stupid enough to think it was important *and* mistake it for family pride. And family honor, Momma, what's that? Don't you know that there's more honor in being a dead Giles than a live one? We have plenty to be proud about in this family, but that pride would also include my mother, *our* mother Gloria, who may not have been *pedigreed*, but she helped love flow through this family from all those dead people on the floor right there. To you, they were only worth what they accomplished. To my mother and father, they were worth the families they nurtured. I have no idea what this family has become, but can I tell you one thing," and by now, she had gotten off the coffee table and circled the piano, only to come around and sit on the piano stool, "true Giles family pride has nothing to do with this toxic thing that is purely your creation. Look at our grandfather, Momma."

Lila went over and knelt beside her mother, who was still sitting vigil for the ruins on the floor. Lila gingerly picked her grandfather's picture from the shards with two fingers while tiny bits of glass tinkled against the fireplace marble. She held the picture practically in her mother's face, then said, "Look at him, Momma! Do you think this man—a man you yourself said was the finest, most beloved colored doctor in all of Baltimore—would have said to his own people, 'Oh yes, come to me and I'll treat you, but only if you're light enough with straight enough hair and from one of the finest colored families in Baltimore?' No, of course he didn't. He treated everyone, and treated them equally. This man went to some of the poorest black neighborhoods in this city, maybe even in *East Baltimore*, Momma, and he treated people who could only afford to pay him with collard greens or butter beans. That's my family lineage, Momma. That's what I come from, not the Giles family lineage you've invented."

Eulelie breathed heavily, as if she were trying to restrain herself from something—striking Lila, screaming, throwing something across the room, firing up her own rage. Something. Through a tightened jaw, tightened lips, and gnashing teeth, but still kneeling in a pathetic heap on the floor, Eulelie said, "Lila, you think your little bit of time on this earth has allowed you to know all the answers to life, don't you? Well, you know nothing! Knowing who you need to know to put a dollar in your pocket and choosing who you'll invite into your home in your world of leisure, these are two entirely different things. Are you really naive enough to believe that the separation of the social classes is my invention?" Eulelie laughed arrogantly, her implied irony meant to berate and to take back just a little of the control Lila had stolen from her. "Well, you certainly give me more credit than I deserve." She got to her feet, sat in her chair and crossed her legs in a way that was a definitive dismissal. It was bombast.

"You be quiet!" Lila screamed at Eulelie, banging on the piano keys to put a somehow appropriate discordant background theme to her ire. *"You just shut up!* All my life I've done nothing but listen to you! 'Yes ma'am, Momma. Right away, Momma. Whatever you say, Momma. You know best, Momma,' " and she mocked herself with such disdain it put a sour scowl on her lovely face. "Now I'm going to have my say and *you* have to listen to *me! You are not to say a word!"*

Neither Gil nor Linda nor Lucretia moved a muscle. They sat staring at Lila, then Eulelie, then Lila, with saucer eyes.

Lila composed herself before saying more. If she were calm, she believed, her mother, her sisters, her brother, would hear her, really hear her. Right now, she knew that they thought—just by the way their fearful eyes took her in—a tiny part of her mind had slipped away. So in a level voice that seemed forced, phony, she said, "And yes, Momma, I do believe that they broke bread with poor people, and dark people, and uneducated people and all kinds of black people. I have to believe that because it's the only thing that can give me pride in this family name. You know something, Momma, when I think about it—and it's embarrassing to admit this about the woman who raised me—but when I really think about it, you're the worst and most dangerous kind of racist. You're actually confused enough to be racist against people who look just like you. I sometimes wonder if your only regret in life is that you weren't born just a little bit lighter with hair just a little bit straighter, and that way you could pass, making your snobbery, your racism, at least seem more complete."

Suddenly Lila was bowled over by a thought from nowhere, and she began to laugh. "And isn't it funny!" she said, practically unable to speak through that chilling laughter. "Isn't it just so, I don't know, funny and at the same time humiliating for you that the woman who you thought wasn't good enough to be a Giles finally came to her senses and realized that the *Gileses* weren't good enough for her? And the saddest part of it all is that it wasn't just you who thought she wasn't good enough. Linda, Lucretia, and I all thought she wasn't good enough. But you know what? We were only able to believe that because of years and years and years of that little voice, *your* little voice, chanting in our brains that being a Giles meant owning the right to look down on anyone who didn't meet your standards. The only problem with that, Momma, is that your standards have never been the true Giles standards."

What she did next went right up to the edge of going too far. She went back to the coffee table and sat again. Then she looked squarely at her mother with more honesty than she ever could have thought possible and said, "Say it, Momma. Say it. 'Sandra is too good to be a Giles.' Say it, damn it! If you're so dead set on this being an honest home, then you *say it!*"

Gil, Lucretia, and Linda sat stark still, too afraid, or too in awe, it was difficult to tell which, to say one word as they watched their mother and sister in a battle of wills, in a grown-up game of stare-down. But it was finally Linda who cried out with a fear that was rare for her, "Gil, call the police! Lila's lost her mind! Call the police before she goes even crazier. Let them take her to Crownsville!"

"*Shut up, Linda!*" Lucretia ordered in a scream.

"I'm not crazy, Linda," Lila said in an even, intimidatingly sane tone, but without looking at her. "I've just finally rescued myself." She turned halfway around so she could see her sisters and said, "You know what we are? We're like shell-shocked prisoners of war who've been too beaten down to believe that we will ever know another way to live. Prisoners of war, you know, will sympathize and even bond with their captors, because they're all the prisoners know. That's what we are, prisoners of Momma's war on *those other* black people. Prisoners of her belief that possessing the name Giles, or Pettigrew, or Van Dyke, or Ballard, or whatever, makes us better than somebody with the misfortune of being born a Hightower."

Lila turned back around to face her mother. Stiffening her back to sit up a little straighter, she made her declaration: "Well, this is it for me. This is where I get off. I've served out my sentence and I am releasing myself. Next week I'm moving to my own apartment."

Eulelie laughed dismissively, as if Lila were some rebellious teenager with fantasies of an independent life she could never realize. "Lila, don't be ridiculous. Your own apartment, well, I'd just like to see that. How do you figure you're prepared enough to be a woman living on her own in the world? You've been sheltered, Lila. You've been sheltered and pampered. All of you have. I'd just like to see you try to survive out there."

Lila smiled to herself, remembering the time when her mother's words could strike her down into a heap of self-doubt. Her mother had no power anymore, though, and Lila

told her as much: "I'll tell you how I figure, Momma. I
figured I could live on my own the day I walked out of this
house with my eyes open and kept them open. And guess
what? There's life beyond that reservoir over there. And you
know what else? There are actually other decent people in
Baltimore other than your little incestuous circle of socialites.
Oh, and by the way, Roger Pettigrew-Van Dyke is a pimp
out in San Francisco."

Lucretia drew in a gasp of air, then let out a burst of
laughter that was impossible to reign. It was so shocking yet
so funny all at the same time, all she could do was laugh
from her belly until she fell limply forward onto her own
lap. She couldn't stop, even as Gil nudged her, poked her,
then pushed her, wanting her to stop, she knew, before he
himself started. After a while she wasn't quite certain at
what she was laughing—whether it was the fact that her
cotillion escort from one of the finest families in Baltimore
was in the business of whores, or Lila's delivery of the news
no one would have ever expected.

Lila continued, though, as seriously as she could through
the sniggers and guffaws coming from Lucretia. "My new
home is over in Charles Village, on Charles Street. A large
eat-in kitchen, beautiful hardwood floors, a spacious living
room, and it's all mine." Before she started her declaration
of independence, it hadn't been her intention to put that
wounded look on her mother's face with the news of her
new apartment, but there it was, and there was a part of
Lila, a part that was a stranger even to herself right now,
that felt vindicated. "I'm going upstairs to pack," she said,
and she walked out of the living room with an internal smile
of which she felt so worthy because she was leaving that
room a different woman than the woman who had entered.

By now Eulelie was out of energy to say another word.
Where would her mind even begin to take in all that had
just happened in that room? The surprise news of Gil's was
rousing enough to drain her, and from that news she was
made lighter than she'd been in weeks, because like Moses

parting the Red Sea, Gil had delivered her to freedom; not
the freedom of truth, but the freedom of silence. At long
last it was over. No more Sandra. No more Camilla. No
more fear of what Camilla might do with the truth. But then
there was Lila, who had heaped on her another heaviness
that Eulelie thought might not ever turn light. How could
it be that in the same day she could gain her freedom from
the truth and lose her daughter to the truth? Life's ironies
would never sit well in her heart.

Gil stood to leave, first kissing his mother, then Lucretia
and Linda. He walked out, closing the French doors behind
him and deserting them in their awkward silence.

Later that day, as evening was about to dispense its calm
over Baltimore, and the dust in the Giles home was settled
and all minds were sane again, Lila, still determined to be
free, came into the house with three boxes. She was hoping
to slip in and up to her room without anyone noticing or
hearing. After what had happened, she assumed everyone
would still be in retreat in their own parts of the house.
Three boxes at one time, though, didn't exactly make for an
unobtrusive entrance, as they bumped and knocked against
the door, the wall, the hall table. The struggle showed in
her face and in the perspiration mixed with the evening's
humidity that pasted her hair to her skin. Finally, she
dropped them in the middle of the hall, careless of who
might hear, then pushed the door shut with her foot.

One box at a time. That was the best way to get them
upstairs. So she picked up the largest one, positioned it in
front of her and went to maneuver it up the stairs. But just
as she was about to mount the first step, Lila was drawn to
look into the room where rage had sent its awesome power
coursing through every conscious part of her being. She
knew that her mother and sisters would call it a spell, but
she knew the truth. Her rage did come up from nowhere,
but unlike a spell, she had the power over her rage to let it
stay—and it stayed until its work was done. That room was
so still now. The storm that had blown all over it should

have brought down the whole house, yet the only thing that as much as whispered that anything devastating had happened was the glass, still strewn over the floor in front of the fireplace. It almost looked deliberate, like some sort of modern art gallery exhibit making an existential statement about anger. *I Walk Alone Without the Past* she'd call it. Then it actually hit her—this mess was still there. Not she, nor anyone else, had seen fit to clean it away. And her mother was certainly the one who told Belva to leave it there.

Lila put the box on the floor without making a sound. She went into the kitchen and got the whisk broom and dustpan that hung just inside the stairwell to the basement. As she went back into the living room, she studied the broom and pan. Everything, even the bristles, were as clean as brand new. This had to be the only home in the country, maybe even the world, she thought, that had a whisk broom and dustpan devoted only to sweeping up nondirt objects.

Plucking a pillow off the sofa, Lila dropped it on the carpet just beyond the fireplace and then kneeled on it. She was pretty certain none of the glass had gotten onto the nearby carpet, but it was best to be safe, especially since she was wearing a skirt. Holding the broom and the pan in each hand, she paused, thinking that once she started, once everything had been swept clean and neat, all would be forgotten, and all that she'd said would have been said in vain. Maybe they needed the reminder of this broken glass forever. Maybe it did need to stay there like modern art, rendering the emotions of that day every time someone put a crackling footfall on that broken glass or looked over at the mess on the floor. But then the empty mantel caught her in the corner of her eye and she smiled, knowing that it was okay to get on with the sweeping.

So she swept, first shallowly, with only a few tiny shards of glass gliding into the pan. With her second sweep, though, the glass tumbled with large-sounding clinks that brought the room to life with the memory of why there was glass in bits on the floor. Every word was in precise focus, and she smiled faintly at her own eloquence. There was nothing, absolutely nothing, she had forgotten to say, or wished she had said. And as she swept and replayed the words from earlier in her mind, she could hear the echo of silence from the hall become muffled by the presence of another.

"Getting rid of the evidence, huh?" Lucretia said from the aperture.

Lila continued to sweep without turning to face her sister, then said, "You're still speaking to me? I thought after today I'd be getting the silent treatment from everybody."

"The silent treatment?" Lucretia said, with a hearty laugh. She mockingly continued, "That's funny, because you know that's not how we do things around here. When you're a Giles, you just pretend nothing at all happened, and then it just goes away." And she was still in the throes of a full-throated laugh.

Lila turned toward Lucretia, then laughed herself. She put the broom and pan down atop the broken glass, stood up and went over to the sofa in a way that said she wanted her sister to join her. "Lucretia, I really didn't plan that, you know. I didn't walk into this room thinking I would get in Momma's face like that and just break it all down. But I'll tell you, Lord knows I've been wanting to do it for years now, for years, I tell you." Lila sat, nodding her head in agreement with herself and clasping her own hands for comfort.

"I guess it was the news about Sandra. That floored all of us."

"Yeah, that was pretty shocking, but that wasn't it. I'm actually glad she came to her senses and decided that being a Giles is not all it's cracked up to be. We are such a dark family, Lucretia."

"I know," Lucretia said, then stopped. She shifted herself so she could look squarely at her sister. She wanted to make sure Lila didn't miss a word. "I agree with everything you said to Momma today about what real Giles family pride should be about. You know, when I saw you and Lionel together at the cotillion being way more intimate with each other than two mere friends ought to be, I really couldn't understand why you hadn't told me about it. And today when you announced that you were moving out, for a split second I was hurt that you would make a decision like that without telling me, and then I remembered everything that you had said before that, and you answered my question of why none of us tell each other anything. I think we've all been so private about things because we've lived in fear of Momma's judgment. She has always set these rules to live by, you know, that don't have anything to do with the way real people behave. As kids, we were all so eager to please Momma that we acted like spies, always so willing to carry little tales back to her so that we just might win her favor. I don't know, Lila, I guess we've all just brought that whole fear of spying and tattling into adulthood. It's something we learned early, and it's really hard to unlearn that kind of survival instinct."

Lucretia slumped back on the sofa so that she was leaning closer to Lila. She took in a long drag of air, then blew it out. "Gosh, Lila," she said. "All this talk of spying and survival instinct and prisoners of war, my God, was it that bad?" she asked, in a way that said she wanted confirmation of what she knew was true.

"You don't need me to tell you, Lucretia. You were there too. You lived it."

"I know, but why didn't it make me as mad as it made you? Why didn't it make me want to just up and move out too? I mean, yeah, I lived it, but to me it was just the way things were. I didn't question it and I didn't want to question it. It was comfortable."

"For me too, Lucretia!" Lila said excitedly. She put her hand on her sister's leg and said, "But something happened. Maybe it was Sandra coming here and shaking up everything that seemed normal and comfortable. Maybe it was the way Momma, to this day, continues to treat us—four grown people—as if we're ungrateful little children whenever we men-

tion our mother. Maybe it's all of it, Lucretia. All I know is
that I have to get out of this house. Lucretia, I'm almost in
my thirties, and I feel that I've already given the best years
of my youth away. I've lost those discovery years of my
twenties where I should have been doing all the stupid things
learning experiences are made of, but I gave them all away
to the loyal service of Momma and I can't get them back. I
don't want to blink and find myself at forty still doing the
same thing. Let me ask you something. Do you question the
way things are?''

Lucretia's eyes lowered to stare into her lap. She took in
another a deep breath and turned her head toward her sister,
but still didn't look at her. "Of course I question it now,
Lila. And I can't help but think that if you had told me you
were planning to move out, I don't know, maybe I could
have gone with you, you know, been your roommate.''

"Maybe you still can," Lila said, with squinting eyes that
held in them the hope that her sister would save herself.

When Lucretia looked up, her face was covered with a
sheet of tears. Of course she should go, but how? Life with
Eulelie, she thought, was not awful yet. Lila wasn't the only
one who had romantic visions of leaving Eulelie's world.
What frightened her to the deepest part of her heart was
leaving prematurely, before things became unbearable, and
living to regret her haste. She'd go away one day, that much
she knew, but like Lila, she would have to inch herself out
on a rope that would eventually have an end. "Maybe I can,
and sooner than you think, but first let's get you packed and
out of here.'' And then, with a half beat skipped, Lucretia
looked at her sister with a gossipy grin and said, "So tell me
the truth. What's going on with you and Lionel Breckenridge? You two are pretty hot and heavy these days, huh?''

"Me and Lionel?'' Lila said with genuine incredulity.
"What in the world would make you think that?''

"I saw you two at the cotillion. You just seemed closer
than I thought you two actually were, you know.''

With a bashful smile, Lila lowered her head, readying

herself to tell the truth. "Okay, well, we've been, I guess, intimate a few times. But only a few times!" she said, as if it would somehow make a difference. "He's really nice, Lucretia, he's really a terrific guy, and he'd probably make a great boyfriend. He's interesting, he's smart, he's sensitive, he really listens to me when I talk to him, you know. And he's—"

"A doctor."

"Please, Lucretia. Don't be crass. Anyway, we're not romantically involved. We've talked about it, but I'm not ready, Lucretia. I feel like I have to start from the bottom and re-raise myself. Do you know what I'm saying?"

"I guess I do. It's like reprogramming yourself, I suppose."

"That's right!" Lila said excitedly, in much the same way she did when her students got it. "So see, you know what I'm talking about. I'm not sure how I'm going to do it, but I have a feeling it's going to have something to do with what our mother would have done. How she would have raised us, and the values she would have instilled in us. And you know what? I know it will all come from my own mind, imagining what our momma Gloria would have done, but maybe that's where I'll find all my answers, Lucretia."

Lucretia went into the hall and picked up a box. She looked into its emptiness, and said to her sister, "Good luck, Lila. I mean it. Maybe you'll find answers for all of us."

✎ We Loved Him 'Cause You Loved Him

A world away from the Gileses, Sandra sat at the table in her parents' kitchen peeling an orange. Waiting for someone, anyone, to come home, she had nothing to do but think about how she would tell them. It would not be easy. Gil was stiff and didn't seem completely comfortable with himself in the presence of her family, but Camilla and Eustace really liked him, probably loved him. Why not? He was likable, even lovable in his own way. Sandra still loved him and wished more than anything that she and he could have had what she had with Joseph. Just then, as she had that thought, a squirt of orange hit her in the face. She plucked a napkin from the holder in the middle of the table and wiped her face, thinking perhaps it was the fates telling her that her wish was pointless. Gil and Joseph, by their very natures, were two monumentally different people. Then she thought about it, Gil, who had the need for perfection and order in every part of his life, and Joseph, who took himself and life a little less seriously. Maybe it wasn't that Gil was uncomfortable around her family, she suddenly thought, maybe he simply wasn't comfortable with himself. It never once occurred to her that this could be the case. After all, why wouldn't he be comfortable with himself? His family was socially and politically correct. He was tall, and handsome in an obvious way; and he was more than a black man with a job—he was a lawyer. He had more than most.

She heard her name called from the other room. Her thoughts were so deep and so imposing, she hadn't heard the front door open.

"Yes, I'm in here, Ma," she said. She stood up, sliding the chair from underneath her, and went into the living room.

"Hi, darlin'. What are you doin' 'round here? We didn't know you were comin'. You gonna stay for dinner?"

"Yeah, sure, if you have enough."

"Have you ever had a meal in this house where there wasn't enough for extra people to eat?" Camilla didn't expect an answer. It was just her way of telling her daughter that home would always be home. "Here, take this bag. I'm goin' out to help your father bring in the rest of the groceries."

Sandra took the bag after plucking a grape from a bunch that lay on the top. She took it into the kitchen and began unpacking the groceries that were so familiar. There was no waiting to find out where everything should go. Since Sandra was a child, Camilla and Eustace, on Saturday afternoon, made their rounds to three markets, every week buying the same thing. Nothing ever varied, not even brands and never amounts—always three pounds of string beans, always two pounds of collard greens, a head of cabbage, and so on—this was their ritual.

Her mother walked into the kitchen, dripping wet and loaded down with three plastic bags filled to the rim—two in one hand, one in the other. She looked as if those bags were stretching her arms down to her knees. Plopping them up on the counter, she noticed, from the corner of her eye, Sandra smiling, almost laughing.

"Somethin's got you in a good mood," she said.

Sandra laughed aloud and said: "No, Ma, it's just that you and Daddy have always bought the exact same groceries every week, without fail. Always the exact same amount, the exact same brands. It's just . . . well, cute, that's all."

"Well, that's just what we do. We never know who we gonna have to feed during' the week, life bein' as unpredictable as it is."

"It is unpredictable, isn't it, Ma?"

"It sure as heck is," her father said, coming in with the last of the groceries. He reached past his wife to tear off a paper towel and dried his face and arms, which the rain had soaked. "Did your mother tell you how, just the other day, outta the clear blue, we get this letter in the mail, no return address, just a postmark sayin' Charleston, South Carolina. It's addressed to both of us. Your mother opens it, and don't you know in it is this check for two thousand dollars from your grandmother with a note sayin' that she thought we might be able to use it to help pay for you and Gil's weddin'. Ain't that somethin'? We don't hear from her in years 'cept when your momma calls down there, and even then all of 'em too uppity to talk for more than a hot second. Then here she come sending us this money. I tell you, you just never know what life has for you 'round the corner."

Sandra looked down at her shoes for help, then smiled,

remembering that Joseph had told her to wear them. They made her legs look even sexier than he dreamed possible, he said. Realizing the memories in her shoes were too much to have on her mind, she looked up into her mother's eyes, which knew, with a mother's radar, that something was on her girl's mind.

"Sandra," was all she needed to say.

"Ma, Daddy, I want y'all to come over here and sit. I need to tell y'all something and I don't know how you'll take it."

"Oh, dear God, Eustace," Camilla said, taking her husband's hand. He pulled her to his chest without saying a word. Everything would be all right. They sat in their respective mealtime chairs.

"Ma, it's not anything to worry about, so please just calm down. Listen, you two, you may have to end up sending back that money to Grandma, because Gil and I aren't getting married."

"What?" Camilla exclaimed. "What happened, child? Was it his mother? What did she do?" Camilla was almost on her feet now.

"Nothing, Ma, I swear. It's just that something happened that made me see that we'd be making a big mistake getting married. You know, Gil never really accepted me for everything that I am. I think he wanted to marry me in hopes of turning a sow's ear into a silk purse."

"My baby ain't hardly no sow's ear."

"Just listen to me, Ma, please. I met someone, over at Gil's mother's house, as a matter of fact. It started innocently enough, he just wanted me to knit him a sweater. But then, as we talked and got to know each other better, we found that we really had feelings for one another, true feelings, you know. He has no interest in turning me into a lawyer or anything. He just wants to be with me for everything that I am."

She paused, waiting for her mother and father to say something. Their judgment was the least of her concerns.

However, she knew that they cared a great deal for Gil, and they welcomed him with wide arms into the family. Camilla and Eustace, though, didn't say a word. They just continued looking at their daughter with blank stares, either out of shock or simply waiting for what she had to say next.

"Ma, Daddy, I know this is a big surprise, because I know how much you love Gil, but I know that you will love Joseph even more. He's so comfortable with himself, and that makes him comfortable with anyone he meets. He talks to every-body and never talks down to anybody. He's really terrific."

Finally, Camilla said: "Well, Sandra, we trust your deci-sion. If you think this is the best for you, then we have to believe that. And as for us loving Gil so much, I can't speak for Eustace, but I loved him 'cause you loved him. Beyond that, if he don't make my baby happy, he can go on about his business."

"Well, exactly," Eustace said. "And besides that, he didn't really fit in with the family, you know. I saw the way he always stiffened up when he walked through the door. I ain't never said nothin' 'cause you loved him, but personally, I didn't think he was the best man for you, anyway. Like your momma said, we loved him 'cause you loved him."

Sandra looked at them with her happy smile, which Jo-seph had put there just that morning, and said: "So, that's that?"

"I guess so," Camilla said. Then she got up and went back to putting her groceries away, secretly delighted that the dark storm cloud, Doralee/Eulelie, had passed on by.

THIRTEEN

✺ Finally, Somebody Gets It

Eulelie sat in her car listening to another Saturday morning's raindrops do their wild dance in sixteenth notes over her head. They played an unfamiliar tune that seemed to come from the mind of John Cage or some such other sensibility that hears all the world's sounds as music. It pulled her deep under its sets of rhythmic spell, each one different from the last by one or two beats. And it was this *plunk-a-plunk-plunk-plop-plunk, plunk—plunk—plop—plunk* that kept her there even though she had driven all the way down to Lexington Market. It wasn't that the rain-music was so hypnotic, it was just that it was great mindless noise whose relentless beats seemingly wrestled thoughts from the depths of the mind.

What would she say? She'd driven all this distance in the rain, and somehow now she did not know why. It seemed to make such good sense that this was what she should do when she climbed behind the wheel. But somewhere between there and here, she had lost her reasons.

Eulelie turned off the car and a feature segment on Louis Armstrong and his early years spent in poverty, while "Hello Brother" played backdrop to a young man's punkish voice that was the antithesis of Satchmo's. There was something about the blueness of this song that spoke directly to her life. Eulelie couldn't think about that, though. She plucked the umbrella from the backseat and was out of the car in one movement. Locking it with the remote, she dashed across the street with a ladies' trot. She snatched open the door to the market with a purpose and started down the aisle, past Pollock Johnny's, past a stand spewing out the most heavenly smell of sizzling Italian sausage with peppers and onions. No other smell in the world could make her mouth water like that of peppers and onions frying in a pan. Those sausages and onions and peppers had so distracted her that she forgot she'd have to pass Mary. This wasn't her week for meat. Mary would be surprised to see her and just might ask what she was doing there. As soon as she thought to avoid Mary by turning into the next aisle she saw, she heard the call.

"Mrs. G! How you doin', hun? This ain't your week for the market. What you doin' here?"

"Mary, hi," Eulelie said, as if Mary were who she was there to see. "I know it's not my week, but I need more of those steaks you sold me last time. The girls just loved them. They were just so tender." Well, that was at least part of the truth. They were tender.

"How many you want?" Mary said, slipping into plastic gloves that looked far too tiny for her meaty hands.

"About four . . . no, make that five. Five would be good," Eulelie said, looking around for a hint of where Camilla might be.

"Lookin' for someone, Mrs. G?"

"Oh, no, just looking around. There are a few new stalls in here, huh?"

"No, nothin' new. Some of these places just changed things around a little, is all."

Mary began chattering away about something, and Eulelie could simply not focus on the woman's point. She did hear *Junior* and *irresponsible* and *so I told Junior's mother.* What is she talking about? Eulelie thought as she waited with impatient fingers drumming away on her purse. Mary tied the handles of the bag into a loose knot, still talking, and handed it to Eulelie.

"Thank you, Mary, dear. This should more than cover it," Eulelie said, handing Mary a twenty. "Keep the rest."

"Thanks Mrs. G." Then, without skipping a beat, Mary said: "And so, anyway—"

"Mary, I wish I had time to chat, but I've really got to run. I'll see you next time."

Mary gave a good-natured, "Awright, hun. 'Bye, now," and let Eulelie get on her way.

Eulelie walked with the swiftness of a mission, looking left and craning her neck right for any sign of a place that might look like where Camilla could work. Did she sell meat? Did she sell vegetables, or maybe fruit? Did she sell crabs, or simply fish? Eulelie had no idea. Camilla could be almost anywhere, selling almost anything. Maybe she didn't even work on Saturdays. "Oh, for goodness sake!" Eulelie said to herself in a whisper. "She probably doesn't work on Saturdays."

She saw a door just ahead of her and decided she'd take it, even though she'd be a good full block and a half from her car. It was worth walking the distance if it meant avoiding the risk of having Mary pull her back into some story about that slow-witted boy Junior. Seeing nothing but the door, Eulelie readied her umbrella, settled her package firmly in one hand, her purse on her shoulder, then stepped briskly toward it. And just as she was about to push through, she heard her name.

"Eulelie," a woman said softly.

Eulelie turned and looked with surprised eyes, then smiled nervously. "Camilla! Hello," Eulelie said, letting the door close.

Camilla was with Margie, who was eyeing Eulelie most dubiously.

"I had actually come here to see you," Eulelie said, "but then I thought that maybe you didn't work on Saturdays."

"I don't," Camilla said, walking over to where Eulelie stood on legs that would not move. "I just came here with Margie to pick up some things. It's funny, you know. I spend

Monday through Friday in this place. You'd think this would be the last place I'd wanna be on my day off." Camilla chuckled, not so much at the irony, but at the awkwardness of having nothing else to say.

Eulelie didn't chuckle, giggle, or even smile, though. She did have something to say. "I'm sorry about what happened between Gil and Sandra." There was something in the way her eyes didn't move away from Camilla's that said she meant it.

That didn't stop Margie, though, from coughing up a doubting, albeit impolite, "*Hmmmf,*" with rolling eyes and a sideways mouth.

Eulelie looked, but said nothing to Margie. A lady ignores such impertinence.

"Well, it was certainly something none of us saw coming," Camilla said. "Anyway, it was probably for the best."

"I suppose. I don't know, though. They just seemed so good together," Eulelie said.

"Hmmmf," Margie said again, this time louder, so as to make it impossible to ignore. Then she added: "He prob'ly didn't even love her to begin with."

Then, looking directly at Margie, Eulelie, in as flat and imperturbable manner as possible said: "Well, it was Sandra who broke it off with my son, dear, not the other way around."

"Yeah, but she prob'ly wouldn't have broken it off if he—"

"All right, Margie, that's enough," Camilla said, knowing that Margie had been just champing at the bit to give Eulelie a piece of her mind. "Besides, it don't matter no more. It's over."

"That's right," Eulelie said.

"Anyway, you said you came to see me."

"Yes, I did." Eulelie paused, then motioned with just a hint from her body toward Margie. "May I speak privately with you for a second, please, if you don't mind."

Camilla turned to tell Margie to make herself scarce, but she was already on her way.

"I'm goin' over to get some chicken wings. Come get me when you ready."

Not even Eulelie found it necessary to hold to the mannered drivel of *Nice to have met you.* She didn't actually meet the woman—there was no introduction, and even if there had been one, it was anything but nice being in the presence of such a boor.

Once they were alone, Eulelie took Camilla's hand and said: "I never had the chance to thank you for not saying anything to Sandra and Gil, and even my girls, about . . . well, you know. . . ." There was no way Eulelie could finish that statement without reducing herself to giving voice to the tragedy of her two selves.

"I know you're grateful," Camilla said.

"Why did you do it? Not tell, I mean." Eulelie needed to know the workings of a benevolent heart.

"I don't know, Eulelie. I certainly didn't want to be a part of this secret, but I suppose if I did it for any reason, I did it for your children. I wouldn't have been able to live with myself if I had destroyed your children because you did some unkind things to my child. I mean, when you add it all up, you could never have hurt Sandra the way your children would have been hurt if I had told them just for the sake of being spiteful. Besides, vengeance is God's to give out."

And just the thought of God's wrath that Camilla tossed off with such easy belief gave Eulelie a chilling start. What did she mean by that? Did Camilla believe that she actually *deserved* God's vengeance? All she'd ever done was love her family.

"That's not my way, Eulelie," Camilla went on. "Those children only know themselves through you. It would be like I was playing God by turning everything they've always found comfort in upside down."

"A lesser woman would not be so kind, so thoughtful."

"A lesser woman I don't know nothin' about. All I know is that those children are in pain for a mother, and you're what they got."

"Of course, and I've been the best mother I could be to them. I wouldn't have loved them any more than if I had given them life myself."

Camilla looked down at her sneakers, then past Eulelie, trying to decide if she should go on. "You know, this may not be my place to say, but it seems to me that your kids would be more sure about who they are if you had let them know their mother."

"Well, Camilla, I appreciate your honesty, but I had my reasons for that." What she did not say, what she would never say, but what she's always known, was that every single one of her reasons were for her.

"I just think everybody deserves to know about the woman who gave them life, whether she's good, bad, or indifferent. You just need to know. It fills in blanks, you know what I mean? You put your own mother away when you became Eulelie, but I think if you look hard enough in your heart, you'll still find a part of her that makes you who you are."

"No. I am nothing, absolutely nothing, like my mother. My mother just accepted her fate of poverty in life and never even dared to dream that life could be different. My sisters are like her, but I'm nothing like that. I saw something better and I found a way to go after it."

"But Eulelie, don't you see, that's just the surface part of who your mother was. What about the way she loved you and your sisters? Can't you see somethin' good in that?"

Eulelie's bottom lip began to tremble. It was too much. Too much of the past. Too much of the pain. Past and pain screaming at her in shame. Her eyes welled with shallow puddles of tears and she fought with everything in her to keep them back. "You don't know a thing, Camilla Hightower. You don't know a blessed thing about what it was like. My momma was too busy being poor to know how to love any of us. She was too busy wiping the noses of white children to hold me on her lap and tell me how special I was, so don't talk to me about finding something of my mother in me, because as sure as I'm standing here, she's not there. And don't you dare try to make me out as the devil just because I want my children to hold me in their hearts in a way that I'll never hold my own mother."

Then Camilla quietly, sympathetically, squeezed Eulelie's hand and said: "I'm not callin' you anything of the sort, girl. I'm just sayin' that you loved those children when they needed love, but just let 'em get to love their mother. A part of those kids is missin', don't you see?" Camilla let Eulelie's hand drop softly, then smiled at her, as if her heart pained too. "Listen, I've got to run. Margie's waiting for me. You take care of yourself."

"Camilla," Eulelie called after her as she turned to walk away. "You will . . . I mean, you won't say . . ."

"It's like I never even knew you," Camilla said.

With that being that, Eulelie walked out of Lexington Market thinking she just might never see Camilla Hightower again.

Moving on to Freedom

Eulelie approached the door that sat wide-open, forgetting for that split second that this was moving day for Lila. Over her head she still carried her umbrella for a rain that had slackened to an annoying spitting drizzle. Folding the umbrella, she stood it on the porch against the wall next to the open door and stepped through. It seemed this day was just a pipe dream of Lila's, even though she'd heard her daughter book the movers and haul in empty boxes and fill them up. Lila's tantrum sat in Eulelie's mind as a hazy memory of which she could only see dull edges, nothing in focus. In the way a mother's heart always can, she had forgiven by virtue of forgetting, and she never spoke of it, because there was nothing to say. Lila had said all she'd needed to say, and that's all that mattered to Eulelie. And now Lila, Eulelie knew, was doing what she needed to do. Still, Eulelie could scarcely believe it even as the door sat open in wait for some man who would come to cart her daughter and all her things off on this drizzly June morning. Her oldest girl was actually seeking greener pastures—much the way she once went seeking hers.

"Lila, honey, can you put these steaks away for me, please?" Eulelie said as she went into the living room where Lila stood waiting at the window. "Why are the doors sitting wide-open? If the movers aren't here yet, close the doors. You'll let flies in the house and I'll have a devil of a time getting them out of here."

Lila hesitated, wanting desperately to say no. She wanted to stand firm in the words of her declaration of freedom she'd made only one week ago and tell her mother that she would no longer fetch and carry. But this was it. She'd won, and there was no point rubbing salt into the wound that would always be her mother's pride. Besides, Lila recognized that the nature of humans was such that her declaration would never, could never, change what took years for Eulelie to become. "Well, okay Momma," she finally said, "but will you keep watch for the movers for me?" Lila took the bag, stopped at the doors to close them, then went off to the kitchen.

Eulelie turned on the radio to the sound of the last few notes of accordion music. A polka music special, she thought; or maybe theme music to a bayou special. Either way, she was fond of accordion music in any style. Even the clichéd "Lady of Spain" could make her head sway to its rolling rhythm on a good day. *"The minute I strap on an accordion, I suddenly become Carl Richter the German instead of Carl Richter the American,"* a man said in a complaining way. Bigotry through the accordion. This could be quite interesting. *"The much maligned accordion,"* another man said, but Eulelie couldn't focus on what else he had to say. Lila's untimely return distracted her. "You didn't wrap them?"

"No, Momma, the movers are going to be here soon, you know."

"Oh, that's all right. The girls can have them for dinner tomorrow."

"The girls? Where will you be?"

"Oh, well, that's what I wanted to talk to you three about. I've got to go down South, back home for a few days. I've got some family business to straighten out that I've been putting off for some years now. It's about time I take care of it. In fact, where are your sisters? Let me tell them." She called for Linda and Lucretia, who were on their way down the stairs, anyway.

"Listen girls," Eulelie started before they had even gotten into the front hall. "I'm going away for a few days. I've got to take care of some business for my family that I've been putting off for some time now. I'll just be gone till midweek or so."

"Down in Columbia?" Lucretia said. "Oh Momma, why didn't you let me know sooner? I would have loved to have gone with you, to see where you grew up, that big house and all. Maybe even meet some of your family that's still around down there."

"Yeah, me too, Momma," Linda said.

"Momma, of all the times you picked, it would have to be the weekend I'm moving, and I can't take any time off right now."

"Well, I've needed to do it, and I just want to get it over with. This isn't a pleasure trip in the least, girls, so don't worry about going. I'm not even going to be there long enough to enjoy myself."

Lila went back to staring out the window for the first glimpse of anything resembling a moving truck. Her patience was gone, even though she'd started watching for them an hour before they were due to arrive. Finally, the truck pulled up in front of the house, five minutes before Lila expected it, no less.

"Here they are," she said excitedly, running to the door to greet them, her sisters trailing behind.

The movers took their time getting out of the truck. Lila

walked out onto the porch, thinking they would assume her impatience and move it along. They did move it along sooner than they would have, but still, not right away. When the two moving men did finally make their way out of the truck, they ambled up the walk as if they'd rather be anyplace else but there.

The driver asked: "Is the truck okay parked there?" He was a beefy man with tree-trunk arms and thighs, and long sausage fingers. His face was red and his bulbous nose even redder. Stringy blond hair that hung to his shoulders worked together with everything else to create the man no one would want to meet on a darkened, deserted street.

"It's fine," Lila said, looking at the truck, which was quite a bit too large for the roomful of furniture she claimed as her worldly possessions.

"How you doin', ma'am?" his partner said, a tall chocolate man with the lean build of a marathon man.

Lila led them through the door then stepped past them to better lead them to her room. This must be their first move of the day, she thought. They smelled fresh. They stood in the hall awkwardly, not knowing where to go. All they knew was that they had a room of furniture to move. They looked with alarm into the parlor—no one had said anything about moving a piano.

"Please be careful with corners, especially on the staircase," Eulelie called to them. "This is only year-old paint on these walls, so it's still quite fresh."

Lila said nothing in response to her mother's command. One of the men just gave a mumbled, "Sure."

"The room is upstairs," Lila said, walking toward the stairs. So they followed her upstairs, the driver somehow making the staircase look as if it belonged in a doll's house. Linda and Lucretia followed the men, staring in disbelief at them as they assisted their sister in her getaway. In their eyes, Lila was treasonous. Be that as it may, they followed. Following them all as they took each step without words was the trailing sound of a man's voice: *"The accordion's dorkiness is what has sustained it . . ."*

Lila led the men to the room. "This is everything. Everything is ready to go. It's all packed."

In the days following Lila's announcement, as she packed boxes and gave things away to Lucretia, Linda could not bring herself to go into Lila's room. So this was Linda's first sight of the room packed, prepared for emptiness. No prints on the walls. No stuffed animals on the shelves. No lace curtains at the windows. No flowery bedclothes on the bed. No bed, just pieces of her bed.

Linda looked on with a face that had been flattened by too many emotions all at once, but nothing specific—anger, betrayal, melancholy, and the one she feared most, jealousy. She feared it most because she couldn't understand it. Moving out never interested her, she reminded herself. Why would it? Life, as she knew it, on Hilton Street was more than good—it was content. And she wanted for nothing. All she had to do was work and take care of her own necessities. If life had to be more complicated than that, Linda thought with a mischievous smile, she didn't want it. Yet she stood there watching Lila go from here to there, from this corner to that corner, flitting around like a butterfly, so happy, so chatty with the moving men. It sickened Linda, and her pique showed in every crag and cranny in her face, which had no trace of the smile of just a few seconds before.

The men looked the room over. "Everything in here is going?" the driver asked.

"Yes, everything." Lila watched as the thin man went over to the floral footlocker in the corner. Her heart jumped. "Please be careful with that. There are breakable things in that. They're all wrapped and secured, of course, but you never know."

"Why didn't you pack 'em in a box?" the man asked.

"Well, it didn't make sense. I'm just going to put them back in there. It's my hope chest. It made more sense for me to keep them in there and just wrap them up."

"What're you hopin' for?"

"Excuse me?" She didn't say it with sarcastic haughtiness. Lila truly didn't understand the question. In her world, everyone knew what was meant by hope chest.

"You said it's a hope chest. What're you hopin' for? What, did you write down everything you're hopin' for in life on pieces of paper and put it all in there?"

"Well, if it were filled with pieces of paper, its contents wouldn't be breakable, now would they? It's a hope chest for when I get married. It's filled with things like my grandmother's crystal glasses, formal silverware, things like that."

"Oh, so you're hopin' for a husband."

His frankness made Linda and Lucretia laugh nervously. Not because what he'd said wasn't true, but because it somehow sounded so pathetic when it was said out loud.

"Naw, I think that's cool. A lotta women don't prepare like that. That's pretty smart."

"Yes, I think so," Lila said with an arrogant tone meant for her sisters. She shot them a disapproving look. They had some nerve, laughing at her, she thought. They were hoping for the same thing. At least she was trying to be independent—what she now believed men wanted in a wife.

The movers started with the bed. The driver hoisted the mattress over his head and carried it down the stairs as if it were a bag of feathers. His partner took the bed frame—two long boards and two long metal pieces. It was clear who would do the most work. But then when they came back up, the thin man took three small but heavy boxes, stacked them atop the hope chest, lifted the whole lot in his arms and carried it out. Unbelievable! This skinny rail of a man didn't look strong enough to carry all of that off. All three Giles women were quietly titillated by his power. The men hauled everything off piece by piece—boxes of varying sizes, two chairs, a chest of drawers, a couple of throw rugs. The room was picked clean. Nothing was left except a few dust balls that had collected behind the chest of drawers. Even her closet looked ruefully barren.

When everything was gone and the men had secured it all on the truck, there was nothing left for Lila but goodbyes. "Well, I guess that's that. Momma's coming over later to help me put the place together."

"Oh, yeah, uh-huh," was all Lucretia said, praying her tears would wait until Lila left. Lila had enough passive guilt coming from her mother and Linda. Lucretia didn't want to add to it.

"Listen, why don't the two of you come over with me now and help me unpack. It'll be fun. You could even spend the night if you want."

"Really, Lila? That sounds like so much fun!" Lucretia said, ignoring Linda's furtive glances, which were attempting to recruit a partner in misery.

"Well I can't," Linda said. "I think the cleaning lady comes today and . . . well, somebody should be here while she's here. You know that's how Momma prefers it. Besides, tonight I've got plans. Maybe some other time."

Lila looked at Linda, fully aware that she was being given the weakest excuse. She gave a smile, more to herself than to Linda, clutched her purse tighter then turned to leave. By the time she got downstairs to the front hall, her body hesitated as if, with its own will, it was having second thoughts about leaving home. Then, over her shoulder, she said. "You know, Linda, stranger things have happened out in the world than a twenty-nine-year-old woman leaving home. I'll see you." Then she beckoned to Eulelie. "Momma, I'll see you a little later, right?"

"Yes, honey," she called from the dining room, "but wait a minute, before you leave, I have something for you." Eulelie walked through the living room and into the hall carrying a china plate. "Your mother's china, you've always admired it so much. I thought you should have it in your new place. I'm going to pack it all up nice and secure and I'll bring it over when we come."

"Oh, Momma, I don't know what to say. You're going to make me cry. Thank you so much." She took the plate from her mother and ran her fingers over it with several back and forth feathery strokes, as if she were actually caressing her mother. Then she clutched it to her breast and smiled the brightest smile at Eulelie, which said the gift was more beloved than gold.

"Well, we don't use it, and it might as well go to you, being the oldest girl and all."

"So, all of you are coming, Momma?" Lila looked at Linda with raised, inquisitive eyebrows.

"Of course we're all coming, Lila."

"I can't, Momma, I've got plans," Linda said.

Lucretia simply smiled, then said, "I'd love to see your place, Lila. And I just might stay the night, if you need me."

"Well, I've got plans." Linda went off into the living room, where she sat on the sofa, not allowing herself to look back at her sister as she left.

Eulelie and Lucretia watched through the screen door as Lila moved down the walk as if she had fire nipping at her tail. They watched her say something or other to the driver. Then they watched her get in her car, start it, and pull away, leading the truck with all her earthly belongings to a place they still could not conceive as real. When Eulelie walked off and up the stairs to her room, Lucretia continued standing, watching, and knowing beneath the surface of her mind that this whole thing, this Lila-leaving-home thing, was the culmination of an intangible happening within the walls of the Giles house, and no power on earth or beyond would ever make her want to search for its root.

From the living room, Lucretia could hear Linda pick up the phone and dial. She spoke in low, hushed tones, only her giggle and scarcely perceptible delightful squeal making it obvious that it was a man to whom she was talking. And when Lila and the truck were too far away to even hear, much less see, Lucretia closed the door, went off into the kitchen, and sat in Lila's seat, trying to figure out what to do next.

Linda flitted into the kitchen a few seconds later. "I've

got a date coming over today. Jeffrey Borders. I told you he'd come knocking again. So you and Momma stay over at Lila's as long as you want."

"Whatever," Lucretia said, not actually looking at Linda. She picked up a dog-eared magazine of her mother's on knitting that sat on the edge of the table and flipped through it—anything to kill time. Lucretia waited, almost prayed for an inspired thought to come with this less than stimulating read. It was futile. Inspiration was not the soul of the world in which she'd always lived. And that wasn't necessarily a bad thing—for any of them. Before she'd even finished the first paragraph of an article on knitting perfect sleeves, she put the magazine down on the table and slumped against the chair's back with a conflicted heart and bedeviled mind. She shifted to one side, only enough to slip her hand in her pocket to pull out two folded pieces of paper she had been carrying with her everywhere for the last week.

Lucretia unfolded and read aloud, but in a whisper only she could hear: "Position of a lifetime for the millennium. Prestigious private school in picturesque Charleston, South Carolina seeks primary school teacher to start in January, 2000. . . ." Then she unfolded the other piece of paper, the crackling filling the room with more noise than she wished, and read her own words, words that someone at that prestigious school should have read by now, words that Lucretia just knew were her ticket out of Baltimore, and out of a world that had stifled her life long enough. Just months away, Lucretia thought. And she closed her eyes and dreamed. Rebirth. Reprogramming. She folded the papers up again and put them back in her pocket, because until her ticket arrived, she and her sister—and Eulelie made three— would continue to go about the hours, the days, the weeks, the months, of living in a realm where secrets and lies, imposture and delusion, would forever live without question or thought.

EPILOGUE

≈ The Prodigal Sister

Doralee was in this strange town in search of a woman she hadn't seen for years. It was time to end the internal torture she had brought upon herself. She had the cabbie she'd hired at the airport drop her off way at the end of the road. Doralee had to feel this place, really feel it, walk it, breathe its air, trample its dust, smell its smells. It was like traveling in a time machine. Nothing at all had changed. There was nothing there that was foreign to her memory. The same faces, worn by age and hard living, still rocked on porches overlooking tiny dirt-patch yards. The same cars seemed to be broken down in front yards, the intended projects of every man for a Saturday afternoon. About the only thing that was different was the road itself—it was black-topped, but there were still no sidewalks on either side. There was just the road, then houses, or, if they were lucky, what passed as a front yard standing between the two.

Doralee knew all those faces peering at her from porches, doorways, windows, her own face hiding from their view under the too-wide brim of a navy-blue straw hat. She was received and followed by mistrustful gazes all the way down the road. Why would they know her? She had long left these people's conscious minds. There was a stranger on the road, and she would be the talk until someone came back with the news as to who she was and where she was going. The last person they expected to see walking down their road in a fancy lady's suit and a big movie-star hat was little Doralee who seemed to have just vaporized more years ago than most could remember.

Doralee saw everybody, but saw no one. There was no way she would let her eyes meet any of theirs. She was back there for one reason, actually two, but in the general sense one reason only, and it had nothing to do with connecting with old neighbors and school chums, telling tales of old times, or catching up while chugging moonshine out of a mason jar. Doralee kept on past the eyes she did not want to see. Her pace was quick, lively, her steps dainty like the queen's. Nothing was going to keep her from her reason for being in this place on which God surely never smiled; at least not in the way Eulelie's life saw His smile.

When she reached the house the first thing she saw was that old tire swing still hanging from the willow tree that was the only beauty bestowed on this tiny spit of earth. The willow grew, tall and majestic, from the dirt floor, its leaves like open arms welcoming her home. There was no grass to be found around that house, only the green in the tree that had once given her the hope of beauty, and the hope of hope in this joyless place. She tried not to see it for as long as she could, but there was no ignoring it, the house that, sadly, looked no different than the house she remembered. There were a few less missing tiles in the roof, and the front window that sat broken and patched with a cardboard box from the time she was ten until the time she left to become Eulelie had been fixed. The porch, though, still looked shaky, buckling with the same rotting wood, which was made all the more unstable with steps that were precarious, at their very best. And the house as a whole needed paint badly. This was once her home. This was where she was raised. What, she wondered, would her children think?

It was only when she opened the gate to step into the yard that she noticed the two women, sitting way over in the corner of the porch. One woman dressed in a five-and-dime housecoat stood, having the bearing more of Doralee's former self than the present Eulelie. In fact, this would have been Doralee without the luxury of easy living to help age her gracefully. It wasn't the spirit of the woman she used to be, though. It was her sister Cora. Cora, whose dry, bloodless skin the color of wheat bread made her look like a puff of dust. And her hair sat atop her head with the straightness of a process and just a distant memory of curl, but nothing else. Around her thin lips was a ring of wrinkles, the culprit of which was the cigarette she held between her fingers; and with that wrinkle-framed mouth Cora formed a perfectly round circle of surprise at the sight before her. As Doralee moved closer to the porch, she heard her sister say, "Well, I will just be damned," and then she blew out a puff of smoke which seemed to linger longer than its natural life for the sake of drama. "It's Doralee."

Anna, who stood next to her, was obviously younger, but more feeble, possibly ill, and possessing the same dowdiness as her housecoated sister. She wore a misshapen Pepto-Bismol pink sweater that had snaggy snits all over it. Her time-weathered, withered, and all too wearied face shattered the long-held truth that *black don't crack*. Still, she offered a ragged-tooth smile that was none too attractive—a bit tentative, crawling crookedly to the right side of her face as if she were just learning how. She stood with a wild-eyed stare saying: "What in the world?" Doralee could possibly have been an apparition brought on by some vision-altering glare of the late afternoon sun.

Doralee got to the porch steps, then stepped cautiously on the first, then the second, then the third, trying to make her body as light as possible until she was on the porch. She looked at her sisters, giving them a contrite half smile. She couldn't believe that these haggard women, looking more like her last vision of her mother, could be her *younger* sisters. "Hello, sisters," she finally said.

At the same time, as if some gail-force wind had just blown into their faces, the two sisters pulled their heads back, giving Doralee a furrowed-brow stare. "Doralee," said Anna. "I always knew you'd come back." And she beamed that unpleasant smile that somehow juxtaposed her soft nostalgic gaze. Doralee had learned a long time ago, through years of looking at that smile, that not every smile was necessarily a pretty one.

Then the other one, her voice laced with bitterness and insult, said, "So, does this mean you ain't pretendin' to be somebody else up there in Baltimore now?"

And all Doralee could do, all she was able to offer her sister in the way of explaining herself, was a slack-jawed gawk that was pregnant with more questions than answers; questions she could not find a voice at that moment to ask.

"That's right, if it hadn't been for your husband up there writin' and tellin' us you was okay, we woulda gone on assumin' you was dead somewhere. 'Course, Anna here always thought you'd gone off to Paris someplace."

"Yeah, you know how you always had those fancy dreams. I thought you was in Paris," Anna said, still with that eyesore of a smile. It seemed as though she still felt a little let down, if not downright sad that Doralee hadn't gone off to Paris.

"What?" Doralee said in utter disbelief. "What are you talking about? My husband? What do you mean?" It was as if she'd just stepped into a parallel universe.

"Your husband, Gilbert Giles. He never told you?"

"Never told me what?" Then she realized, specifics didn't matter. He had never told her anything regarding Cora and Anna. "No, he never told me. How did you find him? When did you find him?"

"We ain't find him. He found us. Got this letter in the mail one mornin' and—"

"What mornin'? What morning?" she said, correcting her own diction. "When did he send you a letter?"

"Oh, gosh, it must've been about, oh, twenty-five years or so by now. Not long after Daddy died, the last time you was down here, that's when you told us that you was livin' in New York. But you wasn't, was you?''

Doralee's mind wandered to that day when she got the news about her father's imminent death. It was the one and only time she had called home to check on her father, who had already begun to ail when she left Charleston some five years before. It's not that she never wanted to call before then. It's just that the more time went by, the harder it became for her to call, to reconnect. It didn't really matter, though, she convinced herself. The important thing was that she called in enough time to pay her respects.

Her eyes squinted as she remembered the fear she felt at the possibility that he would die before she got there, and he did. She heard those words as clearly as if they were being spoken in her ear—*He died of natural causes. He went in his sleep.* But it seemed to Doralee that he died from deep mourning—a broken heart some said—over her mother, who had been dead for five years. From somewhere she couldn't even describe a pang of guilt flashed through her gut as she remembered that the day she buried her mother was the day she left Charleston to become Eulelie. The guilt was big, and for that moment, unceasing; guilt for not mourning her mother properly or guilt that just maybe her sudden departure from Charleston helped kill her father. Doralee hadn't felt this, or any other kind of guilt at her father's funeral. Why now?

Doralee's face contorted into a wince with the memory of being torn between going to her dying father's bedside as Doralee or staying in her Baltimore life, pretending, but being so sure of herself as Eulelie. But her father had only days left on earth, and if she believed in any part of God's word, as Doralee or Eulelie, she believed in honoring thy mother and father.

She broke the news to the Judge. She remembered telling him that she had to go down to Columbia to bury her father. *He's dying fast,* she recalled saying. Of course the Judge was ready to pack his bags and the kids' as well to be by her side while she grieved, and she remembered how she stood firm on not wanting to drag him and the kids to the funeral of a man they didn't know. Besides, he wasn't their grandfather, she'd said. *I'll be just fine. He was an old man, and he was very sick*, she told the Judge.

And she believed, for all those years, that her husband had accepted all her excuses, but now she knew that the look in his eyes when he said, *It's just a pity I never got to know your father*, was actually saying that he didn't believe a word from her mouth. That must have been when he decided to have her followed. It had to happen that way, because at that moment as she stood there remembering his eyes that were saying so much, there was no other way it could have happened.

Staring into the nothingness of air, Doralee quietly said to her sisters, "And, so what did he say?"

"He said he was your husband and that he had four children that you were helpin' him raise. Said he didn't know your reasons for abandonin' your family, but that he prayed in time you'd trust him enough to tell him. I guess you didn't, huh?" Cora looked at Doralee with the eyes of a stranger. She looked off down the road, trying to remember the rest, then said, "Then he asked us not to contact you about his contactin' us because he didn't want you to be embarrassed. He said he just wanted you to come to him and tell him in your own time. He said he loved you. Said you was a good mother. He sent us pictures of the family every Christmas, and once in a while would just send us a check saying he thought we might be able to use it for this or that."

"Wait a second," Eulelie said, waving her hands at her sister. "You were in contact with my husband by mail? You wrote to him?"

"Yeah, that's right," Cora said, stating a fact.

"That just couldn't be, because I got the mail every day, and let's just say I would have remembered seeing this return address."

"No, I didn't write to your home. That would be a little bit ridiculous, don't you think, especially since he didn't want you to know that he was writin' to us. When we wrote to him, we sent the letters to some courthouse."

Eulelie said nothing. She just stared straight, focusing on a spot on the wall just behind Cora's head.

"Anyway, you really hit the jackpot, Doralee, 'cause he really seemed like such a kind and generous man. I liked what I knew about him. He said he was sorry we had to meet in such a crazy way, though that's not the word he used. He used some big word that I had to look up. I can't remember it right now, though. Anyway, he said he hoped we would all meet one day and be one big family."

"Well, that won't happen. He died ten years ago," Doralee said sullenly, though not mournfully, but in a humiliated memory of his eyes, which had looked at her for all those years knowing the truth. That were still looking at her from eternity.

"Yeah, we know about that," Anna said.

"You know about what? Gilbert's death? How would you have learned about that?" They couldn't have possibly known about his death. Supposition, that had to be it. They simply assumed he'd died since they hadn't received any more letters or photos. That had to be it, because any other possibility was simply too much for her mind to accept right then and there.

"Your son, Gil. When his father died, he wrote and told us," Anna said, unaware of the shock and embarrassment she was inflicting.

Doralee's face seemed to lose all color. She stumbled slightly backward, her bottom coming to rest against the porch ledge. "My Gil has known all these years? Oh my God. Oh my dear sweet Jesus, help me." Then, in a panic, she looked pleadingly at both her sisters, fighting back tears: "My girls! Please tell me my girls don't know. Do my girls know?"

"No," Cora said. "And I know that for a fact, because

Gil said his father swore him never to tell those girls, or anyone, Gil said. His father told him that the girls were too fragile. That it's best they not know. Anyway, he mostly told Gil about us 'cause he wanted Gil to continue sending us pictures. You know, keep in touch. Gil said his father wanted to make sure that if we needed anything that we could always contact him. I tell you, he was more generous than any flesh and blood man I ever known."

"Your husband told us about your new name too. Eulelie. It's real pretty. Reminds me of that white woman used to live here in town. Is that where you got it?"

Doralee didn't respond, lowering her head with an abashed shadowy smile. She stood from where she leaned against the ledge. Doralee put her bag down without saying a word and walked over to the door, the same rickety wooden door with four panels of screens, still the same yellowed shade of ecru that had been there since her childhood. She opened it, listening to the same moans, and groans, and creaks that it had obviously been screaming since her childhood, and stepped over the doorsill that emptied directly into the front room. That's what they'd always called it— the front room. Not the living room, or even the great room, just the front room. Possibly, she now thought, to distinguish it from the back and only other room, which was the kitchen. On top of a table that had no purpose, it seemed, except holding the many pictures of her family the Judge, and later Gil, had been sending through the years, her mind filled with her husband's dying moments, which he wanted to spend only with Gil, and no one else. Nothing about that last request seemed at all peculiar, that is until now as she stood stark still, unable to wrench her eyes from those pictures on her sisters' shrine. And then, all at once, the wisdom of her own words, words she had just spoken to Gil about Sandra not more than a few months before, occurred to her. They had always been just as true for her own life. For it had come to pass for her that the only thing secret about her secret was how many people knew.